Vol.12 ADVENTURE No.3

Published by THE RIDGWAY COMPANY

ERMAN J. RIDGWAY, President   GEORGE B. MALLON, Secretary and Treasurer

Spring and Macdougal Streets   -   -   New York City
6, Henrietta St., Covent Garden, London, W. C., England

Entered at the New York Post Office
as Second-Class Matter

ARTHUR SULLIVANT HOFFMAN, Managing Editor

CONTENTS FOR JULY 1916

(Continued on next page)

(Continued from preceding page)

Statement of the ownership, management, circulation, etc., required by the Act of Congress of August 24, 1912, of *Adventure*, published monthly at New York, N. Y., for April 1, 1916. State of New York, County of New York. Before me, a Notary Public, in, and for the State and county aforesaid, personally appeared JAMES F. BIRMINGHAM, who, having been duly sworn according to law, deposes and says that he is the Business Manager of the *Adventure*, and that the following is, to the best of his knowledge and belief, a true statement of the ownership, management, etc., of the aforesaid publication for the date shown in the above caption, required by the Act of August 24, 1912, embodied in section 443, Postal Laws and Regulations, printed on the reverse of this form, to wit: 1. That the names and addresses of the publisher, editor, managing editor, and business managers are: *Publisher*, THE RIDGWAY COMPANY, a corporation, Spring and Macdougal Streets, New York City. *Editor*, ERMAN J. RIDGWAY, 223 Spring Street, New York, N. Y. *Managing Editor*, ARTHUR SULLIVANT HOFFMAN, 223 Spring Street, New York, N. Y. *Business Manager*, JAMES F. BIRMINGHAM, 223 Spring Street, New York, N. Y. 2. That the owners are: (Give names and addresses of individual owners, or, if a corporation, give its name and the names and addresses of stockholders owning or holding 1 per cent or more of the total amount of stock.) *Owner:* THE RIDGWAY COMPANY, a corporation, Spring and Macdougal Streets, New York City. *Stockholders:* THE FEDERAL PUBLISHING COMPANY, a corporation, 15 Exchange Place, Jersey City, N. J. THE BUTTERICK COMPANY, a corporation, 223 Spring Street, New York City, N. Y. THE BUTTERICK PUBLISHING COMPANY, a corporation, Spring and Macdougal Streets, New York, N. Y. J. F. BIRMINGHAM, Butterick Building, New York City, N. Y. WM. H. BLACK, 152 West 91st Street, New York City, N. Y. MRS. THERESA R. CARROLL, 777 Madison Avenue, New York City, N. Y. W. H. GELSHENEN, 100 William Street, New York City, N. Y. CLARA E. KEHOE, 2524 Creston Avenue, New York City, N. Y. H. F. MORSE, 3 West 46th Street, New York City, N. Y. LAURA J. O'LOUGHLIN, 156 Ridge Street, Glens Falls, N. Y. MRS. ARETHUSA POND, 955 West End Avenue, New York City, N. Y. ERMAN J. RIDGWAY, Butterick Building, New York City, N. Y. AUGUSTUS VAN WYCK, 149 Broadway, New York City, N. Y. R. A. VAN WYCK, 149 Broadway, New York City, N. Y. G. W. WILDER, Butterick Building, New York City, N. Y. MARIE A. WILDER, Butterick Building, New York City, N. Y. BEN F. WILDER, Butterick Building, New York City, N. Y. 3. *That the known bondholders, mortgages, and other security holders owning or holding 1 per cent or more of total amount of bonds, mortgages, or other securities are:* (If there are none, so state.) GEORGE W. WILDER, 329 West 108th Street, New York, N. Y. GERTRUDE C. WILDER, 329 West 108th Street, New York, N. Y. JULIA MARLOWE, Hotel Walton, Philadelphia, Pa. THE FEDERAL PUBLISHING COMPANY, 15 Exchange Place, Jersey City, N. J. JOHN ADAMS THAYER, Westport, Conn. JOHN O'HARA COSGRAVE, 128 West 59th Street, New York, N. Y. 4. That the two paragraphs next above, giving the names of the owners, stockholders, and security holders, if any, contain not only the list of stockholders and security holders as they appear upon the books of the company, but also, in cases where the stockholder or security holder appears upon the books of the company as trustee or in any other fiduciary relation, the name of the person or corporation for whom such trustee is acting, is given; also that the said two paragraphs contain statements embracing affiant's full knowledge and belief as to the circumstances and conditions under which stockholders and security holders who do not appear upon the books of the company as trustees, hold stock and securities in a capacity other than that of a bona fide owner; and this affiant has no reason to believe that any other person, association, or corporation has any interest direct or indirect in the said stock, bonds, or other securities than as so stated by him. J. F. BIRMINGHAM, Business Manager. *Sworn to and subscribed before me this 31st day of March,* 1916. A. P. SCHOEN, Notary Public. (*My commission expires March 30, 1917.*) [Seal.]

I0614929

Adventure

July 1916 Vol.12 No.3

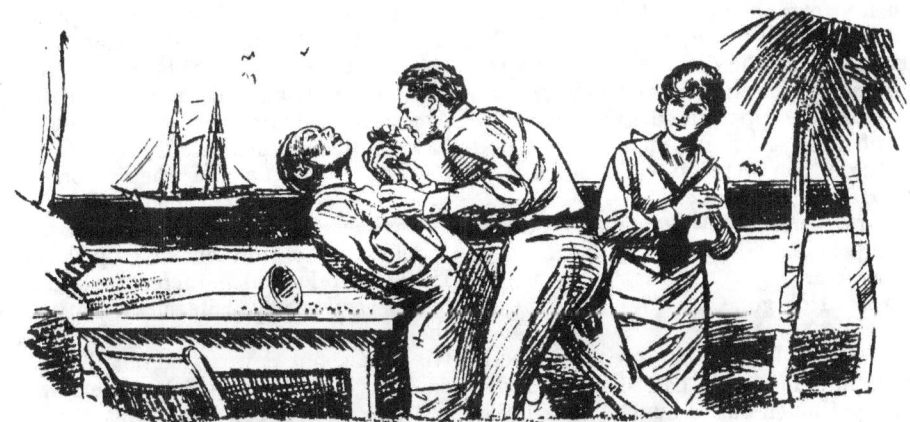

BEYOND THE RIM
A COMPLETE NOVEL *by* J. Allan Dunn.

Author of "The Gold Lust," "The Island of the Dead," etc.

CHAPTER I

THE PINK PEARL

CHALMERS did not go up to the *Times* office when the *Kinau* reached Honolulu. He was his own man for the time being and, being only in his middle twenties, vacations held for him too much of enjoyment to be spoiled by visiting the scene of his daily labors. The waterfront man of the afternoon paper met him with a grin.

"Come back for the shipwreck story?" the reporter asked. "It's a bunk. The only chap alive's a Solomon Islander who's half conscious and half *pupule* (crazy). Can't find out the ship's name or nationality, what she was or where she was bound. Tough luck to spoil your vacation."

"I'll have to cover it anyway," said Chalmers. "I'll take the rest of my holiday out yachting. Tell me, who's the Chinaman getting into the taxi with two others— the middle one. Tuan Yuck's his name, the purser told me. But what do you know about him? He's no ordinary Chink."

"I should say not. Tuan Yuck! He used to be the whole thing in Chinatown, kingpin of the gambling and dope ring, but he got in wrong with his *tong*, got them mixed up in a wild-goose chase after some buried treasure and he lost out all down the line and ducked for the 'big island.' He must have fixed things up to come back. That was all before your time, Chalmers. Anything stirring on the trip?"

"Not a thing. I'll see you later. Where's the chap that's still living from the wreck?"

"Sailors' Home. If he isn't *make* (dead)

by now. The story's dead anyway."

Chalmers determined to cover the story, such as it was, at first hand, to get all there was out of it for his mainland correspondence columns. A wireless message had brought him hurrying back from a holiday trip to the volcano and he wanted to use his own judgment of its news value. He crossed the waterfront, passed through the Fish Market, unheeding the brilliant array of strangely shaped and more strangely colored fish strewn on the stalls like tangible rainbows, and ran up the steps of the Sailors' Home where the derelicts of the South Seas sunned themselves on the wide porch, and entered the superintendent's office.

The official nodded greetings.

"Thought you were on vacation, Chalmers. Have a good time?"

"So far, thanks. Have you got that chap picked up in the whaleboat by the *Lehua*. Can I see him?"

"Taroi? He's gone."

"Gone?"

"It wouldn't have done you much good to see him. He was in bad shape and we couldn't get much out of him. Half stupid from exposure. They were in the boat seventeen days from what we made out of his talk. He was a Solomon Islander from Malayta way, same place Sayers's *wahine* (woman) came from. She translated for us. He's up at Sayers's place now. They took him away yesterday."

Chalmers whistled under his breath. Sayers was a newspaper man of shady character who covered sports for the *Times*. He had lost all caste among his own people by marrying a native woman, one of the tribes alien to the islands that had been imported for labor in the early days of sugar planting. He was an Australian, clever at his work, not to be personally believed or trusted, suspected of too close acquaintanceship with native jockeys and turfmen of uneasy reputation. Chalmers knew him as a fellow-worker and had been in touch with him on yachting events, Chalmers's favorite recreation, and he knew that the list of Sayers's faults did not include an excess of hospitality.

The superintendent grinned understandingly.

"Chap's not expected to live," he said. "Sayers has taken the funeral off our hands. Going to look him up?"

Chalmers nodded.

"Do you know where he lives?" he asked.

The superintendent grinned again.

"Just where you'd expect him to," he said. "In Aloha Alley, back of Kawaiahao Church and opposite the brewery. Know it?"

"Yes. What about the wreck—on French Frigate Shoals. Any one gone out there for salvage?"

"No. She must have gone to pieces by this. There was a big *kona* blowing last week, you know. Nobody particularly interested, you see. There were no papers in the boat; only three dying Kanakas and one crazy one. Probably just a trading schooner. Might have been British or American or Dutch. None of the Consuls have bothered their heads over it. They might be doing the other chap's work. Not much of a story in it, I imagine."

Chalmers left the place a little dispirited, though still bent on following up the story. It began to look as if there were nothing in it. Sayers's native wife might have taken the man in out of sympathy for a fellow tribesman, but Sayers was not the kind to encourage that sort of thing at his own expense. He decided there was something out of the ordinary back of the Australian's sudden generosity and as he determined to solve the problem his spirits rose again.

 ALOHA ALLEY consisted of a double row of primitive bungalows, facing each other across a tangled garden strip of bananas and motley-leaved crotons that skirted a dozen vine-clad royal palms.

The scroll-saw architecture was covered with purple bougainvilleas and orange huapala vines in a riot of violent tropical color. Sayers's dwelling was the second on the right, exactly like the rest, a dozen steps leading to the porch that ran all round the house. The main room extended across the entire front. The windows, like the door, were blinded with green slats, close-shut for coolness.

The whole of Aloha Alley seemed asleep in an afternoon languor. As Chalmers paused outside the door he heard the sound of groans that seemed to be emitted with every breath, a steady plaint for succor that made him open the blinds and step into the darkened room.

Against the farther wall beside a door stood the bed, and beneath the dingy mosquito curtain something writhed and tossed

and moaned. As his pupils became adjusted to the dusk, Chalmers distinguished the figure of a native lying outside the sheets, clad only in a loin-cloth, throwing his head from side to side.

The man's naturally brown face was a grayish hue and twitched continually beneath a frizzly mop of hair, stiffened and dyed a rusty red by constant applications of lime. The place reeked of sickness.

Beyond the door Chalmers heard the loud murmur of two voices, one of which he recognized as Sayers's. The other, a woman's, he set down as his wife's. He was about to knock when his ear caught the monosyllable the fevered man repeated. Chalmers knew a few words of native and this was one universal through all the South Seas—*wai* (water).

There was a grimy pitcher on a chair beside the bed with a grimier glass beside it. The pitcher was half full of water with halved limes and a pebble of ice afloat in it.

Chalmers sat on the edge of the bed, poured some of the water into the glass, moistened his handkerchief with more, set aside the netting and slipped one arm about the shrunken shoulders of the man, raising him gently. The body was burning up with fever. As he dampened the flaked lips the native's eyes opened and rested on him with an expression half of dislike, half terror, that changed to animal gratitude as Chalmers wiped his lips and set the glass for him to drink. Chalmers mustered up his native, remembering the name he had heard.

"*Aloha, Taroi,*" he said.

"*Tarofa oe,*" the man responded huskily, as he made shift to gulp at the liquid. His figure relaxed and Chalmers let him down on the pillow he had reshaken.

It needed no medical expert to tell that the spark of life was at its faintest. A shudder ran through the gaunt figure, the jaw relaxed, then set again with an effort.

The sound of the voices beyond the door was suddenly raised, and a shadow of fear passed over Taroi's face. His claw-like fingers twisted upward to his mop of hair and burrowed in it gropingly. The right hand with something clutched in it reached out, found Chalmers and pressed something hard and round into the white man's palm.

Chalmers looked at it. Even in the dusk of the room he could tell the beauty and purity of the faintly iridescent globule, a pink pearl, perfectly round, the size of a marrow-fat pea. Even as he wondered, Taroi's eyes closed and his hands fell lax on the sheets.

"For Sayers?" asked Chalmers.

As the eyes opened he nodded toward the door. A look of protest widened the native's glance.

"*Aore!*" (no), he protested.

His right hand closed Chalmers's palm about the gem with feeble fingers of fire. The eyes rolled toward the door, the head shook in a final negation, then the body shuddered, the knees were drawn up, the hands clenched and the jaw fell.

Outside, the banana fronds tapped gently at the window. The voices in the inner room were quiet. A fly buzzed loudly.

Chalmers set down the pearl, straightened the limbs of the dead man, drew the sheet over him and replaced the mosquito netting. As he stood beside the bed, with the gem in the palm of his hand, the door opened, a shaft of sunshine pouring through the gap. Sayers stood on the threshold, his wife behind him, the two staring at Chalmers in an astonishment that held them spellbound.

CHAPTER II

THE STORY OF THE SOUTH SEA ISLANDER

SAYERS spoke first, chewing his words as if his mouth were half full, his eyes half closed in scrunity of Chalmers.

"How long have you been here?" The tone was full of suspicion.

Chalmers put his finger to his lips and motioned with his head toward the bed.

"He's dead," he said.

The native woman brushed by Sayers with a loud wail of *Auwe!* The next instant she had thrust them both into the inner room, and shut the door upon them. Chalmers heard the outer door thrown open; another cry of *Auwe!* Then came the swift scurrying of curious feet upon the porch. In the confusion he slipped the pearl into his vest pocket.

"Let's get out of this," said Sayers. "She'll attend to it. The whole crowd of them will be howling all over the place in two minutes."

He led the way through the back door, down a flight of steps and through a gap in the ragged hibiscus hedge to the road. Aloha Alley was wide awake now with all the native excitement of hysteria over death.

"Where do you want to go?" asked Chalmers. "Make it somewhere close by." He was in no mood to walk far with Sayers at any time and his distaste of the man had heightened with the look of fear the dead man had shown at the sound of his voice. "Isn't there something we can do for him?"

"I'll 'phone the coroner," said Sayers callously. "She'll handle the rest of it. He came from the same place as she did. Let's go to the Art Saloon. I want to have a talk with you."

As they went, Sayers surveyed Chalmers with constant side looks of suspicion. Chalmers realized that this was bred of the doubt in Sayers's mind as to how much of his talk with his wife had penetrated the door. This advantage he determined to keep. There was no doubt in his mind now that there was a real story that tied up with Sayers's unusual hospitality to Taroi and the pearl the dying man had given him.

Arrived at the Art Saloon they took one of the private snuggeries and Sayers called for drinks. At his request, the Chinese boy brought two bottles, gin for Sayers and beer for Chalmers.

Native fashion, Sayers drank his liquor neat, avidly, with a desire to get not so much the taste but the kick of the raw spirits. Excess had already trade-marked him. Powerful of build, still of some athletic prowess, his general condition was typified by the white duck suits he wore, constantly renewed by his wife's laundering, yet always limp and crumpled as if he slept in them.

His head, nearly bald, was frizzed with ginger-colored hair, his eyebrows showed faintly and the eyelids were scant in the red rims that framed shifty eyes the color of dishwater. Freckles and blotches covered the skin of face, neck and hands, the latter to the last joint of the stubby fingers. Broken veins showed purple along the lines of his jaw and flecked his nose, which had been battered in boxing contests. His teeth were yellow and distinctly apart behind full lips, half colored by a bristly sandy mustache. He walked and sat with a slouch.

Occasionally he showed flashes of good breeding. His articles, despite their sporting slang, had all the distinctions of an educated man. One quality that showed strangely amid his sordidness was a love of music coupled to an intimate knowledge of the art that had seen him detailed as critic to whatever musical affairs were given that were really worth while.

Chalmers, with the rest who gave any thought to the matter, set him down as the ne'er-do-well of a well-bred Australian family, who had developed the degenerate streak in his nature by self-indulgence, slumping year by year as he lost caste with his own race.

He was game. Chalmers knew that from yachting episodes. But his sporting instincts had deteriorated to shiftiness, though he kept up in talk and writing an appearance of playing square and, as a judge of sporting events, he was eminently an expert.

A love of fair play held Chalmers from a close analysis of the other's faults. There were fifteen years between them, and their thoughts and modes of living held little in common. At present he enjoyed the game he was playing, to outwit Sayers in craftiness and get the story he was convinced was in existence.

"You didn't tell me how long you were in the room," said Sayers, elbows on the table, his tumbler in his hand, a quarter full of raw gin, his colorless eyes covertly watching Chalmers' face.

"I hardly know. Several minutes. I heard you talking and was coming through when Taroi called for water. He was in a bad way, as you know, and died practically in my arms."

"I thought you were on your vacation. Funny I didn't hear you."

"You were talking pretty loudly."

Sayers grunted.

"I didn't suppose any one was in my front room, listening."

Chalmers ignored the suggestion. He took the pearl from his pocket and set it between them on the dark wood of the table. Under the electric lights it seemed to give off a shimmer of iridescence, as the down shows on a peach. Sayers' eyes glittered greedily and his fingers twitched as he reached to take up the gem. Chalmers forestalled him by putting it in his own palm.

"Taroi gave me this," he said.

"He meant it for me." Sayers put out his hand.

"He said it was *not* for you. He was afraid of you. What had you been doing to him, Sayers?"

"Doing! Didn't I take him in from those charity-mongers at the Home and treat him like a white man? I got a doctor for him, my wife waited on him hand and foot and the ungrateful Kanaka dog held out on me. That pearl belongs to me by all rights, Chalmers. I want it."

He thrust his face across the table, his jaw stuck out, his fists clenched, his eyes narrowed, every inch the bully. Chalmers had no fear of him physically; mentally he felt himself the superior of the two.

"He didn't want you to have it, Sayers. I don't know why he gave it to me except that he knew I was friendly. You must have done something to make him dislike you."

"I did nothing, I tell you, but look out for him. The beggar didn't want to talk—I may have coaxed him a bit."

Chalmers mentally glimpsed Sayers urging his wife to bully all he knew out of the dying man, burning up with fever and desire for rest and quiet.

"Who's going to pay for his funeral, I'd like to know?" blurted Sayers. "Who's going to pay for the doctor and his medicine?"

"I fancy you got enough out of him to make it worth your while," said Chalmers. "But the pearl will pay for his funeral. I'll see to that—and a good one. It must be worth a hundred dollars or so."

Sayers snorted in disgust.

"A hundred. It's worth five if it's worth a cent. And—" He broke off short. "There's no need to waste expenses on him; it wasn't his pearl."

"How do you know it wasn't?"

Sayers sat back, emptied his glass, poured himself another measure, emptied that and once more leaned across the table confidentially.

"I don't know how much you know, Chalmers," he began, "or how much you've guessed. But I've had you in mind already over this affair—there's nothing crooked about it," he said hastily, as he noted Chalmers' face. "It's a clear open and shut proposition. I don't imagine you want to grind away for the *Times* all your life, do you?"

"What is it?" asked Chalmers.

"It's your big chance and mine," answered Sayers. "The chance of a lifetime."

"Go ahead," said Chalmers.

"You can navigate, can't you?" asked Sayers.

The question seemed irrelevant, but Chalmers answered it.

"You ought to know," he said. "I took the *Manuahi* up to the coast and sailed her down in the trans-Pacific race, trick and trick with Captain McParland. I passed the Board in San Francisco for the fun of the thing and I hold my ticket. Why?"

"That's where you come in. I've got to have some one who can navigate and one who's interested in the deal," answered Sayers. "You'll see why, in a minute."

Chalmers lit his pipe and sat back comfortably. His news sense had justified itself. Already he felt himself crossing the threshold of the commonplace, sure that the story held for him a personal element, subconsciously inclined already to listen favorably to the proposition that Sayers, his voice lowered and full of concentration, was unfolding.

 "I WAS at the wharf when the *Lehua* came in, that trip," said Sayers. "Honamaku was on board, coming over for the swimming-races next week; but I passed up a talk with him for the story of the wreck. I knew enough of the Solomon dialect to talk to Taroi a bit.

"The others were too near being *make* to talk, but Taroi had chirped up with the soup and champagne they'd been feeding him. They took him up to the Sailors' Home and the others to the Queen's Hospital. One of 'em died that night and the two others next day. I volunteered to get Faleta—that's my wife—to interpret, and they were glad to let her.

"The *Lehua* people didn't know much outside of having picked them up, drifting in the Molokai Channel, Taroi trying to signal with an oar he was too weak to lift and the rest in the bottom of the boat, starved and nutty with thirst. No name on the whaleboat, no papers, nothing for identification."

Chalmers nodded as Sayers poured himself a drink.

"Seventeen days from French Frigate Shoals—four hundred miles," he commented. "They must have been blown down by the trades and then back again in the *kona*."

"Here's the part of the story you don't know," continued Sayers, "aside from what you may have overheard today. Taroi got delirious up at the Home. By the time I had Faleta up there he was talking rot, but I got enough sense out of it to wise her up to listen and keep quiet herself. He was rolling his eyes and chucking himself over the bed with his temperature getting higher all the time, and the doc' told us to come back when he sent for us.

"That was in the evening. Taroi was quiet then and Faleta just translated answers to the questions they put. He wasn't much good at that. Didn't even know the skipper's name—just called him 'kapitani.' Didn't know where the schooner was built or chartered; naturally enough, he didn't bother his head about it. He'd been hired as extra hand at the last minute to take the place of another Kanaka who got sick. What the hospital supe didn't ask for, we didn't tell; and that wasn't all that Taroi talked about by a long shot. He seemed a lot better and they gave us permission to take him to my place—glad to get rid of him. Early this morning he got worse again and—well, you saw him die."

"What about keeping back information from the authorities, Sayers?" asked Chalmers. "I thought you said there was nothing crooked about this."

"There isn't. What I found out wouldn't do them any good without what Faleta happened to know. I'm planning to do more than the authorities would. If I told them what Faleta knows they wouldn't thank me for it, even if they acted on it. I'll tell you the yarn in five minutes if you'll listen:

"The schooner was called the *Manu*. That's South Sea for bird and doesn't tip off where she comes from. There are fifty schooners named *Manu* in the trading line. I've a notion she was Australian, but I don't know for sure. Anyway, her captain owned her. He had got wind from some native he'd helped out of a hole of an island with a lagoon full of pearl-shell, way off by itself, not on the charts or in the directory. He started out to clean it up in a hurry. You know how that is. As I said, it isn't on the map and it hadn't been touched, but once let a hint of a find like that get out and you've got a government gunboat on top of you, claiming it. The Japs 'll swipe anything and you can't argue with four-inch guns; or else it's the British or the Dutch.

"Anyway it's first come, first served with pearling; and this was a virgin lagoon and rich. They ran into the tail-end of a hurricane making the island, and the schooner got blown 'way out of her latitude and got

pretty badly banged up. And they ran short of grub.

"Coming away in the rush they did, they were short on grub and equipment. They didn't dare buy any special stuff before starting. With a fortune lying in the open sea for the first one who grabs it, you can't be too careful not to tip it off. All they had with 'em was one diving outfit and not even a pop-gun on board to make a bluff with, in case they were trailed. And they were.

"A schooner followed 'em and they saw smoke on the horizon the day of the storm that might or might not have been a gunboat; they were 'way off the steamer routes. It threw a scare into the skipper, though he figured the gale would have covered them up.

"They tried out the lagoon. It was a big one—and rich. First day they found a dozen pearls, and Taroi either swiped one of them or found one of his own and tucked it away in that mop of his. It's an old trick. The skipper didn't want to leave the island open and he wanted to make a big clean-up —shell and all. So he decided to stay with his find and sent the schooner kiting up to Honolulu for more equipment, more grub and guns, and ammunition.

"I imagine the mate wasn't the greatest sailor in the world, and anyway he wasn't the first to run afoul of French Frigate Shoals in nasty weather. It must have been a bad smash. You know the rocks shape up at nightfall for all the world like a square-rigger under full sail.

"They went crashing on to the coral with the wind blowing half a gale, and a lee shore at that. The mate got his head crushed in by the gaff falling on it when they struck. Next morning the schooner was still there, what was left of it, and they got the boat that was still in the davits and seaworthy, and started off for nowhere.

"None of them knew where to go, none of 'em had sense enough to save any papers. Seventeen days afterward the *Lehua* picked 'em up.

"The point is—" Sayers' voice fell to a whisper—"there's the captain alone on the island with four kings' ransoms in pearls, and no chance of getting away—unless some one fetches him, and I'm the only one who knows where he is."

"The authorities would send after him from here," said Chalmers. "You don't suppose they'd leave the man to starve?"

Sayers looked at him with scornful amusement.

"No more would I. But they don't know where to go. Taroi couldn't tell 'em. He knew the name of the island, but that wouldn't do 'em any good without the latitude and longitude, for there's a dozen of the same name and I told you it wasn't on the chart. I *do* know where it is from what Faleta found out.

"If you were a man alone with a fortune in the middle of the sea and some one came along and offered to take you off after your own crowd had been wrecked and killed, wouldn't you be glad to see 'em? Wouldn't it be worth something to you?" He watched Chalmers's face narrowly. "Wouldn't you give anything in reason for expenses and a reward rather than sit there and rot on the chance of some one turning up?

"Mind you, I might take the trip without any thought of reward if I had a ship, but I haven't, and ships and crews cost money. It's only fair to be reimbursed, ain't it? You'd do it gladly, I'll bet!"

Chalmers, looking at Sayers, wondered how far his generosity would take him without hope of gain, but the main argument seemed fair enough. The man would be glad to recompense them. He would, in his place, he decided.

"We'll treat him fair and square," said Sayers. "There's enough for a dozen men according to what Taroi says, and if that pearl's any criterion of what the rest are, it's our chance to make a fortune and do a good turn."

"Where's your ship and your money?" asked Chalmers.

The sudden prospect of adventure appealed more to him than that of wealth. This would be getting beyond the rim with a vengeance.

Sayers sat up, relaxing, and poured himself more gin from the now half-empty bottle.

"I'll get the ship and the money. You can put in what's left of the value of that pearl after Taroi's buried. That'll help some. That's your share with your work as navigator," he said. "It'll take three of us. We don't want to noise this thing about or we'll all lose out. Some one'll suddenly discover the island belongs to the States or they'll just naturally grab it first. We'll keep it close. I've got the location of the island. That's my share. We don't need such a big schooner. A couple of Kanakas for crew should fix it. How much will it take?"

"We can't charter a schooner under five hundred a month for an unknown destination," said Chalmers. "We could buy one outright for a thousand, probably—one of the firewood fleet might do. But there's the grub and wages, chronometers and other things. Call it a couple of thousand."

"I've got the man who'll put up the balance of the money and go thirds in the deal. It's too bad Taroi didn't swipe a bigger pearl so we could do this on our own. But the man I've in mind is close-mouthed enough. What do you say?"

"We've got to give this captain a square deal, Sayers," said Chalmers.

"You're going to have your say in the matter, ain't you? I'm not going to take advantage of the man. We'll settle that matter before we start. Are you game?"

"Who's your third man. Do I know him?"

"He's a Chinaman," said Sayers; "a topnotcher. He's down and out in a way and he'll snatch at the chance. He'll keep it to himself and he can find the money. I don't suppose you know him."

"Maybe I do," Chalmers said quietly. "Is his name Tuan Yuck?"

Sayers looked at him in open, if grudging, astonishment.

"I don't know where you get your dope," he said. "But that's the man. You know more than I thought you did about the whole affair. But you don't know the whereabouts of the island. I do! Are you on?"

"Have you seen Tuan Yuck yet?"

"Not yet. He was expecting to be back this week from Hawaii."

"He came over on the *Kinau* with me. I had a talk with him. See him first and then I'll have time to think it over. You know where my place is?"

Sayers continued to look at Chalmers in wonderment. Hitherto, he told himself, he had underestimated the younger man. After this he would have to accord him a more prominent place in his plans. He got up, unaffected by the gin, save as to his breath and an extra cloudiness of the whites of his eyes.

"You're on," he said. "You'd be a fool not to come. As soon as we all three shake hands on it, I'll tell you the name and place of the island and we'll get busy. I'm off to hunt up Tuan Yuck. Good-by!"

"I don't like you overmuch," said Chalmers to himself, after Sayers left, "and I don't believe I'd trust you too far round a corner. But I can't stop you from going on the trip. And if I do go, I've a notion the captain will get a better bargain on account of being taken off. It's a real adventure. It's beyond the rim, all right."

His blood began to tingle with the excitement of the prospect. To sail the uncharted sea as the master of a stout little craft; to play the part of rescuer to a marooned mariner, to share in a well-earned reward!

Chalmers was twenty-five. Destiny seemed to be dropping gifts into his lap. He refilled his pipe, squared his shoulders unconsciously and smoked on, seeing in the smoke-drift the palms of an ocean oasis rising above the horizon in the morning haze.

CHAPTER III

THE PIN-PRICK ON THE CHART

THE three men so widely apart in appearance and opinion, drawn together by the common interest of the venture, sat about a chart of the South Pacific in Chalmers' quarters. The French windows that led into the garden were closed and the blinds drawn.

Chalmers, flushed with excitement as much as the heat, fidgeted with a pair of dividers. Sayers's forehead was dewed with perspiration, he dabbed at it with his limp handkerchief; his scanty thatch of hair was wet on his scalp. Only Tuan Yuck was impassive to conditions.

"It's agreed then," said Chalmers, "that the three of us share equally in the net returns that may be made out of this undertaking from any share of pearls and pearling interest that the captain may make over to us for rescuing him."

"There'll be two sides to that bargain," said Sayers. "He's not going to give us just what he happens to feel like."

"Neither are we going to hold him up," rejoined Chalmers firmly. "It's fair to repay all our expenses and give us a reasonable share, but the man's got to be rescued. That's why I'm in on this. You can't leave a man marooned in mid-ocean on a question of bargaining, Sayers."

"The matter will surely be adjusted," intercepted Tuan Yuck in his silky voice. "I am sure we defer to Mr. Chalmers's philanthropic ideas. I suppose a fifth of what the find is estimated to be worth, to be divided between the three of us, would be called reasonable?"

He held Sayers's eyes with his own and the latter nodded.

"A fair show all round is what we want," said the latter. "Only I'm not in this for my health, Chalmers, nor for the captain's. It's my chance for a stake and I'm going to get all I can. But a fifth ought to make us all fat in the pocketbook. That suits me."

"And I, Mr. Chalmers," said Tuan Yuck, "am in the deal primarily for the money it offers. So that's understood. Frankly, while I admire your impulsiveness, from my standpoint it is Quixotic. A man places himself in a false position. I see no reason why I should sacrifice the opportunity his bad move has opened up to me. Life is a good deal like a game of chess. Some of us may be born pawns and others outrank us in opportunity for action, but even a pawn can work its way across the board to supremacy if it is not too self-sacrificing."

"You talk as if we make our own moves, Tuan Yuck," said Sayers.

"We do," said the Chinaman. "That at least, is my philosophy, or part of it. What is yours, Mr. Chalmers?"

"Why, I don't know that I have one." Chalmers experienced a swift sense of extreme youth in the presence of Tuan Yuck. "To get all there is out of life without hurting anybody else, would about sum it up, I suppose."

"Change that to 'without getting hurt yourself' and you will find it more practical," said Tuan Yuck. "Eh, Sayers?"

"Grab it before the other fellow gets it. That's what I've had rubbed into me," said the Australian. "We'll play fair with the captain, Chalmers. It's only natural to get all we can out of him. So it's all hands round on the deal. Tuan Yuck puts up the money or most of it. Chalmers puts up the pink pearl, and acts as navigator, and I put up the idea and position of the island. No use for papers, I take it. This is a private venture and a gentleman's agreement."

He looked at Tuan Yuck and the ghost of a grin seemed to flicker across his face. If the Chinaman noticed it, he gave no sign.

"The interests are mutual. All of us need each other," he said. "Perhaps we need you most of all, Mr. Chalmers, not only to take us there, but to bring us back again."

"That's right!" exclaimed Sayers, almost with the air of having made a discovery. "So we'll all take a drink to success and call that our signatures. It's understood none of us talks outside?"

"Naturally," said Tuan Yuck. "We can't trust any one. They might get a faster vessel and get there first."

"That's fair," said Chalmers.

Sayers busied himself filling the glasses.

"What do you take, Tuan Yuck?" he asked. "Chalmers, yours is beer, I suppose?"

"Mine also," said Tuan Yuck. "The universal beverage."

"Beer for babes, and gin for grown-ups," answered Sayers, pouring himself a liberal tot of the spirits.

"You'll not find it pay in the long run," said Tuan Yuck, lifting his glass. "Good luck to all of us!"

They set down their tumblers and Chalmers once more took up his dividers.

"Now then," he said, "before we talk schooner and outfit, where is the island?"

THE trio stood up, moved by a common impulse which even Tuan Yuck shared. The big hydrographic chart was held down flat by books placed about its edge and Sayers set the shaded oil-lamp so that a broad circle of light irradiated Micronesia and Melanesia.

Sayers took the dividers from Chalmers, and held one leg of the instrument poised above the map.

"Motutabu is the name of it," he said. "That means the forbidden or tabu'd island, and there are any amount of forbidden islands scattered over the map. Here's one in the New Hebrides, another in the Marshalls and in the Fijis, tabu'd usually on account of some misfortune overtaking the inhabitants or visiting natives. This Motutabu got its name from an epidemic brought on by eating fish, poisonous there, but not in other places. The place has been deserted ever since, though once a colony under an insurgent chief from Malayta lived there. My wife's father was one of them. So was Taroi's. That's how there's no doubt about it being the place."

"Many of the lagoon fish are poisonous during the breeding season," said Tuan Yuck. "It is a natural protection against being eaten by bigger fish."

"Here is Nameless Isle, close to the hundred and seventieth meridian and just under the equator, between the Solomons and the Gilberts," went on Sayers, "and, almost due south—about four hundred miles, I suppose, Chalmers, is Jesus Island. Motutabu is half-way between the two—just about here."

He speared the chart with the sharp point of the dividers while Chalmers and Tuan Yuck bent across the table to look at the mark made in the clear paper of the chart, a spot unknown to the hydrographers, far off the sea routes, a pin-prick that represented to Chalmers adventure, the surge of the sea, the opening up of things worth while; to Tuan Yuck and Sayers the indulgence in many things that neither shared with the other, but which meant ease and comfort to the latter and power to the Chinaman.

"You can take us there?" asked Tuan Yuck, his eyes glowing like polished bronze in firelight.

Chalmers took up his parallel rulers as Sayers gave him back the dividers.

"Easily," he said. "The latitude should be close to five degrees south. It's east of the hundred and seventieth, between the two islands charted. There should be no trouble about finding it. A straight run from Honolulu almost due southwest, a little longer than that from San Francisco to Honolulu. Call it twenty-three hundred miles."

"How long will it take?" asked Tuan Yuck. "Three weeks?"

"If we get the schooner I'm figuring on, the *Aku*—she's carrying algaroba wood from Molokai now, an old boat but in good shape and with good lines—we ought to average eight knots or better. That would mean three weeks. But the trades are uncertain and we've got to figure on spells of light weather. Call it a month."

Sayers' face lengthened ludicrously.

"A month!" he protested.

"And a week more for outfitting," added Chalmers. "The *Aku* is owned by Afong & Company. Tuan Yuck," he continued, "do you know any of the firm? We should buy her outright for somewhere about a thousand dollars."

"I can handle that part of it," said the Chinaman. "And if you will make out your list of stores I'll attend to the financial end of it. The pearl I can sell for at least six hundred dollars."

"A hundred of it goes for Taroi's funeral," said Chalmers.

Sayers shrugged his shoulders as Tuan Yuck replied:

"I'll give you that amount in cash now, Mr. Chalmers. How about crew?"

"Sayers can act as mate. We should have a good man to help steer, and at least one more—natives preferred. Do you know anything about sailing, Tuan Yuck."

"Not a great deal. But I can cook."

The idea of Tuan Yuck preparing meals struck both Americans as incongruous and they laughed.

"I do not mean it as a joke," said the Chinaman. "It is the means to an end. You handle the ship. I'll preserve our stomachs. You will not regret the suggestion, gentlemen, and I will give you something else besides Chop Suey and Chow Yuck! If you will honor me at dinner tomorrow night I will give you a specimen of my skill. I will have arranged for the schooner by then."

He counted out five twenty-dollar gold pieces to Chalmers, took the pink pearl and left with Sayers.

Chalmers remained gazing at the map till it changed to a heaving sea and the matting beneath his feet to a lifting deck. He set himself to marking off the course on the chart but paused before he finished. Visions still floated between him and the paper.

"I wouldn't have picked either of my partners on personal preference," he told himself. "Sayers will bear watching. Both of them, for that matter. I'd like to know more about the inside workings of Tuan Yuck. He is the original Mongolian Sphinx. He might be either a pirate or a philosopher —or both. His eyes are a thousand years old in experience. He made me feel like my first day at kindergarten."

He yawned, completed his work on the chart and went to dream that his head was a pink pearl and that Tuan Yuck and Sayers were throwing dice for the possession of it, a vision that was not altogether as remote from the truth as nightmares usually are.

CHAPTER IV

THE FORBIDDEN ISLAND

THREE weeks of close contact aboard an eight-ton schooner bring out characteristics and breed intimacies or aversions in swift and unerring fashion. To Chalmers, Tuan Yuck remained a mystery. The man lived absolutely within himself to his own complete satisfaction. He was not unwilling to talk, but his conversation was so preeminently born of experience, and so based on selfishness that Chalmers never felt he penetrated the other's screen of self-sufficiency. For Sayers, he felt a growing dislike. The Australian was both slovenly and lazy, and his especial brand of selfishness lacked, somehow, the quality of the Chinaman's.

Sometimes Sayers would show the better streaks of his cosmos. In discussing philosophies with Tuan Yuck, between the three of them, Sayers would show flashes of philosophic brilliancy, born of an education that Chalmers envied, while he wondered at the little permanent result it had against the man's coarser nature. And at times the Australian would bring a zither on deck and invest its strings with a quality that seemed utterly at variance with his character. They had shipped two Hawaiians as crew, a sturdy, good-natured Hercules named Hamaku, and a somewhat stupid, but willing younger man, known only as Tomi, who possessed a high tenor that held qualities many a famous singer would have envied for his higher register.

Some days the wind sulked beneath the horizon, and, after the heat of the day was over, Sayers would play such things as the barcarolle from the "Tales of Hoffmann," or the sextette from "Lucia," and then drift into accompaniments for Tomi, singing native *meles* full of plaintive melody born of coco-palms bending in the trades and surf, crooning lazily to coral reefs.

Then he would discuss the mathematics of harmony with Tuan Yuck, while Chalmers listened with quickening interest as the Chinaman infallibly discounted Occidental methods and accomplishments, and showed the Orient as the very matrix of philosophy and the birthplace of science.

An hour later, Sayers, a bottle of gin before him, would play solitaire until, soddened with liquor, he would stumble to his bunk to sleep away his trick at the wheel, and appear at noon the next day morose and red-eyed until twilight came and his fingers steadied enough to coax a melody from his zither.

With it all, Chalmers's view-point broadened. His vitality, the buoyancy of his youth, and his ardent belief in human impulse and action that were based on real friendliness toward one's fellow man, off-set the cynicism of the Chinaman and the more brutal selfishness of the Australian. A sense of responsibility broadened his mental and spiritual shoulders. He was conscious of a link between Tuan Yuck and Sayers that was at variance with his own ideas of fair play, and, almost insensibly, he became the champion of the unknown captain, marooned by Fate, at the mercy of these mercenary rescuers.

His own dreams were those of youth crystallizing to manhood in the crucible of experience. The wide sea spaces, where the horizon seemed the veritable edge of the world, the vagrant clouds drifting across the sky, the starry infinitudes, the touch of the free-roving winds, strengthened the spirit within him.

Chalmers felt that behind the China-man's impassive exterior there dwelled absolutely human passions held in check until the owner willed to loose them. The shifting of the brilliant eyes behind the immobile eyelids constantly suggested the pacing of a beast within a cage that might open at any moment.

Meanwhile, as a cook, Tuan Yuck achieved wonders. From a scrawny, sea-sick chicken, with a handful of rice and a sprinkling of herbs, he could evolve a curry that, while it wholly satisfied the stomach, seemed, by the sheer savor of the dish, to evoke subtle suggestions of the Orient with all its hidden mysteries of dozing power and knowledge. And yet Chalmers could never lose the thought that, if it suited his purpose, Tuan Yuck would as callously poison the ship's company as he decapitated the chicken that formed the base of his culinary marvel.

He had shaken off the feeling of youth and ignorance with which the Chinaman had first inspired him. Something told him that Tuan Yuck missed the better part of life, had perhaps outlived it in the unknown years of his existence, and he rather pitied than resented him. At the beginning of the trip the Chinaman had produced a chess-board, and challenged both of them, proving them such amateurs before his brilliant, insoluble gambits that they had permanently retired.

Nights, when Sayers shuffled his cards at Canfield and Chalmers wrote up his log and checked his reckonings, Tuan Yuck worked out inscrutable problems on the squares, and at last retired to his cabin, whence the fumes of opium presently came pungently. Chalmers wondered if he sometimes smoked the poppy-seed to escape from his own philosophies.

DAY in, day out, they sailed across the changing ocean without a trail of smoke or the gleam of a sail on the horizon, splitting the angle of the diverging steamer trails that run from Honolulu to Guam, northward, and to the south from Honolulu to Suva and to Apia. Fortune favored them for two weeks with a steady following wind, and then they drifted, a squall sometimes a few miles off, and lifeless, lumpy water all about them, in which dolphins gamboled or chased great schools of flying-fish.

Their way lay through an ocean desert, set only with the scattered isles of Johnston, Jane, San Pedro and Barber, too far off their route for sighting, until they raised the Gilberts and sailed through the group, crossing the Equator and the international date line almost simultaneously as they entered the last quadrangle of their quest.

Chalmers grew daily more certain of some secret understanding between Sayers and Tuan Yuck. The two never seemed to court privacy; there was nothing on which to base his suspicions; but the consciousness deepened that there was something between them in which he had no share. That it in some way was aimed against his own interests or that of the captain, he felt sure, and cautioned himself accordingly.

On the twenty-seventh day the crossing of his Sumner's lines by double observation proved their position to be 171° 47′ East, and 4° 30′ South. He had checked his nooning and dead reckoning by a stellar altitude record, and was sure of his figures.

"Dawn tomorrow ought to show us Mo-tutabu," he announced.

Tuan Yuck looked up more quickly than his wont from his chessmen, and Sayers' nervous hands spoiled the stacks of his solitaire layout. Chalmers thought a look passed between them.

"Dawn, eh?" said Sayers. "That's only five hours away. Five hours from——"

He checked himself.

"Freedom," suggested Tuan Yuck. "We've made better time than we hoped.

My compliments to you, Mr. Chalmers, on your navigation."

Chalmers fancied a tinge of irony in the tone, but he accepted the congratulations.

"Let's make a night of it," said Sayers. "Tuan, I'll match you drink for drink to see who's the better man of the two. Come on, Chalmers, join the tournament."

"I have to relieve Tomi," said Chalmers. "I'll be at the wheel till daylight. Better turn in, Sayers. I'll call you if we sight anything."

"I'll take your wager if you'll match me pipe for pipe," said Tuan Yuck, producing his silver-stemmed opium holder. "No? Then you to your vice, I to mine. You'll call me, Mr. Chalmers?"

Chalmers went on deck and took the wheel. The wind filled the sails, sheeted well out. Above the main gaff the Southern Cross hung suspended. The slow hiss of the water, as it seethed from stem to stern and broadened to the wake, the low croon of Tomi somewhere in the bows, produced a soothing hypnosis.

The hours seemed short until the sky shivered, turned from violet to gray, then flushed in radiant, tremulous pink to port. The western sky was pale green, and, above the sealine, like an etching, showed the fronds of a cluster of palms, the land rise of Motutabu.

CHAPTER V

THE DEAD MAN OF MOTUTABU

THE island of Motutabu was shaped like a broad-bladed sickle, the lagoon lying in the crook of the steel with low hills, thickly set with foliage, rising irregularly behind the emerald water patched with purple where the humps of coral came close to the surface. The handle of the sickle showed as a high, precipitous ridge, crowned with the clustering palms that Chalmers had first seen rise above the horizon.

Down the cliff fell a narrow white plume of water. From the tip of the crescent blade to the shoulder handle ran the line of the reef, accented here and there with creaming surf. Up to the barrier the free sea held the rich blue of a peacock's breast.

There was no sign of human life. A few birds wheeled above the hills, and once a flight of gulls scattered over the ridge like blossoms in a gale, and went soaring seaward bent on breakfast.

The dawn wind was fair from the sea, though light. Chalmers hauled in his sheets, dropped foresail and skirted the reef, looking for an opening.

Sayers and Tuan Yuck, the former in a high state of excitement, the latter impassive as ever, both scanned the shore line through binoculars, while Chalmers, setting his feet in the rings of the mainsail and grasping the halyards, mounted to the crotch of the main gaff, resigning the wheel to Hamaku, as he prepared to con the *Aku* in. His voice came clearly from aloft in the quiet morning air.

"Come up a bit, Hamaku. Little more. Steady. Tomi, come in on your mainsheet. Lend a hand there, Sayers, will you? Keep her up, Hamaku. There's a shore current. Stand by to let go the anchor. Down staysail, Sayers! Smartly. There's a back draft from the point."

The *Aku* glided through the reef passage into the broad lagoon, the chain rattled out and the anchor struck, holding bottom in eight fathoms.

"Give her three fathoms of slack, Tomi," called Chalmers, and slid down the halyards to the deck again.

"Chap must be asleep," said Sayers. "What the devil's that?"

His exclamation was echoed by cries from Tomi and Hamaku, who threw themselves face down on the deck, lamenting loudly—

"*Auwe, ke aitu!*" (Alas, the ghosts!)

Even Tuan Yuck had started at the sight, and Chalmers stared in bewilderment. From the shore all about them came blinding flashes of light in rapid succession, as if a battery had suddenly been unmasked.

There was no sound, no sign, only the silent hostility of unwinking flares. Despite himself, Chalmers felt imaginary hairlifting along his spine. Then, one after the other, the glares were swiftly extinguished.

"What d'ye make of those?" asked Sayers. "Signals?"

Hamaku, still prostrate, broke into a torrent of Hawaiian. Sayers translated.

"He says there are spirits on the island lighting ghost fires."

The Australian himself seemed to half believe the superstition. A memory of Stevenson's stories of South Sea wizards burning fires that had no visible fuel flashed across Chalmers' recollection.

"Nonsense, Hamaku," he said. "No *pilikia* (trouble). *Aitu* no good along *haole* (white man)."

The natives raised their heads above the rail and looked fearfully shoreward. Perhaps the *Kapitani* was right. May be the *aitus* were afraid of the white man. It might be.

Suddenly they howled again. A secondary line of dazzling lights above the first, back in the hills, broke instantly out in brilliant flame. For two or three minutes they glared, too vivid for eyes to meet, then died away. Tuan Yuck set down his glasses.

"Reflections of some sort, picking up the sun," he announced. "There were none in the shadow."

Sayers sighed with visible relief.

"My nerves are in rotten shape," he said, wiping off the sweat from his forehead.

"Obsidian cliffs, I fancy," said Tuan Yuck. "Volcanic glass. I've seen something like it before. Nothing like this though."

The two natives plucked up courage as they sensed the mood of their masters, and the minutes passed without any hostile demonstration from the ghosts or further display of the weird lights. But they absolutely refused to go ashore.

"We'll have to leave them aboard," said Chalmers. "I suppose we all three want to go. We'd better take our rifles and automatics."

Sayers came up from below, steadied by his universal stimulant, refusing the coffee that Tuan Yuck prepared and shared with Chalmers.

The two white men pulled ashore with the Chinaman sitting in the stern, a Winchester across his knees. Sayers tugged at his oar, setting a hard pace even for Chalmers, and the whaleboat made rapid progress over the quiet lagoon. They spoke little, and then in whispers as seemed to befit the occasion.

"Chap must be asleep, I fancy," said Sayers. "We'll be a surprise party. Funny he isn't on the lookout. He must be getting anxious by now over his own outfit."

"There's a pile of shell over there," announced Tuan Yuck. "They've done some rotting out. If the wind had been offshore we'd have noticed it before from the smell."

He leaned over the side of the boat as they neared the beach, a covetous look in his eyes, as he estimated the possible value of the shell that lay undisturbed on the floor of the lagoon, brilliant sea shrubbery waving about the patches, primary-colored fishes darting away as the boat passed over them.

Chalmers' mind was on the marooned captain, sleeping unconscious of his rescuers close at hand. Sayers and Tuan Yuck shared one thought—pearls. That betrayed itself in Sayers' nervous tugs at his oar, and a certain feverish glitter in the Oriental's eyes.

The keel slid softly over the white sand and they sprang out, hauling the boat up the slight incline out of tide reach, their rifles at the carry, hurried with long strides across the beach amid scuttling, rustling land-crabs toward the pandanus and palmetto scrub that shod the hills.

To their right mangroves apparently masked a swamp, and perhaps the exit of a stream. To their left the beach was strewn with irregular masses of coral. They had chosen the only practical landing-place.

With the exception of the faint screams of birds high in the hills, the place seemed invested with a strange silence, that infected them with a feeling of mystery. As they neared the scrub they insensibly slackened their pace.

The quiet was uncanny, utterly at variance with all preconceived ideas of a rescue party. The half-explained incident of the blinding flares still held them to caution. A shout to awaken the supposedly solitary inhabitant might bring a rush of savages or a shower of spears and arrows.

Chalmers, scouting to one side, stopped and beckoned to the Chinaman.

"Here's your volcanic glass," he said.

He had stopped at a mirror propped against a block of coral, a warped looking-glass, cheaply framed, of the type used for trading purposes. Its surface had caught the rising rays of the sun as they had dropped anchor in the lagoon.

"That's a clever idea," said Tuan Yuck. "The man knows his South Seas. You saw how it affected our boys. He's set these all about the place on exposed ledges to catch the sun and leave him undisturbed by the natives. They're not particularly friendly in these waters, and there may be other islands nearer than we imagine. I suppose he has them placed so as to catch the sun all the day round. The man has brains."

Tuan Yuck's masklike face never seemed to change, but a certain quality of hardness entered his glance that indicated his recognition of the brain quality of the captain of the shipwrecked *Manu* did not have his unqualified approval. It simply meant a harder bargain to drive.

Sayers came hurriedly toward them.

"There's a house back in the pandanus!" he cried excitedly. "And a tent behind it. No one in sight, though."

 THEY turned and entered the scrub. The house stood in a little clearing beneath a clump of *hala* that had been left for shade. It was a cozy portable dwelling, that had evidently been shipped for the purpose in hand. Its original roof was supplemented by a thick thatch of dried palm-leaves for coolness. Just back of it showed a small tent with a fly roof against the heat.

The place looked eminently practical and comfortable, yet it, too, appeared invested with unnatural silence. There is a quality of humanity that links itself with man's habitation in lonely places that is unmistakable. Tent and house seemed alike deserted. Something of mystery the trio could not fathom emanated from the spot, intangible, illogical, but plainly making itself felt.

The natural impulse would have been to shout a welcome, but the three men almost tiptoed to the little veranda. Tuan Yuck noiselessly mounted the steps and knocked on the door softly, then with a vigorous tattoo of his knuckles. There was no answer.

If there had been, it would have startled them as unexpected. The window was draped with a *tapa* cloth of mulberry bark that did not quite cover it. The Chinaman stooped and looked through the opening. Chalmers and Sayers still stood on the level ground watching him.

"There's a man lying on the bed," he said, and kept on peering into the room.

Then he straightened up with determination, and the mystery of the occasion seemed to drop from his shoulders.

"Come on," he said abruptly, opening the unlocked door and leading the way into the house.

The room was one of two, a wooden partition dividing them. It was furnished with a pine bureau, a rough table, two wooden chairs, and a sea-chest under the window. An iron bedstead was in one corner. Clothes hung from hooks, here and there. On the chest a diving-suit was laid.

Tuan Yuck pulled down the *tapa* from the window and the rays of the early sun entered, irradiating the room, leveling their direct strength upon the bed where the figure of a bearded man lay in the rigidity that unmistakably revealed the hand of death.

CHAPTER VI

LEILA

CHALMERS stopped half way across the room. It was not his first encounter with death. His newspaper experience had divested it of much of its awe and dignity, but to him there seemed something peculiarly tragic about the sudden withdrawal of life from the man they had come so far to rescue. Possibly the dead captain had been alive when Chalmers had announced the schooner's position in *Aku's* cabin the night before, and had wondered in his last moments where his own schooner was, and if his men would come before the end.

Chalmers' main impulse was that of sympathy for the going-out of the man without a kindly word or friendly hand to minister to his last needs. He forgot the pearls. The long voyage had failed.

Sayers stood by the table, looking at some dishes that held the remnants of a meal. One platter was practically filled with small flat fish, like flounders, that had been fried in meal.

"He didn't die of starvation, that's a cinch," he announced.

Tuan Yuck wheeled suddenly from the bed he had approached.

"Don't touch any of that food!" he cried sharply. "The man has been poisoned."

"Poisoned!"

Tuan Yuck nodded.

"By the same thing that killed off the natives," he said. "The fish in the lagoon. Probably ate them before, a dozen times, without their hurting him."

They grouped about the bed. A brief look was sufficient. The dead captain's face, where his beard left it uncovered, was blotched with livid purple. So were the hands, one on his breast, one hanging over the edge of the bed at the full length of the arm. The corpse was fully dressed.

"Must have got him right after he ate them," said Sayers. "I suppose it isn't catching?" he added suspiciously, drawing back a little.

The rare ejaculation that Tuan Yuck used for laughter escaped him.

"You needn't be afraid, Sayers," he said. "Unless you are scared of his ghost." Sayers shrugged his shoulders. "His capacity for good or evil will end with his burial."

"We've got no time to bother with that," said the Australian. "The Kanakas can bury him. The question is: where are the pearls?"

He commenced to pull the diving paraphernalia from the sea-chest. Chalmers caught his arm.

"The pearls can wait, Sayers," he said. "We're going to give this man burial, and find out what we can about who he is and where he comes from. Haven't you any sense of decency?"

Sayers turned upon him, his wide-set, yellow teeth showing between his drawn-back lips in a snarl.

"See here, Chalmers," he said. "You've been boss of this expedition aboard ship so far, but you're not running it from now on. What you need is to use some common sense of your own, and if you haven't got any I'll show you where to head in."

Chalmers turned to Tuan Yuck. The Chinaman's mouth was stretched in a mirthless grimace, his eyes gleamed in mockery.

"Dead men neither tell tales nor need pearls, my young friend," he said. "I see no reason for wasting any unnecessary time on this island. The man has made his second blunder, a frequent one, I grant you; he has died too soon."

Chalmers looked from one to the other. Sayers' snarl had changed to an open grin; Tuan Yuck stood suavely unemotional. The partnership had dissolved, the pretense of fairness was tossed aside. He was aware that they considered him as but one against two, a youngster incomparably their inferior, whose will was but a small matter to be set aside as if of no consequence compared to their own desires.

But he felt no sense of fear or weakness. His jaw set as his will hardened.

"The man is going to be justly treated, alive or dead. His family is to be considered. It is worse to cheat the dead than rob the living. You two promised me fair play
2

when I went into this deal, and I'm going to see that you live up to the bargain."

His voice revealed the contempt in which he held them, and told of the action that lay behind the words. Sayers' right hand dropped casually toward his hip where the automatic pistol swung at his belt. At an almost imperceptible move of Tuan Yuck's head he arrested the action.

"Time enough to talk of division when we find the pearls," said the Chinaman. "If you are so desirous of ceremonial, Chalmers, why don't you superintend the funeral arrangements?"

It was the first time Tuan Yuck had dropped the prefix of "Mr." in addressing Chalmers, and it appeared to the latter as if the man's whole mask had fallen. A film seemed to have cleared from his eyes, and for a moment his soul looked out, sardonic, sinister, utterly selfish. He moved, giving Chalmers a clear view of the table.

Chalmers had paid no attention to the arrangement of the dishes. Now he saw something that first startled, then reassured him.

"There's one point you two seem to have overlooked," he said with a little ring of triumph in his voice. "This table is set for *two*. There is some one else on the island."

Sayers kneeling by the open sea-chest, tossing its contents on the floor, looked up.

"Why don't you go and find them?" he said.

"I am going to," answered Chalmers.

He swung out of the room, glad to escape from the sordid company it held. Tuan Yuck stood with his hands folded in his loose sleeves, his eyes still sneering. Sayers laughed as Chalmers went out. It was not until he was free of the house that he realized they had shown no surprise at his announcement. It looked as if the secret Sayers and Tuan Yuck had so evidently shared included knowledge of another besides the captain having been left on the island. If that were the case, they evidently held that person of little importance.

"As they do me," Chalmers finished the thought bitterly.

The resentment he had so often felt in the presence of the Chinaman's inscrutability changed to a determined hostility. He understood that caution was necessary. Until he could find the unknown, they were two against one. The native sailors were not to be counted on, save by the side apparently in power. It would not do to declare war too hastily, he decided.

 AS HE approached the tent, the suggestion came suddenly, that whoever had sat at table with the dead captain was probably also poisoned. That would account for the apparent apathy of Tuan Yuck and Sayers.

He hesitated outside the tent. The canvas was in full sunshine. Any one sleeping there must surely have been aroused. Half reluctantly he raised the flap and looked in. There was a cot bed, empty, a camp-stool, a low bureau and a trunk. Chalmers halted as he took in a survey of the interior and drew a sudden breath. On the trunk was a hat of soft white duck, like a man-of-warsman's, but with a quill in it; something that was unmistakably a woman's skirt, and beside it a pair of shoes, workmanlike, but eminently feminine.

A whirl of emotions possessed him. Who was the woman? The captain's wife—if she was not dead? Sayers and the Chinaman would show scant respect for her sex and weakness.

He squared his shoulders with a fresh sense of responsibility. It was no longer merely a question of a dead man's burial and the rights of a dead man's heirs. The woman might be living, suffering.

There was no trace of any one about the clearing, and Chalmers followed a little trail that led across the open toward the hills.

Just within the brush a spring bubbled up in a little basin that had been built up artificially. The path passed it, leading up-hill through a grove of pandanus. Chalmers followed it, coming out on a plateau covered with long grasses. Beyond this the hills, clothed with denser shrubbery from which sandalwood and koa trees sprang thickly, mounted more abruptly.

As Chalmers gazed, a slender figure, clad in white, came out of the forest toward him, knee-high in the waving grasses. Her hair showed radiant in the sun, but her face was pale and the eyes unseeing as the girl came nearer.

Her arms were filled with great, white waxen blossoms and trailing vines. Chalmers caught the heavy, sickly scent of the flowers twenty feet away. They reminded him of a mortuary and he knew they had been gathered for the dead.

At first he thought her blind, so vacant was the gaze of the eyes that were the deep blue of the open sea. Then, suddenly, she saw him standing there. The soul came back into her glance as if recalled from very far away. Her lips parted, the flowers fell to the ground.

One short-sleeved arm was raised toward him in appeal. Brief as the gesture was, Chalmers noticed the blue veins showing faintly beneath the satiny surface, tanned to pale gold.

"Who are you?" she asked.

Her voice held the quality of a linnet's song. The blue eyes were still a little vacant, the lids stained with grief. It seemed as if she were walking in her sleep.

Chalmers stammered a reply, trying to find phrases that would reassure her, all the chivalry of his nature aroused at the sight of her brave helplessness. But his words halted.

"I—why, I—we came to take you away," he said.

"To take us away? Why did you stay so long? You are a day too late—just a day too late. If you had only hurried—perhaps——"

The life in her eyes died out. Her hands groped toward him. She swayed uncertainly as Chalmers sprang forward and caught her in his arms.

He ran with her to the little spring and bathed her wrists and forehead in the cool water. Her head lay on his knees. In the checkered sunlight her hair was golden-brown and, despite the moisture that turned it to little tendrils on her brow, filled with the iridescence of splintered rainbows. The very ghost of a girl she seemed, Chalmers thought, as she lay slim and pale, her breast barely lifting beneath the white middy blouse she wore.

His manhood warmed at the sight of her utter helplessness. He wondered what relation she was to the dead captain. Probably his daughter, he decided, still working to bring her back to consciousness, already appointing himself her champion. As her protector he felt himself capable of handling a dozen Tuan Yucks, a score of Sayers!

He felt her body relax. A sigh parted her lips to which the color was beginning to return. The upper one drooped in a pendule over the pearly teeth. A faint rose tint came into her cheeks, and long lashes fluttered. A wave of tenderness came over him. He lifted the little hand he had been gently chafing, and raised it to his lips in token of fealty. She shivered a little at the contact and her eyes opened, looking questioningly into his.

There was a slight rustle in the thicket. Chalmers looked up to see Tuan Yuck regarding them, his face expressionless, his eyes inscrutable.

"You have found Miss Denman, I see," he said. "Our friend Sayers is still looking for—what he will not find in a hurry, I fancy. We are at your service, Miss Denman."

The girl shrank from him, closer to Chalmers.

"I do not know you," she faltered. "Where is Butler—and the crew? Did you come in the schooner with them?"

She was trembling violently. Chalmers gently took her arm.

"We'll tell you all about it presently, Miss Denman," he said. "We are here to help you. Perhaps we had better go down to the house."

"Yes," she assented, then started back. "Wait," she said. "Where are my flowers? I must get my flowers. They are for my father."

"They are just a little way back," said Chalmers. "Shall I get them?"

"No!" They went back along the trail together and gathered up the blooms.

"Thank you," she said. "My name is Leila Denman."

"And mine, Bruce Chalmers," he answered.

"I don't quite understand," she went on. "You say you came here to help me, and I should be very grateful—but—" her eyes filled with tears and she caught her under lip between her teeth—"I have tried to be brave," she went on, her voice tremulous, "but I could do nothing alone. I could not —even—bury him."

Chalmers longed to take her into his arms and comfort her as one would a child. Her broken phrases called up the horror of her situation, alone with her dead father, forced, in with her frail strength, to plan crude, helpless methods of disposing of the body. It was horrible. He marveled at the spirit that had kept her from madness.

"It will be all right now, Miss Denman," he said, conscious of the poverty of his phrase. "We will do all we can. We came

to rescue your father. We—I—did not know you were here."

As he spoke the suspicion came to him that Tuan Yuck and Sayers had been aware of her presence from the first.

CHAPTER VII

CHALMERS HAS A CLOSE CALL

THE burial of the dead sea-captain took place at night beneath a blaze of stars. Tuan Yuck cajoled Hamaku and Tomi ashore by explaining to them the mystery of the flashing mirrors, and a grave was dug in the deep soil of the first ridge of the hills.

The rude coffin was interred before Chalmers called the bereaved girl from the tent to which she had taken her sorrow after performing the last few personal offices for the dead that she had insisted on carrying out with her own hands. As they reached the grave beside which two great fires were leaping, sending out the incense of burning sandalwood, the Hawaiians tossed into the pit fragrant masses of wood orchids and *maile* vine, then stepped back into the shadows. Suddenly Tomi's sweet tenor chanted softly a native lament to the chords of Sayers' zither.

It was theatrical but somehow it did not seem bizarre. The night-wind waved the palm crests like funeral plumes and set the long grasses shivering on the ridge. The reef below them sighed faintly; beyond, the sea ran out in lonely leagues to where it blended with the starry sky. They seemed very remote from all the world and very close to the things that lie beyond it.

Chalmers stood beside the weeping girl in a silence full of sympathy but embarrassed for lack of words. Across the grave Tuan Yuck in his Oriental, priestlike robes was a mystic figure in the swift alternations of flame and shadow. It was he who had planned the obsequies and had persuaded Sayers into at least an outward show of sympathy. Yet Chalmers felt instinctively that all his deferential courtesy toward the girl covered some hidden purpose of his own to accomplish which it was necessary to win her confidence.

As the music ended Tuan Yuck stepped to the other side of Leila Denman.

"Your philosophies and mine, Miss Denman," he said in his silken voice, "hold many minor differences, but in one main matter they agree—that there is no death. And I think your father, like Robert Louis Stevenson, would choose such a place as this for the last sleep. You remember:

> Under the wide and starry sky,
> Dig the grave and let me lie."

The girl turned to him gratefully.

"Thank you," she said, "and thank you for him, too."

She took his arm and he led her down the ridge. Sayers came forward and joined Chalmers.

"The Chink's a wonder, isn't he?" he said. "You've got to hand it to him. A bit *too* smart for my way of thinking. We've got to keep our weather eyes open, Chalmers, or he'll get the best of us."

There was a quality in Sayers's voice that suggested that the Australian's admiration for Tuan Yuck was not unalloyed with envy. Chalmers determined to foster any spark of ill-will that existed. It might reduce the odds later on if any issue arose over his determination to protect the girl's interests.

"He likes to play the leader," he prompted.

"And he'd like to get a leader's share," said Sayers who had been drinking and whose voice was husky. "You and I have got to stick to each other, Chalmers," he went on. "White against yellow, you know. He's a sly one. A regular Mongolian Mephistopheles, he is."

They had been watching the natives pile a cairn of loose lava boulders above the dead and now they moved on down the hill.

"The girl's a wonder," said Sayers. "Did you notice her skin, Chalmers? Put pearls around that throat of hers and you couldn't see 'em, they'd match that close. And her figure!" His tongue clucked suddenly. "A man might do worse—eh? A beauty like that, fortune or no fortune!"

The reek of gin was on the Australian's breath and Chalmers turned away to conceal his disgust. They had crossed the clearing. Tuan Yuck and Leila Denman were standing by the veranda of the little house. The light of two lanterns showed her face wan and tired. But she held it proudly erect. As they came up she turned to them.

"I don't know what to say to you all," she said. "You've been—just wonderful."

She choked back a sob and stretched out her hand to each of them. Chalmers bit his lip in restraint as Sayers held it while he gazed at her appraisingly.

She turned to him.

"Good night, Mr. Chalmers," she said. "You have been very kind and thoughtful."

Chalmers, who had felt himself a blunderer all day as he tried to express his sympathy in ways that would not jar her sensitiveness, stammered something in reply. He fancied he felt a faint pressure return his handclasp. He watched her go into her tent, saw it faintly illumined through the trees and followed Tuan Yuck into the little house.

SAYERS had already established himself at the little table with his deck of cards and a bottle of gin. He looked up from arranging his layout at Canfield as the others entered.

"Going to stay ashore tonight, Chalmers?" he asked. "I am. I've staked out the cot in the next room. I've no fancy for that. You're welcome to it." He jerked his head in the direction of the bed in which the captain had died.

"There's a hammock on the veranda," replied Chalmers. "I'll use that."

"Going to play sentinel over the lady, eh? All right, you watch me and I'll watch you. She's the best pearl on the island, and so far she's the only one in sight. Some figure, Chalmers. I envy you!"

He broke off, checked by the look in Chalmers' eyes.

"You needn't look at me as if you wanted to murder me, son," he said. "You needn't be jealous of me. I'm a married man. Hang it, I'll lend you my zither to serenade her if you think it'll help you any."

Tuan Yuck interrupted.

"I shall sleep on the schooner," he said silkily. "I prefer my own cabin. And let me recommend to you both the maxim that sex and business do not go together."

"You're a cold-blooded squid," said Sayers as the Chinaman went out.

For the first time the Australian showed the effects of liquor. His blotched face was crimsoned, the muddy whites of his eyes transfused with blood, and the veins on his temples stood out in painful relief.

"Listen, you young Puritan," he said, pouring some liquor into a cup and pushing it across the table to Chalmers, "have a drink for once. Drink to the lady, and no offense meant. An' good luck to you. 'Member what I said? A man might do worse. 'Member what else I said about that slit-eyed yellow devil that's just gone out. He don't pull any wool over my eyes with his smooth tricks."

He drained his own cup and took up his cards, shuffling them in nervous fingers, oblivious of the other's presence.

Chalmers left him, glad to breathe the outer air. He walked down to the edge of the water. The light in Leila's tent was out, he noticed. The lamp in Tuan Yuck's cabin showed like a baleful eye. Back in the dead man's room he heard Sayers singing in maudlin mood:

"Drink to me only with thine eyes,
   And I will pledge with mine;
Or leave a kiss within the cup,
   And I'll not ask for wine."

He strode the full length of the lagoon, responsibility heavy upon him and, taking advantage of the low tide, rounded a promontory that jutted out from the precipitous cliff that formed the handle of the island's sickle formation. He clambered over the scattered rocks at the end of the cape and jumped on to the wet beach.

Instantly he sank halfway to his knees, the sand holding him in a vise, while something tugged at him as if some buried monster was trying to pull him down. He had leaped into a quicksand. Instantly he flung himself forward, spreading his arms wide, flat on the surface as he felt himself buried almost to the hips.

The treacherous sand sucked at his finger-tips. Try as he would he could not free either of his legs. He battled ceaselessly, fighting off the panic that attacked him. As well as he could he raised his head and shouted. The cliff echoed it, a few startled seabirds rose screaming but, even as he called, he knew the uselessness of it. The schooner was too far away, almost half a mile from shore, and he had walked nearly two miles from the landing-place. His only help lay with himself and already he felt that he was weakening, the insidious steady pull of the sand winning its victory inch by inch.

Every effort only worked against him. At last he lay exhausted, his cheek against the sand. Above him the Southern Cross burned in a sky of velvet. The tide was at the slack. Presently it would turn, and long before morning, if the sand had not buried him, the water would act as his shroud. He could hear the ripples lapping as if they were chuckling at his predicament.

Leila would be left to the scant mercy of Tuan Yuck and Sayers. Tuan Yuck, who had said that "dead men neither told tales nor needed pearls," and Sayers, who had leered as he talked of the skin of her throat. And he would be as helpless as the dead captain lying in his grave on the ridge.

He lay quiet for a while, summoning all his energies. His body slowly sank into the treacherous surface. Once more he raised his head and shouted, only to hear the echo from the cliff and the cries of the protesting birds.

He turned his head shoreward. The rock he had jumped from was not very far away. Seaweed fringed its base. By a supreme effort he threw himself in its direction, twisting his body at the waist and struggling to free his legs from the steady suction of the sand. Cramped until rupture seemed imminent, his fingers just touched the fronds of the seaweed—and no more.

Fight as he might he could not gain a hand-grasp. And the pain of his position was paralyzing him below the waist.

His clawing fingers sank deep, his head dropped and the grit entered his lips. He had come to the end of his struggle. The sand clogged his nostrils and his hands twitched convulsively, burying themselves.

They struck something solid beneath the sand—the surface of a submerged rock. Hope marshaled the retreating remnants of his will and strength.

Groping while he raised his body, he found a crevice and wedged his fingers into it. The rock was only a few inches below the surface; his forearms rested on it. He gained an inch, two inches; at the expense of agony, three inches. One more and he clutched a stout stem of kelp weed. It was slippery but it held, and he got a second hand-grip.

In five minutes he had dragged himself clear, crawling to the top of the rock. He lay there exhausted for a while, then sat up to chafe his numbed legs. Far off, the tiny light in Tuan Yuck's cabin winked and went out.

Midway along the tall cliff the waterfall streamed down like a silken scarf in the wind. At the base of the precipice low feathery vegetation grew luxuriantly. The sand was dotted with clumps of lava. Close to shore it was probably firm, but Chalmers was in no mood for further adventure. At the cliff's end a high buttress of rock ran out into deep water. At flood tide the place was shut off from the rest of the island. At all but low tide the quicksand made it unapproachable.

As he rested, Chalmers reviewed the situation. He had cheated the quicksand, but the human odds were still against him. The death of Captain Denman had complicated matters.

He had anticipated Tuan Yuck and Sayers driving a hard bargain with the skipper, but at least it would have been two men against two for fair play. He felt certain that his own ideas of chivalry were not shared by either of his partners. The Chinaman had frankly said that sex and business were incompatible. Sayers regarded womanhood only from the coarser standpoint. The best thing would be, he decided, to wait until Tuan Yuck showed his hand, which he would undoubtedly when the pearls materialized.

The pearls! Chalmers chafed at his own stupidity. That was the reason of Tuan Yuck's kindliness to the girl and his persuasion of Sayers into a semblance of respect for the dead. They wanted to find out where the pearls were before they uncovered their real motives. And as soon as they did, he must be ready to act.

He freed himself from the useless labyrinth of conjecture. He would need all his wits about him on the morrow, and perhaps his strength. Every muscle in his body ached as he made his way back to the house. The lamp still burned above Sayers' head where he had fallen asleep amid the scattered cards.

There was a canvas hammock slung at one end of the veranda and Chalmers rolled into it. Almost instantly he was asleep, and for the first time a girl's face filled his dreams, the face of Leila Denman.

CHAPTER VIII

TUAN YUCK DROPS HIS MASK

CHALMERS awoke before sunrise, with stiffened limbs still aching from the struggle in the quicksand. He had turned in all standing and he now surveyed himself ruefully. Drying sand dripped from him like water, and his usually natty appearance was changed to that of a beachcomber sadly down on his luck.

A glance through the window showed Sayers still asprawl over the table. The flap of Leila Denman's tent was closed. He resolved to swim off to the schooner and secure fresh clothing, coming back in the whaleboat with Tuan Yuck.

He walked to the edge of the water, took off his belt and laid it with the automatic in its holster on a ledge of rocks. Then he stripped and swam out through the cool water with long, luxurious strokes, his tired muscles relaxing, and hauled himself up to the bows by the bobstay.

As he went toward the cabin, he saw Hamaku and Tomi by the taffrail busily plucking the last of the schooner's chickens. The natives responded to his greeting in a surly fashion they had developed of late.

Chalmers took no notice of it.

"Bimeby you bring chicken along shore for breakfast," he said.

Hamaku muttered something and Tomi laughed. Chalmers took the men up smartly.

"What was that?" he demanded.

"Big Boss speak you eat along schooner this morning," replied Hamaku, a spice of impudence in tone and look.

"What Big Boss? You sabe plenty I your boss?"

"Tuan Yuck he speak you boss along ship maybe. He boss along land. We along land now."

Chalmers looked at the man. The native's eyes shifted.

"Tuan Yuck he plenty big *kahuna* (wizard)," he said, half surly, half apologetic.

Chalmers forebore to press the point. It was evident that Tuan Yuck had impressed the natives with his own power through the most effective medium, their superstition. But he determined that Leila Denman, at least, should not come aboard the schooner until matters were satisfactorily arranged.

"You fetch me two, three pail fresh water," he said.

The natives obeyed and sluiced the brine from his skin. He went below to his own cabin, opposite the Chinaman's, and put on fresh underwear, clean duck trousers and a shirt. Then he fished out a pair of shoes, slipped them on and went into the main cabin.

Tuan Yuck's door opened and the Oriental came out, fully dressed. He expressed no surprise at Chalmers' appearance, beyond the slightest lift of his eyebrows at the latter's spruceness.

 THEY rowed ashore in silence, and Chalmers retrieved his belt and pistol. As they walked up the beach, Leila Denman came toward them. Her face was pale, despite its golden weathertan, but her eyes were clear and steady with only the faint trace of weeping about their long-lashed rims.

She greeted them cordially with perfect self-possession, with something almost boyish in her erectness and the way she gave to each her cool, slim hand.

"I don't know, Miss Denman," said Tuan Yuck, "whether Mr. Chalmers has told you that I am the *chef* of this expedition, but such is the case. And if you will breakfast with us aboard the schooner I can promise you broiled chicken and some excellent coffee. Perhaps you will give us some Motutabu *papayas* in exchange?"

Chalmers, standing beside him, caught the girl's glance and slightly shook his head.

"I am not so lacking in hospitality," she answered, accepting the cue without hesitation. "Though I must admit the chicken sounds tempting. I have almost forgotten what one looks like."

Chalmers, watching Tuan Yuck, thought he saw disappointment in the Oriental's eyes. But it did not show in his voice as he replied.

"That will be delightful. But you must let us provide the chickens." He turned and gave an order in Hawaiian to the natives, who started for the boat.

A hoarse shout stopped them. Sayers, sodden with liquor, unkempt and morose, slouched off the veranda and joined them. Leila bestowed an involuntary look upon his uncouth figure in the crumpled, dingy ducks, that made the Australian flush and mutter something about changing his clothes before he shambled down the beach and went off to the schooner.

The meal was served out-of-doors at a table placed under the *hala* trees. Leila Denman sat at one end, facing Tuan Yuck, with Chalmers at her right, opposite Sayers. The Australian gave evidence that his principal mission to the schooner had been to satisfy his appetite for liquor. He ate nothing, but sat with his hairy fingers beating a nervous tattoo on the table.

The Chinaman waited for the Hawaiians to clear away before he spoke. The quality of the Oriental's mood showed in his glances. His face was bland as ever, but his eyes held the hardness of orbs of polished metal. A sinister sternness seemed to emanate from the man as hidden flame or ice might make itself manifest.

To Chalmers the morning was rife with a prescience of malignancy that pressed on him even as the air. He sat with his mind alert, his nerves tense for action, waiting for the move that should determine what that action was to be.

"In the matter of leaving the island, Miss Denman," said Tuan Yuck at last. "Is there any particular place you want to go—Sydney, for example, or Honolulu?"

He spoke with grave courtesy, but to Chalmers, question and tone alike were tinged with mockery.

"I hardly know," she answered. "I have practically no relatives." Chalmers saw a swift glitter in Tuan Yuck's eyes. "I have no mother—we were quite alone, father and I."

Sayers' tongue clucked suddenly and his restless fingers pressed on the table till the tips whitened.

"You should consider that you are quite an heiress," went on the Chinaman, "that is, if the character of the shell already rotted out is any criterion, the lagoon should hold a fortune. The shells on the beach are typical pearl oysters. Aside, of course, from what your father found already?"

The inflection of the speech made it a question. Leila answered it readily.

"He found a great many," she said. "Some of them I believe are very valuable, though I am no judge."

Sayers's dull eyes sparkled. The glitter in Tuan Yuck's gaze intensified.

"Ah!" he said, simply but the ejaculation was far from colorless. "I should like to see them. I may be able to give you some idea of what they are really worth."

The girl got up from the table and went into her tent before Chalmers could prevent her. Sayers's glance followed her greedily, his jaw was thrust forward. The veins on his forehead seemed to writhe, and his big stumpy-fingered hands worked as if they already clutched the gems. Tuan Yuck sat immobile, his glittering eyes the only sign of life in the masklike face. Chalmers leaned forward speaking in a low voice.

"There is to be no bargaining," he said firmly. "Her heritage is all that is left her. You know our agreement?"

Tuan Yuck turned his baleful eyes toward the speaker. The shadow of a smile, or a sneer, flitted across his face.

"What agreement?" demanded Sayers hoarsely.

"You called it a gentlemen's agreement, Sayers," said Chalmers. "At all events I intend to see it carried out. We are not going to rob the dead or cheat the living while I can prevent it."

Sayers's retort was stopped by the reappearance of the girl, bearing a shallow wooden bowl. The Australian's tongue showed between his teeth like a panting dog's, his face was patched with purple, his eyes bloodshot, gazing on the calabash as if hypnotized.

Leila Denman set the polished bowl of native wood on the table before Tuan Yuck. It seemed to be nearly full of a milky opalescence. Sayers stood up and looked at it. He gave a bellow of disappointment.

"Those ain't all?" he demanded.

The girl looked up with surprise at the rudeness of his tone.

"These are only the seeds and *baroques*," she said. "I always carry the real pearls here to keep them in good condition."

She put her hand into the opening of her middy blouse and pulled up from her breast a bag of soft leather, untying the narrow silk ribbon that suspended it from her neck. About the collar of her blouse she wore a black silk handkerchief. This she unfastened and spread out on the table. On to it she poured out from the bag a number of shimmering globules that shone with satiny luster as they rolled a little way here and there and settled into groups.

Chalmers, who knew little of pearls, held his breath at the beauty of the nacreous mass of varying color, silver and rose and azure. The sunshine checkered the table-top with gold, and in it the pearls seemed to be alive, so vivid was the iridescence. A few were small, the majority larger than the pink pearl of Taroi. At least a dozen were the size of husked hazel-nuts and two, almost perfectly matched for size and shape, were as big as marbles, glorified, transcendent marbles, rosy-silver of hue with a bloom that seemed almost fuzzy in its refraction.

Tuan Yuck's eyes blazed. Sayers, his hands gripping the table, rocked gently to and fro as he stood licking his feverish lips with the tip of his tongue.

"There are fifty-nine of them," said Leila Denman. "They are beautiful, aren't they?"

TUAN YUCK, with fingers that trembled ever so slightly, drew the black square of silk with its precious contents slowly toward him. Sayers, breathing hard, followed every inch of the Chinaman's movements with fascinated avarice as Tuan Yuck delicately turned over the pearls with his pointed fingers.

"It is hard to fix values," he said. "All these are exceptionally well shaped and they are wonderfully alive, owing to your plan of keeping them close to your body, Miss Denman. These pearls—" he set apart six of the gems—"are easily worth twenty-five hundred apiece. There are ten at least worth much more than that. This matched pair I have never seen equaled. Their value is only to be estimated after they get in the market. I might miss the price they'll fetch by thousands. Roughly speaking I do not believe I am exaggerating by saying that the lot should represent between one hundred and fifty thousand and two hundred thousand dollars."

Leila Denman's face matched the palest of the pearls despite her tan. Chalmers gasped. Sayers moistened his dry lips with his tongue before he could speak in a voice that squeaked ludicrously.

"And the lagoon!" he ejaculated.

Tuan Yuck lifted his shoulders in a non-committal shrug.

"These may have come from an exceptionally rich patch," he said. His voice had lost its silkiness and sounded sharply vibrant. "Pearl oysters are sick oysters and the sickness often runs in colonies or patches. The lagoon may yield as many more like these, or less. Or it may hold pearls to almost fabulous values, like the lagoon of Faleita where Nacre Williams harvested over four million dollars before he stripped it. Lagoons are lotteries."

He replaced the pearls gently, one by one, in the little bag and placed it on top of the seed pearls in the calabash in the center of the table.

"You are a very rich young woman, Miss Denman," he said.

The girl set a hand to her heart.

"It seems so unfair," she said. "Father risked his life for them. If it was not for them he would be alive. All that money, and none of it of use to help him."

"Pearls ain't much good on a desert island," said Sayers, looking hungrily at the bowl with its precious contents. "They ain't pills, you know."

Leila Denman looked at him but he seemed unconscious of his grossness. The man had coarsened rapidly in the last few hours. He laughed at what he esteemed a witticism.

"They wouldn't have been good for anything except to play marbles on the beach with, miss," he went on. "I'll warrant you'd be glad to trade 'em for a home trip."

Chalmers set his jaw, clenching his fists till the nails scored his palms. The pieces were being set on the board.

"Put your pearls away, Miss Denman," he said.

She reached for the bag but drew back her hand as Sayers clapped his big palm over the top of the calabash.

"Hold on a minute," he said. "There's no use beating about the bush. When your schooner got wrecked, miss, and all hands lost, I was the only one who found out where you and your father were stranded—lost in the middle of the ocean. You'd both of you have rotted if it hadn't been for me. I got up this expedition and Tuan Yuck there financed it. Young Galahad there," he nodded at Chalmers, "was navigator. We were all in the deal. And it wasn't a pleasure trip. It cost money and we expec'. returns on the investment."

"That seems only fair," said the girl, trembling a little as she sensed the growing excitement. "How much do you want?"

"The expenses have been about two thousand dollars," broke in Chalmers. "The schooner can be resold for something. Give these men five thousand apiece for their investment returns, as they call them, and that will end it."

Sayers laughed loudly. Tuan Yuck's eyes danced behind their slitted lids like a mocking devil's. He said nothing, content while Sayers played his game.

"And you?" asked the girl, turning to Chalmers.

"I want nothing," he answered.

"To —— with you!" cried Sayers. "Because you are stuck on a pretty face do you think our brains are addled? This is a business proposition. It's all—or nothing!

Chalmers' hand dropped to the grip of his automatic. Leila Denman looked at Tuan Yuck sitting opposite to her, bland, motionless, his cold glittering eyes the only signs of life or interest.

"You see," he answered her look, "our impulses are entirely mercenary. Chalmers has suffered a change of heart, quite natural at his age."

"You promised fair treatment and no bargaining!" cried Chalmers hotly.

Tuan Yuck emitted a derisive sound like a goat's bleat.

"You are still very young," he answered.

"We're wasting time," said Sayers. "I want to get at that lagoon. When we're through with that you two can get a free passage home, or you can stay behind and play Adam and Eve for all we care. Meanwhile I'll take care of these."

He lifted the bag in his left hand as Chalmers sprang to his feet, leveling his pistol at Sayers' head. The Australian drew simultaneously and fired as Chalmers pressed the trigger.

There was only one shot. The action of Chalmers' automatic had been choked by the quicksand. He heard the bark of Sayers's gun and felt the heat of the flame from the barrel as he vaulted across the table and crashed into the startled Australian. His swift leap had disconcerted Sayers's none-too-steady aim, and the bullet had gone wild.

Chalmers rushed his man who was still staggering from the impact. Sayers fired again wildly and in the same fraction of a second Chalmers' right smashed viciously up and landed on the Australian's jaw, straightening him for a second before he began to sag like a half-filled sack of meal and pitched forward senseless under the table.

The girl stood wide-eyed. The table was strewn with the scattered seed pearls and *baroques*, but the bag of pearls had vanished. Tuan Yuck stood at the other end of the table imperturbable, his arms folded. It was not his policy to interfere while others played his game, and the elimination of Chalmers or Sayers, or both of them, fitted in with the moves of his opening play.

"Have you got them?" asked Chalmers.

She shook her head, looking at Tuan Yuck.

Chalmers whirled. The Oriental's elbow twitched and Chalmers flung himself upon him, pinning his arms to his sides and grappling for the gun concealed in the long sleeves, twisting him round and bending him over the table until it seemed as if the Chinaman's back must break.

Tuan Yuck struggled fiercely but silently. Writhing, he snapped at Chalmers with his teeth like a mad dog, frothing at the lips, his eyes glaring, the mask of his face distorted with rage and pain. The pressure of his spine against the table-edge beneath Chalmers' weight paralyzed his nerve centers. His body collapsed beneath Chalmers's weight, his arms grew limp and the automatic fell to the ground.

"Give me that gun, Miss Denman," panted Chalmers.

The girl came swiftly to his side, knelt and picked it up. She was trembling, but she controlled her weakness and thrust the pistol into Chalmers' groping hand.

"I've got the pearls, too," she said. "They fell out of his sleeve."

Tuan Yuck, as his cracking spine got relief, suddenly shouted aloud in Hawaiian. Chalmers clamped his left hand over his mouth and rammed the automatic's muzzle viciously under the Chinaman's armpit.

"I'll kill you, cheerfully," he said, "if you don't keep quiet."

Tuan Yuck knew that he meant it. "Let me up," he whispered. "You've broken my back."

"Put up your hands!"

Tuan Yuck obeyed with a groan as Chalmers suffered him to stand up. His eyes gleamed as he straightened. Leila Denman cried out in swift alarm—

"The *Kanakas!*"

Chalmers, grinding the pistol-muzzle into Tuan Yuck's ribs, heard the soft pad of running feet on the firm sand behind him. It was Hamaku and Tomi coming to the rescue of the Big Boss.

"Tell them to stop," he said to Tuan Yuck. "In English! Quick!"

The Chinaman sullenly obeyed. The natives halted half-way down the beach.

"Tell them to go back—down to the water. Watch them, Miss Denman."

"They're going," she reported.

"All right. Now, do you think you can get me Sayers's gun? Take off his belt."

The girl was behind him and he did not see the strained look on her face nor the effort with which she pulled herself together. The loss of her father, the disclosure of the intentions of Tuan Yuck and Sayers, culminating with the swift turmoil of the last few minutes, had taxed her strength to the utmost. She did not trust herself to answer, but knelt beside Sayers, prostrate under the table, unfastened his belt and dragged it from beneath his body. He moaned a little, and she hurried back to where Chalmers still held the pistol against the Chinaman's body.

"He's coming to," she said.

"Quickly then," he answered, unconscious of everything but the need of haste. "Take the pistol out of the holster. Put down your arms," he commanded Tuan Yuck. "Now give me the belt, Miss Denman. Hold the gun against him. Arms close to your sides, Tuan Yuck. Now, Miss Denman, I'm going to strap him up. Remember he wouldn't hesitate to kill us. Fire if he makes a move. Can you do it?"

"Yes."

She bit her lips in the attempt to steady her voice. Chalmers cast a swift glance at her. Her face was deadly white, but her chin was uptilted and her eyes narrowed with determination. He swiftly ran Sayers' belt about the Chinaman's body, cinching it until the leather sank into the flesh.

"That holds him," he said triumphantly. "Now for the legs." He used his own belt to truss the other's ankles and leaned Tuan Yuck helplessly against a tree. "That's all over," said Chalmers. "Now for Sayers. Bravo for you, Miss Denman."

Even as he spoke the girl swayed, her eyes closed, the pistol dropped from her hand and she swooned. Chalmers caught her about the waist as she fell. Under the table Sayers was dragging himself up to his knees. Down the beach Hamaku and Tomi had jumped into the whaleboat and were pulling furiously for the schooner.

Chalmers thought rapidly. Hampered with the unconscious girl, the odds were against him. The rifles they had brought ashore the day before were still in the house, but there were more aboard the schooner. If Hamaku had gone for them they might be picked off at long range unless they sought cover.

He lowered the girl gently to the ground

and picked up his own pistol from beside the table, as Sayers got waveringly to his feet and lunged toward him. Sidestepping, he brought the butt of the automatic down on the top of the Australian's head. Blood spurted and Sayers fell like a log.

Chalmers thrust all the guns into the bosom of his shirt and stooped to pick up the girl once more. Tuan Yuck still leaned helplessly against the tree, his eyes malignant as a shark's. The thought came into Chalmers' brain to kill both him and Sayers and make an end of it. For a second he hesitated.

A bullet came whining through the little grove high above his head. Hamaku had remembered the other rifles and was firing from the deck of the schooner. Another shot came lower but wide and to the right. With the girl in his arms Chalmers ran to the house, the bullets trailing him, sped up the veranda steps and into the house where he laid Leila on the bed.

The Winchesters were leaning against the bureau. He pumped a cartridge into the lever of one of them and knelt by the door to aim. Hamaku had jumped into the boat and was crouching in the bows while Tomi rowed for the shore.

Guessing at the range, Chalmers fired. The bullet hit the water and ricochetted, skipping over the surface close to the boat.

Hamaku replied and the shot smashed the window of the house, thudding into the wall above the girl and going on through the frail woodwork. Chalmers wondered at the native's skill, then remembered he had been a member of the Hawaiian National Guard. The flimsy house was only a protection in the way it might hide them from his aim.

He took the senseless girl from the bed and carried her into the next room and put her on the floor for safety. Back at the door again, he found the boat had landed under the cover of some rocks between which Hamaku and Tomi were now crawling toward the clearing.

CHAPTER IX

CHECK FOR TUAN YUCK

THE minutes passed in a silence that was ominous. The trunks of the *hala* trees, though neither big nor thickly set, yet afforded a cover that made accurate shooting difficult. The beach itself, while fairly open from the front of the house to the water, was strewn with masses of lava and coral rock, behind which a whole company might advance in open order and never expose themselves.

Once the natives succeeded in getting in touch with Tuan Yuck and Sayers, the odds would be four to one; three to one actually, as far as firearms were concerned. They had brought six Winchesters on the trip besides the three automatics. These last, one out of commission until it could be cleaned of the sand, were in Chalmers' possession with three of the rifles. But his supply of cartridges was limited. And, if the others attacked simultaneously on three sides, they could riddle the house with every chance of at least crippling the girl and himself.

One hope lay in the smash over the head he had given the Australian with the pistol. He hoped he had put him seriously out of commission.

Either of them, he thought, would have had no compunction in killing him in cold blood. They had tried to. It would not have been murder if he had retaliated in kind. But the girl might not have so considered it. He wondered how much she thought him tarred with the same brush as the others. Their plan of getting money for the rescue, even on a compromise basis of reward, appeared to him now entirely too mercenary for him to have ever considered. That was the reason why Tuan Yuck and Sayers, reading him aright, had concealed their knowledge of the girl, fearing he would be overscrupulous.

They had used him as a catspaw. He burned with resentment at the thought. They had treated him as a youngster, but from now on they would find him a different person to deal with.

If only he could get on even terms! The Hawaiians were evidently under Tuan Yuck's control. That the Chinaman was absolutely treacherous was assured. He believed that the Oriental's crafty brain held a determination to ultimately take the entire treasure for himself after he had used, first Chalmers, and now Sayers to secure it.

Chalmers watched with every sense alert. He did not dare leave the doorway lest the natives should make a successful rush across the open to liberate Tuan Yuck.

And all this time the girl lay unconscious. He was not afraid for her life, save from a stray bullet, understanding the exhaustion under which she had broken down, but it seemed heartless to make no attempt to revive her. Yet she was safer as she was, he concluded, listening for a sound from the other room.

It was oppressively hot. The perspiration ran off his forehead into his eyes. His palms were slippery on the rifle stock, and his thin clothes, saturated in spots with moisture, stuck to him unpleasantly. It was not yet noon, but a thermometer on the door-jamb registered 110°. There was a vague mistiness in the air that grayed the usually vivid shadows of the trees, and the sunshine seemed to have lost its brightness, though not its power for heat.

Two shots came together, wide-angled from his right. One plowed a furrow across the planking of the veranda in front of where he crouched. The other, doubtless fired by Tomi, had either hit a tree or gone wild.

He could see nothing, but the location of the firing bothered him. It meant that the two natives were working round to the back of the house. There was plenty of brush there to conceal them and no windows for outlook. It meant also that they were not going to risk themselves across the space in front.

There was a side window in the other room and he went swiftly to it, hoping for the chance of a lucky shot. His blood was up and he had no compunctions about firing to kill at the men who, from sheer lust of gain, were willing to shoot the girl and himself in cold blood. He was equally determined that they should not lay a finger on the girl's inheritance as long as he could prevent it. He wondered, grimly, what Tuan Yuck had promised Hamaku and Tomi.

Leila Denman stirred as he crossed the room, opened her eyes and looked dazedly about her. As she caught sight of Chalmers, kneeling beside the window, rifle in hand, terror joined the nausea that swept over her. For the moment all the events that had brought her to this pass were blotted out.

"Who are you?" she asked, staring at him. "Where is my father?"

She raised herself on one elbow as Chalmers turned toward her. A bullet suddenly sent the lower pane of glass shivering to the floor.

"Lie down flat!" he commanded. "It's all right, Miss Denman, please do as I tell you."

He caught sight of a brown figure bounding from a clump of coral to the undergrowth and fired hastily through the broken window. The bushes waved and rustled and he realized with a swift qualm of apprehension that he had missed and that Tuan Yuck would soon be released and their refuge made untenable.

While he hesitated, desperately seeking for some plan of action, the girl sat up, despite his protest, and then got to her feet.

"I'm all right now," she said. "I remember everything. They are firing at us. Give me a gun. I can shoot, too. The cowards!"

He looked at her in surprised admiration. The color had come back to her cheeks and lips and the sparkle to her eyes. Mouth and chin were set, every line of her lithe figure expressed determination.

"You must not expose yourself," he said. She flashed him a look.

"I am not going to faint again," she answered. "I despise myself for it. And I am not going to let you do all the fighting. Give me the gun I took from that man."

A bullet came from the left, straight through outer wall and partition, humming between them where they stood.

"That's Tuan Yuck," said Chalmers.

The girl neither blanched nor wavered, even when a second missile came from the opposite direction and the upper half of the window tinkled on the floor. They were surrounded. The shell of the portable house was powerless to protect them. With three rifles pumping their contents, the place would soon be like a sieve. It seemed a miracle to Chalmers that neither of them had been hit. The situation was desperate, almost hopeless.

He swept the girl back into a corner.

"Listen," he said. "We're in hard case. But there's a way out. They are after the pearls. If we give them up——"

She stamped her foot.

"Give me something to help fight with!" she cried. "I wouldn't give them up if they were a handful of pebbles. What good would it do. I'd rather be dead than trust myself to them. They are brutes, both of them. Give me a gun."

The room darkened visibly. The daylight had given way to the gloom that precedes an eclipse. Through the door the sky back of the trees was a deep blue-black.

"Chalmers!"

It was Tuan Yuck's voice, speaking from the back of the house, clearly audible through the flimsy walls. It has a vibrant quality that was chilling in its utter lack of human attribute.

"It's no use, Chalmers," the voice went on. It was impossible to distinctly locate it and Chalmers, his finger on the trigger, cursed inarticulately at his impotence. "*Force majeure* rules, Chalmers. We'll give the girl and you passage to where you can get in touch with Honolulu or Sydney. But we want the pearls!"

"No!"

The girl's voice rang out shrilly before Chalmers could formulate an answer.

"As you like." Tuan Yuck's voice retained its even pitch. "Perhaps you'll think better of it presently. Bring up those dry palm-boughs, Tomi."

 THEY were going to burn them out. The house would flame like a torch.

"No you won't!" The new voice was hard and rough. It was Sayers, recovered from the blow on his thick skull, furious at his defeat and eager for revenge. "You can fill that young fool's carcass full of lead if you like and I'll help you. But I want the girl."

"You heard," said Leila in a tense whisper. The room was dusky with the weird midday half-light. Chalmers could hardly distinguish her features. "Where are the pistols? I may need one—for myself."

Apparently powerless, Chalmers felt like an animal as the jaws of the trap clip home. The world seemed out of joint when chicanery and avarice held them at their mercy. It was not for himself he cared. He would have wished nothing better at the moment than to have rushed out and gone down fighting, content if he could win his way to hand grips.

But Leila! A picture flashed before him of her helpless in the power of Sayers. He slipped noiselessly into the other room and brought back the pistols. One was for the girl, one for himself when they came to close quarters at the last. And one of the three was the automatic that had failed

him before. It would not do to make a blunder now.

"I'll give you one minute to make up your minds," called Tuan Yuck.

"You can't hide behind a girl's skirts, Chalmers!"

That was Sayers. Leila snatched one of the pistols and fired through the wall in the direction of the sound. Chalmers tried one of the remaining guns. The action resisted his pull and he tossed the weapon aside, gripping the other. He contemplated a swift dash for the boat. They might successfully run the gantlet and perhaps gain the schooner.

"Hamaku! Tomi!"

"*Ai.*"

That hope faded as the native answered the Chinaman. Both Kanakas were posted close to the veranda.

"Have you got the pearls?" he whispered. "Perhaps we can make better terms."

"They are here," she answered. Chalmers could barely see the movement of her hand to her breast. "They would not keep any terms. They are no better than wild beasts."

He groaned as he acknowledged the truth of her reply. Resistance was useless. They were lost unless a miracle intervened in their favor.

"Time's up," called Tuan Yuck.

The twilight turned to dark as blackness rushed up from the sea and behind the hills, shutting out the sickly sun and enveloping the sky from horizon to zenith in a pall of ebony. A bolt of lightning fell athwart the sky and the rooms blazed blue. A terrific peal of thunder crashed immediately overhead with deafening oppression, there was a sudden rushing in the trees and the tropical torrent broke loose, the rain falling in sheets that battered down the foliage and pounded on the corrugated roof with increasing fury.

Tons of water descended. The earth was covered almost momentarily with a hissing torrent. The thunder seemed to peal incessantly and flash after flash ripped the ebony curtain of the saturated clouds. The lagoon was lashed into torment under the heavy drops and the shrubbery beaten down and stripped of its leaves.

The two stood awed before the rage of the elements as the artillery of the thunder roared, reechoing among the hills, while flash after flash wrapped the scene in a weird, sudden brilliance, then left it black as the pit. Between the peals, the rain fell with an uproar that forbade all attempts at speech. She had set her hand upon his arm and the little fingers clutched hard but did not tremble.

The fury of the storm increased until it seemed as if nothing could resist its violence, certainly nothing human could think of anything but shelter from the battery of the rain. The thought that the besiegers might attempt entrance sent Chalmers to the open door with ready rifle. Leila followed him.

In the blackness they could not see the rain, but they heard the battering smash of it above their heads and the hissing splash with which it fell into the ground that was unable to drain off the vehemence of the flood.

A streak of fire ran down the sky seaward and seemed to fuse into a coruscating mass that made them shield their eyes, but not before they had discerned four figures, drenched, half-drowned and bowed double, close to the waters edge. The downpour had driven them to the schooner for shelter. There was no danger to the ship in the lack of wind, and even the greed of Tuan Yuck and Sayers was not proof against that pitiless drenching.

Chalmers cupped his hand close to Leila's ear.

"They are trying to find the boat," he called. "We've won."

She shook her head.

"God won for us," she said as he bent to catch the words.

Chalmers smiled grimly. Not that he failed to respect either her reverence or the Power that had intervened in their favor, but Tuan Yuck's philosophies came into his mind.

He would call it "an unfortunate coincidence," he thought.

Coincidence or miracle, it had effectually called check to the crafty Oriental's game.

CHAPTER X

SAFETY HAVEN

IT RAINED all the long afternoon. The thunder and lightning died away after half an hour that seemed five times as long, but the steady downpour continued until night merged with the somber darkness of the day. Chalmers lit the lamp in one room while they remained in the other, but no shot came from the schooner.

He prepared an impromptu meal from canned goods that were stored in the inner room

He found some tins of salmon and sardines but Leila asked him to put them back.

"I shall never see fish again without a shudder," she said.

Chalmers set them aside, blaming himself for his lack of thought.

"You see I cooked that last meal," she said. "We had eaten those same fish many times before. Father—" her voice wavered—"was very fond of them but I had grown tired of them. He coaxed me to eat some but I refused, and then——"

She broke down and Chalmers sat dumbly awkward. Her head was on her arms as she sobbed and he reached over and put his hand on one of hers. She turned it palm upward and let it lie in his like a child seeking consolation.

"Let me cry," she said. "It will do me good. I don't mind crying before you."

Chalmers felt strangely warmed. The little speech showed how she appraised him.

"I am glad," he said softly, and her fingers closed about his.

Presently she sat up and smiled at him while she wiped her eyes.

"Thank you," she said. "It helped— lots. You won't think me a baby?"

All the protectiveness in Chalmers mingled with the admiration he had for her beauty and her bravery, a feeling that, had he had time or inclination for analysis, would have amazed him with the vigor of its far-reaching growth.

"A baby!" he exclaimed. "I think you are a—a wonder," he concluded somewhat lamely.

Leila Denman, being a woman, read the look in his eyes that he himself was unconscious of, even as she supplied the ardent nature of the word he had checked on his lips. She smiled at him again, not wistfully this time, but with the spirit that prompted it so blending with his own that for the moment he forgot time and place, the peril they were in, everything but the girl with her red lips parted, her blue eyes now violet between the long lashes with a light in them that challenged every element of his manhood, her hair beneath the lamp like peacock-copper matrix in the sun.

So, while the rain poured pitilessly down upon the sodden, protesting ground, they talked through the long afternoon—she with tales of her paldom with her father and their life together in the South Seas; he of his work as a newspaperman.

"I have always wanted to get out of it," said Chalmers. "My first job was in San Francisco on a daily. The city editor was my father's best friend until dad died——"

Leila slipped her hand into his in sympathy with the loss that seemed to bring them closer, and the touch sent the blood tingling to his finger-tips and he felt the pull at his heart from the swift flooding of his veins.

"He told me one day I would never make a newspaperman," he went on frankly. "Said I lacked the instinct and doubted if I would ever get the knack, and congratulated me on it. I didn't see it that way as it was the only thing I could do, but he said he wished he was out of it. Said if he was my age he'd quit it if he had to drive a hack.

"Get out of it son," he told me. "It's a rotten game. You have to stand by and see your best friend knifed one day, and a man you know is a blackguard, praised to the skies the next. We are like flies in a saucer we think is the world, half muddled, half intoxicated over some stale beer we think is news. Get out beyond the rim of the saucer while you're young and husky. Do things; don't write about what other people do."

"I think I should have liked him," said Leila softly, "and then?"

Chalmers gave a wary glance into the veil of driving rain.

"Then," he laughed, "he offered me the chance of a newspaper job in Honolulu. I couldn't see how that shaped up with his argument, but he said it didn't call for a real, first class metropolitan reporter, but carried a good salary and that Honolulu was close to the rim of the saucer anyhow. So I went. The work was easy and, with the correspondence for mainland papers, the pay was good. I came back in the middle of my vacation to cover the story of a shipwrecked crew——"

"Our schooner?"

"Yes." And Chalmers told the story of Taroi and his partnership with Sayers and Tuan Yuck. "And so," he said, "that is how I came here."

"Beyond the rim," she concluded.

Chalmers looked at his watch. It was seven o'clock.

"It's time to get busy," he said. "I'm going to offset any interruptions.

"Can I help you?" she asked.

"Yes, by figuring out what we have to take. All that's most necessary. It's quite a walk and we won't be able to take many trips."

"But what are you going to do?"

"I'm going to take a little swim out to the schooner and put their ferry system out of commission."

"You mean you're going to steal their boat?"

"I don't know yet whether I can do that. It depends on conditions. But I'll promise to run no real risk."

He expected a protest, reluctant as he was himself to leaving her alone while he ran a hazard that he purposely made the least of. But she put an eager hand upon his arm.

"Let me go with you," she said. "I can swim like a fish. Really. And there's my bathing suit in my tent. Let me, please. I can help, I know, if it's only to keep my eyes open. There's no danger for me. I could swim all the way under water easily."

But Chalmers was adamant. His plan held dangers that he was not willing to have her share unnecessarily.

"You can be more help doing what I asked you to," he said.

"Truly?"

"Truly."

"Aye, aye, sir," she saluted in mock humility.

Chalmers was seized with a sudden desire to tell her how adorable she was, but there was serious work on hand and he merely registered the picture she made, adding to a gallery in his brain already better stocked with the same subject than he was aware of.

With the fatty part of some canned meat he carefully greased every inch of an automatic and slung it round his neck by a lanyard improvised from twine.

"It's a bit of a handicap," he said, "but it may come in handy. Now for a knife."

His own sheath-knife he had left behind when he stripped it with his pistol-holster from the belt before he bound Tuan Yuck.

Leila took one down from a shelf and gave it to him.

"It was father's," she said. "Here's a belt. I wish you'd let me come along."

"I wish you'd have a list of what we need to take by the time I come back," he parried, as he greased the blade of the knife and tested its keenness. "I'm going to carry this in my teeth like a pirate," he said laughing. "*Au revoir.*"

Leila watched him as the rain and dark enveloped him and turned back into the room with a sigh that was not altogether unhappy. She took counsel with herself concerning the lightening of her grief and, reasoning, blushed; blamed herself for lack of loyalty to her father in forgetting her grief; blamed herself again for lack of loyalty to Chalmers and his sympathy and so, womanwise, set aside the argument by getting things together for the trip to the cliff.

CHALMERS could hardly tell where the beach ended and the lagoon began. The ground was a foot deep with water racing from the hills and augmented by the rain. The latter was slackening perceptibly and he lost no time getting into deep water.

The surface of the lagoon was pitted with tiny spouting fountains beneath the fall of the heavy drops. They beat a tattoo on his head as he swam steadily out in the direction of the unseen schooner, nearly half a mile from shore.

The sky was black and starless. He seemed to be swimming in a black globe half filled with ink. There was no sign of the vessel and he began to wonder whether, in the dark, he was not swimming in a circle, when, close ahead, a dull light broke through the mist.

Paddling cautiously he made out the loom of the schooner, bows to the ebb tide. The whale-boat trailed alongside, its painter fast to the foremast stays, its hull directly beneath the port-hole from which came the light.

It was open. The vertical rain fell past it without entrance. Out of it came an acrid, pungent odor, beaten down toward the water by the rain. Chalmers recognized it as opium. He had already recognized the cabin as Tuan Yuck's. He wondered whether the Chinaman was under the influence of the drug. If he was, and Sayers drunk, he might board the schooner, overawe Hamaku and Tomi. . . .

"Your methods are too crude Sayers."

Tuan Yuck was awake and Sayers at least sober enough to be talked to. Chalmers clasped the stem of the whale-boat, drew up his knees, kicked vigorously downward and climbed like a cat into the boat.

"Yours are too —— slow to suit me," Sayers was saying as Chalmers crouched quietly down below the open port, straining to hear every word above the patter of the rain. Even as he listened he felt the downpour lessening. There was little time to waste, but the next sentence arrested him.

"You'll find them surer in the end, Sayers."

The silky tone seemed to hold a menace that the Australian missed or ignored.

"Well my way is going to be your way, tonight," he answered truculently. "D'ye think I'm going to stand being hammered over the head by that young cub without a comeback. And you, trussed up like a prize turkey for basting! A wise-looking bird you were." He broke into discordant laughter.

"The rain's slacking up now," he went on. "Listen to it on the deck. We ran off like a couple of drowning rats. But we're going to finish this affair before I sleep. We'll cut that young gamecock's comb and his throat into the bargain to stop his crowing. I'm not the one to be made a fool of by a half-baked man and a girl. If you're too yellow for the job——"

Some gesture or expression of Tuan Yuck's must have halted him, Chalmers fancied.

"Yes my friend, what then?" The Chinaman's voice almost purred.

"No offense, Tuan Yuck. But what's the use of shilly-shallying. There's four of us, ain't there? We can go ashore and settle the whole thing. You can handle the Kanakas. I'm going to sleep with my share of those pearls under my pillow tonight. And Chalmers'll sleep in the sand. There's a million or more in the lagoon, you say. We can clean that up and none the wiser. Dead men tell no tales. You said that yourself. We'll leave the mirrors on the island and it'll be Motutabu to the end of the time. As for the girl——"

He broke off again.

"As for the girl?" repeated Tuan Yuck quietly, with peculiar emphasis.

"Why—ha, ha! That's a good one. You don't mean to tell me you—" The sentence ended in the discordant laugh. "I'll tell you what we'll do about the girl," he said gaspingly. "We'll gamble for her!" But you'll have to roll your sleeves up when you deal the cards. Come on, the rain's quit. Let's turn out the Kanakas."

CHALMERS glanced at the port-hole above him in the wish that he could reach it and settle the matter with his greased automatic, there and then. But it was impossible. The rain had suddenly dwindled to a scanty sprinkle.

The cloud curtain was rolling up to the north like a great awning and the stars were showing through the frazzle of its rack. He had meant at first to row the boat ashore under cover of the rain and hide it in the mangroves. But with the passing of the storm he would undoubtedly be seen even if the noise of the oars passed notice. And under their fire he would infallibly be killed or desperately wounded before he half-way reached the shore.

He drew out the case-knife and swiftly severed the painter. Then with both hands he tugged at the plug. The bottom boards were already afloat with rainwater and, as the boat slowly drifted sternward with the ebb, the water from the lagoon gushed in. Chalmers slid over the side, tilting the gunwale before he let go and shipping water enough to make the boat commence to settle as it sluggishly followed the current.

He heard Sayers calling for Hamaku and Tomi and blessed the reason that still kept them in the forepeak. The Australian's curses died away as Chalmers filled his lungs and, with a glance to sight the lamp where Leila was working over the preparations for their exodus, swam hard under water shoreward.

When he came up he turned gently on his back, cautiously paddled till his head was toward the beach, dropped his legs and raised his head ever so slightly, still stroking against the ebb with his arms.

Sayers was on deck swearing at one of the natives who held a lantern aloft. Chalmers chuckled as he thought of the severed line that had been found. Against the white of the reef surf he could distinguish the rim of the whale-boat almost awash. It disappeared as a shout came from Sayers

and some one dived from the stern of the schooner.

Chalmers turned on his chest again and once more swam under water, repeating the process until he felt the sand. He had swum to his left and crawled out on the beach close to the rocks at the side of the landing.

Half-way to cover he was discovered by the eyes watching for him. The *ping* of a bullet on the lava warned him, and he dived into a sand lane between the rocks, safe from the futile shots that followed him.

Bent double, he hurried up the beach, keeping well covered and shouting to Leila to put out the lamp that might be a target for a random shot. It was extinguished and the house was lost against the background of the hills.

Leila was waiting for him at the foot of the steps and he warmed to the anxiety in her voice.

"I was afraid they'd killed you," she said.

"Not this time, nor the next," he replied jauntily with a boyish ring to his voice. "But I've sunk their old whale-boat and they'll have a fine time getting it up again. Only I've left my shoes down there and those rocks cut like the devil."

She murmured her sympathy. Chalmers laughed.

"I can get you a pair of dad's," she said. "They'll be better than nothing."

"That's all right, Leila!"

She did not resent the name but caught at his hand as they crouched down by the steps.

"They'll stop firing soon," he said. "Tuan Yuck won't waste cartridges. He knows we've won this trick."

"Won't they swim ashore?" she asked.

"Tuan Yuck can't. The main boom caught him one day and he nearly drowned before Hamaku got to him. Sayers always gets cramps. That's one thing we can bless his drinking for. The Kanakas won't tackle it alone. They think we had that storm made to order."

"It's a wonder they didn't hit you. I was terribly frightened."

"Were you?" He pressed the hand he still held. "They didn't see me till I landed. I swam under water. The only thing I worried about was a shark."

"A shark! They never come in the smaller lagoons. Dad said they are afraid of getting trapped by the tide."

3

"Don't they?"

There was something in the way Chalmers said it that made the girl look at him in the dim light the stars gave in the clearing.

"Was that the reason you didn't want me to go?" she asked.

"One of 'em," he answered, feeling rather foolish. "Did you get any things together? We must make a start. We'll keep in the brush and along the edge of the mangroves. Then there are rocks to the point that will cover us."

 AT THREE o'clock Leila Denman collapsed. She had been limping uncomplainingly for the last half hour.

Chalmers, packing double burdens, was almost played out. "There's a lot more I'd have liked to have brought," he said, "but I doubt if we could make another trip before dawn."

Leila, lying flat on the sand, her head pillowed on the crook of one arm, gave a weary little sigh. "I can hardly move," she confessed. We can get along with what we've got, can't we?"

"I think so," said Chalmers and went prospecting.

"Here's a cave for you with a nice smooth sandy floor," he said. And another for me right next door. That bedding from the house is dry. I'll fix it for you."

"Good night, Leila," he called presently after she had crept wearily into her cliff dwelling.

"There's no danger," he went on to assure her. "Sleep tight. The lagoon here is too shallow for the schooner. It'll take them all morning to get that boat up, if they're lucky. Tide's coming in and it's all hunky-dory. Everything's safe in our little haven. Let's name it 'Safety Haven.' That's the ticket."

There was no answer.

"Poor kidlets, she's tuckered out," he told himself remorsefully. "And I'm wide awake." Even as he formed the thought he yawned. "Not so wide awake after all," he concluded. "Good night, Leila," he said aloud softly.

The repetition of her name roused her.

"Good night," she said.

"All comfy?"

"Yes, thank you. Good night, Bruce."

And, with that music to accompany his dreams, Chalmers too fell asleep.

CHAPTER XI

MONGOLIAN MAGIC

THE TRADITIONAL pair of strange bulldogs had little more in common than Tuan Yuck and Sayers aboard the schooner next morning. While the Chinaman showed no outward signs of irritation he was chagrined at the success of Chalmers in cutting off their shore communication.

Sayers openly growled and barked and vowed to get even. His head seemed split apart and the liquor he absorbed increased the aggravation until he vented his ill-temper upon everything in sight, glowering with bloodshot eyes and cursing the Kanakas as they hurried out of the way of his wrath, and finally spilling his spite against the armor of Tuan Yuck's impenetrability.

"A nice mess," he growled. "The only boat we've got gone to the bottom and hell and all ahead to get it up, if we can do it at all. It's all very well for you to sit there sneering at me like an ivory Buddha in a bazaar. It was no fault of mine! I'll tell you flat to your face that I don't like your attitude, Tuan Yuck, with your 'wiser than thou' smile. I didn't sink the boat, did I? I wasn't to blame for it any more than you, was I? Then don't look so —— superior about it, because for two pins I'd change the look on your face and make the change permanent."

He had advanced his head with its undershot jaw and glaring eyes close to Tuan Yuck's across the cabin table, set with his own untasted breakfast and the Oriental's emptied dishes. Tuan Yuck did not move a muscle, the narrow eyelids were partly closed and behind them the dark eyes sparkled like a snake's, never moving from those of Sayers.

The Australian's bullying speech was mostly braggadocio, spoken not only to relieve his feelings but to reassure himself. He was conscious both of an increasing distrust of Tuan Yuck, and of a certain fear that was gradually growing within him and strengthening a conviction that before the trip was ended the two of them would come to open warfare. This belief was born of his own half-planned determination to possess himself of the Chinaman's share of the pearls—once they obtained them—and an instinctive, prophetic knowledge that Tuan Yuck held the same intent.

It was with a strong effort that he checked his outburst. His nerves were jumping with the reaction of the liquor and he knew that physically he would collapse after one fierce spurt of energy. How much strength there was in Tuan Yuck's frame he did not know; it was the enigma of the man, bodily and mentally, that controlled while it enraged him. Besides there were yet the pearls to gain and the contents of the lagoon to reap. He could not handle the situation single-handed and he could not count upon the natives. How much they were under the Oriental's control he was presently to learn, but hè already sensed that any act on his part would range them against him—unless he could catch Tuan Yuck unawares and single-handed—when the time was ripe.

The man's mind was like a stagnant gutter, never flushed, holding all the impurities that came to it and breeding more. The thought of being the possessor of unlimited wealth inflamed his selfishness with plans of debaucheries that included a circuit of the world and an orgy of wine, women and song, a vague mixture of intoxication that was a blend of the satisfaction of the vices one part of him wanted to wallow in, and a revel in the hearing of music and the operas that the remnant of his spiritual consciousness craved.

He reached out a trembling hand to refill his glass and knocked over the square-faced bottle of gin. Tuan Yuck caught it with a swift movement before it spilled and set it upright.

"That's your main trouble, Sayers," he said quietly, as he set it down. "If we are going to pull together in this thing we both of us need all our wits."

"What about your dope pills?" sneered Sayers.

"I use opium to quiet my nerves," said Tuan Yuck evenly, "not to set them on edge. Did you ever notice that it did me any harm?"

Sayers' half-muddled brain caught the logic of the retort. The Chinaman was right. He needed all his wits, not so much for joint action as to remain on even terms with his partner.

"You're right," he said, hesitating, with the bottle-neck clinking against his tumbler, "but I can't chuck it altogether—not right away." And he gulped down the liquor.

The hint of a smile passed over Tuan Yuck's countenance and faded.

"I didn't mean to do that," he said. "I only counseled moderation," he went on with eyes that mocked the Australian's endeavor to pull himself together. "When I said last night your methods were crude, I meant that you drink too much and forget to eat. You spilled the fat on the fire when you made a grab at those pearls——"

"While you were wasting time in words. The thing had to come to a head. What was the use in beating about the bush?"

"If we had promised everything and the girl had come on board, would it have been any harder to have eventually got what we wanted?" asked Tuan Yuck quietly. "Now, we have a fight on our hands and, so far, they have got a little the best of it."

Sayers looked at him in resentful appreciation.

So that had been Tuan Yuck's plan—to get the girl and the pearls aboard; to let Chalmers navigate until they were close enough to their destination to dispense with his services, and then . . .

"You're a better pirate than I am," he said grudgingly. "Why didn't you tip me off to your scheme?"

Tuan Yuck showed his teeth in a blank smile at the compliment.

"It seemed the obvious move," he answered. "I imagined you figured it out the same way."

Sayers pushed back the bottle and started to get up, holding his head in both hands as he did so.

"I've got to cut out the booze," he muttered.

Tuan Yuck, watching him, chuckled internally. The Oriental was a firm believer in the axiom that lookers-on see most of the game. His policy was to wait until the right moment, and then usurping the board, make the move that left him the ultimate conqueror.

"I can give you something for that headache," he said. "And presently you can eat something."

Sayers' bloodshot eyes viewed him suspiciously as he disappeared to his cabin, emerging with a lacquered box in his hand nearly full of greenish-gray tablets. Tuan Yuck placed two in the Australian's half-reluctant palm, and, with a quizzical look, that showed how well he read the other's thoughts, put one into his own mouth.

"The Mongolian equivalent for hasheesh," he said. "Let it dissolve on your tongue."

Even as the pastils liquefied, Sayers felt their soothing effect. His head cleared as if by magic, his nerves steadied, and his pulses began to beat with a regularity that soon invigorated him.

"You're a wizard!" he exclaimed. "There's a fortune in those, Tuan Yuck! 'Morning After' tablets. Worth their weight in gold. And you could charge that much for 'em and get away with it."

"They cost more than that," Tuan Yuck answered dryly. "And as they are the most insidious of drug composites, they are likely to form a habit that is decidedly expensive and dangerous."

Sayers looked covetously at the little box.

"It's great stuff," he said. "I feel fit. Hanged if I haven't got the beginning of an appetite already. If I can get some food into my system presently I'll be in fine shape. Now the first thing to do is to get that boat up. That's going to be some job. I wish I had Chalmers by the neck and could make him do it. We'll have to make Hamaku dive and get a rope on to it. Then we can rig a line at the end of the main gaff and swing the spar out so as to get a fairly up-and-down haul, and snake her up with the capstan. We can do that as we lie without getting up anchor, and making sail on this flood-tide and trying to moor dead over the boat."

Tuan Yuck eyed him curiously.

"How good a sailor are you, Sayers?" he asked.

"Good enough to handle this schooner in everything outside of navigation," he boasted, feeling the increasing exhilaration of the drugs he had swallowed. "I can sail her as close as Chalmers any day in the week."

"Ah! You could make Nameless Isle at a pinch?"

"That's easy. Or to the Solomons for that matter. Just sail sou'west. You couldn't miss 'em. If the winds were steady I could come close to sailing all the way back, following up the course Chalmers laid out coming down. Yes—sir. Oh, Hamaku!" he called up the companionway. "You can handle him better than I can," he said to Tuan Yuck. "Tell him what we want."

Tuan Yuck explained, talking Hawaiian fluently, as did Sayers. Hamaku shook his head.

"I am no diver," he said. "I could not swim down to six fathoms with a rope and fasten it. My lungs are not big enough. And there is no height from which to dive."

"You can carry weights," said Sayers. "Put the line under your arms, Hamaku. You can take the chicken-coop or a grating for a raft, and paddle it out over the boat."

The Kanaka continued to protest. Both he and his fellow were still cowed by the storm, and the second win of Chalmers in sinking the boat. It was their disposition to always be with the victors.

"I am no diver," he repeated sullenly.

"Hamaku!" Tuan Yuck's voice held a vibrant note of command. Hamaku shifted on his feet, his head hanging.

"Look at me!" commanded the Chinaman sharply.

The silky tone sounded like the snap of a whiplash. The native lifted his eyes with evident reluctance, caught the challenge of the gaze that held his own and mastered it while the stronger spirit of the Oriental took possession of the Hawaiian's. For a moment Hamaku's will resisted, then his dwindling protests of "Aole! Aole! (No! No!) stopped like a well trained servant waiting for orders, as impassive as his master.

It was the first time Sayers had witnessed a demonstration of Tuan Yuck's control of the natives. It was the first time he had ever seen hypnosis at close range, and he was inclined to be skeptical.

"Will he do anything you tell him to now?" he asked.

"Anything I will tell him to."

"Going to keep him in the trance while he dives?"

"No. He'll be a better judge of what should be done than I can be. But he thinks I can control him at any minute."

"Then it's bunkum?"

"Not at all. I'm going to speak aloud what I will him to do, so you can judge for yourself. Tuan Yuck tore a loose leaf from the end of Chalmers's carefully kept log-book and folded it into a narrow strip.

"Pick up this dagger, Hamaku," he said in a low voice. "You are afraid of Mr. Sayers. This will protect you. You can kill him with it if you hate him enough. See, he is asleep. Now you are not afraid of him any longer. Creep up on him. Be careful. Make no noise. Now! Strike!"

The Australian, with a fascination touched with awe, saw the emotions change on Hamaku's face from fear to convulsed hatred, then to cunning as, clutching the paper, he inched towards him. As the Hawaiian raised his arm for the blow, Sayers, despite himself, threw up his own arm in defense and clutched the descending wrist.

Tuan Yuck shouted a sharp command, and clapped his hands. Animation returned to Hamaku's eyes and confusion left him shamefaced, as Sayers, feeling almost as foolish, let go his wrist, and the mock weapon fluttered down.

"What have I done?" asked the native.

"Nothing. Go and get ready for the dive."

Hamaku left, cringing as he passed near Tuan Yuck.

"I thought you had to make passes or use something to dazzle them," said Sayers, trying to affect a nonchalance that he was far from feeling.

"Not always, with a good subject. The stronger will is sufficient. I might have to with you. Shall I try?"

Tuan Yuck's eyes mocked Sayers', as their glances met. The Australian doggedly endured the power that seemed to pour from the Chinaman's darkly glittering orbs until he felt a sudden desire to yield in answer to the imperative statement that rang in his brain in one repeated sentence: "You are not so strong as I am. You are not so strong as I am."

He passed his hand across his forehead, summoning all his will to throw off its oppression, and his vision cleared. The room had been gradually filling with a mist out of which shone two points of light. Now he knew that these were Tuan Yuck's eyes, still mocking, and that the mist was the hallucination of his own brain.

"I'm going to rig up that tackle," he said shortly, rousing himself.

As he went on deck, still conscious of the Oriental's jeering gaze, he resolved to find some way of offsetting the latter's influence over Hamaku and Tomi. The prospect of having a knife stuck between his ribs at the will of Tuan Yuck was not a reassuring one.

"I've got to go slow on the booze," he told himself again, "and when I sleep it'll be behind a locked door or a long way from Mr. Yuck. I think I'll stay ashore nights after this, though I suppose I needn't worry till we've got our hands on something worth

letting blood over; and then, my worthy Confucian, you'll find more than one can play that game."

CHAPTER XII

SAYERS FINDS A WEAPON

HAMAKU achieved a raft with a wooden grating. To this he attached a spare halyard, coiling the slack and making a loop of the loose end to slip over his neck and beneath one arm. He freighted the little craft with two pigs of cast-iron ballast, took one of the oars that had floated out of the boat when it sank, and which he had recovered with the bottom-boards the night before, and paddled off to where they had seen the whale-boat vanish. The schooner lay between him and the shore as a bulwark for possible bullets, but he worked quickly.

He soon located it in the clear lagoon, lying on a patch of sand between the live coral. Sitting on the edge of his raft, he adjusted the line for smooth uncoiling, weighted himself with a pig of iron in each hand, and, as the grating tilted, slid gently down to the bottom, the line snaking off the float above him.

It was well over two minutes before his head bobbed up with a triumphant grin of white teeth.

"*Hiki no!*" (All right!) he called, and swam back to the schooner, towing the grating with the halyard fastened to it. Climbing aboard, he spliced it to the spare line Sayers had reeved through a block at the end of the main gaff, running down the spar through the throat-halyard block to another at the foot of the mast and so forward.

The two natives set their strength to the bars of the little capstan, the line tautened at an obtuse angle, and the whale-boat came slowly to the surface, then above it, while Hamaku ran out on the main boom and, as the water spilled, handled the slackened line until the boat once more rode on the water, and communication with the shore was reestablished.

Tuan Yuck had been busy with the binoculars. He noticed the removal of the tent, and picked out its furniture still standing amid the trees. The mounting sun sucked up the moisture that the overladen earth had been unable to carry off.

Leaves that had drooped beneath the downpour revived, and everywhere the wet surfaces reflected the light, so that the magic mirrors were hardly noticeable. A steamy mist hung over the mangrove swamp.

Nowhere could the Chinaman gain a hint of the whereabouts of Chalmers and the girl, though he was certain they had broken camp. Landing was dangerous until they were discovered. Tuan Yuck's policies called for the making of ambuscades, not attacking them.

At Sayers's suggestion, Tomi climbed to the main spreaders for a wider view. He had hardly reached his perch before he called down to them that he saw smoke at the foot of the cliff. From the deck it was not to be distinguished from the mist above the mangroves.

Sayers looked at the mast and grunted. With the sails furled there were no rings to serve for foothold. Tomi had gone up it like a cat, planting his bare feet against the mast and grasping the halyards.

"I can't make that," he said, "and I'm too heavy to haul. We could get you up easy enough, Tuan Yuck?"

"Why not?" assented the Chinaman. "I'll chance a stray shot."

The throat halyards were cast loose, a loop made in them for Tuan Yuck's foot, and, with Hamaku and Sayers hauling, Tuan Yuck, steadying himself by the peak halyard, was readily lifted to the side of Tomi, where he focused his glass on Safety Haven.

The height enabled him to look over the cape and see a portion of the beach, ending in the farther promontory. It was high tide, and he was quick to appreciate the value of the place as a base of defense. The glass revealed the steep, flinty sides of the nearer headland, impossible to climb, and the masses of rock on the beach beyond from behind which an attacking party could be driven off without exposure. There was no sign of an encampment save where, close to the foot of the waterfall, a thread of smoke proclaimed the presence of a fire, masked by boulders and the verdure at the foot of the cliff.

"Our friend, Chalmers, possesses more military strategy than I gave him credit for," he said to Sayers when he regained the deck. "He seemed to have chosen a good place for defense. I'd like to get a closer look at it. I wonder how they are off for supplies. They've got plenty of water."

"They'd pot us if we took the boat," said Sayers. "Let Hamaku swim in. He may be able to sneak up between the rocks and get a look at them, and a line on how they are fixed for grub."

Hamaku took his instructions willingly enough, reassured of Tuan Yuck's power to compel ultimate obedience, and slipped quietly over the side for the long swim that meant nothing to his aquatic prowess. Sayers watched him start, then announced his intention of eating breakfast.

"I'm going to fill up on a square meal," he announced. "First time I've felt like touching food for three days, thanks to your pills."

Tuan Yuck looked at him curiously as he went below with more of vigor and purpose than he had shown for many days. The Oriental's shoulders lifted in the barest suggestion of a shrug as he went to the rail and trained his glasses on Hamaku's steady progress.

The sound of a shot and its echo from the cliff brought Sayers on deck.

"Did they get him?" he asked, hurrying to where Tuan Yuck stood gazing through the binoculars.

"I think not. I told him to look out and dive at the flash. I lost sight of him in the dazzle on the water just now. He's probably swimming underneath—there he is."

Sayers took the glasses and picked up Hamaku's head, like a seal's, close in by the cape, before the native dived again.

 IN HALF an hour Hamaku was aboard, unhurt but excited and eager for commendation.

"They saw me," he said. "Just a little way the other side of the point. I did not see them—only the flash of the gun. So I dived quick and swam under water. There is fresh water off the point," he went on, proud of his knowledge. "I felt it cooler as I swam through. Then I tasted, and I knew for sure. Plenty of fresh water coming up from the bottom, just off the point. That means a quicksand when the tide is low."

"They're in there. That's the main point," commented Tuan Yuck. "And if it's hard for us to get at them, it's just as hard for them to get out. You're a good boy, Hamaku."

The native beamed with pleasure.

"Yes, Hamaku, you're all right," seconded Sayers. "Well, we can work the lagoon for pearls and starve them out at the same time. Which reminds me I haven't finished my breakfast."

He went below, beckoning Hamaku to follow. In the cabin he poured out a generous measure of gin.

"That was a long swim, Hamaku," he said. "You did well. Take this."

The Hawaiian's eyes glistened as he took the glass.

"Thank you," he said in native, and tossed down the raw spirits with gusto.

"Have another?" asked Sayers, with the bottle ready tilted.

Hamaku beamed in gratitude at the unexpected access to the liquor he loved. It's warmth spread over his body, and he looked at the Australian as a starving dog might look at a man who tosses him a meaty bone, a glance that held readiness to serve, almost affection.

"This is just between you and me, Hamaku," warned Sayers, as the Kanaka set down the glass. "You understand?" He tossed his head upward meaningly.

Hamaku nodded.

"I tell my tongue not to speak," he said, and went on deck, carefully avoiding any proximity to Tuan Yuck.

Sayers smiled. He had found a weapon to offset Tuan Yuck's power over the natives.

"He can't keep 'em hypnotized all the time," he muttered. "Lucky I brought plenty of gin along. There's nothing they won't do for that." From force of habit he poured himself a drink, hesitated, then swallowed it. "Can't do any harm on a full stomach," he told himself. "But I mustn't let it get the better of me."

At which speech, Tuan Yuck, could he have heard it, would have smiled.

CHAPTER XIII

THE LAUNCH IN THE MANGROVES

THE sun, streaming in through the bushes that fringed the mouth of Chalmer's cave, awakened him. His eyelids felt as if they were filled with a mixture of glue and sand, and each joint protested against coordinate action. He had packed every pound he could carry on the trips from the clearing, and he was still sore from the quicksand. But his mind, once roused, was speedily alert, and forced his sluggish limbs to action.

He picked up a rifle and, stepping cautiously, not to disturb the sleeping girl, made his way toward the headland that divided Safety Haven from the main beach and lagoon. The tide was washing the end of the cape, covering the quicksand and the scattered rocks as he sought for some place to climb the barrier, and get a glimpse of the enemy's operations.

The lava ridge was less steep on the side of Safety Haven, and he managed to pick a trail to the top. He had brought the glasses of the dead captain from the house, and with their aid he easily marked the cautious steps of Hamaku and Tomi, moving carefully on the schooner's decks, so as not to disturb their masters below.

"They haven't turned out yet," he commented. "That gives us an hour or so before they'll bother their heads about us."

He left his rifle in a shady crevice of the lava, where it would be handy when he returned for later observation and, unencumbered, swiftly climbed down to the beach again after one comprehensive view of their little dominion. There was driftwood among the rocks and he picked some of it up, still soaked with the rain, and set it to dry in the sun for a fire.

On his way back to the caves he made a hasty visit to certain rock-masses he had noted from the top of the ridge. Despite the almost boyish frankness of Leila Denman, he realized the delicacy of the situation, if they were forced to live in the intimate contact their quarters demanded; and he wanted to spare the girl's sensitiveness as much as possible. Presently he found what he wanted, a series of rocky rooms, high-walled, open to the sky, indeed—which meant nothing in that climate and season—all connecting, two of them floored with sand and shells, the largest of the latter broken, but many perfect and exquisitely tinted.

The third chamber was reached by natural rocky steps, leading to the rim of a lava bowl some ten feet in diameter, nearly filled with sea water, crystal clear and green as an emerald. A ledge of rock ran part way 'round the interior of the basin, an ideal platform for a bather.

Chalmers, smiling at his own folly, whimsically looked for the sea naiad who should, by rights, have inhabited the pool. All the rocks showed traces of wave action; the outer entrance to the rock chambers was an arch.

All signs pointed to the fact that Motutabu had once held a higher sea level. The beach of Safety Haven had undoubtedly long been exposed to the wash of ruder waves than the quiet ripples of the narrow lagoon that rimmed it now, though the sharp uneroded spine of the headland seemed of later origin.

Chalmers was in no mind for geological problems. He was delighted with his find of a complete suite of rooms which would insure absolute privacy for Leila Denman. The problem of their defense and existence, ever present as it was with him, was constantly disturbed by thoughts of the girl, remembrances of some turn of her head, the intonation of her voice, the color of her hair, her eyes, her lips, the piquant pendule in the upper one. He caught himself whistling softly, and thinking the words:

"And dark blue is her ee."

He checked himself with an embarrassed laugh.

"Anybody would think I was in love," he said aloud. A friendly gull, perched on a near-by rock, cocked a black eye at him, stretched its wings in a suggestive imitation of a yawn, and flapped away as if disgusted, with a throaty squawk of disdain that sounded exactly like—

"You are."

The resemblance was so startling that Chalmers called after the bird:

"What did you say? I wonder if I am," he asked himself.

The broaching of the subject, like the sounding of a dominant chord, seemed to set a hundred suggestions and instincts vibrating in harmony with the suggestion. The visions of her, mute in his arms, refusing to give up the pearls to Tuan Yuck, fighting with him pluckily against the odds, came to him in swift succession. He felt again the pull at his heart that had come at the touch of her fingers closing on his, and then flushed at his own foolishness.

"She's got no eyes for you, my boy," he muttered. "And if she had you've no right to think of her. If we get out of this muddle she'll be worth a quarter of a million, to say nothing of the pearls in the lagoon."

"I'll bet I'm a sight," he added, not altogether irrelevantly, as he passed his hand over his sprouting beard and looked ruefully at his besmeared ducks. "I'll have to make another trip to the schooner if it's only for a razor—not to mention other things."

All thoughts of Leila vanished from his mind as he confronted their necessities. Their supply of food was limited, aside from fish, which Leila would only touch as a last necessity, but his chief fear was lack of ammunition. He had only the cartridges that were left in the chambers of the rifles and the automatics. Tuan Yuck would be sure to think of that sooner or later, and, in the meantime, threatened attacks must be warded off.

"Good morning, Sir Sober Face."

He rounded a pile of rocks to meet Leila, her bright hair coiled, a flush in her cheeks, and her eyes alight with friendly greeting.

"I thought you were still asleep," she said gaily. "So I've gone about my duties on tiptoe. Look. Here's our kitchen, with a shelf just the right height for a pantry, and here's our dining-room. I've stocked the pantry, filled the kettle from the waterfall, and all I need is dry wood."

"That's easily supplied," said Chalmers, falling into her mood, "and if you go with me I'll show you a suite of rooms with boudoir, sun-parlor and private bath that I've taken an option on in your name. There was an impudent mermaid in possession, but I made faces at her, and she flapped her tail at me and ran—I mean swam."

So, talking nonsense, forgetting for the moment, with the privilege of golden youth, their present perils, Chalmers showed her what he called in jest, "Number One, Beach Avenue."

As Leila Denman finished looking delightedly about the place that Chalmers had found for her, she turned to him and held out her hand.

"I want to thank you, Mr. Chalmers," she said. "You've been more than kind. I —I can't tell you just what it means to me. When I think of how friendless, how defenseless I might have been, and all you have done for me—of your thoughtfulness—I wish I could reciprocate it. I *do* appreciate it."

Her eyes dewed with grateful tears, and Chalmers, stopping himself on the point of some such idiotic declaration that "one smile of hers was worth a lifetime of toil in her behalf," felt his own moisten and a lump come into his throat.

"I haven't done anything," he said as soon as speech was easy. "Nothing that I wouldn't have done for my own sister—or any one else's."

"Why, then I'll have to adopt you as my brother," she said.

His face fell involuntarily, and her's brightened, such being the way of a man with a maid, and *vice versa*. Then she laughed.

"Where's the firewood?" she asked.

Chalmers flushed guiltily. They were back to the caves already.

"Hurry up," she called gaily as he turned away. "Call at the grocery store and get some eggs—brother!"

There was a mocking emphasis on the "brother" that he did not altogether object to. It showed she was not altogether in earnest about the relation, he thought. Then Fortune favored him. Close to where he had set the driftwood in the sun he saw some telltale furrows in the sand. He had seen similar ones before on the quiet beaches beyond Pearl Harbor, on Oahu, and he swiftly utilized a piece of wood as a spade, and carefully upturned a dozen globular objects of a dingy white, covered with leathery skin—turtle's eggs, not to be despised as an auxiliary to an island menu, and an assurance of future sustenance.

Breakfast was a meal where happiness attended appetite, and it was not until the shrinking shadows warned Chalmers time was speeding, that he resumed his full measure of responsibility.

"I want you to keep in your rock-rooms or your cave," he said, "until I come back."

"Why can't I come with you?"

"I don't believe there will be anything interesting on hand," he answered. "Only a nasty climb which I have made before."

"Very well, ungallant one," she pouted, then changed, noting the gravity of his face. "You'll promise to let me know if it looks interesting or if I can help?" she asked.

"Surely."

He climbed the wall of the cape once more and watched the hauling aboard of the sunken whale-boat. He was tempted to try a shot, but the sun was in his eyes. Gazing against it he failed to see the approach of Hamaku until the native had actually passed the headland and was heading shoreward for the little beach. He cautiously leveled his Winchester and sighted until the bead on the muzzle of the rifle dropped into the notch of the hindsight and aligned with the black dot of the Kanaka's head. His finger instinctively pressed the trigger until the last ounce of resistance was reached.

Then mercy reasoned with the will to kill and he aimed ahead. The bullet splashed close enough to send Hamaku plunging down like a porpoise, and swimming beneath the surface back toward the schooner. From above, Chalmers could see the motion of his body, purple in the green shoal water, wriggling like an eel.

"He'll warn them that we're on the lookout," he told himself. "I can watch the rocks at low tide. There'll be a moon soon of nights by the time the ebb shifts 'round to daylight, and then I'll have to make a boom of palm-trunks. At present I'll sleep afternoons while Leila plays watchwoman, and keep sentry nights myself."

A call came to him, and he saw the girl running across the beach toward the cape. He waved at her in assurance of his safety, and climbed down to meet her.

"You're not hurt?" she asked breathlessly. "I heard the shot."

"Not I," he protested, and told her what he had seen. "They'll not trouble us for a while," he asserted. "We'll have to keep a smart lookout, that's all."

"I can do my share?"

He nodded. She was looking at him in a way that made him a little uncertain of what he was saying or doing.

"Steady, boy," he muttered. "Steady. You're on duty—on honor."

She saw his lips move, and her face blanched as she stretched out eager hands.

"You are hurt?" she declared. "What did you say? I couldn't hear you."

"I was talking to myself," he returned, vexed at his indiscretion. "Just foolishness."

"Oh!" she said, and her eyes lost their anxiety for another expression, less intimate, yet full of understanding.

"You are invited to my beach boudoir," she said, "to discuss the situation, and decide upon the division of watches."

"They'll try to take us unawares, I imagine," he told her when they had settled themselves. "Failing that, they'll probably go ahead and clean up the lagoon of pearls. Then they may try and navigate the schooner somewhere themselves—Sayers thinks he knows more than he really does about sailing—or they'll make some sort of an offer to us."

"Which we'll not accept."

"I don't know about that."

"We can't trust them. You know that."

"I wouldn't if there was any other way of getting you off the island. We can insist upon terms for our own protection."

"But there *is* another way," she said, while Chalmers stared open-eyed. "We brought two whale-boats on our schooner. One of them had an engine in it and a mast and sail, and father kept it for our use. After the natives landed here the first time Dad hid it in the mangroves near where we came when we moved to Safety Haven. It's there now, with several cans of gasoline!"

"That's fine," said Chalmers. "I'm sorry it's in their territory. I hope they don't take it into their heads to go nosing in the mangroves and find it."

"I don't think they could," she answered. "Dad dragged it up the creek and off to one side. It's covered with vines, and a lot of those have sprouted. I could hardly see it when he pointed it out to me."

CHAPTER XIV

SAYERS GOES PEARLING

CHALMERS and the girl sat snugly ensconced in a niche on the edge of the ridge, watching the whale-boat put out for shore, all four of the schooner's occupants aboard. Save for some broken branches unnoticed in the general wealth of foliage, there was no trace of the storm, except that perhaps the air held more of coolness and the atmosphere more of clarity, so that the whole island appeared to have had it's face washed, and to be basking in the sunshine.

Peaceful as the scene was, it held all the elements of tragedy. Death, under the long grasses on the hill, love in the pocket of the lava ridge, greed and murder and lust in the boat on the lagoon.

"It would be easy enough to pick them off from here," said Chalmers half in earnest, cuddling the stock of the rifle that lay beside him.

Leila shrank away from him a trifle, doubt and consternation in her eyes.

"You wouldn't murder them?" she asked.

"No, I suppose I wouldn't," he answered.

"That's the worst of it. They'd pot us without a scruple. Fighting fair with men of their caliber is handicapping yourself pretty heavily. I wonder what they're up to now?"

Sayers and Tuan Yuck, each carrying a rifle, were walking up the beach towards the clearing; Hamaku, also armed, remaining at the boat with Tomi. Leila focused the glasses upon them as they disappeared in the house for a few moments, and came out again bearing what looked like clothes.

"It's father's diving suit," she said.

"Then they are going to let us alone for a while and go after the pearls in the lagoon," said Chalmers. "I wanted to bring that suit along the worst way last night, but I left it to the last on account of its bulk. If I was either Sayers or Tuan Yuck I'd hate to have to be dependent on the other's hand on the air supply."

"It is a patent suit," said Leila. "It has a compressed-air cylinder you fill with that rotary pump Sayers is carrying. It supplies air for thirty minutes after it's charged up to capacity. It's a bit complicated. I fancy they'll have some trouble with it."

"It looks as if they are having it now," he said, watching the two figures in consultation, presently joined by the natives. "They seem to be scrapping as to who's going to put it on. It'll have to be one of them. They'll never get the natives to trust themselves inside that gear. Sayers loses the toss," he announced. "Wonder if he's going to waste time and air wading in from shallow water."

"Dad used to go in by the rocks where the shell is. They go down like steps. When the natives landed here he was under water. I was in the house working, and I didn't see them till the big double canoe sailed into the lagoon. I didn't know what to do. There were fifty of them, at least, armed with spears and bows, big men, smeared with paint, horrible looking savages. And there was Dad, unconscious of it all, liable to come up any minute in the middle of them.

"While I was looking some of them jumped out on to the beach and suddenly they shouted. The crowd broke, and I could see Dad coming slowly out of the water all wet and shiny, the metal gleaming on the helmet, and the two great eyes goggling, like a sea monster. It was weird. To the savages it must have been terrible.

Dad kept on rising, walking up the rocks, and, just as he left the water and started toward them they could stand it no longer. Some of them were on their knees, but they jumped up with the rest, scurried into the canoe, and paddled off in terror.

"Dad told me afterwards he saw they were frightened from the first. He said they probably took him for Maui, their great god, who lived in the sea and built their islands. He was afraid that I would show up somewhere and dispel the idea that he was superhuman, or they'd see the boat. After that he kept the launch hidden and arranged the mirrors. They never came near the island after that, though we used to see them sometimes far out at sea. Dear old Dad!"

She set her chin in the hollow of one hand and gazed pensively toward the ridge that held her father's grave. Chalmers, not wishing to intrude upon her grief, sat silently watching the investment of Sayers with the diving equipment, over the handling of which there still seemed to be considerable discussion.

Finally, Hamaku left the rest and ran along the rocks at the edge of the lagoon, looking searchingly into the water. He shouted, and the little group joined him, Sayers lumbering along in the center. At the rocks the Australian sat down, his feet swinging over the water, adjusted the necessary weights, and put on the lead-soled shoes. Then he knelt and lowered himself awkwardly backwards, disappearing gradually below the surface. Tuan Yuck and the two natives got into the boat and paddled slowly toward the place where Sayers had submerged, the Chinaman peering over the side.

"Directing him and keeping tab on him at the same time," thought Chalmers. "That's some scheme for supervising pearl fishing. I wonder what their luck is going to be?"

Leila touched him on his arm.

"Look!" she said tensely, pressing the binoculars into his hands. "There—far out where the clouds end."

WHERE a pearly mass of trade-wind cumulus showed its sharply defined curves against the blue, Chalmers saw a sail that gleamed for a moment like gold in the sunlight. In the field of the powerful glasses it showed as a double canoe, joined by a high platform, outrigged on either side and driven by a great square sail of fine matting.

The canoes were filled with paddlers, and dark forms lounged on the deck. As he watched, the war-craft grew larger and came swiftly on before the wind. Then it swung around, the canoemen churning the sea into foam as they paddled and backed water to assist the maneuver. The big sail was lowered and quickly raised again and the great canoe raced off on the opposite tack, gradually disappearing until it was only a speck on the water.

"It's lucky they didn't come in close enough to sight the schooner's masts," he said, "or they might have been tempted to investigate. A crowd like that would be a nasty lot to tackle. I suppose they saw the reflections of the higher mirrors and it scared them off. There comes Sayers out of the water. Tuan Yuck doesn't seem to fancy the shell he's brought up."

The boat had been beached as Sayers emerged and emptied from a net bag on the sand the oysters he had found. Tuan Yuck kicked them with an emphasis that was contemptuous even at that distance. He picked up a shell and showed it to the Australian, apparently giving him a lecture on the subject of pearl oysters.

"He's picked out the wrong kind," said Leila. "It's always a distorted, crumpled shell that holds a pearl. The smooth, symmetrical ones never hold anything larger than seeds. He is going to try again."

Sayers picked up the bag and the air-cylinder was recharged. This time he sat astride of the boat's bow and let himself drop to the bottom on a signal from Tuan Yuck.

"Perhaps there are no more rich patches in the lagoon," said Leila. "It often happens that way. It would serve them right."

"It wouldn't suit us best just now," said Chalmers. "We've got a fine position, but——"

"But what? Won't you tell me exactly what you think of the situation? Please."

He looked at her calm face, the unwavering eyes and steady hands.

"All right," he said. "That's only fair. Let's thrash it out together.

"We've got to look at it from both sides. As they figure it, it's a question of us having the pearls and they the schooner. The lagoon is a side issue. They've seen what you carry in that bag." He nodded toward the black ribbon about her neck, nearly concealed by her blouse. "They think sooner or later we'll capitulate and give up the pearls for a passage. Or they may starve us out. Or they may try and rush us. They want the pearls first and last, hook or crook. And they care very little what happens to us.

"We've got the launch, unknown to them as long as they don't find it. That's to our advantage. It's good for a long voyage, barring storms. So we can eliminate the schooner. We don't want it. If we had it we could hardly handle it without help. But they are going to watch us as closely as we keep tab on them. It's a good deal of a deadlock. My best hope is to take them by surprise or that they start a quarrel between the two of them. The most serious thing is lack of ammunition. I've got to get hold of that somehow—and soon. But we'll manage somehow, don't you worry?"

Leila Denman smiled back at him. She was beginning to appraise him, and ranked him far higher than he dreamed. Through all the whirl of events since his arrival she had been inclined to look upon him as frank, impetuous, generous, courageous, but, after all, a good deal of a boy. Now as she noted the set of his lean jaw, the gray of his eyes, like hardened steel, while he calculated their chances and faced them, she felt an absolute sense of protection, and recognized him not as merely manly, but a man, in every stalwart seventy-two inches of him.

His unshaven beard furred his sunburned face, his duck clothes were rumpled, torn and grimed, but they did not hide the well-muscled strength of his broad shoulders nor the litheness of the waist above the narrow hips. Altogether Leila found him very good to look upon. She made a permanent decision in favor of aquiline noses and straight hair, dark brown and closely trimmed to the well-shaped skull.

"That's the way he must always wear it," she told herself, then, noting his steady glance, blushed, afraid he might have read her thoughts.

Suddenly the lava ridge upon which they were perched vibrated and swung beneath them. The crests of the hills seemed to waver. The still water of the lagoon flowed like a splintered mirror. A rasping, grinding sound as of thunder came from the interior of the island. A myriad birds rose and wheeled, screaming.

The boat below them made frantically for the schooner, looking, with its outspread moving oars, like some frightened water-bug. The schooner plunged at its cable like a startled horse at the halter-rope and brought up rocking in the troubled water. The whole place seemed to move as the clear sky above them pitched, and for a second the sea-line tilted as one sees it through a ship's porthole. Then came the grinding noise again with a rasping jar as if the island had been adrift and suddenly had run aground.

Leila had naturally stretched out both arms to Chalmers in her terror, and he, as instinctively, had enfolded her in his own.

"It's all over now," he said, holding her for a moment longer while she still trembled.

Her head was on his breast and the fragrance of her hair filled his nostrils and left them spoiled for all other perfumes.

"It's silly of me, isn't it," she said as he released her. "But that was my very first earthquake and one seems so utterly helpless. Thank you!"

She blushed again while her eyes pleaded with him to ignore her confusion.

"Look there, Leila," he said pointing to the lagoon.

A strange figure, gleaming with the water that ran from the harness it wore, the sun making bursts of radiance on the metal of his helmet, Sayers broke from the water, stumbling clumsily to the sand where, anchored by his weighted boots, he stood swaying, shaking his fists at the boat and raving impotently while he strove to unfasten his helmet.

It was a ludicrous sight and Chalmers guffawed outright, the girl joining in the laugh and forgetting her own fright.

"It must have given him a rare scare under the water," said Chalmers at last.

"He'll not want to go pearling again in a hurry," suggested the girl.

Chalmers' face lost all traces of laughter. The tremor was likely to force matters to an issue all around. The natives would believe this a fresh proof that Motutabu was bewitched, and that might lead to a decision to leave the island, which would infallibly be prefaced by a determined attempt to get the pearls.

Ammunition was a prime necessity. He

must devise some means of securing it. He was not greatly alarmed about the earthquake, unless it should be repeated. The island was evidently of volcanic origin and might have been affected by a main disturbance a thousand miles or more away.

Nor was he discouraged at the odds against him. Chalmers was essentially human. He had enough of the true gambler in him to enjoy the game the more as his stake diminished. Any fool could ride a winning horse, he believed, and he possessed another attribute that stood him in good stead, an increasing desire to fight back harder and harder as the contest grew more difficult.

On the beach, Sayers was showing that he was made of sterner stuff than Chalmers had credited him with. As the boat came back for him, he succeeded in freeing himself of his helmet and at the same time his opinion of Tuan Yuck's desertion of him.

"So you *are* a yellow cur after all," he shouted, "a sneaking, cowardly Mongolian mongrel. Thought I was dead and hoped it too, I suppose. You low-lived, Oriental hound!"

His language grew more livid at Tuan Yuck's imperturbability.

"The water was safer than the land, my friend," said the Oriental suavely. "If we had tried to jump out on the beach we should likely have broken our legs. Anyway, we could not help you until we saw you. Also the boys were frightened at first, but I have convinced them that this is nothing more than happens in Hawaii every month. If you do not want to go down again I will put on the suit, though, as I warned you, I can not go very deep on account of my heart."

The logic of the speech was good, but Sayers, convinced that Tuan Yuck had meant to desert him, could not recognize it. The incident renewed the determination he had made to stay ashore nights and let Tuan Yuck go off to the schooner. But he said nothing of that thought for the moment.

"I didn't say I was going to quit, did I?" he growled. "I didn't forget to bring up my haul, either. Look at those. Are they any better?"

Tuan Yuck toed over the oysters and shook his head.

"Not worth opening, Sayers. A *baroque* or two, perhaps. Even that is doubtful.

Good for shell only. We'll have to try another patch."

Later in the afternoon Chalmers saw the boat take Tuan Yuck off to the schooner, leaving Sayers, now freed from his diving-garb, on the beach. The boat returned in a little while and the two natives carried up some stores and set them down on the sand. The Kanakas started to leave, but Sayers detained them and they went up to the clearing, coming back with material from which they started a fire blazing in the dusk.

A case was broached and a bottle passed round. Tomi's voice was lifted up in song and the others joined in. The Australian took up his zither that had been brought in the boat and soon native songs of questionable delicacy were being roared out.

Here was Chalmers' opportunity. Sayers and the natives, between the attractions of the gin and the singing, were evidently ashore for a night of it. Tuan Yuck would be on the schooner alone, and sooner or later must succumb to the seduction of his opium pipe.

A voice called to him out of the darkness below him:

"Dinner is served, Sir Sentinel. Look out you don't fall coming down."

"What is the program for tonight?" she asked presently. "Why so serious and silent? Who takes the dog-watch? And, if I do, am I supposed to bark at all intruders?"

"I'm going to swim off to the schooner tonight," he said. "Sayers and the boys are ashore and Tuan Yuck will be in poppy-land. I'm going to build a raft after dinner and I'm going to bring back some ammunition and a lot of other things, including a razor."

"All right," she said. "What time do you start?"

"I'll have to go just before the end of the ebb and come back on the flood."

"And that means?"

"About midnight."

"I'll be ready."

"There's no need for you to stay up."

"Indeed there is. I'm going with you."

CHAPTER XV

LOVE LEAVEN

CHALMERS' protests were unavailing. Leila Denman's arguments were both convincing and numerous.

"I am not going to be left alone on this

beach imagining all sorts of dreadful things happening to you," she said. "If there should, I want to be there. They can't be more dreadful than what would happen to me if you didn't come back. I can swim as well as you can. Wait till you see me. I've got my bathing-suit, and I can really help you."

"There seems to be a mutiny in full progress," Chalmers answered, "but I've got to quell it. Some one's got to stay on watch here."

"Pouf!" She dismissed the reason with a charming moue, like the puff of an imaginary cigarette. "We can watch them ever so much better from the lagoon. You are afraid I'm going to be a hindrance—I'm not. You are going to make a little raft, you said, for the things you are going to bring back?"

"Yes, ammunition, some clothes, my charts, the chronometer, and, if I can get away with it, the schooner's compass."

"You are going to climb aboard and get them?"

"Naturally."

"And how are you going to load up your raft without help?"

Chalmers laughed.

"Fairly won," he said. "It would take me ever so much longer by myself. I'll give in—as long as we know there are no sharks. But you must promise to stay in the water."

"Aye, aye, sir! The mutineers return to duty," she said gaily.

"Having achieved their point," he countered.

He marveled at the buoyancy of her spirit, at the sheer pluck of her. That she was not in the least disillusioned concerning the dangers that hourly surrounded them he was assured. Yet, in the face of them all, in the prospect of being left to the vicious whims of Tuan Yuck and Sayers, should he fail her, she was the gay comrade, the gallant "pal" who insisted upon her full share of the perils.

And she trusted him. The thought was an elixir. To its inspiration the subtle alchemy of his body responded, charging the blood with energies that gave new strength to his muscles, invigorating every nerve and sinew till the whole coordinated like the parts of a perfect machine.

Both were heart free, both ripe for the friendly virus with which Cupid tips his arrows, and that ubiquitous godling chuckled at Chalmers's attempts to regulate his passion as the two built their little raft by the light of their fire, the blazing stars and a sinking moon.

The setting could not have been completer for romance. Each was conscious of the proximity of the other and felt little rippling thrills of delight as they came into casual contact over their work. But to Chalmers, the pearls that nestled in her bosom, gaining fresh luster from the magnetism of her young body, seemed as insuperable a barrier between them as if they had been the actual boulders of an impassable wall.

Without conceit, he recognized that both of them were seeped in an exaltation of spirit that made life seem very sweet and free from care, despite their dangers. He was not blind to the fact that Leila shared the emotions that possessed him as their hands met, or that a certain adorable shyness that was both a lure and a promise shone sometimes in her eyes; but he hugged the thought that he would be dishonorable to take any advantage of a mood that might pass, hugged it as the Spartan boy held the fox that gnawed his breast.

She was an heiress; he had nothing ahead but the earnings of a profession to which he was not accredited by nature. So he controlled himself as best he could and checked the growing impulse to tell her how sweet and brave and altogether desirable she was. Once, when the mischievous wind whipped a perfumed strand of her hair across his face, he deliberately went away from her on the idle pretense of looking for more driftwood, though the raft was then complete, and stood dizzily facing the lagoon to fight it out.

"You came pretty close to being a cad," he told himself. "Another second and you would have kissed her. A fine protector you are for a lonely girl."

A tiny voice—it was Cupid's—whispered, "She would not have minded." And he thrust it from him as unworthy. Whereat Cupid, counting his remaining arrows, laughed, knowing well the power of that beneficent venom on their tips, composed of elements allied to hope and youth and health that would crystallize to happiness.

Leila recognized his restraint, guessed partly at its reasons, admired it and was piqued at it at the same moment. At times she devoutly wished the pearls were still at the bottom of the sea, though her father's spirit, strong within her, fiercely resented the giving of them up to their would-be possessors, and, womanlike, she loved them as gems and for what they would bring, and could not see why such a dower should make her less desirable.

So Cupid, well satisfied, left them there beneath the stars, and winged his way to other targets.

IT was close to midnight before their task was ended and the little float of driftwood and boughs, compactly lashed together, carried to the water's edge ready for launching. The rays of Sayers' fire flickered beyond the cape and the sound of ribald voices came to them now and then in the quiet night. The scattered rocks at the foot of the headland were clear and the ebb was nearly at its limit.

"We'll pile it up with seaweed," said Chalmers, "and let it drift down on the current. It runs nearly as fast as we can swim. All we have to do is to guide it. We'll keep low in the water, and if any one should be on the lookout they'll take it for a loose mass of weed. It's about time to start."

"I'll be ready in five minutes," said Leila, disappearing into her cave with one of the lanterns they had brought from the clearing.

Chalmers took off his shoes and with his case-knife hacked off the legs of his grimy trousers well above the knee for freedom in swimming, promising himself a new outfit from the schooner. Tuan Yuck by this time would be well under the influence of opium, he imagined, and there would be little trouble or danger about securing what he wanted. He discarded his shirt, tightened his belt and stood up stalwart and ready for action.

While he waited he examined the clip of cartridges in the automatic handle, re-greased the weapons and the blade of the knife and replaced the latter in his belt. The pistol was on a lanyard ready to put round his neck at the end of the swim. For the trip it would ride on the raft.

Leila came to her cave-mouth, trim in her bathing-suit, and looked at him admiringly as he stood by the light of their fire, gazing seaward. He looked very capable, very handsome, in a manly way, she thought.

"I'm ready," she said.

He looked at her approvingly.

"I'd slip off that skirt when we get into deep water," he suggested.

"I will," she answered. "I'm not going to be handicapped."

They waded quietly into the water, impressed with the necessity for caution, and pushed the raft before them into the swing of the current. Seaweed was piled upon it, trailing in the water. The moon had sunk, the dim mass of the platform was hardly distinguishable as it floated down the star-sown lagoon toward the cape.

They made as little motion as possible, fearing the phosphorescence they disturbed might betray them by its regular flashes. Leila slipped off her skirt and they swam in water that was as warm as midday and luminously alive. Green fire swirled from them as they paddled easily along, their hands resting on the raft. Bubbles and streaks of liquid flame the color of burning alcohol broke along the sides and in the wake of the float.

The blaze where Sayers and the two natives caroused burned brightly. The three still chanted in snatches, and boisterous laughter punctuated the songs. The voices were obviously those of drunken men whose debauch was soon likely to end in heavy sleep. Reefward, the masts of the schooner showed faintly against the sky. As they drew near to the hull they looked in vain for a light in Tuan Yuck's cabin. Everything seemed set for the success of their undertaking.

Chalmers guided the raft to the bows and, clinging to the bowsprit stays with one hand, fastened the raft by a line already attached to it.

"Hang on here," he whispered. "I'll lower the things down to you. I'll be as quick as I can."

"All right," she answered softly, and he deftly swung himself up and clambered over the bowsprit.

The tide was on the turn and Leila prepared to keep the raft from bumping at the schooner's side. Presently the influence of the flood swung it clear as the schooner slowly responded to the shifting current. She let go of the stays, resting her folded arms on the raft, her body in the warm water, and waited for Chalmers' reappearance. Farther aft, the open porthole of Tuan Yuck's cabin remained dark, like the socket of a blind eye.

On deck, Chalmers, treading lightly as a cat, stepped to the open companionway and stealthily descended into the cabin. He had no light, but he knew the familiar position of everything, and there had been no changes. He listened at the door of Tuan Yuck's cabin. Inside, he could hear the Chinaman breathing heavily. The door was light proof.

He tiptoed into his own cabin and found an electric torch, safe where he had left it. He touched the contacts and the ray shone out brightly.

CHAPTER XVI

THE RAID ON THE SCHOONER

THE raft was laden to its full capacity as Chalmers descended into the cabin for his last trip. He had built it so that the deck rode high above the water, and he blessed its buoyancy as he lowered the things he selected, slung in a bag improvised from his oilskin coat, to Leila, who stowed them deftly on the float.

The cartridges he had found in their original stowage under a locker seat and these he took first. Then followed canned goods from another locker, the bulk of his personal belongings—including the razor— the schooner's log, the case of charts, the chronometer, his sextant, and, last of all, the compass, which he unscrewed from the binnacle post.

It was not his intention to leave the schooner destitute of steerage implements. Now that he knew of the launch in the mangroves, it was his first desire that Sayers would muster up enough cocksureness to take the schooner under his command, providing they could be persuaded to give up the pearls as too difficult to procure, content perhaps with what they found in the lagoon.

But there was a spare compass in the cabin and he wanted the more reliable instrument. He took the automatic on its lanyard from his neck and lowered it to Leila, together with the electric torch. As he prepared to slip over the side and rejoin her, elated at the success of the raid, he remembered Tuan Yuck's rifle. To secure it would be to reduce the enemy's efficiency by one third. He had taken all the spare loads for the Winchesters save what might be carried in their belts.

"Just a minute," he called down to the waiting girl, hardly discernible beneath the curve of the bows, her face a dim gray oval looking up at him with eyes that held the sparkle of the reflected stars that spangled the water all about her. "Never mind the torch!"

He remembered where the rifle stood when he had first noticed it and determined to take it. As he reached carefully for it in the velvety blackness, he fancied he heard a faint hissing, sputtering sound, like a noisy fuse.

He stopped, every movement arrested, intent upon the strange sound. Suddenly his spine tingled and he knew that he was not alone in the cabin. His senses, almost supernaturally alert, telegraphed to his brain that a door had been opened, ever so softly, behind him—the door of Tuan Yuck's cabin. He crouched rapidly, circling about in the same motion. He heard the swift intake of a breath, the swish of an arm in a silken covering above his head and, grappling for his foe, found only vacancy.

Which side of him the Oriental stood he could not tell. The cabin was in pitchy darkness through which his sight strained helplessly. How Tuan Yuck was armed he could only guess. The rifle was useless in this kind of *mêlée* and he reached for his knife. Instantly two hands that seemed made of steel clutched at his wrist and twisted skin and flesh in opposite directions. In the swift agony of the attack his tortured tendons were momentarily paralyzed and the knife fell tinkling to the floor.

He heard the scuff of Tuan Yuck's foot as the weapon was kicked away at the same instant that he managed to tear himself free, and groped for his opponent's arms. They writhed from his grasp with a vigor that astounded him. In his first struggle with the Oriental, in the clearing, he had been surprised at the other's wiry strength where he had expected flaccidity. But then he had held him pinioned and now the Chinaman was taking the offensive. He pursued Tuan Yuck, bumping against the fixed table in the center of the cabin, unable to obtain more than the briefest grip on the arms that warded him off so effectually.

The uncanny presentiment came to him that the Oriental's eyes possessed the faculty of seeing in the dark. The next second he was sure of it. The steely hands caught him again, one at the right wrist, the other high up, pressing a nerve that left the arm numb and helpless. A swiftly thrown-up knee was applied to his elbow, an instant more and his arm would have been broken, but Chalmers kicked out viciously in a wide circle and swept Tuan Yuck's legs from under him.

Both crashed to the ground together. Chalmers was amazed at the tiger-like ferocity with which Tuan Yuck strained against his hold and the claw-like grip that tore at his muscles, fighting always to reach his throat. The thought flashed that this fury must be born of opium and would diminish.

He held his own as they writhed on the floor of the cabin, waiting for the right time to exert all his strength in one explosive impulse. The moment came and he rolled uppermost, his fingers feeling for the other's throat. As they twisted, Tuan Yuck's head struck the post of the table with a thud, his form suddenly grew limp and his struggling arms fell outstretched on the floor.

As Chalmers instinctively relaxed his hold, Tuan Yuck's chest heaved upward and his whole body came to sudden life. The crafty Oriental had seized upon the sounding but comparatively harmless blow as a ruse. His right arm eluded Chalmers's swift pounce and twisted upward like a snake. Chalmers brought his left knee down hard upon the other's right biceps, striving to keep his poise upon the writhing form, but the action was too late.

Tuan Yuck had found the knife, perhaps his cat-like eyes had seen it! The blade slashed Chalmers's shoulder. He could hear the squeak of the steel against his collar-bone. By some miracle of luck the plunging point was diverted in the scuffle and the blow was only a glancing one.

With the shock of the wound Chalmers's fury outmatched that of Tuan Yuck.

"You yellow devil!" he exploded pantingly as he held the other's wrists in his clutch at last, squatting upon his chest, each knee in the hollow between the Chinaman's upper and forearms. The warm blood

that ran down his left arm angered him. He held but one desire—to gain possession of the knife and drive it home, the primal instinct of a man fighting for his life.

Tuan Yuck's teeth gritted and the reek of his opium-tainted breath came upward as he spat in Chalmers's face. He flinched at the nastiness of it and the Chinaman with one mighty effort set his foot against a locker and, so braced, upset Chalmers's balance, smashing the latter's head against a locker.

Now their positions were reversed though Chalmers still held the other's wrists in a vise-like grip, dizzy as he was from the blow and the loss of blood. Already he felt a faintness growing upon him as Tuan Yuck pressed his advantage. His grasp was almost automatic now, and it was the hand of the arm that was wounded that resisted the tug of the Chinaman's right wrist to be free and deal the fatal blow.

Hitherto he had thought of nothing but the fight. It had taken only a minute or two of swift, strenuous struggle in the dark and there had been no time to consider other matters. Now, as he lay prone, his strength ebbing, the thought of Leila waiting in the water outside, only a few feet away, maddened him to fresh effort. Tuan Yuck met it with a cackling laugh.

"Yellow devil, am I?" he said. "I'll send you to a white man's hell, you young fool."

Chalmers's fingers seemed nerveless. He could no longer fill his lungs beneath his opponent's weight.

THERE was a swift pattering on deck, a rush of feet down the companionway, a circle of brilliant light that searched the gloom and caught the blade of Tuan Yuck's knife as the Oriental plucked his wrist free at last and started the lunge that would end the fight.

The sudden glare from behind startled him but did not halt the blow. Swiftly as it descended, the girl was quicker and the tube of the lamp came down clubwise, the heavy bull's-eye of the lens striking the base of Tuan Yuck's skull with all the force her strong young arm could muster.

Tuan Yuck pitched forward, his head striking the floor beyond Chalmers's shoulder, the knife driven into the floor of the cabin, where it snapped off short. The ray of the lamp went out with the blow and Leila's efforts failed to relight it.

4

Chalmers, roused from his swooning condition by the torch ray and his recognition of Leila, struggled to free himself from the incubus of Tuan Yuck's weight. Leila, kneeling on the floor, assisted him to rise.

"Quick!" she said. "Tuan Yuck has signaled ashore. They are coming in the boat!"

She gave her strength to him as his will fought its way back to full consciousness and supported him with her shoulder as he staggered up the companionway and across the deck to the rail. A confused shouting came over the water. The fresh air helped to revive Chalmers and the emergency rallied his forces, though his head ached furiously.

"Are you badly hurt?" Leila asked anxiously.

His forearm rested on her shoulder, one of her slender arms was about his waist. He braced himself to stand without her aid.

"I'm all right," he said. "Come on, we've got to be getting out of this. We might hold them off, I suppose; but we don't want their old schooner."

He essayed a laugh and hurried forward, reeling a little as he went.

"You're bleeding," she said with a half-checked sob.

The revelation of her tenderness did more for him than any surgery.

"It's only a surface slash," he said. "The salt water will help, and we can patch it up when we get back. There's nothing serious. I got a whack on the head that did the most damage."

He proved it by straddling the rail and, hanging to it by his uninjured arm, slipping into the water. Leila was there before him, ready to aid. The salt water smarted, but it acted both as a tonic and as an astringent and he reached the raft easily enough.

"You'll have to cast it adrift," he said. "Pull the loose end."

She tugged at the slipknot, the rope fell with a little splash and the raft began to fall away from the schooner, the flood-tide bearing it back toward the cape and Safety Haven.

Inshore, there was splashing and confusion, the shouting of orders by Sayers and the drunken babble of the two natives. Spurts of pale flame flashed up as their oars beat the phosphorescent water in an effort to get the whale-boat straightened out for the schooner.

Chalmers floated full length, his right hand on the raft for support. Beside him Leila, with a steady scissors stroke of her legs, drove the raft onward, aided by the tide.

All their attention centered on their own craft, the Australian and his Kanaka aids failed to see the raft, succeeding at last clumsily in getting the whale-boat in line for the schooner, Sayers cursing loudly at every inefficient stroke and the natives answering him in the coarse familiarity of mutual drunkenness.

The flood was strengthening and the raft was soon beyond the headland and in the home waters of Safety Haven. They found bottom off their starting point and stood upright. An indistinct murmur from the schooner barely reached them.

"How do you feel?" asked Leila. "Can you walk up to the caves?"

"I'm not even wobbly any more," he answered, not with absolute truth. "I've stopped bleeding. But I'd better stay down here to repel boarders in case they try to start something. You might fetch down a rifle. We'll want to stop them at long range."

"I'll bring two," she answered, "and something to dress that wound."

Grateful for the chance to more completely pull himself together, Chalmers sat on the beach, his back against a rock. Aside from a little light-headedness he felt fairly fit. The slash from Tuan Yuck had evidently severed no important veins nor arteries and, though his shoulder was stiffening, he felt no severe pain.

"Flesh wound, I guess," he soliloquized. "Pretty lucky for our side. The darling!" He closed his eyes and saw again the ray of the torch, the flare of it on Leila's face as she raised her arm for the blow. "The darling!" he said again, more loudly.

Leila, coming quietly and swiftly down the beach, lantern in hand, heard it. Her heart bounded and she kissed her hand to him in the darkness.

"Did you call?" she asked.

"Me? Why, no," he answered.

Her lips silently formed two syllables that by daylight might have been recognized as "stu-pid" though coupled with a smile that robbed them of any sting.

"Here are the rifles," she said. "And

now, if you'll sit still, I'll dress your wound."

She set the lantern on a rock and cut his sleeveless vest away with the scissors she had brought. The blood had not stiffened owing to the soaking of the return swim, and the wound showed clean-lipped and pale. With strips of plaster she dexterously strapped the edges together and applied a cooling salve, above which she laid a pad of cotton and bound the shoulder up with a broad bandage.

"I brought our surgical kit along last night," she said. "The salve is wonderful. It's made from native herbs. If you don't have to use your arm any more tonight that cut will be healing up by tomorrow. Really, it's not very deep."

"I thought it wasn't," he said. "I used my arm after it happened and I knew there was nothing very much the matter outside of the loss of a little blood. And that won't hurt me. Tell me, how did you arrive on time to give our Oriental friend that most prodigious swat in exactly the right place?"

"I didn't know where I hit him," she said. "I struck blindly. You had just left me. I had the torch still in one hand when something made me look along the ship's side and I saw Tuan Yuck's head stuck out of his porthole looking forward toward me. It disappeared and I pushed the raft under the bows, hoping he had not seen me. Then his arm was thrust out. There was some sort of a torch in his hand that broke out into a crimson flame."

"A Coston signal," said Chalmers. "That's what I heard sputtering. He must have taken them in his cabin for emergencies. Go on!"

"As soon as it started to flare I slipped my finger through the ring on the torch, reached up for the stay with that hand and drew myself up out of sight. They were shouting on the beach and I knew they'd be on board in a few moments, so I managed to scramble over the bows somehow, with the torch still in my hand, and started to warn you.

"I heard you scuffling in the cabin. I didn't know what else to do—I'd left the pistol on the raft, like a ninny—so I went down into the cabin and flashed the light on, and when I saw you underneath and covered with blood I—I struck at the back of his head. I wish I'd killed him!" she ended passionately, her eyes blazing in the lantern light; then she bowed her head on her knees and sobbed.

Chalmers looked at her helplessly. He wanted to gather her into his arms and comfort her, but reached over and patted her shoulder instead.

"Don't cry," he said.

She lifted her head and looked at him as if he had struck her. Then she bounded to her feet.

"Perhaps I did kill him," she cried. "I hope so. I hate him. I hate all men!"

Astounded into silence and inaction Chalmers saw her disappear up the beach.

"I wonder what I've done?" he asked himself, not knowing that his sin was one of omission, not commission.

He sat there a little wearily, his rifle across his knees, watching the point. There was no sound from the schooner, the night seemed very quiet after the excitement of the fight and he was very lonely.

There was a light step at his side, felt rather than heard, and he turned his head to see Leila. She had discarded her bathing-suit and wore her linen skirt and middy blouse, with her hair braided in long plaits that hung over her shoulders and bosom. In her hands she carried two mugs of steaming liquid.

"I left the soup kettle on the ashes when we started," she said demurely. "This will do you a world of good. I brought one for myself, so we can drink it together."

The aroma of the thick soup was supremely grateful. The draught heartened him. He marveled at the swift change in the girl's demeanor and wondered how many Leilas there were in the one dainty body. But, acquiring wisdom, however tardily, he said nothing.

"That soup has made me drowsy instead of waking me up," he said. "I've got to keep awake, you know. And we've got to haul up that raft."

He yawned prodigiously.

"I'll pull up the raft," she said. "You've got to rest your arm. It will be easy on the rising tide."

When she came back he was asleep under the influence of the veronal she had mixed with his soup. She smiled, lifted his head gently and pillowed it on her lap, then, with the rifles handy, leaned back against the rock and kept watch until long after dawn.

CHAPTER XVII

SAYERS MAKES A PROPOSITION

CHALMERS was furious with himself when he awoke and saw Leila's tired face and the eyes that had purple shadows beneath them, and he was even disposed to be indignant with her when she confessed that she had drugged him.

"Suppose they had tackled us?" he asked.

"I only gave you five grains," she said. "I could have awakened you easily enough. You simply *had* to get some rest. You are the mainstay of the camp, you know." She smiled at him wearily as he helped her with his sound arm stiffly to get up. "How are you feeling?"

"Bully! And I've got the appetite of a shark. If you'll help me pack some of these canned things up to the caves, we'll get breakfast and then you'll turn in and get some sleep. That salve is wonderful. I can use my arm, and my shoulder only feels a bit stiff."

"You'll wear that arm in a sling, sir," she said with a pretty show of authority. "I'll fix one for you as soon as I've dressed your wound."

"That isn't a wound," he protested. "That's only a scratch. I'll bet it isn't a circumstance to the way Tuan Yuck's head feels this morning. Mine's stopped buzzing, thank Heaven. I wonder what their next move will be? Did you see any signs of them?"

"Neither sight nor sound."

"Well, we've got all the spare ammunition. That shoe that pinched is on their foot now.

"What did you do with your pearls last night?" he asked later, as they ate their breakfast.

"I buried them in the cave. I've got them on now." She pointed to the ribbon about her neck. "If dad hadn't worked so hard to get them and planned what they were going to mean for me, I'd give them up if they'd only go away and give us a chance to follow later. I'm a little afraid of this island after that earthquake."

"No use worrying about that," he said. "What did your father plan for you with the pearls?"

"Oh—we were going to travel lots. And then he wanted me to have clothes, I suppose, and all the things a girl wants."

"Humph!"

Chalmers set down his mug of coffee and gazed gloomily in front of him. Leila looked at him for a moment, her eyes tender.

"Don't be silly," she said softly.

As he looked up she blushed scarlet, jumped up and ran to her cave. She paused at the entrance and spoke over her shoulder.

"I'm going to sleep for a while," she said. "Take care of yourself."

Chalmers's shoulder hurt more than he had acknowledged to Leila but the native ointment really possessed great curative qualities and the slash when it was dressed showed every sign of healing by first intention. But he managed to sprawl his way up to the lookout.

The beach was deserted. So, to all appearances, was the schooner. The whaleboat trailed alongside, the oars sticking up from between the thwarts as they had been left by the natives overnight. Through the glasses he made out the ashes of Sayers's beach fire, with empty gin bottles scattered here and there in the sand.

"Headache of more than one sort aboard the schooner this morning, I fancy," he told himself. "They are not likely to disturb us for a while, at least."

He clambered down again and busied himself removing the cartridges and the rest of the load on the raft up to his cave, where he stored them with satisfaction, burying the shells in the sand. Working with only one hand, the morning was well gone by the time he had finished the task.

Leila came out from her cave soon after noon, refreshed from her sleep, smiled at him and passed to her rock apartments, returning presently fresh from a dip in the mermaid's pool, her golden-brown hair streaming down to her waist, full of rainbow iridescence.

She perched on a rock beside him.

"You don't mind if I let it hang down while it dries?" she asked him.

"No, I don't mind," answered Chalmers dryly.

She looked at him quickly, as if trying to read his mood.

"You look all fagged out," she declared. "And I'm feeling fresh and rested. Nothing's happened?"

"Not yet. I think they are all glad to lay

off for a while. You must have given our friend Tuan Yuck a pretty hard smash. He's not the sort to put off trying to get even. Sayers and the crew will probably sleep all day. We're tolerably safe as long as we keep a good lookout. We may run a little shy on the menu, but we won't starve. All we have to do is to watch the front door. And that reminds me, did you notice the alarm-clock I lowered down to you in the first load for the raft?"

"I did. And I was afraid the thing would go off. I could just imagine it ringing away and I turned the alarm switch off, though the clock wasn't going. What's it for?"

"For our watches. It won't do for either of us to watch all night and be sleepy all day. We can split the night up into tricks. It isn't dark until seven and the days are getting longer. We'll make the first watch from dark until midnight, then midnight to four in the morning, and a short trick from four until daylight. We can make up lost sleep in the afternoons."

"You'll let me do my share, as you promised?"

"Surely. We'll alternate. I'll take the first and last tricks tonight and tomorrow morning—and tomorrow it's your turn. The alarm-clock is for the one who's sleeping. One of us must be on the beach or up on the headland all the time. Daytimes there's little danger of surprise."

"Then you'll turn in for a nap now, while I keep a lookout?"

"I will," he consented. "I am tired. You're the best kind of a partner, Leila. Fire, if anything shows up. We can afford the cartridges now, thank Heaven."

She flushed with pleasure, picked up a rifle and went down to the lagoon.

CHALMERS was roused out of a sound sleep by the signal, sounding like an explosion to his sleepy ears. He jumped up, wincing as he forgot to favor his damaged shoulder, and raced down the sand between the rocks, pistol in hand. At first he could not see Leila, and his heart sank within him at the thought that she had been surprised or surrounded. Then he heard her calling to him from the aerie on the headland.

"There's a boat putting off from the schooner and heading this way," she called down to him. "The natives are rowing and Sayers is steering. He's got a white flag on a pole. They stopped when I fired in the air, but they are coming on slowly."

Chalmers considered rapidly.

"It can't do any harm to see what they are up to," he said. "Better come down, Leila. We'll wait for them on the beach."

She climbed down lightly and stood by his side. In a few minutes the whale-boat showed, rowing slowly past the cape. The lagoon between there and the reef was barely fifty yards across. Chalmers challenged them.

"Way enough there," he cried. "Keep your oars in the water. Don't come in too close. Sayers, put your hands up! Cover him, Leila."

She lifted her rifle obediently. The natives, backing water, held the boat almost motionless as Sayers held up his arms.

"Don't shoot, Miss," he grinned. "This is a peace mission. Flag of truce, you know."

"You keep your hands up, just the same, Sayers," commanded Chalmers. "You boys row in till you touch bottom. You'll have to wade ashore, Sayers. I'm taking no chances. Don't put down your hands till I tell you, and the first one who takes his hands off those oars gets a hole through him."

The Kanakas rowed carefully into the shallows and the Australian got out awkwardly into the water, his hands above his head.

"I'm not armed, Chalmers," he said. "I'm trusting you."

"I'm not trusting you," retorted Chalmers sternly. "Come on up on the beach. That's close enough. You boys back off and row up and down slowly till we call for you. No monkey business."

A look at his face convinced Hamaku and Tomi that strict obedience was a very urgent necessity and they followed out his instructions, rowing gingerly up and down a short distance from shore, the whites of their eyes showing ludicrously as they watched the rifle that the girl handled with grim precision.

"Turn around, Sayers."

As the Australian showed his shoulders, Chalmers walked up to him, placed the muzzle of his pistol in the small of his back with a convincing firmness and, taking his left arm from the sling, felt for any weapons the other might carry.

"Honor bright," said Sayers. "I'm playing fair. Glad your arm isn't entirely out of commission. You put Tuan Yuck properly on the shelf. Walloped him with that light-stick of yours, didn't you? I found it smashed after we got there and got a lamp going. Can I put these down now? Thanks. If you don't mind, I'll take a seat."

He settled himself comfortably on a rock.

"Don't mind if I smoke a cigarette, do you? I've got the makings." He started to roll one, but the tobacco shook out of the paper in his nerveless hands. "I don't suppose you've got a drink, have you? There's a bottle in the boat."

"It can stay there," said Chalmers shortly. "What's the idea, Sayers?"

The Australian leered evilly, and there was a malicious gleam in his bloodshot eyes.

"Visitors not welcome, eh?" he said. "I don't know that I blame you any."

Chalmers took a step toward him.

"No offense!" Sayers hastened to say deprecatingly. "You mistake my meaning. Now this is what I've come for."

He had bunglingly achieved a cigarette at last and now lit it, crossing his legs, blowing out a cloud of smoke, and looking keenly at Chalmers.

"You don't like Tuan Yuck and you don't like me. That's granted," he commenced. "You don't think we've got anything in common, but there's one thing we both agree upon—neither of us have any use for Tuan Yuck."

He paused to notice the effect of his words. Leila called a crisp word of warning to the natives who had slowed up in their rowing, evidently trying to listen.

"You work well together, you two," went on Sayers. "I'll say that for your side. We don't. If I'd known you were so close to murdering that Chink last night I'm —— if I'd have tried to help him. I suppose, though, the two of you would have stolen the schooner if we hadn't come off. I see you took most everything you could lay your hands on as it was." His eyes roved to the raft on the beach close by.

"I've got to hand it to you, Chalmers," he said half grudgingly. "You're smarter than I gave you credit for. That's where I was a fool. I ought to have tied up with you instead of with Tuan Yuck long ago. That's all right," he deprecated as he caught the look in Chalmers's eyes. "We may get together yet.

"Tuan Yuck's a crook," he went on. "He'd double-cross the devil and come close to getting away with it. He's for Tuan Yuck first, last and all the time. He's tried to turn the Kanakas against me. As it is I daren't let 'em out of my sight or he'll hypnotize 'em. And I wouldn't trust myself on that schooner with him for sour apples.

"Now see here, Chalmers." He leaned forward, trying to speak convincingly. "You've got Tuan Yuck sized up. You couldn't believe anything he promised. You've made a fool of him into the bargain. He's crazy mad to get even. His head is so stiff from that wallop he can't move it. And those eyes of his ain't pleasant company at the best of times. Now you can trust me because I've got to trust you. I'll give you the best of it.

"I don't believe there's any more rich shell in that lagoon. I brought up a dozen samples from different patches yesterday and they were all blanks. I don't give a solitary whoop if there's a million in there. I want to get shut of Tuan Yuck, and off this island. If you want to come back to the lagoon later, well and good. The girl's got plenty to pay all expenses and set us all three up.

"Now here's my proposition. Split the pearls into three shares. That means one for me and two for you if you play your cards right. Hold on! No offense, I tell you. I'm just using my eyes. A blind man could see she's in love with you—and ought to be after all you've done for her."

"Go on," said Chalmers grimly.

"Now don't go to getting huffy, Chalmers. I'm talking sense. I deserve something. I started the trip. The girl would have died here if we hadn't come. I supplied the information, didn't I?"

"What do you propose to do with Tuan Yuck?"

"Do with him? Do what you like with him. Feed him to the sharks. Leave him here to make faces at himself in the mirrors if you're tender-hearted about hurting him. You take up my proposition and I'll attend to Tuan Yuck. I know what he'd do to me if he got the chance.

"I could sail the schooner back to the Gilberts at a pinch," he went on, his face smoothing from the convulsed snarl it had worn when he was speaking of Tuan Yuck.

"But you've got the pearls and you've fixed yourself properly to keep 'em. I don't want to go empty-handed. Tuan Yuck'll do both of us dirt. You know that. Now you and me and the girl can fix it up nicely. You can't leave here without the schooner. Now what do you say?"

Chalmers said nothing but motioned toward the boat.

"I'm too high, am I?" asked Sayers. "Then cut my share in half. You can land me anywhere you want to where I can get in touch with the outside and go on. Don't be a fool. Say the word and I'll agree to turn over Tuan Yuck. He's doped with opium now in his cabin."

"Call the boat in, Leila," said Chalmers.

"Hold on, now. The girl's got some say in the matter. Do the fair thing, miss," said Sayers as the girl came within easy earshot. "Make it your own terms. I leave it to you."

"I wouldn't give you one of those pearls if I never left the island alive," said Leila, looking at him with utter contempt in her eyes.

"You see, Sayers," said Chalmers. "There's your boat."

"I see all right," said the Australian, his face vicious with the sudden hate that flared into it. "It'd please both of you better to stay here honeymooning, I suppose."

Leila shrank back.

"One more word like that, Sayers, and I'll put a bullet through your head as you stand." Chalmers's finger was on the trigger as he spoke.

"All right, then. I'll go. Remember, I gave you a fair chance on your own terms." He waded out to the waiting boat and stepped in.

"You'll keep your hands up until you've passed the cape," said Chalmers.

Sayers spat venomously into the water.

"I'll come back," he said. "I give you warning. And you won't see me coming till I've got the drop on you."

Chalmers laughed.

"Pull away, boys," he said. "Smartly now. Don't drop your oars by any mistake."

The whale-boat swiftly surged down the lagoon, the oars bending under the tug of the demoralized Kanakas, anxious to get clear of the trouble. As it passed out of sight Chalmers turned to Leila. She was leaning on the rifle, shivering as if cold.

"Don't let anything that blackguard said affect you, Leila," he said.

She looked at him with eyes that were cold with rage.

"Why didn't you kill the beast?" she asked, and ran swiftly from him up the beach.

Chalmers followed slowly, perplexed and unhappy, wondering a little why he had not done as she suggested. The man was not fit to live. If he had only been armed!

Ahead of him Leila turned into the archway of her rock house and flung herself face down on the sand. He hesitated, then went on slowly to the caves.

He dismissed the threat of Sayers's last words as idle, but the Australian had brought up more clearly than ever the delicacy of the situation of Leila and himself. Now, he thought, there would be another barrier between them, and he made up his mind to be more circumspect than ever in word and deed.

"Something will have to break soon," he told himself, "with Sayers and Tuan Yuck at odds. I suppose the next thing will be overtures from Tuan Yuck."

CHAPTER XVIII

THE COUNTER CHECK

AN HOUR from midnight Chalmers heard the sound of oars and saw from his station on the lava ridge the blur of the whale-boat crossing the lagoon, its progress punctuated by the little spatters of phosphorescence where the oars dipped. The moon was down and it was hard to distinguish figures even through the night-glasses, but he counted four that landed the boat and went up the beach toward the house.

A light appeared in the window. In about fifteen minutes the two natives returned to the boat, lit a fire and disposed themselves to sleep.

Sayers and Tuan Yuck remained in the house. Evidently there was to be no recurrence of last night's debauch. Before long the window was darkened. The enemy was disposed of for the night.

Presently he heard the distant tinkle of the alarm-clock in Leila's cave and hastened down to meet her. He would gladly have eliminated her from the night watching, but he knew that she was happier in doing it, and his own chance to secure a fair measure of sleep increased the element of safety.

He saw the lantern dancing over the sand and between the rocks like a will-o'-the-wisp, though to himself he called it a love-light. She met him with her eyes wide open and sparkling with excitement.

"Twelve o'clock and all's well," he chanted.

"Including your shoulder?" she asked.

"Nearly. It's just sore from hurrying up to heal. I can use my arm well enough. They are asleep, or at least they've turned in for the night. Take the glasses and watch our front door. No need to climb the cliff. Where's the clock?"

"In your cave entrance, set for four o'clock. You are not to be late, sir. I still have my beauty sleep coming to me."

"I think you've had it," he said involuntarily.

Leila applauded with softly clapping palms.

"You're improving," she called after him in a low voice as he strode off, vexed with himself at having crossed the line of neutrality he had set.

The faithful clock awakened him and he sent her back to bed. The stars were still bright, but the mysterious stir of dawn, so prescient in even the loneliest of deserts, was in the air. Imperceptibly the constellations paled and the deep purple of the sky faded. He clambered to the lookout once again. This day, he felt sure, would see some crisis in their affairs, and he wanted to be forehanded.

A light shone in the house. About the dull embers of the fire he could make out the prostrate figures of the Kanakas. They stirred as the man who sleeps in the open always does with the coming of dawn, still half-conscious, then sat up, stretching and rubbing their eyes as a call sounded from the house.

It was Tuan Yuck's voice. He came out, followed by Sayers. In the still morning Chalmers could hear the latter grumbling. The horizon to the east was turning olive-green, with the suggestion of orange beginning to tinge it below the rim of the sea. The golden stars were now white points of light that trembled and disappeared in rapid succession.

The four men busied themselves about the boat and Chalmers picked up his rifle,

alert for any advance. The orange turned to salmon color. Little clouds, high up, suddenly flamed to rose. Birds awoke, chirping in the hills. The sun was due.

Sayers was putting on the diving-suit and Chalmers, reassured, set down his rifle. They were going pearling before breakfast. Apparently they had determined to make a thorough prospect of the lagoon. That might mean that they were inclined to give up the attempt for the pearls that Leila held, if they found anything worth while in the fresh shell.

Chalmers had doubted whether Sayers's overtures had been made in good faith, inclined to suspect that it had been a ruse of Tuan Yuck's to get them away from their base. Now the pearling maneuvers puzzled him. It was not like Tuan Yuck to forego a speedy revenge, he thought, and yet the Oriental's infinite capacity for biding his time was hard to estimate.

The boat put off; Sayers, equipped for diving, astride the bows, Tuan Yuck steering, the natives rowing. They proceeded obliquely toward the outer reef, reaching it at a point nearly opposite the lagoon. Tuan Yuck appeared to be giving final directions for Sayers's guidance.

Tomi, at bow oar, handed the Australian an implement that Chalmers guessed was for the purpose of loosening the oysters from their bed. He took it and slipped into the water, hung for a moment by his hands, and disappeared just as the sun showed an arc of red gold above the sea-line and then shot up as if propelled, a dazzling disk of brightness. The bird-chorus swelled. Early gulls wheeled out to sea. It was day.

The boat came back to the beach and landed Tuan Yuck, then returned to the lagoon and drifted, as the Kanakas began to eat. Tuan Yuck walked up the beach to the house. They were breakfasting after all. Sayers, Chalmers reasoned, had probably taken his usual morning's meal out of a glass and bottle. There would be no attack on Safety Haven that morning.

Chalmers went noiselessly up to the caves, intent upon lighting the fire and preparing breakfast while the girl slept. He went to the waterfall and let the cool water cascade upon his head, then filled the kettle.

Fearing that the crackle of the burning twigs might disturb Leila, he made the fire away from the usual place, choosing a spot close to the cliff wall between some fallen boulders. Above him the precipice lifted sheer. Seaward the lagoon was hidden by rocks, but with Sayers exploring the bottom for oysters and Tuan Yuck doubtless busy emulating his own example of getting breakfast, he had no present fear of interruption. He piled the twigs, struck a match and soon the preliminary smoke of his fire went streaming up the face of the cliff.

If he had followed its ascent he might have marked a yellow face with eyes cruelly intent upon him shining in it like candles through the eyeholes of a mask. Tuan Yuck was lying prone upon a slope that edged the cliff, sprawling at the peril of his life, his feet hooked into a crevice of the rock, his hands taloned about some scrubby growths, straining his neck like a venomous snake about to strike.

Chalmers opened a jar of sliced bacon that he had commandeered from the schooner on their raid, humming a tune below his breath.

Turtle eggs and bacon, coffee and ship's biscuit, a jar of marmalade to follow! He smiled as he thought of Leila's delight at the unexpected tribute to her frankly keen appetite.

ON THE cliff, Tuan Yuck edged back from the verge and looked at his rifle regretfully. The angle of fire made it useless unless Chalmers ventured away from the face of the precipice. Tuan Yuck's clothing was torn. The climb had been a hard one.

Sayers would not have attempted it, but the Chinaman had believed it feasible and chose it as his part of the attack which was to raise the siege. The excitement of trying the lagoon bed for pearls had put off his attempting it so far, though he had carefully sized up the possibilities of the climb from the deck of the schooner through binoculars.

Now he was here, and for the present, impotent. His eye caught a boulder lying almost loose in its bed near the beginning of the slope. He tested it with his arms, then his shoulders, cautiously. It resisted. Using the butt of his rifle he pried at it again. It shifted a trifle and he smiled evilly. Then his eyes roved seaward. Something was disturbing the water in the narrow lagoon of Safety Haven.

Tuan Yuck squatted on his haunches complacently, as a yellow toad watching for flies. Some one else, as usual, was going to play his game.

The still surface of the lagoon broke silently as a gleaming object appeared, the diving helmet of Sayers. The Australian's shoulders showed, then his body as he advanced, bent from the waist, wading out of the water. In one hand he held the implement which Chalmers had noticed.

He had walked unseen along the bed of the lagoon from the point where he had slid from the boat near the outer reef, perhaps a quarter of a mile of submarine progress, safely hidden beneath an average of eight fathoms. Now he was masked by the maze of boulders from any casual gaze of Chalmers or the girl.

Sayers sat on a low ledge by the water's edge and took off his rubber gauntlets, then his helmet, taking deep breaths. His face was scarlet. It was slow work over the uneven bottom and he had nearly exhausted his supply of air in his endeavor to get as far up the lagoon as possible. He looked cliffward and saw Tuan Yuck, who waved his arms and motioned downward to where the unconscious Chalmers tended his fire.

Sayers wagged one hand in reply and divested himself of the rest of his suit and his heavy shoes. Then he severed the tightly bound cords that wrapped an oilskin coat about the object he had brought ashore and disclosed a rifle. He worked the lever, opening the slide gently to make sure of a cartridge ready for action.

Barefooted and bareheaded, clad in a singlet and trousers, he sprawled full length on the sand and writhed up between the rocks like the reptile he was, carrying the rifle clear of the sand, lifting his head cautiously now and then to take his directions from Tuan Yuck, who stood far enough back to avoid any risk of Chalmers catching sight of him, semaphoring a signal for murder to the Australian.

Chalmers poured the superfluous grease from the frying-pan and set the bacon on some hot ashes. Breakfast was ready.

He stood up to call Leila, looking toward the mouth of her cave, and found her already standing in the entrance, her face frozen into an expression of fear and horror, the rising sun full in her eyes that stared through the blinding rays at something behind Chalmers—a cruel face, blotched with debauchery, the cheek cuddling to a gunstock, an arm stretched across the top of a rock to steady the aim, the rest of the body hidden behind the lava barrier.

"Toss up your hands, —— you! Up with 'em. Don't you stir out of that cave, missy, or I'll spatter his brains against the cliff."

Chalmers turned his head, raising his arms. The tone of the Australian's voice warned him that the threat was not an empty one. Raging inwardly, but impotent, he faced Sayers's taunting face.

"I told you you wouldn't see me when I came," sneered Sayers with a derisive chuckle. "I suppose you thought you had all the brains, as well as all the virtue, eh! Well, now I've got you where I want you. Too good to associate with me, are you, you and your innocent‑faced charmer? Keep your eyes up, too!" he snarled as Chalmers's glance shifted to the rifle slanted against the cliff. "So! Well, I'm going to send you where, if you're as holy as you pretend, you'll be twanging a harp inside of the next minute. Say your prayers, you —— hypocrite, for I've got the drop on you. Don't you move, missy—ah!"

The girl had raised her arm. She held a hand-mirror and the level sun-rays concentrated in its field. The quicksilver flung them back into the bloodshot eyes of Sayers. Dazzled, he flung a hand up in protection.

"Quick, Bruce, the rifle!" shrilled the girl.

Chalmers stooped swiftly. Above, Tuan Yuck, hearing the outcry, pried at the boulder with his riflestock. It left its bed sluggishly, slid down the first slope, braked by the crumbling tufa, and fell, striking Chalmers high upon the shoulders. He crumbled beneath the blow, dropped, the earth whirling, a fiery rush of comets before his eyes, and lay prone, the boulder beside his senseless, prostrate form.

 CHALMERS came slowly to his senses, his mind, groping through a fog of pain, slowly connecting with the sluggish nerve-centers. He was lying in the sand, his lips gritty with it, salty with his own blood.

Memory asserted itself and he strove to rise. His body from the waist up seemed rigid. His neck when he tried to raise his head burned with agony. But Leila's last cry communicated itself to his rousing faculties, and he persisted, lifting himself on his forearms and looking about him with eyes that gradually regained their function.

The long shadows of the rocks had retreated half their length as he grasped at the rough surface of the lava and dragged himself to his feet. The realization of what had happened came back in a rush while he stood swaying, his dull glance searching for the girl and then for his enemy.

Somewhere in his brain-cells lurked the registration of a shot. He looked for his rifle. It was gone, and his fumbling glance could not find the handle of his automatic in his belt. His wound had reopened and his shirt was drenched with blood. He tried to call to Leila, but his parched throat failed him and there was an intolerable pain where his neck set into his spine.

With his teeth set into his lower lip to prevent his jaw from sagging, he tottered like a drunken man among the rocks, supporting himself by their friendly sides, pistol in hand.

The beach was vacant. A huddled heap of white lay at the water's edge, a burnished mass spread out beside it like seaweed—or hair. With an inarticulate cry he staggered toward it and fell on his knees beside the unconscious form of Leila.

There were dull marks about her neck, upcurved between the dimpled chin and the huddled bundle of her body. There was a crimson ring about it where the neck ribbon that had held the bag of pearls had been rudely torn away.

With a hoarse cry of rage strangely blended with tenderness Chalmers gathered her up in his arms, strong for the moment in his fury at the brute who had mishandled her.

Her head fell back, the eyes closed, the long masses of golden-brown hair trailing to the sand. With the last remnants of his strength he bore her to the caves, stumbling at every step, and set her down upon the sand, falling over her on his hands and knees. He chafed her wrists and beat upon her palms, hoarsely calling her name. Then the sky descended upon him like a pall and he fainted.

CHAPTER XIX

LEILA LOSES HER PEARLS

WHEN he opened his eyes again it was to find Leila bending over him, his head raised in her arms, the pungent smell of brandy assailing his nostrils. He suffered a few burning drops to pass between his lips and swallowed them with difficulty.

It was cool and dark with a light shining somewhere on Leila's face. As she raised his head on her arm and begged him to drink again, he saw bright specks against a field of ebony and realized they were stars. The sting of the brandy in his throat reached his stomach and a delicious warmth spread through him.

"Where am I?" he asked, knowing it was his own voice that spoke, but not recognizing its feeble, faraway tone.

"Thank God," she said, and something warm fell on his upturned face, followed by another drop—Leila's tears.

"Don't cry," he muttered. "I'm all right." The shrill clarion of the alarm-clock sounded. "It's my watch," he said. "I must get up, Leila. They may be coming any minute now."

He took the cup from her in trembling hands and drained it, memory and strength returning.

"Have they gone?" he asked, sitting up with a violent effort. "Get me a rifle."

"Oh, lie down," she said. "Lie down and rest. They've gone. Everything's all right now—now you've come back again."

Her voice quavered and dissolved in tears. He slipped a feeble arm about her.

"Come, Leila, dearest girl," he said. "I'm not hurt. See! Don't cry! Don't cry. I'm fine—just a bit wobbly." He forced a laugh. "Have they really gone? What's happened?"

She got to her knees beside him.

"You must rest," she said. "Wait."

She brought a roll of something soft and placed it under his head.

"It's rotten to be a girl," she said. "To cry like a fool."

"I'm glad you are," he whispered.

She set a cool palm on his lips and he kissed it. She withdrew it, not very quickly.

"You mustn't talk," she said. "I'm going to get you some soup."

But her face glowed as though the lantern-light had been suddenly quadrupled.

"Did they get the pearls?" he asked.

"Yes. Hush!"

She was back in a moment, blowing on a cup of soup, tasting it with puckered lips to test the heat while he lay quiescent, looking at her contentedly. The pearls were gone! In spite of everything, the loss soothed him and brought new vigor to his veins.

The barrier was down! Then came the revulsion.

"It was my fault," he said.

"It was not," she protested fiercely. "Tuan Yuck threw down a rock from the cliff. It struck you as you stooped for a rifle. But you must not talk. Take this."

He suffered himself to be fed, spoonful by spoonful, satisfied to have her minister to him. When the cup was ended, he sat up despite her remonstrance.

"I'm fine now," he said. "I'll take some more of that if you have any. My shoulders and neck are stiff, but there's a whole lot of life in me yet."

"Don't sit up, please," she said, slipping her arm about him. "Oh, are you sure you are strong enough? Here's some more broth."

He watched her as she flitted out of the cave and back again.

"Now then," he said, as he finished the second cup, "tell me."

There were hollows under her eyes; he saw faint shadows of them in her cheeks.

"Tell me," he repeated. "Are you sure they're gone?"

"Sure," she answered. "In the schooner. I saw it sailing away."

"They've gone!"

He sat up of his own accord, invigorated at the news.

She brought a box and set it back of him, wadding it with the improvised pillow.

"You drink some of that soup," he ordered; "with some brandy in it. Now!"

She smiled at the assertion in his tone.

"Aye, aye, sir," she answered.

"When the rock hit you," she said presently, "I forgot Sayers and ran toward you. He—Sayers—jumped over the rock and rushed at me. I dodged, thinking perhaps I could get at the rifle, but I was half stupid, thinking you were dead, and he cut me off. His face was horrible. I ran the only way I could, toward the beach, with him after me. If you're going to grit your teeth and get excited," she interrupted herself, "I'll stop talking."

Chalmers relaxed and reached out his hand to grasp hers as she extended it.

"I don't remember what he said," she went on, and Chalmers, seeing by her averted eyes that she lied, reregistered the vow he had already sworn; "but he caught up with me at the water's edge and spun me around with his hand on my shoulder. He put his arms about me and lifted me. I beat at his face and scratched it, but he laughed and crushed me against him. Then I bit him—ugh!" she brushed her free hand across her lips. "He swore at me and started to carry me out into the water. The boat with the natives in it was coming toward us.

"Some one shouted from the cliff—Tuan Yuck. I couldn't hear what he said, but Sayers stopped and turned round. Then Tuan Yuck called again—something about 'leave the girl.' Sayers shouted back. His face was bloody where I had scored it and all asnarl with rage. He swore at Tuan Yuck, and the Chinaman stood up on the edge of the cliff pointing one arm at us, and his voice sounded like a trumpet."

"I wonder why he interfered?" said Chalmers. "What did he say the last time?"

"It wasn't complimentary." Leila smiled at Chalmers, who sat with both fists clenched, the bone of his jaw showing white through the flesh. "But it saved me, or what followed did, though I don't know why he did it. Sayers hesitated for a moment, and a shot plunged into the water beside us. Tuan Yuck stood with his rifle to his shoulder. Sayers cursed again and tore the ribbon from my throat. I hit up at him, and he struck at me——"

"—— him!" said Chalmers. "When I catch up with him I'll kill him with my bare hands."

Leila looked at him with a little thrill of primeval ecstasy. Here was a man who had fought for her, who would kill for her. An ancient strain of savagery surged up within her, the glory of the pristine woman for the protecting male. Then civilization conquered.

"I hope we never see him again," she said with a shudder. "That was all I knew," she went on presently, "till I came to, outside the caves with you by me. The pearls were gone."

It was Chalmers's turn to tell what he knew. He made short work of it.

"And then?" he asked.

"I tried to revive you, but I couldn't. And I was afraid. I was afraid you were going to die. I didn't know how badly you were hurt. I was afraid they would come back. I went to the fall for fresh water after a while, and I saw the schooner standing out to sea, close to the reef, with the natives hauling on the foresail.

"I fell on my knees and thanked God for our deliverance and—" she lowered her voice to a tremulous whisper, dulcet to his ears with its tenderness—"I prayed you might be spared. When I came back you moaned, and presently you went to sleep. Then I knew my prayer was answered."

Chalmers's eyes softened. His hand sought hers. "God bless you, dear," he said.

They sat for a little while in silence.

"Last night," she said after a pause, "I was most afraid of all. There was a terrible earthquake. It kept on, shock after shock, for a long time. The clock stopped. I was afraid the cave would fall in on us. And when it was light, this morning, I saw that part of the big cape—not the one we watched from — had fallen into the sea. And there's a big split in the cliff behind us. The waterfall has almost stopped flowing and I believe the whole island has sunk. The waves came almost up to my rock chambers at high tide and the pool you found for me is full right to the brim."

"A tidal wave," said Chalmers.

"I looked at the pool again this afternoon when you were quietly asleep, and it hadn't gone down."

"Poor Leila! You must have been terribly afraid."

"I was," she smiled rather wanly. "But I'm not now. Only it's so terribly hot I'm afraid it isn't all over."

Chalmers pressed her hand.

"It is hot," he said. "But I'm feverish. You must be, too. What time is it?"

She looked at the clock.

"Half-past three," she announced. "It will soon be morning."

"Why did you set the alarm?"

"I was so sleepy," she confessed shamefacedly, "and I wanted to wake every little while, so I set it."

She swayed wearily and he put his sound arm about her.

"You darling!" he whispered.

She murmured something in return and put up her head to his. Her mouth drooped pitifully, appealingly. Her eyes were wistful, her glance seemed to melt into his, and their lips met.

With a little sigh of absolute comfort she nestled close to him and closed her eyes. He held her tightly, with a savage desire to shield her from all perils, and in a little while her soft breathing told him she was asleep.

Chalmers gradually shifted his position and presently she lay with her body relaxed, her head on his breast, content to know that he had taken up once more the rôle of protector.

He felt ineffably tender to her, weary as he was. The moments passed, marked by the comfortable ticking of the clock, and soon he himself was asleep beside her. In his dreams, made more real by her presence, he passed with her—always with her—far beyond the rim of ordinary things into a fairyland of perpetual youth and happiness.

It was dark when he opened his eyes again. The air was oppressive on his lungs. The dream had turned to a nightmare of them alone on a turbulent ocean, tossed by the waves.

The nightmare was a reality. The solid earth rocked beneath them. Leila was wide awake, clinging to him in terror. He sat up in the blackness and his hand struck the upset lantern. The glass burnt him. It had only just gone out. Leila's arms were about him.

"An earthquake," she gasped. "I can't breathe. I'm stifling."

"Matches?" he asked.

"By the lantern."

His groping hand found the box. He struck a match that seemed to burn dimly, and relit the lantern. The clock was still going. It was six o'clock—daylight.

Filled with swift dread he arose and held the light above his head. The front of the cave was filled with débris. The cliff had fallen in upon them and blocked their exit. Another tremor threw him headlong, close to where Leila crouched in terror, crying:

"Bruce! Bruce! Where are you? I am so afraid!"

CHAPTER XX

THE LAST OF MOTUTABU

CHALMERS stood up, holding the lantern at arm's length.

"Why, this is my cave!" he said, surprise in his voice.

"Yes," she answered. "It was the nearer to where you fell. I couldn't lift you. I had hard work getting you here, out of the sun."

"Why, then we can get out of this yet," he said, "unless——"

He began to dig with his hands at the sand.

"Ah!" he cried in a relieved tone, "here they are. I buried them in case they might raid us sometime."

He brought up the extra cartridges for the rifles and automatics.

"I suppose they took the Winchesters," he said, "while you were senseless. Sayers wouldn't leave them lying around. He knew we had them, and the automatics. But he didn't find these shells. And there's the rifle I left on top of the ridge. He probably overlooked that."

While he spoke he worked at the smaller calibered cartridges for the pistols, wrenching at the bullets with his back teeth and twisting feverishly to get them free with his fingers, emptying out the powder on to his neckerchief.

"I can do that," said Leila, reaching for a shell.

"No, you can't," he answered. "I'm not going to open all of them. There isn't time. My knife's on the schooner, confound it. It broke off, anyway. Give me that saucepan."

She handed him the pot in which she had brought his broth. He smashed it against the rocky side of the cave and wrenched off the handle.

"Dig a hole with this where you can find loose earth," he said. "Near the bottom of the opening, if you can. You can clear it out with that spoon. Make it as deep as possible. I'm going to try and blast a way out! There isn't air enough in here to waste time."

She set to work diligently, scraping and rasping at the fallen débris. Presently she exclaimed. Her crude tool had broken through into a cavity. She enlarged the hole with the iron spoon and thrust in her arm.

"There's quite a big space here," she said, "but it's all hard rock beyond."

"Never mind. That's more than I hoped for," he replied.

He had moistened half of the powder he had obtained with the soup that remained in the pot and smeared the thick paste heavily upon a long strip torn from the handkerchief. Then he half filled the pot with rifle cartridges and packed sand tightly about them.

"The handle," he said.

Leila passed it to him. It was hollow. He straightened out as best he could the end flattened by the girl's digging, ran his fuse through it, made a space between the cartridges and set into it the stiff cardboard case that had contained the bullets for the pistols. Into this he poured the rest of his powder, carefully plàced the end of the fuse into it, ran the tube of the handle down to the top of the case, repiled cartridges closely about it and filled the pot to the brim with sand, ramming it down hard so that the handle projected from it with the other end of the fuse showing loose.

He attacked the opening she had made until it was large enough to pass the pot through to the space she had found, and packed that as tightly as he could with sand and small fragments of rock. The extreme end of the handle he left clear and trailed the remainder of the fuse through a little trench he scraped and bridged over with the thin wood from the boxes which had held the Winchester shells.

With the sweat streaming from him in the close atmosphere of the cave, he filled in the tunnel compactly. Only the extreme end of the fuse now showed dangling from the opening of the groove, the rest leading back to the pot holding the larger shells.

"It's a poor bomb at the best," he said, "but it *is* the best we can do. Come back here, Leila!"

She followed him to the rear of the cave where it turned sharply to the right and ended.

"We'll stand here," he said. "I don't know which way those bullets may fly. I don't know, Leila, exactly what is going to happen. It may bring down more rock and bury us absolutely, but it's the only chance. I hope the fuse works. I haven't made a spit-devil like that since I was a kid."

He tried to speak lightly, but his tone carried the tension he felt.

"Stay here," he told her. "Don't move till I join you. There's no danger."

She had caught at his arm. He gently but firmly released it and hurried back to the fuse, lighting it with a match.

It sputtered, almost died out, then spat sparks bravely. He bounded back to the cave end and stood in front of her, pressing her back against the rock.

He could feel her quick breath on his neck, her heart pounding against him. He reached back both hands and found hers. She gripped them hard.

So they stood silently for what seemed an hour of tense waiting. Chalmers groaned. "It's gone out," he said. "I'll have to try it again."

The air was hot as well as scant and their lungs burned as they labored. Leila's grasp loosened and her body grew limp against Chalmers.

There was a roar, a concussion of the air that hurled them flat to the back of their rocky alcove and a sound of falling fragments thudding on the sand and against the sides of the cave. The place was full of the salty tang of exploded powder.

 CHALMERS leaped out into the main cave. Light poured through a jagged hole at the mouth and fresh air stirred the vapor of the powder-smoke. He tore at the opening, eagerly yet carefully, lest he disturb some key-rock of the pile and close the way to liberty once more. The bomb had done its work well and he was soon able to enlarge the aperture enough for exit.

He crawled through, found another pot and raced to the fall for water. There was only a thread left of the cascade, but he half filled the vessel and hurried back with it to where Leila lay at the end of the cave. The dash of it in her face revived her, and his assurance of the success of their mine roused her to her feet to follow him out to the free world once more.

Even on the beach the air was overwarm. The sky was the color of a tarnished copper bowl, the sun fogged to a tawny blue, rayless and dull. As they stood leaning against the face of the cliff, weak with effort and the foul air of the cave, the ground rocked beneath their feet. A harsh rasping thunder sounded from the hills, the farther headland wavered in its outline and a great mass of it tore apart and fell into the sea.

Leila gasped in terror.

"Come on!" cried Chalmers. "We've got to get out of this!"

He caught her hand, and started to run toward the water when a second shock threw them on their faces. It lasted longer than the first, with a recurrence of the grinding thunder in the hills.

He got to his knees. The seas were mounting beyond the reef, high crestless waves of oily brown that rolled across the coral barrier and sent the lagoon water surging far up the sand. Behind them the cliff had split apart showing a raw wedge where protruding rocks quivered and crashed down upon each other in a cloud of red dust.

Then the tremor ended. Thousands of birds wheeled shrieking and squawking above them. The sullen sea slid greasily over the reef and claimed another fathom of beach.

"Come, Leila," he called.

She crouched on the sand with her face buried in her hands. He shook her roughly by the shoulder.

"Come on. I can't carry you. We've got to swim round and get to that launch."

His intentional rudeness roused her. She raised a face blanched with terror, reproach in her eyes.

"The island is sinking," she said. "We can't escape."

"Nonsense," he answered, though his own secret fear matched hers. "Don't be a coward, Leila."

The words stung her like the blow of a whip and she sprang to her feet.

"What am I to do?" she asked, her eyes resolute.

"Swim round the point. Get the boat back here, load it with what we most need, and make for the open sea."

She nodded comprehension and splashed into the lagoon ahead of him, loosening her outer skirt as she went. The back of Chalmers's neck was stiff, but his shoulder had ceased to trouble him and the danger called out all his reserves of strength. Leila reached shore first, racing into the mangroves.

"Here it is," she called, tearing at a thick growth of vines and disclosing the outlines of a twenty-foot whaleboat, stanchly built, covered with canvas. Chalmers, joining her, stripped off the covering.

"Gasoline?" he questioned.

"In drums," she said. "Four of them, back of you."

He freed them from the tangled growth and rolled them away from the boat. The keel was set in the sand and he rocked at it until it loosened.

They slid and dragged the boat over the sand to where a stream ran sluggishly among the mangroves, launching it at last. Then they returned for the gasoline, rolling down the drums and tipping the boat to get them inboard.

There was a water breaker in the stern and Chalmers submerged it in the creek to fill it, first scooping up the water to be sure it was fresh. The creek was shallow and they waded beside their craft, dragging it over the little bar where the stream entered the lagoon and tumbling into the boat as they reached the deeper water.

"Can you row? There's no time to fuss with the engine."

Leila nodded and seized an oar, keeping time to Chalmers's stroke. Well out in the lagoon, rowing furiously back to their own beach, the boat shuddered the length of its keel as if it had struck a shoal, yet kept its momentum. The roar came once more from the interior. The side of a hill wavered, the dense forest glided downward and vanished in a valley, leaving a scar of brown earth where once it had waved in tropical luxuriance. A blind breaker lifted them shoreward, while they tugged to bring the boat bow on, and rolled high up the beach. A second followed and they rode it. The shock was over.

They ran the boat well up the beach, sprang out and hauled it higher for safety from the threatening waves. Already the water was far above the regular boundary of high tide and this should have been the ebb.

They raced up to the caves and swiftly gathered up stores and a few clothes, stowing them away in the boat with frantic speed. Three trips they made, fearful every second of the return of the earthquake.

"That's all," said Chalmers. "I'll get the chronometer and compass. They are in my cave. Stay by the boat."

In the cavern the sight of the unused cartridges reminded him of the Winchester in the lookout. He did not know what perils might be ahead of them and determined to secure it. He gathered up the shells and took them along with the instruments.

"I'm going to get the rifle," he said.

"I'll get it!" cried Leila.

She started to run for the cliff, determinedly forgetful of her fear, bent upon proving to him that she was not a coward.

"Come back!"

As Chalmers called, a wave advanced far beyond its predecessors, clutched at the boat and threatened to set it adrift. He jumped to steady it and Leila was already clambering up the headland before he had it under control. A minute more and she was down again, climbing with the grace and freedom of a young chamois.

"Here it is," she said breathlessly, "and the glasses."

They rowed hard for the reef-opening across the troubled lagoon, indistinguishable now from the outside sea save where the great waves suddenly reared themselves as they reached the wall of the reef. There was nothing to mark the passage, but Chalmers knew the bearings that the earthquake had mercifully spared, and, keeping a tall palm on the first ridge in line with a notch in the farthest hills, they cleared the lagoon and fought their way to the open sea.

A steady wind blew from the land and Chalmers determined to take advantage of it. The engine, installed beneath a roughly built-in but practical and weather-proof hood, needed more time to connect than they had then to spare, so he resolved to set up the mast that lay in the open cockpit by the exposed shaft of the screw, a lugsail rolled about it.

"Can you take both oars and keep our head to the sea?" he asked Leila.

"Easily," she answered and he passed her his oar, going forward with the mast where he stepped it through the forward thwart and stayed it to the gunwales and hoisted the leg-o'-mutton sail, first reefing it as the wind was appreciably strengthening.

His back was to the girl as he worked, her face, while she tugged at the heavy oars, toward the island.

The breeze caught the sail and filled it. The boat leaped to its impulse and Chalmers prepared to go aft and steer. They were free at last, in a well-built boat that, with careful handling, was well fitted for open sea-work, barring a gale.

Leila uttered a cry and he turned. Above Motutabu a cloud of birds still circled, loath to leave, afraid to stay. Beneath them, as he gazed, the outline of the island changed, the hills crumbled and fell in, the sea seemed to be dashing upon the lower ridges. He sprang aft.

"Ship your oars!" he cried, and as the girl obeyed he seized one of them with which to steer.

The rudder was still unshipped but he knew their danger. Motutabu was sinking into the sea and its disappearance would be inevitably followed by a local storm. Leila covered her eyes.

"It's gone!" she said.

Chalmers knew that her terror was augmented by the memory of her father's grave, once on the hilltop, now beneath the waves.

But their peril was too imminent for words.

The waves rose all about them in sudden confusion, tumbling angrily at cross purposes and gradually assuming the circular motion of a whirlpool. A furious wind blew out of where the island had gone down. He blessed the forethought that had made him reef the little sail, striving to prevent the steering oar from being torn from his grasp, and to keep the boat from being drawn into the vortex. They were on the verge of the circle and, aided by the great gusts of wind the little craft fought gallantly up the oily crests, tipped with greasy spume, and down the shifting hollows, where the wind failed for the moment.

At length the mad turmoil of the sea gave place to a regular succession of waves, running strong and high but holding little menace to the buoyant whaleboat. The breeze that had blown them due east from the island gave way to a steady northeast trade and Chalmers hauled their course, sailing as close to the wind as the boat would point.

Giving over the steering oar to Leila for a while, with instructions how to keep it set against the seas, he shipped the rudder and tiller. He had belayed the sail forward; now he ran its sheet aft over the engine housing to where he could handle it from the stern.

"Now we are shipshape," he announced. "If the sea goes down presently we'll overhaul the engine. I'm afraid I'm not much of an expert at it. Are you, Leila?"

"I know something about it. I've run it," she answered apathetically.

Her eyes were darkly circled, but she smiled pluckily back at him.

"Thank you for calling me names, when I funked things on the beach," she said. "I am a coward, you know."

Chalmers flushed.

"I apologize," he said. "And I think you are far braver than I am."

"Then we're even. Where are we going?"

"I think we'd better make the Gilberts. Byron Island, perhaps. That's British. What speed can we make?"

"A little over ten knots."

"Bully! We'll get there in a little over two days, after we get the engine going, if the gasoline holds out. Meanwhile if you'll take the tiller, I'll stow our grub and stuff."

He put away the things in shipshape order and arranged the boat canvas covering so as to turn the engine housing into a cabin. There was plenty of space in the double-ended craft, open save for wooden hood built before and above the engine and the voyage of five hundred miles did not seem so formidable. He set up his compass, arranged his sextant chronometer and then unrolled a chart upon the engine hood to confirm their position before dark.

"We've no log but we can get along without that," he said, as he resumed the tiller. "The Ellice Group is nearer than the Gilberts, perhaps, but I think we'd better tackle the latter. Look at the sunset, Leila. It's like the flare from a volcano. Perhaps it is. There must have been some great disturbance somewhere. Motutabu didn't sink of its own weight.

He talked lightly, hoping to divert her. She smiled faintly at him as she sat drooping on a thwart. It was a frightful position for her, he realized, orphaned, absolutely alone, save for a friend of a few days, racked by her sorrows and the trials they had gone through, dependent upon him for safety and comfort. It was not the moment for love-making nor did he think of it, feeling himself powerless to console her.

"I've fixed up a sort of cabin for you," he said. "Don't you think you'd better lie down for a while. We'll get something to eat presently."

She started to obey listlessly.

"You'll call me for my turn at the rudder," she asked.

"As soon as the sea goes down enough," he said. "It's tricky work in the dark. Try and sleep a little."

She disappeared behind the canvas curtain. Chalmers sat at the tiller, nodding for sleep and shaking his head fiercely to keep awake, tired in every ounce of him. But he remembered the night that she had put the veronal in his broth and watched for him and shook off his drowsiness.

The flaming sky in the west, metallic in its radiance as fire reflected from copper, died down, the seas lessened and a star or two came out. Behind the canvas he could hear Leila sobbing softly.

In a little while weariness had conquered her grief and Chalmers sat alone by the tiller holding the whale-boat to her course away from sunken Motutabu with its pearl lagoon and the grave of the man who discovered it, his eyelids weighted with sleep but his heart stout within him as becomes one

5

who has faced perils and mastered them, not merely for his own sake, but another's.

CHAPTER XXI

ENGINE TROUBLE

LEILA came aft a little after midnight. "I'm a pig," she said, "sleeping all this time. But it's done me a world of good aside from making me thoroughly ashamed of myself. How it's cleared up! The stars are wonderful, and I can read the compass by the moon. What's my course, Captain Chalmers?"

The few hours rest had given her a grip on her courage once again and she was her old audacious self.

"Turn in, skipper," she said. "I'll call you at eight bells. You'll have to trust me. We left the poor old alarm-clock behind in the hurry."

He found some clothes arranged to pad the bottom boards and with his head on the same pillow she had used, still fragrant with her hair, floated off into restful unconsciousness.

They had breakfast when she called him and then started to overhaul their engine. Finally adjusted and oiled from a supply they discovered in one of the drums, they filled the gasoline tank, primed it, and Chalmers, practically his own man again, heaved on the fly-wheel. There was a spatter and a buzz and then—inaction. They tried again and again, applying all their mutual knowledge without results, while the boat rocked gently on a breezeless sea.

At last, spattered and smeared with grease, they looked at each other in sympathetic disgust. Leila wrinkled her brows.

"The batteries are all right, we've got a good spark, the cylinders are clean, carbureter's in shape, gasoline I know was strained before it went in the drums. It's just sheer perverseness. It was always like that. It would run like a clock for days and then when you most wanted it, sulk till it got to feeling better."

Chalmers laughed.

"Don't make faces at it," he said. "You look demoniacal with those smuts on your cheeks and chin. Give it a rest."

"You have a large one on your nose," she answered. "I'm not going to give in to the beast."

He straightened up, cramped from stooping over the engine. Then he reached quietly for the binoculars. The field showed him a double canoe, its mat sail flapping above the platform deck that swarmed with men, paddles flashing as the men in the canoes forced the craft along toward them.

"I wonder if they got blown out of their island," he asked himself, "or if it sunk under them like ours. They don't seem particularly friendly. Let's hope it's curiosity, though I don't like the armory. And not wind enough to fill a fan. We're still in the woods."

The canoe was coming up rapidly, the natives brandishing their spears. Chalmers picked up his Winchester, filled the chamber and spilled a lot of cartridges where they would be handy. Leila turned at the rattle they made.

"Your friends the savages," he said. "It seems we are not out of our troubles. But I'll handle them. I'm not going to let them get within arrow range if I can help it. You've got your hands full with that engine. Coax it. If you can get it to running we can laugh at them. At present we look over-easy."

He sighted, resting the barrel on the gunwale, crouching well down, and fired. The bullet went high through the sail but he depressed his muzzle and the next sang true. One of the savages on the platform tossed up his arms and fell into the sea, while the others yelled and brandished their weapons. A score of arrows whizzed toward the whale-boat but fell short half-way.

Three men were down now but the canoe came on. Fire as he might, they would reach them, with overwhelming numbers, within a minute or two. He began trying to pick off the paddlers, but every time he paused to refill the magazine the gap between them closed ominously.

The barrel burned his fingers. Behind him he sensed Leila throwing over the wheel, repriming the stubborn cylinders, while she talked to the engine as if it were a refractory child. Twice she got a response that failed as soon as it had raised hope.

The arrows were coming thick now, feathering the sides of the boat, singing over him as he crouched.

"Lucky they haven't sense enough to try a dropping shot," he muttered. "Wonder if they're poisoned. Ah! I got you."

A tall Micronesian, bushy-haired, tinkling with brass armlets, who appeared to be the leader, spun about and fell from the deck into one of the canoes. There was instant confusion and the craft halted while Chalmers pumped shot after shot into the mass of them. Then they came on again, only fifty yards away. The air filled with their imprecations.

JUST then the engine coughed, snorted, coughed again, and settled down into a steady *puttera-pattera* that was music to Chalmers's ears. The screw churned the water and the whale-boat lurched ahead.

"Keep back there!" he called to Leila. "We'll be out of it in a minute."

He cautiously crawled aft and tossed the loop of a sheet about the tiller to steady it. A howl of rage came from the Micronesians. They plied their paddles at double speed and for a few seconds held their own while the bowmen sped their arrows. But the relenting engine warmed to its work and the whale-boat was soon out of range.

Chalmers gave them a few parting shots.

"Want to try your hand?" he asked Leila jestingly. "Careful with those arrows, they may be poisoned. There's the start of a nice collection for a museum. I'm sorry I ever abused you," he apologized to the engine with a mock bow. "You're all your sales-agent ever claimed for you. Listen to that ragtime purr, Leila. *Puttera-pattera*, my name's Pat. Catch it? Go ahead Pat, and patter along to Byron Island."

Leila laughed at his nonsense as he wanted her to.

"You're much too ridiculous for dignity," she said.

"Do you prefer me dignified?"

"Sometimes. I was quite afraid of you on the island at times, when you ordered me about like a cabin-boy."

"I was afraid of you, too," he confessed.

"Not now?"

"Not now. You're not an heiress any longer."

"Oh!"

"I shouldn't joke about your losing the pearls, Leila, though I'm afraid the chances are slim of ever seeing them again. Do you feel very badly about losing them?"

She looked him squarely in the eyes. Her own held a twinkle, almost an invitation.

"No," she answered. "I'm really rather glad."

Looking at him while she slowly and adorably reddened, she saw his eyes change to a stare of incredulity.

"What is it?" she asked.

"It seems incredible," he said, "but it's the schooner. And she's headed this way, as much as the wind will let her. She's hardly got steerageway. There's something wrong aboard of her. The sheets are hauled in and there's no one at the wheel, apparently. Give me the glasses.

"There's some one now in the bows. It's Hamaku. He's waving a cloth. There's Tomi, beside him. They don't know who we are."

"You'll not go near them?"

"I'll go near enough to find out what's up. They wouldn't be coming back for nothing. There must be something that's upset your calculations. I've got a score to even with Sayers. Your pearls are aboard."

"I told you I didn't want them. Don't go near them."

"You lost the pearls through my fault, Leila. I should have thought of that diving-suit. It's not going to be my fault if you don't get them back again."

He spoke with decision. It was his duty, as he considered it, to recover Leila's fortune, and he tingled at the hope of getting his eyes on Sayers. Leila sat silent as he steered the launch toward the schooner. As they neared it he called out to Hamaku.

The native started as he heard his name, spoke to Tomi, peered at the launch from under his hand and sprang into the water from the bowsprit, swimming swiftly toward them.

"Eh, Kapitani," he said as his fingers clutched the gunwale. "Eyah, Kapitani, plenty pilikea aboard."

"Climb in," ordered Chalmers.

The dripping Hamaker came lithely overside and sat on the thwart his skipper indicated. His face was drawn and gray instead of its usual healthy brown, and his body twitched.

"Now then," said Chalmers. "Out with it."

"*Sayasi* (Sayers), he *make* (dead). Tuan Yuck he nearly *make*, too. One, two night ago they play cards together for pearl. Last night Tuan Yuck he win—everything. Sayasi he laugh and call for gin. I bring. Sayasi he say, 'All right, you too smart for me. Then very quick he pull out gun and shoot Tuan Yuck. Big Boss he fall on floor and not move. Sayasi he got up and laugh some more. Then he take big drink of gin. Me, I keep back where he not see me. So then Sayasi he kneel along Tuan Yuck on floor and he say, 'Last man he laugh more loud.' Tuan Yuck open his eyes and say, 'Yes, —— you.' He strike at Sayasi with knife quick like that, all same cat. Knife he cut Sayasi all through stomach. He *make*, right away. Too much blood he lose.

"Tuan Yuck he no can move his legs. He make me pick him up and put him in cabin. He no eat. All the time smoke *lele* pipe. Very soon I think he die. So I frighten. I try make boat go along back Motutabu."

Chalmers looked at the native searchingly. It was evident he was telling the truth. He restarted the engine and ran alongside the schooner. Tomi came to the side, his eyes bulging with terror.

"God bless it, you come Kapitani," he said. "Too much *pilikea*."

"Up you swarm, Hamaku," commanded Chalmers, "and get out the "side-ladder. You'll stay here for a few minutes, won't you please?" he asked Leila.

"Yes," she answered, pale at the mental picture of Sayers lying in his own blood on the cabin floor, much as she hated him.

The two natives under Chalmers' orders rolled the stiffened form into canvas and sewed it into a rude sacking. This they weighed with ballast and carried it up the companionway, where they slid it quietly into the sea from the opposite rail to which the launch lay. Then they cleared up the cabin while Chalmers went for Leila. The door of Tuan Yuck's room was closed.

When he came down with the girl, Chalmers, armed with the automatic that he had picked up on the cabin floor close to the dead body, opened Tuan Yuck's door.

The Chinaman lay in his bunk, smoking. His skin had the look of dirty wax; his glittering eyes seemed to have lost their luster.

"Ah!" he said as Chalmers entered. "So you have the last trick after all. Our Australian friend got me with his pistol, the same one you hold, I fancy. I'm done for, Chalmers. You couldn't do anything for me if you would. The spine's injured. I'm partly paralyzed. More every hour. I can just raise my arms to smoke. It's a good vice. It helps."

"Where are the pearls?" asked Chalmers.

"So mercenary! Where are they? Ask me after I'm dead, Chalmers. I won't tell you while I'm alive."

His eyes held a mocking light.

"Are you there, Miss Denman," he called. "I did you a good turn once when I made Sayers leave you behind. I did it selfishly. I didn't want to be bothered with a woman. You see I figured on winning out from Sayers. It was clumsy of me to lose. Now do me a favor in return. Leave me alone until the end. It won't be long."

"We will, if you tell us where the pearls are," said Chalmers.

A smile that was half sneer broke the mask of Tuan Yuck's face. His voice had grown feebler.

"I've hidden them, Chalmers. They're aboard. But I don't think you'll find them, even though you search me after I am dead. But if you look in the right place you'll find them."

His eyes held an impenetrable enigma as he puffed at his metal pipe with its bamboo stem and jade mouthpiece. His eyes closed. Only the movement of his chest and the curl of the acrid smoke that issued from his lips showed life was still in his body.

Chalmers hesitated. He could not torture a dying man. Leila set a hand on his arm.

"Come away," she said. "We do not care about the pearls."

Half an hour later Hamaku came hurriedly on deck.

"Kapitani, you come quick," he said.

Tuan Yuck was dead in his bunk, his jaw fallen. A lacquered box lay on the counterpane between his nerveless fingers.

"I hear noise," said Hamaker. "I come in quick. He try to swallow pearl. I think he choke. Look!"

He put his fingers into the dead man's mouth and drew out half a dozen of the pearls. The rest were in the box and spilled upon the covering of the bunk. Tuan Yuck's last trick had failed him.

THE wind was fair and the schooner sailed as if eager to leave latitudes that had held so much of danger and distress. Leila, in reaction from the terrific strain to which she had been subjected, kept closely to the cabin Chalmers overhauled for her.

He himself was glad of long lazy hours in the sunshine, drowsing off the consequences of his own ordeal. His shoulder had healed almost completely, thanks to the magic of Leila's ointment, and the stiffness and pain at the base of his neck disappeared as the great bruise made by the falling boulder took on all the colors of a dying dolphin.

On the afternoon of the third day, Leila, a little languid, but smiling, faced him on deck. In her hand she held the little lacquered box.

"I want you to take half these pearls," she said and frowned as Chalmers shook his head.

"I insist. You've saved them time and time again. If you don't, I swear, I'll toss them overboard this minute."

He temporized but the girl was determined. She walked to the rail and held her hand with the box in its palm above the water.

"Promise," she said.

Her eyes looked at him tenderly, invitingly, wistfully. They held a hundred variants of the one theme in their liquid depths. And in those depths Chalmers' last remnants of pride dissolved.

"I'll take them," he said, "but I'll give them back to you again."

She stepped backward, her face changing.

"Why?" she faltered.

"As a wedding-present, sweetheart," he whispered.

THE PEACE HAT

by Thomas Addison.

Author of "Come-On Charley," "Too Much Business," etc.

FOUR men's hats — tan, green, blue and black — were ranged in a row on a table under the frowning eyes of Mr. David Miller, sales manager for The Blatchford Hat Manufacturing Company. They were all of a pattern, these hats: low, soft felt crowns with a five-inch flexible brim. The like of them, Mr. Miller reflected bitterly, could be found nowhere under the broad canopy of the chill March heavens except in the topmost loft above him. They had lain there two years; thirty gross; sixty-five hundred dollars' worth of good material, unsalable, a dead loss.

The door opened and a slim young fellow stepped into the office. He had a clean, wholesome, well-featured face, with steady brown eyes and a head of thick chestnut hair which, though barbered to an inch, curled in upon itself rebelliously. Altogether rather an engaging and a decidedly alert-looking young chap was Mr. Barry Howard, junior salesman of the Blatchford Company. Miller motioned him to a chair.

"I want to talk with you, Barry. But first take a squint at these hats, please."

Barry picked up one of them, the tan. He scanned it closely and with an odd expression.

"What's the idea?" he asked. "I haven't got them listed. Something new?"

The sales manager grunted.

"Never mind about that. How do they strike you? Honest now."

Barry replaced the hat on the table.

"Well," he said slowly, "I can't see anything in them, Mr. Miller. With that crown the brim is a riot." He grinned. "Back in the hills they might go for umbrellas, but in my territory—ouch! It scares me to think what would happen if I showed them."

Miller scowled at the monstrosities.

"That's what they all say, every mother's son of the selling force. See here, Barry. You haven't been with us long; let me tell you about this hat. We call it the dodo among ourselves. It's one of the mistakes we make in this business now and then. We try to anticipate a style, or create one, and get stung. Mr. Blatchford tried it two years ago; had an idea he'd revive the old wide-awakes, with modern improvements, and here's what he shoved at us. Fell flat as a flounder. Couldn't give 'em away. And we've got forty-three hundred of them upstairs!"

Barry made a little hissing sound through his teeth.

"Two years! And you didn't make them over?"

"Mr. Blatchford wouldn't listen to it. He has never sent out seconds. But it's a sore point with him, these curios. And here is a stock-taking coming on with that junk to be red-inked again on the inventory. Last year he didn't come down for two days after he had seen it."

Barry wondered what all this was leading

up to. He had not been called in, he knew, for an idle chat on ancient history. Something was wanted of him. So he said:

"Whatever it is I'll do it if I can. Go on, Mr. Miller."

The manager's face brightened. This was talk he liked to hear. He passed a cigar over to his salesman and lit one himself. His manner became intimate.

"It's this way, my boy. This beautiful line of dodos cost us one-fifty apiece to make. We'd be glad to see the last of them at half that. It would tickle the old man to death. Everybody's had a hack at the job, and nobody's got away with it. I'll be frank with you—it's the big joke in the shop. And it's your turn to get the laugh or—" he paused for emphasis—"put it over on the rest of us. What's the answer?"

"Oh, I see!" exclaimed Barry softly. "Here's where I step into the limelight."

"It is. Can you hold it?" The other stabbed the question at him with a pencil he was fingering.

The young man thoughtfully viewed the array on the table. There was an intent look in his eyes.

"Meant to sell at three and a half; two-fifty to the trade, if I'm right," he observed at length.

Miller nodded.

"Right as nails, only—well, you've heard of the place that's paved with good intentions. Seventy-five cents will take 'em away now, my boy, and with three cheers and a blessing. And I'll say to you there's quick promotion for the man who can work off this bunch of old bonnets for us."

The word, though he had used it often enough himself, appeared to strike Barry at this moment with singular force. "Bonnets!" He cast a rapid eye over the hats. A wild fancy seized upon him, stirred him to action. He reached out for a hat—the blue one—turned it over and over in his hands, studied it and finally laid it carefully on his knee.

"Maybe I can do it," he said to Miller, who was regarding him with curious attention. "I must do a bit of thinking. But let me get the business end of it straight. You'll ship them out at seventy-five cents —the entire lot?"

"Thirty gross. Yes."

"And do I get the difference on all over your price?"

"The deuce!" Miller looked at him searchingly. "What have you got up your sleeve?"

"Not a thing," laughed Barry. "It's in my bean—just a hunch—floating around like a chip on the water. And I've nothing more than a thread to anchor it with. It may not work out. Do I get the difference?"

The sales manager hesitated. Barry, as he had had occasion to know, was shrewd and resourceful. He might be able to run the hats out at a dollar. It would be handing him a clear thousand.

"Why, you see—" he began, but Barry cut him off.

"Oh, well," he offered indifferently, "it's a fool idea anyway. I was going to put in a hundred or so of my own to try it out. But of course if the house doesn't care to see me make a few bucks on the side——"

He pitched the hat he was holding on the table, and got up.

"Stop!" snapped the other. "Don't be so fast, young man. I've decided to go you. Seventy-five cents to us—net, you understand; and a million to you, if you make it. How's that?"

Barry reclaimed the blue hat.

"I'm on," he answered. "I'll just take this bonnet home with me tonight and ask Effie what she thinks of it. My sister. If she was put to it, I'm betting Effie could make a Paris model out of one of my old four-in-hands and a feather-duster."

"But, Barry, this is a man's hat!" ejaculated Miller. "How the dickens?"

"That's the idea," said Barry calmly. "I'm going to make the women wear them. I'll tell you more when I've doped it out."

 MILLER rang for his stenographer when he had run through his mail next morning. She came in with her hat on, a blue one. She was a brisk and business-like young person in general, but today, for some reason, a trifle flustered. Miller glanced at her sharply.

"What is it, Miss Joyce?" he demanded. "Anything happened? You haven't laid off your hat——"

He pulled himself up, catching sight of Barry smirking in at him from the door. He turned his eyes on the girl again. The truth burst upon him.

"Well, I'm hanged!" he rapped out. "Your hat—it's the dodo!"

"It's a dear!" sparkled Miss Joyce. "I want one for myself."

"Not so bad, if you ask me," boasted Barry. He came forward. "Effie's idea. A twist of red velvet around the crown, and the brim caught up with a knot of it. And the same scheme for the other shades—colors to suit. Simple, cheap and striking. Am I wrong?"

"It's stunning. I wouldn't have thought it," trilled the stenographer. "I'm sure it will sell."

She had the hat off now and was musingly considering it, in the way of women with such things. Miller spoke to her.

"Never mind the mail for the moment, Miss Joyce. I'll call you when I'm ready." When she was gone he said to Barry: "Your hat looks good. What next? Of course you can't put anything of the kind across here in the city."

"Hardly," assented Barry. "I'm thinking of trying it on at Blanton, up the river. It's out of my territory, but it's a mill town —thirty thousand—and half of them women. They are making good money. Mills running full time. Everybody happy. I am going to breeze up there and look over the ground; take with me a crate of the bonnets, trimmed. The rest, as they are, can follow by boat when I wire for them. Only a night's trip."

"Yes, yes," barked Miller impatiently. "But the stunt—how are you going to sell them?"

"I don't know," confessed Barry frankly. "I've got to pull off something that will make a stir—make talk. I'm not quite clear about it yet." He looked quizzically at his chief. "All the same, I've fifty dollars in my clothes that says to any man I'll do the trick."

Miller leaned back with a pleased smile. The youngster's nerve got to him.

"I'll be glad to lose that bet," he chuckled. "What are you going to call this—er— new line? It must have a name."

Barry showed a set of strong white teeth.

"Well," he drawled, "with everybody wishing this murderous war was over, and praying for it, I've got a hunch that ought to make a kill. The Peace Hat—how is that?"

This time Miller laughed aloud.

"Fits like an elephant's hide. But what's the difference? My wife wears a poke she calls the Roccoco, or something with just as much sense to it. The Peace Hat! Fine! Slide out of here, boy. Get busy. And if you fall down——"

"You'll hear me all right," grinned Barry. "I'll make a noise."

II

IT WAS the second day of April, a Monday. Barry, carrying a bandbox, walked into Beach & Brown's Department Store in Blanton. It was the biggest establishment of the kind in those parts. Barry noticed one of their windows was given over wholly to a showing of Spring millinery. Inside it chanced to be Mr. Beach himself whom he accosted.

"I've a proposition to make to you," he said to the gentleman. "There's money in it."

Mr. Beach, a puffy, pompous little man, with a peevish eye and rasping voice, scowled at the bandbox.

"Hats?" he squeaked.

"Yes; ladies' hats. Something they'll eat up. Let me show you——"

"I won't look!" puffed Mr. . Beach. "We've got our line in. Loaded up. Didn't you see the display?"

"But," argued Barry, "I've got something——"

"Keep it, young man, keep it," rasped the other. "We're loaded, I tell you. You can't give me anything in hats. Good day."

"Oh, all right," returned Barry cheerfully. "I hope you'll find tomorrow just as good — but I'm betting you won't. So long."

That plan had not worked, and he had not counted on it over much. Now for the next move. He made his way to the office of the *Evening Leader*. It was the favorite sheet with the mill people, somebody had told him.

"I am going to spend some money with you," he said to the business manager, one Mr. Alder, when he had introduced himself and his house. "We are pushing a special line of women's hats, and it depends a good deal on your fashion editor how much space I take. She ought to know who's who in this town."

"The cream," Mr. Alder assured him earnestly. "I'll call Mrs. Cook down from upstairs."

He came back presently with the lady, a person of uncertain Summers, chastened to a meek demeanor by her secret knowledge of the endless caprices of her sex. Barry opened his box.

"This, Mrs. Cook," he began, gravely important, "is something absolutely new in Spring styles for the ladies. I favor blue myself, but we have three other shades—tan, green and black. In view of the fact that the women of the whole world are praying for the end of hostilities in Europe, we have called this creation the Peace Hat. It is one of the best quality of felt and, as you see, simple yet effective—distinguished, is the word."

The fashion editor made little throaty sounds intended to express a surprised admiration.

"It is certainly a new idea," she murmured. "And, really, it's rather fetching."

"Ripping!" put in the business manager. "How much space will you want, Mr. Howard?"

"In a moment," said Barry, waving him down. "Our appeal, Mrs. Cook, is to the working women—the great throbbing heart of the social structure. Say, don't forget that, please. It's a good line, and I want some fancy writing about this hat. Now, who is the most popular girl in town I can get to wear it—to start the style here?"

Barry, in an absent way, drew from his pocket a comfortable-looking roll of yellow-backs and toyed with it.

"Rosalie Martin!" exploded Mr. Alder.

Mrs. Cook nodded assent.

"Yes, Rosalie Martin by long odds. The mill girls adore her. She is the secretary of the Working Women's Club, and the mainspring of the movement to raise funds for a new building. If we could get her to do it——"

"We've got to get her!" Barry cried out tumultuously, for a great light was beating in upon him—another clamorous hunch. "I want her picture in the paper wearing this Peace Hat."

"Why, as to that——"

Mrs. Cook paused. A doubt assailed her.

"Leave it to me," said Barry quickly. "All I ask is an introduction. Here!" He peeled off a fifty-dollar note and passed it to the business manager. "Put me down for that much space right now. There'll be more to follow. And say to Miss Martin I've an idea I can help her swell that building fund. A thousand dollars, very likely. Or more. It's up to her."

Mr. Alder stared at the bill in his own hand, and at the roll in Barry's. It was convincing.

"Have Mr. Howard meet her at your house tonight," he suggested to his editor.

"Do," begged Barry. "You can reach me at the Blanton. And, Mrs. Cook, if you like this sample it will please me mightily to see you in it. Thank you; the pleasure is all mine." He started off, then stopped. "Oh, I forgot. The price of the hat—" to decide this had teased him until now—"is only four dollars. You might mention it in your write-up."

He went away in jubilant mood. He held, he believed, the key to his problem. It would be a killing, nothing less.

BARRY hunted around for a vacant store in the shopping district. His luck was with him. A building was being remodeled. The ground floor with two immense show-windows was finished, but men were still at work on the upper floors. A banner over the door announced that the Blanton Furniture Company would move in April fifteenth, occupying the entire premises.

Barry made a note of their address. He also noted that Beach & Brown's store was directly across the street. It made him laugh to look at it.

At eight that night he was sitting in Mrs. Cook's parlor talking with Miss Rosalie Martin. Four Peace Hats were scattered over the piano. Miss Martin had laughingly tried on all of them. She was a tall young woman one would glance at twice in passing; not so much because of her comeliness —and she was not lacking in that—but by reason of a carriage that singled her out of a crowd as a stately cup yacht would be singled out from among a fleet of tow-boats.

"Lord," breathed Barry to himself, "she'd give class to a Quaker sunbonnet!"

"But I don't understand the motive back of this," the girl was saying dubiously. "Why should your company give us a dollar on every hat? It doesn't seem——"

Barry checked her with an apologetic hand.

"It's not the company's idea. It's mine; and I'm not a philanthropist. I make my living selling hats. Through the usual channels I might sell a hundred or two of these Peace Hats here; but it occurred to me when I learned of your club that I could use it to help me sell more hats. Incidentally it would help the club. Before going on let me ask if I've made my position clear?"

Miss Rosalie Martin's fine eyes smiled on him. This frank, business-getting young man appealed.

"You have," she replied simply.

"That's good," said Barry, warming under her gaze. "Here is the proposition from A to Izzard, and as brief as I can frame it:

"I am giving your club the middleman's profit—one dollar. And I'm going just a bit further because I think it will sell more hats. They don't come trimmed. I've had a few fixed up for show purposes, but the buyer trims her own hat. A quarter of a yard of velvet will do it, in the style you see. All right, I will allow the buyer fifty cents for trimming, and that's liberal. In other words, she gets a four-dollar hat for three-fifty, one dollar of which she knows goes into your building fund. She is contributing that dollar herself, and she'll have a hat which—I pledge you my word—she can't get anywhere under the sun but from me."

Mrs. Cook spoke.

"Rosalie! They ought to go like hot cakes."

A small wrinkle showed between Miss Martin's eyes. She was puzzled.

"But I don't quite see how you are going to do it—sell the hats. Where? When? The mill girls are at work during the day," she said to Barry.

"Oh, that's easy," he assured her confidently. "I'll get a vacant store, lay a lot of boards on wooden horses to hold the hats, and you'll furnish the girls to sell them— girls you can trust. I'll pay them two dollars a day. We will keep open evenings with an extra shift. And—I say, Miss Martin—we'll have music, four or five pieces."

This was an eleventh-hour inspiration.

Miss Martin's brow lost its wrinkle. She leaned forward eagerly.

"How many of these hats have you, Mr. Howard?"

"Only enough with me to fill the windows. I'll have to wire for more. How many, for a guess, do you think we shall want?"

"Could you get a thousand? That means a thousand dollars for the fund. Could you get that many?"

"Yes," said Barry, after a meditated pause.

"And if we should need them, do you think—" she put the question anxiously— "you could get two thousand?"

"I'll try," said Barry bravely.

"You see," she went on, "we have a mass-meeting at the club tomorrow night to hear reports from the soliciting committees, and——"

"You will wear the Peace Hat, Rosalie?" Mrs. Cook's reportorial instincts quickened.

"Yes; and I will tell the girls the proposition you have made, Mr. Howard. I believe—I really do—that they will go wild over it."

"They will have read about it in the *Leader* by then," proclaimed the editor. "It's *news*, Rosalie, dear! A clean scoop for us, because, of course—" she looked at Barry—"not a word of this is to be breathed to any one until our first edition is out."

Barry strove to maintain a benevolent calm.

"Not a word," he promised. "And in the morning, Miss Martin, I'll have a man at your house to photograph you as you are leaving it with thé hat on." He showed his teeth in his boyish grin. "A snapshot, you know. Nothing posed."

The girl put back her head and laughed.

"Oh, of course! Well, if you think it will help, I'm willing. I'll try not to assault the camera-man."

Barry stopped in the telegraph-office on his way back to the hotel. Barry was nothing if not an optimist. He wired Miller in these words:

Ship all the hats by Tuesday's boat. The dove of peace is cooing in my hand.

III

THE Blanton Furniture Company saw no reason why they should not pocket fifty dollars for the use of their vacant new store for a week. Their lease ran from April first. Barry's offer was like finding money, and they closed with him.

He had the place swept out, got in men to put up improvised counters, draped a lot of bunting around the walls, and from a florist secured some mounted white doves— typical of peace—with the view to suspending them in the show windows. And then he moved in a piano.

By Tuesday night all was ready to take down the sheeting from the windows and reveal the display of sample hats. But Barry decided to wait till the following night, when the sale would start. Curiosity, properly whetted, has a value to be counted in dollars and cents.

The *Leader* had come out with a cut of Rosalie Martin in the hat and a vivid story of the plan to swell the building fund of the Working Women's Club. Every mill girl in town had read it, had pored over Rosalie's picture. They paraded by the store after supper and took in avidly the huge banner Barry had hung up in front:

THE PEACE HAT
Big Sale Begins Tomorrow Night
Seven O'clock Sharp
Music

Barry went around to see the morning paper, the *Herald*. They would have to say something about the sale, willy nilly, for, as Mrs. Cook had shrewdly pointed out, it was news. The Working Women's Club was a factor to be reckoned with in the city's economic development. It represented a combined purchasing power of many thousands of dollars. But Barry had concluded that a few dollars expended with the *Herald* would enlist its active support in lieu of a cold chronicling of facts it could not ignore.

"Better send some one tomorrow night to see the opening," he prompted as he rose to go. "I've an idea there will be a rush."

The man he was talking with laughed with a secret amusement.

"It's a joke," he explained. "Fred Beach, of Beach & Brown, owns that store you are in. It's funny to think of your bucking his hat department. I don't see how the Blanton Furniture people came to let you have the place. Did they know it was for hats?"

"Sure. I told them," said Barry. "Guess they didn't think of Beach. But it's too late now." He grinned comfortably. "I've got them signed and sealed."

Barry put in a busy day, Wednesday. The hats had come. He ordered up a thousand and left the balance in storage at the wharf. Miss Rosalie Martin and a squad of capable girls came down and helped him unpack the hats and arrange them on the counters.

They worked behind locked doors, for Barry had a suspicion which, however, he kept to himself, that he would hear from Mr. Fred Beach. But nothing happened. When all was in readiness Barry voiced to Rosalie a thought that he had been quietly mulling over. He said:

"This sale is going to be a success. I want a local manager for it, some one to count up and handle the club's end of the money. It's worth a hundred dollars to me to get the right person." He added slyly: "The money could be given to the cause. Do you know anybody who would like the job, Miss Rosalie Martin?"

"Here!" she answered earnestly. "If you could have seen those women at the meeting last night. Success! Just wait. Do you think you could get another thousand hats?"

Barry smiled.

"I'll tell you something, Miss Martin. I took a chance. I've thirty-three hundred more down at the steamboat warehouse. It's every last one to be had for love or money. Can we sell them, do you think?"

"If we don't, I'm no good at a guess," she came back spiritedly. "Watch!"

They bared the windows at five o'clock. A crowd gathered about them. And it grew. At seven the doors were thrown open. The music struck up, and "I Didn't Raise My Boy to Be a Soldier" brought a cheer from the street.

It seemed to Barry, viewing the scene from a corner inside, that the big store was instantly filled. And the crowd outside grew greater. Police were detailed to handle it. A lieutenant struggled in and spoke to Barry.

"You'll have to pass this bunch out through the rear or there'll be a riot," he yapped.

"Help yourself," said Barry. "I'm glad you are here."

Then he chuckled. Mr. Fred Beach was pushing his way to him. And he had a rough-looking man in tow.

"Why, hello!" Barry greeted Beach genially. "You must have read the *Leader*. These are the hats I wanted to sell you Monday."

"Where's your license?" growled the man with Beach.

Barry showed the paper.

"Did you think I'd forgotten it?" he reproached. "I'll have it framed if you say so."

Mr. Beach made an impatient gesture.

"Serve him, Lynch, serve him!" he rasped. And to Barry: "You're enjoined from holding this sale here. The Blanton Furniture Company's lease stipulates that the premises are not to be sublet."

"Oh! So you waited until now to cut loose, did you?" drawled Barry. "That was thoughtful of you. Just a minute, please. I want to speak to my manager."

He turned his back on Mr. Lynch, who was poking a paper at him. He caught sight of Mrs. Cook passing by, and made his way to her.

"Beach is trying to close me up," he said to her urgently. "Get Miss Martin, won't you—quick! And there ought to be somebody from the *Herald* here. Get him, too. Thanks." He returned to Beach and his minion. "If you really want to put this thing through," he remarked pleasantly, "why go ahead. I'll accept service. I think, though, you are making a mistake."

"Lynch! He's accepted. Close the place," squeaked the merchant.

"Wait!" Barry's tone was hard now. "Don't be a teetotal fool, Beach. And here's my manager—Miss Rosalie Martin. You know her, I believe."

Rosalie, accompanied by Mrs. Cook and the *Herald* man, had come up. Barry explained the situation to them. Rosalie's eyes flashed. She looked Beach over with cold scorn.

"Why," she cried, "this comes with fine grace from you, sir. You've grown rich off the working women of this city. They have put thousands into your pockets, and what have you, on your part, done for them?" She made a sweeping gesture drawing, as it were, the two reporters into closer confidence with her. "He subscribed in his firm's name seventy-five dollars to our building fund. There's appreciation for you —generosity—gratitude! And now that we have the chance to put a large sum in our treasury, he would prevent it. Take note of it, please, you of the press. Here is a public-spirited citizen indeed!"

Mr. Beach squealed an angry response.

"It's simply a scheme of this man's to unload a lot——"

But Mr. Lynch stopped him. Rosalie's voice had reached outside their circle. Women were pressing toward them. And there were the reporters!

"You're in wrong, Beach," muttered the constable. "Let's get out of this."

Mr. Beach himself seemed of a sudden to sense the situation. He glanced around uneasily and essayed to speak again. Rosalie interrupted. She held out her hand to Barry.

"Help me up on one of these counters. I'll tell this crowd what has happened."

"No—no!" stammered the puffy little man with a frightened air. "It's not necessary. I was hasty. Er—ah—go on with your sale, Miss Martin. I won't interfere."

Mr. Lynch instantly melted from sight. But Barry caught Beach by the arm and drew him aside. His eyes were intent. He had a "hunch," as he would have named it to Miller.

"Here's a tip for you," he whispered. "We are allowing these women fifty cents for trimmings. Hang out a sign at your shop 'Big Bargains in Peace Hat Trimmings.' Advertise it in the papers. Get some of this coin we are turning loose here. And by the way, maybe we can make a deal to let you in on this sale. Watch us tomorrow. If you should happen to want to talk with me, just send a boy across. Good-day —evening, I should say."

Barry unceremoniously left the little man and plunged into the crowd.

IV

THE boy came across at noon the next day. Mr. Beach had watched the sale. Mill girls stayed away from work to buy Peace Hats, fearful lest the supply should give out. Society women discovered it was a public philanthropy to buy and help the cause. And men bought that the women might acclaim them.

Barry's lips twitched as he passed into Beach & Brown's under a banner advertising bargains in Peace Hat trimmings. Mr. Beach received him in his private office. His manner was ingratiating.

"That deal," he remarked, his voice oiled, so far as he could manage it, of its ear-splitting asperities. "You said last night——"

"Oh, yes," responded Barry carelessly. "I believe I said I might let you in on this sale."

"Well? What's the proposition?" asked Mr. Beach, himself striving for a casual tone.

Barry considered a moment. He knew his mind, but apparent deliberation has its uses when wits are pitted one against the other. Finally he said:

"We had only thirty gross of these hats to begin with, and you see how they are going. We are well into the second thousand. They'll be sold by night. The rest are down at the steamboat wharf—twenty-three hundred. Here's the warehouse receipt with the agent's notations of the number I've withdrawn. Make me an offer for what is left and take over the sale from tonight. I ought to be away from here now."

"Twenty-three hundred?" Mr. Beach looked doubtful. "That's a lot of hats."

"Man alive," exclaimed Barry, "I could sell ten thousand. You know it. The women have simply gone daffy over them."

Mr. Beach smiled craftily.

"When did the Blatchford Company start to making women's hats?"

"When I showed them how," rejoined Barry composedly. "Does that answer you? What is your offer?"

"A dollar and a quarter."

Barry thrust out his chin at him.

"Mr. Beach, you are not subscribing now for the women's clubhouse; and I'm not seeking charity for myself. This is a four-dollar hat—understand? And the women are paying that, less fifty cents for trimming. A dollar goes into the building fund. That leaves two dollars and a half, gross, for me. And the hat cost one-fifty to make. Here! I haven't time to haggle with you. Take them at two dollars, or leave them. Just as you please."

Mr. Beach drummed with his fingers on his desk. The price would allow him a quick profit of eleven hundred and fifty dollars, with but small selling expense, and advertising all done.

"Well, I'll take you," he decided, and opened his check-book.

"Draw one payable to me for forty-six hundred dollars, and the other to Miss Rosalie Martin for twenty-three hundred," he requested smoothly.

"What?" shrilled the little man. His pen fell from a paralyzed hand.

"It's the Working Women's Club share," said Barry. "In advance. I've a notion Miss Martin would like it that way. After last night I'm afraid— You get me, don't you? If Miss Martin should draw out of the sale——"

"Well, well, have it as you say," creaked the other fretfully and picked up his pen.

"Good!" applauded Barry. "And I say! It will sound rather neat for you in the papers, paying in advance. It's really a gift you are making, come to think of it. I'll see they treat it as such."

"Why, yes, it is a gift, certainly," simpered Mr. Beach, basking in this cheerful light thrown so unexpectedly and inexpensively upon him. "You might impress it on Miss Martin, if you will. I don't have to do it, you know. But to help——"

"Sure," Barry soothed. "She will understand. Come over and see her. Thanks. The place is yours from tonight."

Barry quietly slipped around to the bank and bought with his check a bill of exchange. And he had Rosalie's certified. Both actions evinced the respectful esteem in which he held Mr. Fred Beach. Then he went around to the *Leader* and told them the news. After which he imparted it to Rosalie.

"Why, this is perfectly fine of you," she praised, as she took the check. "And you are going away tonight?"

"On the twelve-o'clock train. I wish— I'd be awfully pleased—if we could have a little farewell spread at the Blanton, you and I and these girls, after we close. Will you?"

Her frank eyes dwelt upon him kindly.

"Yes," she consented, and added, "I am sorry you are going."

"Now I'm sorry," he mourned. "But it's not so far. Maybe I'll come back—if I'm asked.

The color rose in her face, though she laughed.

"Who knows?" she said.

BARRY sauntered into Miller's office the following morning with a nonchalant air he hoped would create an impression. It had with Miss Joyce who was tittering over his shoulder. But he received a surprise. The sales manager flung down a newspaper he was reading and burst into a storm of reproaches.

"The dodos! Why in thunder did you leave that lot at the wharf?" he blazed. "Fifteen gross!"

Miss Joyce incontinently disappeared.

"Why did you do it?" barked Miller.

"Because—" began Barry.

" 'Because!' " Miller choked him off angrily. "Because you didn't have the gumption to take them away. And they were not insured!"

"Say!" Barry was startled. "What's this you are giving me? You don't mean——"

"I do. The wharf was burned to the water at one o'clock this morning. Here it is in the paper, with the losses."

Barry dropped weakly into a chair. Miller stared at him, for he was laughing crazily and mouthing strange words.

"Oh, by jiminy, this is rich! Poor old Beach! He's out sixty-nine hundred dollars. I'd give a farm to see him." He struggled for composure. "Mr. Miller, I sold those hats to Beach & Brown yesterday noon. At two dollars. Had a hunch. The thing was too good; it scared me. I sent you the Blanton papers about the sale. Here's a statement showing how we stand. The factory's share is $3,225, mine $6,375,

and Rosa's—the club's—$4,300. Awful, isn't it?"

Miller glanced at the paper, then fixed his eyes on the grinning boy. A slow chuckle welled up to his lips.

"You infernal young robber!" he gulped.

"There was some talk of a promotion before I left," said Barry pertly. "I'm waiting. And I'll trouble you, Mr. Miller, for that fifty, if it's quite convenient. I promised it to Effie."

The sales manager reached for a paper weight.

"Out of here, you throat-cutting thug!" he shouted. "Go see the old man. And take this statement with you. He'll very likely give you anything you ask for in the shop. Beat it, or the next thing I know I'll be shaking hands with you."

CASSIDY'S CONSOLATION KICK
by Hugh S. Fullerton.

Author of "Ole Lekker's Ride," "Peterson and Forseille (not Inc.)," etc.

WHEN Winter fastens its cold fingers upon the upper lakes and the straits, the bays that break in upon the defending line of sand mountains are first to freeze. Along the outer edges of these frozen bays a breastwork of white is thrown up as the cakes grind to white powder against the edge of the shore ice, and as the spray freezes upon this ridge, it rises higher.

Floating floes that drift against this ridge are caught and chained fast by the cold when the gales blow. When the lake is calm the field of ice throws out a thin skirmish line, which strengthens and thick-

ens until the waves no longer can crush it and throw it back, and along the edge of this new ice-field another ridge is thrown up to grasp and hold the floes.

Each advance of the ice is marked by a level, unbroken plateau of white, and each battle with the gales is revealed by a ridge of contorted, shattered, upheaved blocks, showing how desperately the waves strove to drive back the invader.

During late November and December the lake holds its own and sometimes with one mighty attack it smashes the advancing drive of ice and hurls it, crushed and mangled, back upon the sand-dunes. But when

Winter comes in its full strength a great plain of ice is locked against the shores.

Sometimes one may climb to the top of one of the dunes and far out over the waste of whiteness may see the blue of the open lake, dotted with the white of floating islands of ice. And if one takes a field-glass and climbs to the tallest of the dunes near Ludington or Manistee or Frankfort, one may see, far out near the edge of that great white plain, a row of little black dots. These are the homes of the fishermen who spend the Winter on that arctic waste that you may eat fresh fish.

 OLSON had whisky in his hut, which was located three miles off shore between Big Point Sable light and Manistee. Cassidy had none in his shack, which stood on the ice seventy-five yards to the north of Olson's.

The worst of at was that Cassidy knew Olson had the whisky.

It was mid-January. The shore ice was heavier and smoother that Winter than in ordinary years. Cassidy and Olson were neighbors in Summer, when they lived in shacks along the river's edge and went out in the tugs to bring in whitefish and trout. They were friends and neighbors in the Winter on the floes. A few hundred yards a week they had dragged their shanties outward over the ice-pack since early in December—and the catch had been good.

Their homes were much alike. They were the size and the architecture of large packing-boxes, made of heavy planking and covered inside and out with tarred paper to keep out the cold. They were mounted upon runners so that they might be moved from place to place and dragged back to land when the floes broke up in the Spring. Inside of each hut was a small stove which furnished heat and upon which they boiled coffee all day and cooked fish and bacon.

On the Saturday preceding, Olson and Cassidy had dragged their hand-sleds across the ice and up the frozen river to Manistee, where they had sold their fish. The market price was high, so Olson and Cassidy got drunk together very harmoniously. True, they fought each other several times, but that was because they could not find any other fishermen who wanted to fight, and it was all in the best of fellowship. To get drunk and not to fight is not the code of the fisherman.

Each had purchased a case of beer to take back on to the ice. Odd as it may seem to landsmen, many of the ice fishermen prefer drinking beer to whisky when they are on the floes, because the beer warms them, while the whisky, after its first flush of heat, leaves them colder. Olson usually drank beer, but this time he was drunk, and he purchased, in addition to his case of beer, four quart bottles of villainous whisky which was half alcohol colored with logwood, which he preferred to the whisky of commerce.

Olson and Cassidy were half drunk when they faced the west wind and dragged their sleds, loaded with provisions, drink and tobacco, out across the waste of ice.

Two miles out they stopped to rest and to drink a bottle of beer and, by accident, Cassidy saw the whisky on Olson's sled. He thought nothing of it at the time. He did not understand the psychology of desire for drink resulting from knowledge that drink is near. He and Olson had been friends and mates for years and neither had ever refused the other a drink.

They reached their shacks, started their fires, treated each other to a bottle of beer and resumed work late in the afternoon. The wind was strong and straight from the west. The skies were clear and the cold was biting and numbing. Their bodies, suffering from the reaction after the drinking bout, felt the cold more than they usually did.

Olson was tired. He fried a fish with strips of bacon, smoked for a time and decided to retire for the night.

Preparations for retiring were simple. He drew off the hobnailed rubber-and-leather shoes with their heavy felt boots inside, drew on a fresh pair of thick woolen socks and crawled into his blankets. The thirst that follows a drunk was upon him. He reached out into the darkness, found a bottle of beer and drank it. The beer failed to satisfy his craving for drink and, after a time he crawled out of his blankets, opened a bottle of whisky and drank long and deep. Then he sighed contentedly, crept back into the blankets and went to sleep.

Cassidy was undergoing similar experiences, and in addition the knowledge that Olson possessed whisky disturbed him. Ordinarily, knowing there was no whisky nearer than Manistee, he would have gone to sleep with no thought of drink, but the knowledge that Olson had four quarts of it in his hut was too much. Olson scarcely had fallen into a sound sleep when Cassidy kicked upon the batten door of his hut.

"Ole!" yelled Cassidy. "Lave me hov a dhrop av booze."

"Vot in —— you ban vake me up for?" demanded Ole angrily. "Ay got no booze."

The dénouement was as shocking to Cassidy as it was unexpected. Never before had Ole refused Cassidy a drink. He had, in fact, been very generous—as generous as Cassidy had been with him. Cassidy knew that Olson lied. Besides, he wanted the drink. He kicked upon the door again and Ole swore and ordered him away.

"Ye're a dirthy liar, ye blank-blanked Skowhegian!" said Cassidy and strode away over the ice.

 OLSON had been insulted. To call a man a Skowhegian on the ice is an insult not lightly to be passed over. Olson started to roll out of his blankets and go out upon the floe to fight Cassidy. The sound of the wind roaring made him hesitate and the warmth of the blankets tempted him. He decided to forego vengeance until morning, took another long drink from the bottle and went to sleep.

Cassidy returned to his shack, drank a bottle of beer and brooded over Ole's refusal to give him a drink of whisky. The unneighborly conduct of Olson had wounded his pride—and besides, his longing for hard drink was increasing. He knew that McIndoo, whose shack was a hundred yards or such a matter, had Scotch whisky in his hut. Cassidy did not like Scotch whisky. He said it tasted like the creosote they use on the bottoms of the boats.

Nevertheless, after brooding for a time over the conduct of Olson, Cassidy's longing for hard drink caused him to forget his hatred of Presbyterianism and Scotch whisky, and he rolled out of his blankets and went across the ice to visit McIndoo. He found McIndoo sitting up, playing upon his pipes, kicked upon the door and was admitted.

Together they consumed a bottle of Scotch whisky and during the consumption Cassidy told McIndoo that Olson had four quarts of whisky and that he had refused to give him a drink. McIndoo sympathized with Cassidy and Cassidy warmed to

him, declaring that a Swede was stingier even than a Scotchman.

The next morning Olson awoke to discover that three quarts of whisky which he had cached under the hut between the runners had been stolen. The half-empty bottle by his side was all that remained. Olson took a large drink from this bottle, went across the ice to where Cassidy was fishing and accused him openly of being a thief.

They fought. Cassidy was knocked down. His head struck upon a rough corner of an ice cake, cutting the head open to the skull and, while Cassidy was down, Olson kicked him with his hobnailed boots, which is perfectly ethical according to the code of the floes.

Two days later, when Cassidy's wound was healing, they fought again and Cassidy knocked several of Olson's teeth down his throat with a lump of ice hurled at short range. In addition Cassidy called Olson names reflecting upon Olson's maternal ancestors, from the first to the tenth generation. Olson spat out a loose tooth and flung an epithet extremely insulting to a person of the Roman Catholic faith.

It is true upon the ice, as in other places, that when men fight they must not attack either women or religion, and that, as in many places, the less religion a man has the more bitterly he resents any slur cast upon it. Cassidy, not having been in church since his christening, rose in righteous wrath to defend the faith. They fought until pried apart and carried to their respective huts.

As the Winter gripped the upper lakes more tightly the feud between Olson and Cassidy waxed more and more bitter. In the saloons, on the dock, on the ice, wherever and whenever they met they fought. For Olson swore Cassidy had insulted his mother and Cassidy vowed Olson had assaulted the fair name of his church. Cassidy charged that Olson was a line cutter and a fish thief, which are offenses not lightly to be condoned on the floes. Olson retorted that Cassidy was a whisky thief and, in the eyes of the fishermen, stealing whisky on the ice is a capital crime.

The ice was very heavy that Winter and the little shanties out near the edge of the land pack moved further and further out into the lake until the dunes were only hazy scallops, fringing the purple skirts of the skies, and the lights on shore were but pin-points.

The middle of February found Winter's grip stronger than ever. By day the sun shone upon the dazzling whiteness of the ice and its rays were flashed back without softening the surface that rang like steel when the ice-augers or axes bit into it. By night the cold was numbing. Twenty, twenty-five, thirty degrees below zero the thermometers registered.

Fish drawn upon the ice flapped for a minute and were frozen stiff. Men grew quarrelsome, surly, or silent according to their natures. Those who dragged their sleds over the ice to Manistee drank deep and brought back strong drink to deaden their sufferings from cold. There was little visiting back and forth among the little black shanties. The sociability and the rough, good-natured play that had marked the early weeks of Winter were gone.

When darkness came the men crawled into their blankets, doubled themselves in the attitude of half-closed jack-knives around their little stoves and slept. If they were lucky enough to have whisky they drank alone. They quarreled at the smallest slight, and fought at the least pretext.

Cassidy and Olson still lived side by side near the edge of the floe. If either had moved his shanty further from the other, it would have been construed as a sign of cowardice. They no longer fought each other. They had discovered that neither could whip the other, save by resort to murder. Neither would have hesitated at the commission of murder had he been able to furnish proof of self-defense and, on the ice, self-defense is somewhat more strictly interpreted than it is in the courts.

On February twenty-fourth a warm, damp wind came from the southward over the ice. It blew gently all the afternoon and the fish were biting more freely than they had in many days. At nightfall the wind rose higher and the sound of the waves roaring in the open lake grew louder.

By midnight a gale was raging. The waves, driven by the wind and by the weight of the open water, crashed against the outer barrier of ice a hundred yards beyond the shanties. The ice was rumbling and occasionally a sharp report indicated that it was cracking.

John the Polack, who was scorned as the most timid of all the men on the ice, heard the rumblings and, not long after midnight he arose, chopped the runners of his hut free from the ice and dragged it back across the floe to beyond the second ice-ridge. The pressure of the heavy sea was forcing water under the great floes. The field moved uneasily and groaned.

Occasionally there was a report like the firing of a saluting gun, and again a heavy booming noise. Lights were flashing around the shanties long before the pale daybreak came over the dunes. The fishing-colony was making hasty preparations for a landward flight if the ice-field started to break up. They knew the pressure of wind and wave from the west would pack the mass tighter, but that, if it started to break up, the level field would be transformed into an inferno of upheaved and contorted ice.

Men worked desperately chopping the runners out of the ice and dragging the shacks shoreward. By daybreak half the colony had moved nearly a mile shoreward and were camping back of the high ice-ridge on ice six feet thick.

Olson emerged from his hut shortly after daybreak. He sniffed the wind, glanced around over the litter of tin-cans, empty bottles and rubbish left by the retreating fishermen and then turned his gaze toward Cassidy's hut. Cassidy had not moved. He was fishing. Olson studied the skies for a few moments, glowered toward Cassidy and prepared to catch fish. He knew more wind was coming and he felt the splattering drops of warm rain. Under his breath he cursed Cassidy for a brainless fool and proceeded with his fishing.

Before long the rain came in driving sheets, warm and steamy and the water gathered in puddles in the depressions in the ice and steamed until a veil of light fog spread over the surface of the floe. Out in open water the seas were running higher. The waves broke in spray clouds above the top of the ice-barrier and slatted down upon the ice, forming ponds that spread steadily. Olson got a tarpaulin, covered himself with it and continued to fish, watching Cassidy and cursing him.

When night came only Olson and Cassidy remained near the outer edge of the floe. Even French George, reckoned the most daring of them all, had dragged his hut shoreward. Some of the men had dragged their huts beyond the first sand-bars, deserted them and gone ashore to wait until the ice broke up or the storm ceased and left the floes solid.

The wind shifted to the west during the night and blew harder and harder. The rain had ceased and the swell in the open lake was heavier. The sound of ice breaking was like the noise of a battery of quick-firers in action, and all around the floe grumbled and groaned and heaved. Toward midnight the wind shifted back to the south and blew a hurricane.

The strain on the shore pack-ice was relieved, but great masses that had been cracked loose moved along the edge of the pack into clear water. The sound of these floating masses crashing against the pack was like a far-away artillery bombardment. Olson got up at daybreak and peered out of the door of his shanty.

"Vind she ban shift off shore purt soon," he muttered to himself. "Ay tank ve ban —— fool to stay."

Seeing that Cassidy had not stolen a march on him and moved shoreward, he returned to his shack and went to sleep. An hour later a series of violent upheavals of the ice, a sickening lurching accompanied by a series of explosions that sounded as if a battery of five-pounders had opened fire, caused him to sit up suddenly. The upheaving movement ended suddenly and was followed by a rocking movement.

"By Gar, ve ban drift!" he exclaimed.

An instant later he had drawn on his heavy felt boots and sprang out upon the ice.

A huge cake of ice, perhaps two hundred yards wide and a quarter of a mile long had split off from the main pack and was being driven to the northward, scraping and bumping against the solid floe. The break had been along the line of the second ice-ridge, and the weight of the outer ridge tilted the floating mass upward. The floating floe was scraping and grinding and, with every collision with the shore-ice, great cakes were torn loose, ground into smaller chunks that formed a drifting, swirling mass of pulverized ice, across which passage to the shore-ice was impossible. Olson watched the turmoil for a minute then, inspired by sudden resolve, he turned and ran to Cassiday's shack, kicking upon the batten door.

"Yim!" he yelled. "Yim—ve ban float!"

"Git away from thot door, ye Skowhegian son av a fish gutter!" yelled Cassidy. "Oi've known it for an hour."

"Ay ain't ban no visky thief!" screamed Olson, angered by the surly reception of his well-intended warning.

 CASSIDY came from his hut roaring like an enraged bull. In his hand he carried a curved fish-cleaning knife. Olson saw the knife and with an angry bellow he leaped to meet his foe.

Cassidy struck with the knife as Olson's arms seized him around the waist. The knife slashed downward through many garments and bit to the bone along the back of Olson's shoulder. The two men went down. Over and over across the ice they rolled, locked in each other's grips. The knife was lost. Olson's huge arms were crushing the breath out of Cassidy's lungs, and Cassidy's fingers were clutching at Olson's windpipe.

Neither man spoke. Their hoarse gruntings and deep breathing gave evidence of the desperation of the conflict.

With a great effort Olson lifted Cassidy and turned him over. An instant later Cassidy heaved upward and flopped Olson onto the ice. Over and over, first one on top, then the other, they struggled, sliding down the slanting floe until they were in the half-congealed water of one of the ponds formed by the spindrift.

Exhausted, they lay upon the ice, face to face, locked in each other's arms, breathing into each other's faces and glaring into each other's eyes. They were waiting to recover breath and strength for the final settlement of the feud.

Olson was first to regain his breath.

"Ay ain't ban no Skowhegian," he said slowly.

"Thin don't be callin' me no booze thafe," said Cassidy.

"Ve ban —— fools fightin'," said Olson.

"We are thot," agreed Cassidy hesitatingly. "Until we git ashore."

"Ve ban hav fine fight then," said Olson, releasing his hold around Cassidy's body.

They arose stiffly and stood together, looking shoreward, while Olson held a lump of ice to the cut in the back of his shoulder and Cassidy nursed his torn ear. Far away they could see the dim outlines of the sand-dunes and the spidery tower of the wireless station. Between them and the land ice was a lane of open water, flecked with small cakes of drifting ice, and the lane widened with each slow revolution of the floe upon which they stood.

"Ve ban in vun —— of a fix," said Olson. "Vind she off shore. Ve blow across lake."

"Av this cake breaks up we'll not make Green Bay," said Cassidy.

"Ay ban vish Ay had some booze," said Olson with sudden longing.

"Would ye be after givin' me a bit av a dhrink av it?" demanded Cassidy.

"Sure Ay vould, Yim," said Olson. "Ay ban give you half. Ay ban sleepy that night Ay say Ay ban got none."

"Thin why the —— didn't ye say so?" demanded Cassidy hotly. "Oi thought ye was stingy wid it."

"No," said Olson, "Ay yoost ban drunk and sleepy. Ay no ban vant to get up."

They ate together at noon on the ice in front of Cassidy's hut. The floe was riding the waves far out in the lake. In the afternoon the wind blew harder from south·east and they drifted more rapidly.

Toward evening the floe split with a booming sound and the smaller section, after bumping and grinding upon the larger, distanced it.

Cassidy and Olson held a consultation. They agreed they would drag their huts close together upon the strongest point on the floe lest the ice break between them and they be separated. Darkness found them with their huts hauled close together, sitting in the open doorways, scanning the horizon in faint hope of seeing the smoke trail of some freighter. Cassidy dressed the knife-wound in Olson's shoulder, washing the frozen dried blood away with ice-water, and they slept in peace.

The next morning after breakfast they were strolling around on the ice when suddenly Cassidy stopped and commenced to swear.

"The —— scut av a Scot," he said. "'Tis for the loikes av him thot two good min hov been fightin' all Winter."

Upon the spot where McIndoo's hut had stood, amid a litter of empty tin cans, empty Scotch-whisky bottles and rubbish, Cassidy had found two empty bottles that once had contained the whisky stolen from Olson's hut. The evidence was conclusive, for never had McIndoo drank any but Scotch whisky unless some one gave it to him, or he stole it. Cassidy kicked viciously at the rubbish and uncovered a full bottle McIndoo had hidden.

"Ay alvays ban know you no booze thief, Yim," said Olson.

"'Tis by the grace av God, an' worth fightin' for," said Cassidy reverently, as he held up the full bottle.

That night, while the half hurricane blew them further and further out across the lake, they broiled their fish over one fire, ate together and drank from the bottle. When it was empty they went to sleep, sitting up in their blankets in Olson's hut.

 ALONG the river bank at Manistee, in the shacks where lived the fisher-folk, Olson and Cassidy were mourned as dead. Those who had known them related their virtues, which were chiefly those of fighting men. The gale subsided, the cold returned with the calm and the shore-pack's wounds made by the storm were healed by the cold. Then came a blizzard out of the straits, a howling, screaming blizzard that swept the snow over the face of the floes and hid the scars of its battle with the winds and waves.

On the seventh day, out of the northwest came Olson. The blizzard had driven their floe back from midlake and against the shore-pack off Portage Point.

Olson staggered along the shore-ice, far out. On his back he carried Cassidy, whose leg was helpless from being caught and ground between crunching ice cakes over which they had fought their way from the floe to solid ice. All day Olson had carried and dragged Cassidy, until at dusk he reached the hut of a fisherman on the ice off Portage light, thirty miles north of the place they had gone adrift.

The fishermen dragged them ashore on sleds. Doctors amputated three of Cassidy's toes that had been frozen, treated the frost-bites from which both had suffered and patched up Cassidy's leg. Three days later Cassidy and Olson returned to Manistee and were greeted as ones arisen from the dead. They were very drunk in a saloon when McIndoo entered.

"Ye shall take the pleasure av batin' him up, Ole," said Cassidy, as he held McIndoo in his grip. "But after ye hov baten the dirthy scut av a Scotch booze-thief, will ye be affther savin' me wan kick av him wid me good fut?"

Ole nodded, and when he had finished his part of the task, and McIndoo lay upon the floor, Cassidy spat upon his hands and took full measure of revenge in one kick.

OLD DAD by George L. Catton.

Author of "Under the Skin," "The Years Between."

IT IS calling me now, that luring, demanding, irresistible call; the two short blasts on the whistle of a train pulling out—the "Highball." There's a tingling itch in the soles of my feet for the old, free life of a tramp; for the two endless shining steel rails, and the grit and the eternal ties of the "road."

And in the next room, Bricks is not asleep. It is calling him, too. I heard the bed creak when he sat up, and the crack of the match when he lit his cigarette. It is calling to him as it is calling to me, as it calls to all who know it, from the day we leave it—if we ever do—till the day leaves us and we check out.

It came up just now on the soft night breeze from the railroad yards on the flats and brought back to me all those six years I spent between the rails; brought back the old longing that a year's absence even hasn't dulled; and to Bricks in the next room and to me, it brought back Old Dad.

Who was Old Dad? Was he a last survivor of the bad men of the old bad West of fifty years ago, who held up steam trains with a cracking rifle and robbed the mail-coaches and the passengers; ambushed pack-trains out of the hills, shot down the guards and got clean away with millions in bullion from the mines, or stopped a stage-coach with a revolver in each hand and fled across the Rio Grande with a pack-horse sweating under an express box? Or was he just a common "knight of the road," a tramp lured on to the grit and held there by the Highball?

There are some victims of the "Two Short Blasts" who go out and stay a few months, till they get tired, and take root on a two-dollar job or go home to father like the "Bull" did. They're the "Cats." You can tell them by their soiled clothes and the grime on their necks. There are some, like myself, who finally locate the best little girl in the world and settle down to slave out "a home for her beyond the strife," as Riley puts it.

There are some who "jog back into the ruts of the righteous for a blowout every time they make a good stake," as Bricks classifies himself. And then there are those, the very small minority, who go out, stay out, and check out, on the road. Who is he? Where did he come from? What is his name? Nobody knows. For it is one of the most strictly adhered-to creeds of the road to ask no questions.

Yesterday you saw him beside the coffee fire in the jungles at Seattle, Washington; next October you will run into him asleep in the shade beside the tank at Spofford, Texas; at Christmas he will nod his head to you in the sand-house at Worcester, Massachusetts. Or maybe he'll stay on one two-hundred-mile branch line till every last shack gets sore on him and he's got to shift. And always he's an old man, white-haired, inoffensive, and as silent as his past. The younger boys look at him and call him

Dad. Old Dad was one of those, and Old Dad was Bricks's pal.

Bricks gets his name from having red hair. He's about as big as an oak post, but he's got the wide nostrils and pugnacious jaw of self-assurance and tenacity of purpose, and an analytical mind for untangling knots. And I wish I had his education—I don't mean technical schooling—he can read and write—but his knowledge of the earth's odd corners, personally taught at the expense of a hide full of scars and an accumulation of very expressive expletives.

It was strange that a man like him would make a pal of a silent old fogey who never had anything to say, never gave an opinion, and who was so ancient they called him Old Dad. But he did, and they worked together for years.

 A VERY little, very silent, very bent old man Old Dad was, not as tall as Bricks, shriveled like a frosted apple, and about the same color. He'd come out of the old-time wild and woolly West we figured, because of the prehistoric Colt seven-shooter he toted, and his shifty, ever-watchful eyes. We couldn't get behind him, out of his sight, no matter how we maneuvered. But he drank tea always instead of coffee and smoked a pipe, and that didn't jibe with our reckoning.

He could speak Mexican-Spanish like an Oaxaca peon, till the palone dogs would quit growling at him, and his English was perfect when he used it, which was about once a month when he would get back pickled from his regular drunk. And always in the jungles he sat apart, a little away from every one else, with his back to something and his eyes half closed.

It was in that position he passed out. The Bull found him in the San Antonio jungles, propped up against a stump, his eyes half open and his pipe still warm in his hand. He had died as he had lived, alone, unknown.

Those days I was high-pitching the two-ring trick in the small towns in the panhandle and making expenses, and at the Spring carnival in San Antonio and the New Orleans Mardi Gras and saving every dollar to quit the road. There was a little girl in Toronto, Canada, where the Bull came from, who was waiting for me to come back and help her keep her life's most important engagement.

Bricks and Old Dad were splitting the customs on, and the difference in price on, drawn-work and tanned furs between the *hombres* of Lampasas and the tourists in San Antonio, and clearing fifty a week apiece. The Bull was, to quote Bricks, "feeding his two-hundred-odd of uselessness on lumps, soiling six feet three inches of nice clean grass while the sun shone, and slinging the bull the rest of the time about his old gent's vast brick-yards and unholy millions." The Bull was the biggest man all around, the worst-tempered, and the strongest off the mat that I ever saw.

When the Bull found Old Dad dead in the San Antonio jungles he went through his clothes and discovered a paper that he figured was a map of the location of the old man's savings, but he didn't have the gray matter in his dome to make foot or fist of it, so he took it to Bricks, Old Dad's pal. Bricks and I were sitting by the coffee fire in the Laredo jungles when the Bull pulled in. He reached for the can and added his handful of coffee.

"Old Dad's kicked off," he growled. "I found him a stiff in the Santone jungles."

Bricks looked up and I could see by his set jaws he was beating down his surprise and disappointment. Bricks had been waiting there two days for Old Dad to come back from his monthly toot and cross the river for the bundle. He watched the Bull's face for a moment, then:

"Whisky or mescal?" he asked.

The Bull set the coffee-can back onto the fire and reached for his makings.

"Neither!" he snapped. "Just croaked natural with the weight of his sins and that old gat he toted."

Bricks frowned. He didn't like the Bull's disrespect for the old man, and I saw his eyelids pull down a trifle.

"What did you get when you frisked him?" he queried.

"Not a —— dollar!"

Bricks's jaw set itself again.

"Was that all?"

The Bull frowned and pulled an old black leather wallet out of his pocket.

"And a map of the old gink's plant," he admitted grudgingly. "But it would take a Philadelphia shyster to dope it out." And he drew a folded paper out of the wallet.

Bricks felt in his pocket for his makings and rolled a cigarette. He lifted a blazing stick and lit it.

"Maybe I can," he proposed indifferently.

"What's the split if you do?" The Bull spread the map out on his knees and studied it seriously.

Bricks got up, piled some wood on the fire and sat down again.

"Fifty-fifty?" he suggested questioningly.

The Bull eyed Bricks a moment, then he scrambled to his feet and I distinctly saw the long handle of Old Dad's ancient seven-shooter sticking out of his hip pocket when his coat swung back.

"Good enough!" he growled, "But——"

He looked at me questioningly.

Bricks saw the interrogation.

"The Dreamer stays," he answered. "We might need him, and if we do I'll split with him."

I shook my head.

"Can't do it, Bricks," I laughed. "I've been trying to make you boys believe for two months that I'm going to quit. I'm going North tonight to get married."

Bricks grabbed my hand and shook it warmly.

"A wise gink!" he ejaculated. "But you'd better stick and see this through. For all we know, Old Dad might have a million planted somewhere, and a quarter of it would buy a kid a new pair of kicks."

I shook my head again.

"I'm due on the eighteenth," I returned. "This is the twelfth and I've got to see a tailor. I've got to hurry."

He nodded his head understandingly and spread the folded paper out in the light so we all could see it. Then I understood why the Bull couldn't make horn or hoof of it.

Old Dad's paper was a map taken from a Southern Pacific time-table folder, with the map on one side and the stops and table of times on the other, and there wasn't an added mark on the map side. We all went over it carefully, but Old Dad hadn't touched it. Then Bricks turned it over.

Old Dad had used a pen to draw five little circles in a row straight up and down, and to the left of the middle one, about two and a half inches, he'd made another circle and put a dot in the center of it, and we could barely see them there among all the letters and figures of the stops and times. That was all.

"Old Dad never intended any one to find

his plant, if that is a map of its location, "I laughed.

"It'll stay where it is till the old fool comes back for it himself!" the Bull supplemented snarlingly.

But neither he nor I figured on Bricks's analytical mind. Bricks folded it carefully again as it was folded when the Bull took it out of the wallet and turned it around, studying it in detail. Then he knocked the ashes off his cigarette and deliberately held the red end to the corner of the folded map.

I thought at first he intended to destroy it, and so did the Bull; but he held it there only a second, then he unfolded the map and spread the left half across his knee. He chuckled.

"Old Dad's plant is just a little north of Presidio del Norte," he announced quietly. I looked where his finger pointed and understood.

Originally the map had been folded in four long ways to fit into the time-table folder, and Old Dad had folded it across, had nearly doubled it in half to shorten it so it would fit into his wallet. When Bricks folded it in the old creases and scorched the corner and opened it out again, the brown spot his cigarette had made came exactly on the intersection of the two-fold crease-lines on the left half of the map. And that spot was just a little north of Presidio del Norte on the Rio Grande.

The Bull got up and looked at Bricks.

"Will we go?" he asked respectfully.

Bricks slipped the map into his pocket.

"We'll catch the 'ten-ten' tonight for San Antone," he replied. "Coming, Dreamer?"

"I'll leave you at San Antonio," I answered. "I've quit the road."

Six days later I was married here in Toronto, and it is just a year since I left Bricks and the Bull in San Antonio. In that year I thought I had succeeded in fighting down the memory of the Highball and its luring, demanding call, but today I ran into Bricks. This afternoon, unexpectedly, in the last place I would ever expect to find him, I ran into Bricks and——

I had been looking forward for weeks to the sale of unclaimed baggage, freight and express that the railway company held annually in Markham's auction rooms, so when the day came I was quite annoyed because I was delayed and missed the first of it. There is an enticing maximum of chance in exchanging laboriously won real tangible dollars for a trunk or a box or a crate whose contents one has no conception of, and sending it home to open all by ourselves. Then, too, there is that very brief moment of breathless suspense when, after prying off a lid or breaking a lock, one finds he has paid out a half a dozen long green dollars for——

My next-door neighbor once paid eighty cents for a box that proved on opening to contain five thousand Turkish cigarettes, and at the same sale bid seven dollars for a trunk full of old photographs. At the sale previous he risked two dollars for a trunk full of burlesque makeup for chorus girls, and got the laugh from the crowd for raising another man's bid to thirteen dollars for a barrel that yielded up thirty pounds of rice hulls and ten little Chinese idols that he sold to a curio dealer for two hundred dollars.

So when I walked into the auction rooms and found I was a half hour late, I was mad clear through. But I forgot it when I saw two husky men straining to lift a big copper-bound trunk on to the counter where the auctioneer stood, and I drove my fist down into my pocket.

The auctioneer looked the trunk over and faced the crowd.

"Twenty dollars? Fifteen dollars? Ten dollars? Give me a bid for it!" he called.

I FELT the money in my pocket and began to figure how much I would risk on it. It might be full of molded cement samples—my neighbor told me of a man getting stung on those things last year. It might be full of stones— some crook going to do a hotel out of a week's accommodation. It might be full of— It was that unknown content that had brought me to the sale, that made me want to bid. But I hesitated, and a voice back in the crowd, a voice I recognized instantly as Bricks's beat me to it.

"Four bits!"

I whirled around, but I'm short and I couldn't see over the heads behind me. I tried to wedge a way back, but I've got soft since I left the road and that crowd wouldn't be disturbed again. I turned back to the auctioneer. I'd wait till that trunk was sold and follow it back in the lane the baggage handlers made when they carried it out.

The auctioneer brought his big red fist down on the end of the trunk with a snarl of assumed rage and ignored Bricks's bid. He gets five per cent. commission.

"Here's a locked trunk as good as new that must have cost a hundred dollars, and full of the Lord only knows what, and can't get a bid on it!" he roared savagely. "Look at it men! Copper bound and banded, with a double-forged steel lock that a safe-blower couldn't blow, and weighs like —— "

"Four bits!" It was Bricks's voice again.

The auctioneer straightened up with a gesture of despair and glared at the bidder. Then he brought his fist crashing down on the trunk again and leaned out over the grinning crowd.

"Four bits! Fifty cents!" he sneered sarcastically. "I'm bid a half a dollar for a hundred-dollar trunk full of——"

"One hundred dollars!" There was no mistaking that voice.

I jerked my head to the right and there, standing head and neck above those around him, and wearing a high silk hat, was the Bull, and I knew by the direction of his gaze that he was looking at Bricks. Then a voice behind me caught my ear:

"What on earth does Albert S. Townsend want of somebody else's old trunk?"

I turned around.

"Who is the big man in the silk hat?" I asked.

The talker laughed.

"That's Albert S. Townsend, junior," he answered, "He owns the big brick plant down on the flats."

I turned back to the auctioneer. The Bull's old boast had not been a boast after all.

I knew the plant. I had seen Albert S. Townsend senior's death written up in the papers a few months back; that meant the Bull was a millionaire. Once again I tried to get back to Bricks, but I couldn't make it.

"One hundred dollars!" the auctioneer had recovered his voice. "I'm bid a hundred dollars for a——"

"Five hundred real iron dollars!" That was Bricks.

I pulled my hand out of my pocket. There was something doing here between Bricks and the Bull, and I was out of the bidding now. When it was over I'd see Bricks and have a long talk with him.

The auctioneer grinned; his commission was five per cent.

"Five hundred dollars!" he bellowed. "Five hundred once! Five hundred twice! Five——"

"Six hundred!" The Bull's voice held a note of anger now, and, as he turned his head to glance at Bricks, Bricks bid again:

"One thousand milled-edged scads!"

The crowd gasped. The auctioneer opened his mouth to take up the new bid, but the Bull beat him to it. And in his anger he dropped back into the vernacular of the road.

"One thousand, one hundred bucks!" he rasped, and turned square around to face Bricks; and in his little brown eyes I saw blazing the hate of the beast that wants to kill and is caged.

"Fifteen hundred of the long green!" drawled Bricks.

There was that note of determination in Bricks's voice that had usually ended a discussion with me in the old days, and a big tone of amusement. Bricks was enjoying himself. The Bull shot one swift glance at the trunk and faced Bricks again.

"Sixteen hundred beans!" he roared.

The auctioneer grinned. It was plainly evident to all that Albert S. Townsend was near the exploding point.

"Two thousand of the needful!"—Bricks didn't hesitate a second.

"Two thousand one hundred shiners!"—Neither did the Bull.

"Three thousand nice, clean, untainted, not inherited, gold dollars!" Bricks drawled it out with a very pronounced insinuating tone.

Then the Bull let go.

Without a word, his face purple with rage—rage that looked comical indeed in a silk hat—he drove his massive body through the crowd in Bricks' direction.

The crowd surged back. I climbed up on the counter beside the auctioneer so I could see over their heads. The trunk, the cause of it all was forgotten in the excitement of a coming fight.

Bricks stood behind the stove leaning lazily against the wall, his eternal cigarette hanging on his lip, his jaws set in a tantalizing grin, half amusement, half sneering defiance. Always particular about his front, he was even better dressed than the Bull; his clothes were not so loud, showed his better taste.

The Bull, raving with rage, turned loose and, towering a good ten inches above Bricks, doubled up his ponderous fists and shook them within an inch of Bricks' face.

"You—you—you—" he stuttered idiotically.

Bricks rested his hand upon his hip like a sissy and I saw the thumb holding back the edge of his coat for a quick reach to his hip pocket.

"Oh, Mister Bull, I wouldn't say that!" he lisped affectedly.

That was too much. That grin, that lisp, that tone of voice and that name put the teeth on the raw edge of the Bull's rage. I tensed forward. I didn't want to miss anything in the coming scrap that I knew would end but the one way, if Bricks pulled his gun.

But the Bull's road experience came to his aid. He saw that hipped hand of Bricks's, and remembered Bricks' ability to take care of himself just in time. He quit stuttering. He thrust his blazing face down and forward till it was within four inches of Bricks' sneering nose.

"Five thousand dollars!" he exploded.

"Ten thousand!" Bricks taunted.

"Fifteen thousand!" the bull roared.

"Twenty-five thousand!" And Bricks drew a match across the top of the stove and lit his cigarette.

For a second I thought the Bull would go crazy, but he didn't quite. He just drew back about six inches, pulled a long breath and:

"Fifty thousand dollars!" he screamed.

Bricks raised his hand, picked the cigarette butt off his lip and with a spring of his finger flipped it against the wall. He pulled out his watch and glanced at the time. Then, with the Bull's hate-white rage-purple mottled face within four inches of his mouth, he opened wide that mouth:

"It's yours, Bull!" he yawned.

The Bull glared. His mouth worked savagely. His great hands clenched and unclenched. Then his high silk hat toppled off his shaking head and fell with a thud at Bricks' feet. A long sigh went up from the crowd. It laughed.

I can't understand why, but it did. That crowd laughed, held its sides and shrieked with laughter. Then to the Bull came swift realization of the fool he had made of himself. He stiffened up and whirled around. He pulled a check-book out of his pocket and strode through the jeering crowd to the auctioneer.

I jumped down and made my way toward the stove, but the crowd jostled me and I had to fight my way through. When I got there Bricks was gone. I raced out the door forgetful of the sale and everything else. I wanted to see Bricks. I wanted to talk to Bricks. I wanted to know what was in that trunk.

I found Bricks in Otto's café down on the corner, and he recognized me instantly. His hand shot out and fastened on mine.

"The Dreamer! Well I'll be —— !" he greeted, his face all smiles, "I knew you were up here somewhere, but I didn't know you were holding down this burg or I'd have dug you out this morning."

"Bricks, for the love of pete, what was in—was in——"

I started to stutter, then back across the year that had gone, came the six years I had spent on the road, came the old freedom and the rocking sway of the rattling train and the rush of the wind in my face, and it jerked back into my mind the creed—mind your own business. I dropped his hand and held up the old two fingers to the bartender.

Bricks laughed understandingly.

"Old Dad sure was a wise old gink," he said almost gently, his face growing grave again. "And I found his plant, Dreamer. And the Bull and I found——"

He stopped and laughed again.

"You saw me stick a knife into the Bull's goat?" he asked.

Then I grabbed him by the two shoulders, pushed him on to a car and brought him out home here. He had supper with us and has promised faithfully he'll stay with us till the Highball gets to calling too strong again. He's in the next room smoking and thinking of Old Dad. He says that trunk that the Bull, Albert S. Townsend, paid fifty thousand for, arrived here in Toronto containing a plant, but he won't ever be sure the plant was Old Dad's.

Now I am going to ask Bricks to tell you about that. Being his own personal experience, he can tell it better than I:

I HOOKED up with Old Dad because he could chatter the Mex and I couldn't, and I needed some one to do the jewing over the river for the drawn-work while I peddled it in San Antonio. (This is Bricks. The Dreamer is in there walking the floor with the kid.)

Before we started the grift I had a hunch there'd be a roll in it, but I didn't think it would pan out as well as it did. It wasn't a month before we were splitting a hundred fifty-fifty, every seven days. Old Dad sure was a hicky at beating an *hombre's* price down to a frayed jitney and getting across the river with the bundle. He seemed to be able to spot the custom's flies by their kicks.

I was sliding my fifty over the blotter in the First National every week, Old Dad was planting his. Every month end he would slip away and come back half soused and flat. He'd have to borrow from me for his tea and tobacco. Old Dad never would mix, drunk or sober, and I knew he couldn't blow two hundred dollars on booze and mop it up all by his lonesome in the four days he always stayed away. But why he was saving it, and where he was planting it, I never thought to ask him.

We'd been pulling that fifty per nearly three years, and my bank license had begun to look big enough for Australia or maybe India again, when I got wise that Old Dad was starting to slip. He must have been seventy when Bryan started running for president, and the mescal he was lapping up was going to his head higher and worse every trip.

One day he teeters into the Laredo jungles where I was waiting for him to come back, steers his back up to a stump and flops down. He dives into his coat pocket and hands me a paper all folded up, and comes away with a string of that fancy language he used.

"Over the natural course of human existence the will of man has no jurisdiction," says he, thick like and slow. "If anything untoward, anything definite should occur, not stipulated in our arrangements, burn the right-hand bottom corner of that paper."

I slipped the paper into my pocket and later on, when I was alone, I took a slant at it. It was entirely blank.

"Old Dad's going." I told myself.

But a month later when the Bull told me he had croaked and showed me that map, folded just like that paper had been folded I changed my mind. Old Dad had been slipping all right and he had known it, but not the way I doped it. And he had tried to put me wise before he passed over.

So it wasn't a guess or any wise-guy work

when I scorched that map of Old Dad's and located his plant a little north of Presidio del Norte, and I aint wise yet whether it was his plant or not that the Bull and I dug up there, and I don't suppose I ever will be.

When the Dreamer left the Bull and me at San Antonio, we caught the race special for Juarez and dropped off at the K. C. intersection. Two days later we pulled into Presidio del Norte on the rods of a rattler and bought two shovels and a mattock. We figured Old Dad would pick out the most isolated section he could find to plant his money in, and according to the burnt spot on his map it lay about ten miles up the river, so we paid a dirty *hombre* about three times what it was worth for a little warped rowboat as big as an armadillo work-basket and packed a weeks' grub into it.

Next morning at gray streaks we started up the river, taking turns cussing and sweating at the oars, and made ten miles as close as we could figure by ten o'clock. But the little stone houses and dobes along the bank didn't show any signs of thining out so we kept on a couple of miles further and pulled into the bank to take another slant at the map. We figured we must be getting close to the spot, but there were still a few smears of onions, tobacco and beans, and a grape vine or two sticking up beside the dobes and piles of stones, and there wasn't a thing in sight that Old Dad could have represented with five little circles.

Here and there along the bank was a banana-plant or a bunch of thorn-bush, but that was all. Then, all at once, it hits me that those five little circles on Old Dad's map were drawn in a row straight up and down in the column of stops on the time-table, between the two column lines. That meant they were between the two banks of the river, in the water.

I leaned over the outside of the boat, and there, grinning, up at me, was a half-ton pebble with its nose a foot under water. It must have been sticking out six inches in July. I showed it to the Bull. He got excited and I had to take the oars.

We pulled up along the bank, keeping our eyes on the water, and about a hundred feet farther there's another the same size, and farther up another. We kept pulling, looking for the fourth, but there wasn't anything bigger than a sack of tobacco beyond

that. We turned around and rowed back to the first one we'd found and there, sitting on the bank, was the oldest woman I ever got my eyes on. I'll bet my last red, she was a century young when Jim Bowie got his at the Alamo. The Bull looked at her for all of two minutes steady, then he turned to me with an "It-ain't-so" expression on his map.

"Mother of Moses!" he exploded.

"Nothing doing!" I came back. "She's the wrong color and too ancient for that."

"And that face, that map!" he went on, paying no attention to me. "Say Bricks, is that a human map or an old scar?"

"Scar on what?" I laughed. "There ain't nothing there for a scar to grow on."

And I wasn't so far out at that. The old girl wouldn't have dared to go out in a ten-mile draft if she wanted to stick around home. Sitting there on the brown sand with a bunch of cactus behind her, she looked just like a wart on a horse's hock.

And she was watching us like she thought we had come to swipe her beans.

We were so busy sizing her up that we wer'nt watching where we were drifting, and the first thing we're wise to we're half out of the water sitting on another of those pebbles.

I pushed the boat off and we rowed down another hundred feet and found the fourth. The fifth was sticking up out of the water a little farther down. We'd found the five little circles.

I stopped rowing and spread the map out on my knee. I pointed to the sixth little circle that Old Dad had drawn, the one with the dot in it about two and a half inches to the left of the five.

"And this one is—" I started to say.

Then I caught sight of the old señora again. She was sitting up on the bank exactly opposite the middle stone of the five.

I looked at the Bull, and he looked at me and shook his head.

"Guess again!" he growled. "Old Dad never would have drawn a circle to represent that. Maybe he meant the dot for it. We'll go and ask her."

But the old girl didn't wait for us to land. We hadn't more than stepped out on to the sand before she got up and scuttled away sideways like a crawfish so she could keep her eyes on us while she was going. We climbed up on to the higher bank and took a look around.

A hundred yards back from the river was a pile of stones that had been a house in Crockett's days. To the left of that were two dobes and a couple of patches of something green, and behind was a handful of post-oak with a row of little hills beyond.

And sitting in front of one of the dobes was a *hombre* with the biggest lid I ever saw.

The old girl reached the dobe while we were standing there and started waving her arms and screaming something at the *hombre*. Pretty soon he got up and the Bull let a whistle out of him.

We'd thought the old woman was little and ancient, but that *hombre* must have been her grandfather. He looked exactly like a big-top mushroom with that big sombrero on, and walked like if he'd been in a hurry he might have made a furlong in a fortnight. He didn't have more than twenty feet to go to reach the door of the dobe, but we got tired waiting for him to make it and sat down to have another look at the map.

According to Old Dad's drawing, that sixth circle was on the bank somewhere opposite the middle circle of the five, but when the old señora shifted there wasn't anything left on the bank. One of the dobes or the pile of stones might have been that sixth circle but I didn't believe Old Dad would take any one into his confidence; in fact, I was surprised at his making his plant anywhere near where any one lived. Then I saw he'd drawn that sixth circle in the column of times on the time-table, and inside of it was the time 6:05. I showed it to the Bull.

"That circle is six hundred and five something from the middle one of the five," I explained.

"Feet, maybe?" he suggested.

"More like paces," I argued. "Old Dad didn't have a tape line on him when you frisked him, did he?"

He shook his head.

"No, but if he'd made his plant here he'd have to slip up at night to bury it so those peons wouldn't see him," he came back. "And it's a cinch he'd not go far from the river soused or sober. Maybe he added the six and five and it's eleven feet from the middle circle?"

"Or eleven paces?" I saw his argument but I stuck to mine.

The Bull shrugged his great shoulders as if to say, "have your own way," and I got up and went down to the water's edge. As well as I could judge the middle stone of the five was four paces out from the bank. I was about the same size as Old Dad so I put my heel in the water and paced the other seven. Then the Bull brought the shovels and the mattock and we started to dig.

The old señora had been sitting in front of the dobe in the old man's place all that time, but when I stuck a shovel into the ground she got up and hustled for the hills behind. That made me suspicious. When we stopped for dinner she was still away.

We'd dug a hole ten feet square down a yard by that time and found nothing, and all the time the Bull had been arguing with me that we were in the wrong place because the earth and mesquite roots hadn't been disturbed "since the old clucker was a chicken," as he put it, but I had kept our shovels going. There was a big idea beginning to sift into my dome. When I looked back at Old Dad and his shifty eyes, his ancient Colt seven-shooter and his age— when I looked at that old señora and that ancient man of hers, and that pile of stones that once had been a house—when I added all those circumstances together I kept the shovels going.

About five o'clock we struck. The Bull drove his mattock into the bottom of the hole and pulled up about a foot of rotten leather.

"Buffalo hide!" he ejaculated, picking it to pieces with his fingers.

"*Sh-h-h-h!*" I closed him off.

Sitting on the ground, fifty feet from the hole we were digging, was the old girl back again.

 THE Bull straightened up and turned loose a string of rough stuff at her that would have riled a fixed-post policeman, but she didn't understand English or wasn't caring, for she never batted an eye. Then my suspicion grew out of its teens.

I ran my hand over my hip to make sure my gun was willing to work and started the shovel going again. The old girl might have known what it was we were hunting for, but being shy on its location she couldn't dig it up or get any one to dig it up for her. She couldn't see the bottom of the hole from where she was sitting, but I had an idea she knew what was down there, and just the minute we started to take it away she'd begin something of her own. I didn't like that late absence of hers. I'm not a looker after trouble, but I believe in signs and in meeting them more than half-way.

In five minutes we'd uncovered and pulled away a yard of that rotten leather, and under that was a rusty iron box with four big padlocks, one on each corner, that the present-day safe-blower would pick with a weiner. And the box itself must have weighed a good one hundred pounds, empty. It was all the Bull and I could do to lift it out of the dirt when we got our hands under it.

Three feet long it was, by two wide, and fourteen inches deep, and covered with rust scales that we could lift off with our fingers; but for all that, those old blacksmith padlocks were hanging on like a bull-snake to a rattler. The Bull picks up the mattock to knock them off, but I stopped him.

"Nix!" I admonished in a whisper, jabbing a finger in the old girl's direction and sitting down on the box. "We'll take it over on the U. S. side to open it. Wait till it gets dark and we'll throw it into the boat and pull across."

He growled a little about an old fool of a woman, but he caught my drift and let his curiosity and excitement wait. We'd found Old Dad's plant according to his map, after a lot of work, and we couldn't afford to take any chances. We climbed up and sat on the edge of the hole with our feet hanging inside and rolled our cigarettes.

We'd left the boat in the water tied short to a wild banana-plant with everything in it but the mattock and the shovels, and we hadn't any further use for them. We'd had a late dinner and weren't hungry. We were all ready for a quick getaway. But the longer I sat there, watching the old señora watching us, the harder it hit me that we were going to have some fun before we reached Presidio del Norte. My blood was racing across my ears so I could hear it, like it always does just before something happens.

We were only about twenty feet from the water, but that box weighed all of two hundred and a half and there wasn't a handle on it of any kind. There wasn't anybody in sight but the old woman before dark and after that we couldn't have seen them if there were.

The moon wouldn't be up till after midnight and it was darker than the hell-hole on a County Farm. The only way we knew the old girl was still there, was by laying our heads on the ground and spotting her against the sky-line, and I suppose that was the way she was watching us.

About half-past nine I reversed my gun, leaving the barrel sticking out of my pocket. I don't care about killing white or near-white men if I can get away without, and I've found the butt of the new automatic as good as a short hammer in a close mix. Then we dropped into the hole, got under the box, hoisted it out and——

"*Schre—eel*" the old girl let go.

She dug up a screech that echoed out over the water like a grinding truck-wheel on a frosty switch.

We scrambled out and I shot a glance at the hills, but I couldn't see twenty feet. The Bull grabbed up one end of the box and I the other. We started for the boat. Behind the high bank, ten feet lower down, rose up six husky peons. I could count them against the sheen of the ripples on the water. They were so close I caught the glint of their knives. But we beat them to the boat.

The Bull jumped into the water and swung his end up on to the stern. I heaved myself over on the other side of the stern and the box was in the boat.

The Bull whirled around. He drew back his powerful arm and drove his fist square into the face of the first *hombre*. The *hombre* rose up and fell back on his neck. The second one let drive at me with a streak of steel and ripped my coat sleeve to the shoulder. I crashed the butt of my gun into his mouth.

The third tripped over the one the Bull had dropped and sprawled on his face. The Bull stamped on his head and ground his face into the sand. Then he swung on the fourth. He missed. They clinched. I got busy with the other two.

They came at me together with a foot of knife swung back and an arm up to take my blows, but they were too yellow to close in. First one would drive at me and jump back, and then the other. I kept dodging and trying to get close enough to one of them to drop him; but they were too quick for me.

Then one of them nicked me on the hip. That got my goat. I reversed the gat.

The one on the right went down with two

slugs in his feet, I couldn't have missed them at that distance if I'd tried. The other turned, when the gun flashed, and ran. I whirled around to help the Bull, but he didn't need it. The fourth *hombre* was in the river and the Bull was in the boat, holding his head under water. The whole scrap hadn't lasted two minutes.

I untied the stern rope, threw it into the boat and swung my foot overside.

"Quick!" I yelled. "Get those oars into the locks!"

The Bull let go the *hombre's* hair and leaned forward to give me a hand, I thought, but——

A million little sparks sprang out of nowhere. The boat and the sheen on the water danced wildly. The sand ran out under my feet. Everything began to fade out slowly like the power going off an incandescent. I could feel myself slipping away.

"Hang on, Bricks! Hang on, Bricks!" I tried to yell at myself, but I couldn't get my mouth open.

Then everything came back suddenly— jerked up short it seemed. I was sitting on top of one of the groaning peons and three of my front teeth were swimming around in my mouth. Out on the river, twenty feet away, the Bull was pulling down-stream like a fly-cop was after him. Then I got wise.

The Bull had sunk his great fist into my face when he leaned forward. He was getting away alone with the box.

I jumped to my feet and pulled my gun. I could get him quite easy at that distance against the ripples on the water. Then I slipped my gat back on my hip and started on the run for Presidio del Norte. I'd beat him in and be waiting for him when he got in.

I didn't.

Every time I left the water to look for a road or a short cut across a bend, I lost the river in the dark and wasted hours unraveling myself from onion beds and bean patches and cactus entanglements. Finally the moon came up and I reached Presidio hours behind the Bull. He had the current behind him and pulled an oar like a launch screw.

The first thing the Bull would do, I figured, was to get a line on the first train across the river, but he'd have to get the stuff in that box into something that wouldn't attract attention, before he could take it on a train.

So when I reached the depot and found the first train, for five hours getting ready to high-ball, I started on a still-hunt for the Bull. I found him in the baggage-room, checking a big copper-bound trunk on a ticket as long as his leg. I kept out of his sight and followed him aboard the train.

The Bull must have seen me get up after he'd hit me and start down the river after him, but he knew me well enough that he was safe while he was in a crowd. No doubt he felt quite easy after he got on the train and the wheels started moving.

I found him in an empty smoker, hanging half out of the window to look back to the depot for me. He didn't hear me till I got my gun into his ribs. He dropped back into his seat like some one had hit him in the face.

"Well I'll—" he ejaculated.

"Sure!" I blazed. "If you don't cough up the check for that trunk—quick!"

He reached into his vest pocket and pulled out the check. He held it up and made a pretense of kissing it good-by on both sides. Then with a lightning jerk he flipped it out of the window.

I shot a side glance after it, and down below the river stood out in the moonlight. He'd known well I wouldn't pull trigger on a moving train crossing the water.

I jabbed him again with the gun as a reminder.

"Now the gat!" I snapped.

He reached back to his hip and grinned. He handed me Old Dad's ancient seven-shooter.

Back of the smoker the vestibule door slammed. I slipped both guns into my pockets and dropped back into the seat facing the Bull.

"Tickets please?"

It was the con and right back of him was the auditor. They looked at my ripped coat sleeve and swollen mouth, and at the Bull's dirty face and grinned. The Bull dug into his breast pocket and handed the con that long ticket of his.

"Toronto, Canada," says the con, tearing off about a foot of the ticket and giving it back to the Bull.

The Bull was going home to pa. I pulled out a roll that chased the con's sarcastic grin into a pleased smile.

"Toronto, Canada, straight through!" I barked; I was going home with the Bull.

But the con couldn't give me the ticket; I

had to get off at Fort Worth and buy it from the agent. And all the way I sat opposite the Bull and kept an eye on him. When we stopped at a lunch station he'd get off and I'd stand beside him while he ate, eating too, and I never opened my mouth to him.

AT ST. LOUIS while we waited for Wabash connections, I bought a new coat in a clothing store where he was fitting on a new hat and collar and tie. At Detroit I sat down at the same table in a restaurant, and then, just to have some sport with him, I let him get away from me.

I hung back till he was a block ahead and slipping up a side street walked back to the square. I took a ferry over to Windsor, and when his train came in and started to pull out again, I strolled into the coach where he was sitting, all smiles, and flopped down facing him. Pulling out of London I brought out Old Dad's revolver and gave it a once over.

I've seen some badly used weapons one place and another, but that old Colt was the worst victim of neglect I ever did see. There were seven cartridges so badly rusted into the cylinder that I would have needed a hammer and a punch to drive them out. The barrel was packed full of dirt. The butt was chipped and scarred where Old Dad had been using it to break up firewood, and the trigger-guard was clean gone. I rubbed the top of the barrel above the cylinder on the seat to clean off some of the rust and dirt and found the maker's name: Samuel Colt, 1839.

I slipped the old relic back into my pocket and tapped the Bull with my foot.

"No wonder you didn't pull it in the scrap!" I jeered.

He didn't answer; just kept looking out of the window.

"What did you want it for anyway?" I asked.

He didn't pay any attention.

"I'll put it in the trunk when we get to Toronto," I taunted.

But that didn't move him either, so I shut up and let him alone.

At the depot, here in Toronto, he hustled into the baggage-room with me right behind him.

"I've lost the check of my trunk," said he, holding up one of the baggage-smashers. "How am I going to get the trunk?"

"Bring the key and identify it by its contents," and the smasher grabbed up his truck and hurried away.

I looked at the Bull's face; he was very disappointed. That gave me a hunch. If he'd lifted the old iron box intact into the trunk, all he'd have to do was to describe the box and get the trunk without further trouble, but it was very evident he didn't want to expose the contents, so he must have opened the iron box and dumped the contents into the trunk.

When he left the baggage-room and climbed into a taxi, I took the elevator to the third floor and put in my application for a job in the baggage-room. I knew I couldn't get the trunk without the check, and that was beyond recall, and I didn't know what was in it, so I couldn't identify it, but I'd find out what was in it if I could just get my hands on it for a while.

They took my name and address, the color of my hair and eyes, my age, height and weight, and if they'd thought of it they'd have taken my Bertillon. It was worse than joining the army. And Ananias didn't have anything on me in answering those questions. The next morning they put me on.

Along about three in the P. M. down comes the Bull, all dolled up with a silk hat on, and tries to get the trunk again. But he wouldn't tell the baggage boss what was in it—so he didn't get it. I kept back so he wouldn't see me, and after that I didn't see him again.

I tried for a solid month to get at that trunk when no one was around, but I never got a chance, and all the time I was wondering why the Bull wasn't trying to get it. Then I learned about the unclaimed baggage sale and got wise. The Bull knew I couldn't get the trunk, no way. He didn't want to identify it by the contents. All he had to do was to wait for the sale and buy it for ten or fifteen dollars at the most. That gave me an idea.

I took an impression of the locks and got two keys made to fit. I bought an old second-hand trunk, loaded it and sent it down to the depot on a baggage-wagon. In a month that trunk of mine was in the unclaimed room with the copper-bound trunk of the Bull's.

Then I waited till I could get into that room when no one was looking. I waited eight months. I had begun to think I would have to wait for the sale myself and that would put me out on my idea. One day there was a wreck out in the yards and in about a minute the baggage-rooms were empty.

It didn't take me a second to get that copper-bound trunk open. And when I lifted the lid, when I saw the contents——

I jerked Old Dad's map out of my pocket and spread it out under a light. Then because I was looking for it, I found what I'd missed.

When I burned the right-hand bottom corner of that map with my cigarette, it had been folded double in four, so that when I opened it out again the burned spot came about the middle of the left half, on the intersection of the twofold creases. But there were twofold creases crossing the same way on the right half of the map too, that the cigarette hadn't touched. And they crossed about two miles east of San Antonio.

"And the San Antonio jungles are just two miles east of the city," I was saying to myself. "And Old Dad died there, and the jungles are in a long gully, and there are five fireplaces in the gully."

And next morning I bought a through ticket for San Antonio and rode the cushions.

I didn't lose a minute buying a spade and getting out to the jungles when I got to San Antonio. The jungles looked like a desert without Old Dad and the Dreamer. I put my heel at the outside edge of the ashes of the middle fire of the five and paced off eleven paces. The ground was flat and undisturbed.

I went back to the fireplace and set my heel again. I paced off six hundred and five strides that time and put my last foot into a pile of brush. I dragged that away and found a little mound of fresh earth.

In five minutes I uncovered an old fifty-pound lard can with three two-quart glass sealers in it, packed in grass. I opened them and pulled out three rolls of First National Bank bills, and a note written in Old Dad's little cramped hand. I counted the money. There was exactly eight thousand dollars in the three rolls. Then I read the note. It ran:

DEAR BRICKS:—

The Dreamer has been telling us for months that he is going to quit the road and get married. But he knows the call of the Highball which, after all, is but a call to new scenes, new excitements, new ad-

ventures; and always when he hears the two short blasts of the whistle, his blood will run hot and he'll want to be up and away. He's got a long, hard fight ahead of him, a fight I lost.

Bricks, as man to man, I ask you—see that the Dreamer's wife gets the enclosed money, so that if he loses the fight at times, his children will not want for anything while he's away."

Sincerely yours,
OLD DAD.

I came back to Toronto and got here on the day of the sale. The Dreamer has told you of that. But the Dreamer was a little late for the sale, and so was the Bull. Before they came I bought my trunk, the second-hand one that I had changed the contents of the Bull's trunk into that day in the baggage-room, for eleven dollars, and sent it up to my boarding-house. If that auctioneer had known what was in it, he'd have had apoplexy.

There were seventeen bars of refined silver as long as a policeman's night-stick; four bricks of red Mexican gold as big as a two hundred cigar-box, and seventy-five thousand dollars in Confederate paper money that weren't worth the ink it took to print them; but I'll bet the Bull thought they were real money.

Tomorrow I'm going to get the metal weighed up. I'm going to add another eight thousand dollars to Old Dad's and give it to Mrs. Dreamer to buy a pair of corduroy strides for the Dreamer when the Highball gets to calling him, and give her Old Dad's note. And I'm going to let them think Old Dad left the whole thing when he heard his last Highball.

So when the Highball came up from the railroad yards on the flats a while ago, it brought to me in the next room and to the Dreamer sitting here at the typewriter— Old Dad.

Who was Old Dad?

Was that rusty iron box that the Bull and I dug up on the bank of the Rio Grande a plant of his? And did he duplicate his old scheme of marking a plant when he buried the savings of his last three years in the San Antonio jungles? Or was it mere coincidence that the crease lines on Old Dad's map crossed just where they did on the Rio Grande when he folded it to mark his San Antonio plant on the right half? I've seen stranger things.

Who was Old Dad? I don't know. All I know is, he left Mrs. Dreamer eight thousand dollars. And whoever buried that box above Presidio del Norte left it to me. Wasn't there four red gold bricks in that box? And ain't my hair red, and my name Bricks? I can almost hear him say after he'd covered it up:

"There—that's four Red Bricks!"

I wonder did the Bull, Albert S. Towns-end, have that high silk hat on when he opened that copper-bound trunk that he paid fifty thousand for? And I wonder did it fall off when he saw those forty-two nice white Townsend bricks I put in it when I changed its contents into my trunk that day in the baggage-room? I wonder!

REVOLT

BY HERBERT HERON

THE cities of dead courage and despair
    Have sapped my strength; and I must go to share
  The vigil of the hills beside the sea,
And breathe again an unpolluted air!

My life is numb: I can not bear the weight
Of crowded human misery! My fate
  Shall be unrolled where Truth is nearest earth,
In some old seaward forest, lone and great——

Where mountains wake and listen to the rills
And laughing streams; where boundless beauty fills
  My heart with songs like David in his joy,
Who shepherded the singing of the hills.

My soul is roused from sleep: I will not stay
A slave of Time! My spirit soars away
  And bids me follow where the ocean winds
Blow out across the starlight and the day.

I will not be a captive! I am free!
I see far off the gleam of liberty.
  And plunge down through the valley of the night
To hail the red dawn rising from the sea!

GASTON OLAF

A THREE-PART STORY. PART TWO
by Henry Oyen.

Author of "The Snow Burner," "The Man-Trail," etc.

Havens Falls is one of the last lumber settlements on the St. Croix River, Wisconsin. In it, one faction, led by *Devil Dave Taggart*, lumber king, is working to keep the town lawless so that decent people, who might investigate his timber operations, will not live there.

Richard Hale, Dr. Sanders, and *Rose Havens* lead the respectable element. But they are losing out, when into the settlement rushes *Gaston Olaf François Thorson*, a fighting young giant of French-Norse descent, with his partner, *Tom Pine*. *Gaston* saves *Miss Havens* from the insults of "*Red Shirt*" *Murphy*, leader and driver of *Taggart's* lumbermen, who are derelicts from every camp in the North, working under *Devil Dave's* wing, since he will protect them from the law. *Gaston* whips *Murphy* in a saloon, which to *Gaston's* surprise forces *Rose Havens* to believe him a common brawler.

Gaston hires out to *Taggart* as boss in Murphy's place. He finds the timber tract about to be cut, suspiciously well guarded by *Taggart's* men; also that back in the woods *Devil Dave* has a fine house where live two women who carouse with him, and whom he tells *Gaston Olaf* are his sister and niece.

Gaston decides *Taggart's* is no white man's outfit. He and *Tom Pine* leave it. On their way to Havens Falls they come upon *Hale*, who, while trying to approach *Taggart's* timber territory, has been shot in the leg. They rush him to the settlement. There *Gaston* learns that *Devil Dave* is really stealing timber owned by *Rose Havens*. And he has been aiding in the theft! Now he must line up with one side or the other.

CHAPTER XIV

TAGGART'S SYSTEM

FOR a space there was silence in the room. Then the doctor's voice, incredulously:

"Oh, my stars! Robbing a girl, alone with her mother! The grinding old devil! Has he got the nerve, the heart, to do a thing like this? H'm, h'm! Of course. Nerve and heart to do anything. Devil Dave has. But this—this is beyond the limit."

"I was afraid he'd do it," said Hale. "That bunch of pine always was a thorn in his side. It was the one valuable piece of timber that old Havens managed to hang on to, to leave to his daughter when he died. Taggart had managed to freeze, or swindle, or buy him out of everything else except

that and Mrs. Havens's homestead quarter section here in town.

"Taggart's point of view is that this country belongs to him. It angered him to think that some one else possessed the best piece of timber around here. He tried to buy before Havens was buried. As executor and agent I had to deal with him. He said: 'Sell to me for five thousand dollars, or you'll never log a foot of that pine.'

"I told him twenty-five thousand would be nearer a fair price. 'But five thousand is better than nothing,' he said. I asked him what he meant. He said: 'Nobody touches that timber but myself. Try to log it and see. You've got just this Winter to log it in, too, because if it isn't mine by next August dry spell a fire'll go through it that won't leave anything standing but stumps.' We tried to log it this Winter. We couldn't even get men to go up and clear space for a camp. I've got a small sawmill outfit here. I can't get men to set it up. Taggart warned them—that was enough. Our hands were tied.

"I knew Taggart never intended to send that timber up in smoke. Not that he'd have any compunction about it, but he's too avaricious. He's been in a cold rage ever since the sale was refused him. His men began to make things rougher in the settlement at once. Then this new crew came in. I suspected something then. When I heard it given out that a new camp was to be started within eight miles of town I knew something was wrong, because there isn't any pinery that near town that hasn't one of Taggart's camps in it.

"The men got drunk and got out of hand. Murphy got drunk, too, and lost his grip on them. He tried to start them for camp the second day. They laughed at him. Murphy was done for. He'd never have got them out.

"I began to hope the crew would go to pieces, and it would be too late to get another together in time to get much logging done before Spring. Taggart didn't have another man who could handle that crew. He could have done it himself, but that isn't Taggart's way. He has others do his dirty work for him."

"And that was me," interjected Gaston bitterly. "I came along, and Taggart fooled me into becoming his tool."

"This morning I hooked up and took a drive, following the tracks of the sleighs," continued Hale. "I guess they'd expected maybe I'd do something of the sort. Maybe some one noticed me leaving town; Taggart's Indian can run faster than a horse can travel. Well, we found out, anyhow, thanks to you fellows. Taggart's started to rob the Havens of everything they possess."

"Hah? Everything? What do you mean?" cried Dr. Sanders.

"There's five thousand dollars mortgage against that timber, secured by Mrs. Havens's homestead," said Hale. "The mortgage is held by the bank down at La Croix."

"Well? What of it?"

"If Taggart succeeds in his steal there'll be no lumber, no money, and the mortgage on the homestead will be foreclosed."

The doctor laughed in desperation.

"H'm, h'm. Cunning little Devil David! How like the man! Puts you between the

7

devil and the deep sea, and he's both of 'em. H'm, h'm. Octopus, devil-fish. Very complicated. This needs thinking about."

"Thinking ——!" said Tom Pine. "Ain't these women got any men-folk of their own?"

"They have not."

"Well—" it was a very simple matter to Tom, and he spoke matter of fact—"they's four of us here. Since these women ain't got no men-folk of their own, we got to stand by 'em and see they ain't done wrong. So we just draw lots, the four of us, to see who puts a bullet through old Taggart's head or makes him quit."

To Tom's surprise his suggestion was received without any enthusiasm. Even Gaston Olaf shook his head.

"Those good old days are gone, Tom Pine—here, anyway," he said.

"Why be they?" demanded Tom. "He's doing lone women dirt, ain't he? Why shouldn't somebody get him?"

"Because things have changed, old fire-eater!" replied Dr. Sanders with a tinge of regret in his voice. "The old order passeth; law and order taketh its place—at least let's hope so."

"Law and order!" snorted Tom Pine. "Well, I never felt comf'table where they was too much of that around. Out in the woods no hairy old wolf like Taggart could sneak the grub-bag away from a couple of lone women, if they was any men around, without getting a lung blowed out of him, and you know it. And just because he knew that'd happen to him he wouldn't go try it. Here—'law and order' you sez; 'things has changed.' Well, I should say they has! Gaston—Gaston Olaf—I believe you've changed, too."

Gaston did not reply. He realized the impossibility of making Tom Pine see things as he saw them now, since he had sat at table with Rose Havens and her mother in their home. He had not changed. Men do not change so suddenly, so radically, so dramatically. But in some men a portion of their true self long lies dormant, awaiting the crisis of circumstances to bring it into active control of their personality.

Gaston had not changed. He had lived only at the dictates of one side of his nature so far, the care-free, unthinking, reckless *coureur de bois* side of him, the side of him which made a laugh of life, which had kept his quick feet on the Restless Ones' trail with never a thought of tomorrow, never an idea of remaining any longer in one spot than was pleasant to his vagrant fancy. But back of him there was also a long strain of severe, sober-minded Norsemen, a breed which even in the days of its sea-robber glory held so stern a passion for the Home and the Law that peasants rose and sorrowfully slew their hero-kings who dared to transgress the Law or violate the Home. Wherefore Gaston Olaf, at the ordered, home-table of the Havens, had hungered mightily; and wherefore now he shook his head while Tom Pine uttered his lawless suggestion.

"You've got a sheriff in this county, haven't you?" he asked; and Tom Pine looked at him in disgust.

"A sheriff! Hell's fire and six-bits, Gaston Olaf! What's come over you?"

Hale smiled bitterly and looked at Sanders.

"H'm, h'm! A sheriff? Oh, yes. Yes, yes; of course the county's got a sheriff," said the doctor. "He's down at La Croix. I think he—h'm, h'm—tends bar down there. Taggart keeps him, because sometimes he finds a sheriff handy to do his dirty work."

Gaston stood looking heavily at the floor for a long time.

"So that's the way it is," he muttered at last. "Then I guess 'Devil Dave's' got the drop, hasn't he? I take it you fellows here ain't got an idea that he can be stopped?"

The doctor shrugged his shoulders. Hale looked away.

"Have you?" insisted Gaston. "Get down to hard-pan—not what you hope, or expect, but the solid facts—have you got any idea of a way to stop Taggart from stealing this girl's timber?"

"Sure they have!" sneered Tom Pine. "The law—law'n order. They'll have the law on him, won't you, gents?"

"We will go to La Croix and take it into court, of course," said Hale.

"Which," said the doctor, "considering that Taggart owns the court, too, isn't much of a hopeful move."

"Not for immediate action," admitted Hale. "But the case will be on record. Taggart won't control the court much longer, if we manage to get the decent element on top, as we hope to do. Then there will be opportunity for justice to be done."

"Talk! Nothing but talk. You can't lick Taggart with your mouth. While you're going to law Taggart will have the timber chopped down, the drive down the river, and the logs sold. He'll be stronger than ever; he'll be so strong that you fellows won't dare to make a chirp. Can't you see what this is? It's his notice to you fellows to pack up and travel. It's his way of letting you know that this country is his and that he'll do just as he pleases, take what he pleases, and the law can't touch him. No, that won't do. If he isn't licked on this job, you'll never lick him. And you can't do it, can you?"

"I don't see how we can," admitted Hale.

"Neither do I. You aren't the kind of fellows to lick one of the old breed like Taggart. That ain't saying anything against you; you're good men in town. But Taggart's an old wolf of the woods. It'll take one of his own kind to have a chance against him. You can't get an old wolf's scalp if he knows you're hunting him."

Gaston's lids were narrowed to mere slits, and his eyes were peering out of the window with a far-away, wistful look in the blue of them.

"Boys, are you satisfied now that I'm a white man? All right. Then that's understood; so no matter what happens you'll know it's—square. No matter what. The man who beats an old wolf like Taggart has got to make funny-looking trails. All right."

He moved briskly toward the door.

"There's no use saying anything to the girl about what Taggart's at. No use worrying her before it's necessary. There's only the four of us who know. We'll keep it so, eh?"

Hale nodded.

"H'm, h'm. Got something up your sleeve, Thorson?" asked the doctor.

Gaston thrust out his long arm, stiff and hard as an iron bar.

"Sure!" he laughed. "Take a feel of that."

CHAPTER XV

GASTON HAS A SCHEME

ON THE long wooden bench beside the door of Mrs. Olson's hostelry Gaston Olaf seated himself in the sun, pulled his cap far down over his eyes, and sat staring apparently at the rubbers on his feet. Tom Pine, as was his wont, seated himself at

Gaston's side, bit off a chew, spat into the snow, and waited.

He knew these moods, did Tom Pine. They came at regular intervals and contrasted strangely with the buoyant scheme of life as normally pursued by Gaston Olaf. While in their grasp Gaston's boyish laughter was stilled. The impulse to be up and going, to be playing, to be blowing off steam in some wild fashion, was dead or dormant for the time being. Gaston, on such occasions, sat by himself, serious of mien, wanting to be left alone.

"He's Norwegian today," said Tom Pine on such days, and waited patiently for the mood to pass.

Despite Gaston's incredible weakness in suggesting an appeal to a sheriff, Tom sat contentedly by his side, placidly chewing, holding his peace, waiting. It was pleasant enough there in the sun, and Tom knew that Gaston's thoughts were working in a fashion that presaged immediate action.

When Gaston roused himself he did it slowly, heavily, in contrast to his usual lightning-like movements. He drew his long legs up slowly, straightened his shoulders, and pushed back his cap.

"Tom," he drawled, "we got to get back in that camp."

"All right," agreed Tom. He realized that it was no time to differ with Gaston now. "It's a rotten place for a white man to be, but I 'spect you got an idee?"

Gaston nodded.

"We got to get back in good standing. We've got to be Taggart's men again. To do that you got to get good and drunk."

Tom Pine's mouth and eyes opened wide with amazement.

"Get drunk? You mean it, Gaston Olaf?" A smile wreathed his lips. "Well, if I got to do it, I s'pose——"

Gaston rose with him.

"What! You're going to get drunk, too, Gaston Olaf?"

"Not much. You see, it's this way, Tom: you suddenly discovered you had to have liquor this morning. So you streaked it for town. I took after you, to bring you back. You're drunk now, understand, and I'm just drinking with you to keep you in good humor, so you'll come back to camp peaceful. Understand?"

Tom stared and blinked, and a look of admiration spread over his countenance.

"You old son of a gun!" he breathed in awe.

Suddenly he lurched into the street, threw his cap in the snow and leaped on it.

"Wow!" he bellowed. "Turn me loose! Nobody gets me back to camp till I've drinked this settlement dry. Wow! Come on, boys! Let 'er roar!"

SO THEY proceeded to "let 'er roar" a little in the good old fashion of the bad, old river towns. They surged together through the door of the nearest saloon. They leaned against the bar upon which Tom Pine's mallet-like fists beat in a fierce tattoo.

"Licker! Licker! Licker!" The voice of Tom was strident and drunken. "Whoopla! Out with your poison! Let it come hot an' quick. I'm off the res'vation, and they ain't no foreman going to get me to camp till the last drink's drinked. Money? Come outside an' take it out of my hide like a man."

Tom drank and surged out again, while Gaston paid and hurried after.

"Give the boys something. Give 'em all something. Belly up, boys. 'S on me, an' any man refuses to drink with me's got to put me on my back."

They were in another place now, and Tom Pine was more belligerent than ever.

"Come on; let's go back to camp," insisted Gaston loudly. "You've had enough."

"Enough?" The liquor had really begun to work in Tom's veins, and he was drolly conscious that he was only half acting. "Enough? For me? Hoh! Got to make the rounds first."

So they made the rounds, swinging through one saloon door after another, drinking sometimes, sometimes skilfully quarreling and leaving before the drinks were ordered. In Jack McCarthy's place they saw Charley, the Indian, in a corner, and there they came so close to blows, apparently, that they parted company, Tom to fume over his liquor at one end of the bar while Gaston drank a small glass of beer with McCarthy at the other end. The Indian slipped out unobserved.

"S'prised to see you back in town so soon," offered McCarthy tentatively. "Anything go wrong out at camp?"

"Nothing but that thing there," replied Gaston, with a disgusted nod at Tom. "He's a corker, that little partner of mine is. Wouldn't drink anything to speak of yesterday when we were in town. But this morning, just as the work got started, the thirst hit him. Nothing to do with him then except throw him down and tie him up. I happened to be away from camp a few minutes, and when I came back he was gone.

"He's my partner, you know, and he gets bad if he gets on a bat all alone. I just naturally had to come after him, trying to catch him before he hit town. He'd come across this Hale with a hole in his leg before I caught him. He wouldn't go back then—too good a chance to get a ride to town. Well, he's my partner. I had to come along to watch him; but I'll have him back in camp tonight or break his little back."

McCarthy winked and lowered his voice.

"No need to do that. Any time you're ready to start we'll slip a few drops o' medicine into his drink and he'll go to sleep like a little babe."

"We'll try it later, maybe. He's bound to make the rounds. When he's through mebbe he'll listen to reason."

From McCarthy's the way led back toward the hotel. At each step Tom grew more vociferous, and a crowd began to follow along. In the last place the little man called himself content and willing to start back to camp; so out they came tumbling, arm in arm, and lurched down to the stables. There the stableman, laughing at Tom's efforts to help him, hooked up a light team, and the drive to camp was begun.

In the tamarack swamp, two miles out, they met Taggart, with Charley, the Indian, in the cutter beside him. Gaston saw that the latter was wet with perspiration and knew that he had run out from Mc-Carthy's to meet his employer.

Taggart was thoroughly sober now. He sat sunk down in the cutter, his chin on his chest, his eyes cold, elusive. He did not pull up as the sleighs swung out to pass in the narrow road. He did not even look up.

"You'll never go far with such a partner, Thorson," he whined as he whisked past.

Gaston gave a great sigh of relief. Indian Charley apparently had repeated the tale Gaston had spun for his benefit in McCarthy's, and Taggart had accepted it, never crediting Gaston and Tom with sub-

tleness enough for guile. That danger was past.

"And now," thought Gaston, "we'll see if a young wolf can out-fox an old one."

CHAPTER XVI

TOM PINE IS PUZZLED

IN THE next two weeks Gaston Olaf satisfied Taggart that his judgment of the young man had not been amiss. As a man-driver and company bully of a rotten hell-camp, Gaston proved himself well up to the difficult Taggart standard. Murphy, the camp-boss, laid out the work; Gaston flung the men at it.

Sometime in his career Murphy undoubtedly had learned the logging business under masters of the craft. His skill in directing the work so that the logs went rolling out on the ice of the lake with the least confusion, marked him for an expert logger. As a handler of men he was hopeless, the men reading the constant fear in his eyes and laughing at him when he attempted mastery.

They did not laugh at Gaston. He had set his foot too firmly on their necks in the beginning. When he shouted they jumped, and he shouted often. His manner was changed. He laughed but seldom, and a certain fierce grimness had taken the place of his old recklessness. Often he paced to and fro behind a crew, hands behind his back, head thrust forward, apparently oblivious of their presence. But let them slacken a moment in their work and:

"Hi! Wake up, you rats! Want me to put the corks to you?"

No crew of true lumberjacks—the cockiest type of worker in the world—would have stood his driving for one day, and not for a minute would Gaston have attempted to drive them so.

But these were not true lumberjacks. They were beaten, broken men, or men with a price on their heads, who knew they were safe only under Taggart's protection.

At rare intervals one of them, the strength coming back to his heart and muscles through enforced abstinence and hard labor, ventured to grumble. And then the others looked at him after Gaston had dealt punishment and bent their backs lower in toil.

At times Gaston went away by himself. Tom Pine saw him sometimes at a distance, tramping feverishly up and down between the pines, his hands clenched behind his back, head forward, eyes on the ground. Sometimes at night he was seen so. He did not sleep well. Tom Pine, attempting to chaff him out of the mood, was rebuffed.

"Dry up. Can't you ever get over talking and thinking like a boy?" Gaston was very curt. "Boy's talk! Silly nonsense! What kind of talk is that for grown men to have in their mouths?"

Tom Pine did not understand. Here were he and Gaston Olaf bent on saving this pine for that girl down in Havens Falls, and yet here was Gaston Olaf doing his best to get the pine down in a hurry, doing his best, apparently, to serve Taggart's ends. For under Gaston's dynamic driving the crew of bums was rivaling in its daily output that of a crew of real lumberjacks.

Each day the dark carpet of logs spread farther out over the white Winter covering of the lake. Each day the clearing grew larger, the number of pines standing were fewer.

"Gaston Olaf," Tom burst out testily one morning as he noted how the cut was growing, "I know you ain't no Swede, and I don't go for to call you one, but I do put it up to you that you certainly don't seem to be showing no more brains than if you was one."

"So?" Gaston did not laugh, but merely stood and waited for Tom to explain.

"You bet. Here we're out to help these lone womenfolk save their pine, and instead of doing it, here you're driving hell-bent-for-election to get the stuff down—playing right in Taggart's hands."

"Yes?"

"Well, ain't you?"

"Am I?"

Tom Pine swung away in disgust.

"Hell's-fire-and-six-bits! I'm your partner; you got a right to let me know your scheme, but I'll be —— if I ask you what it is."

Gaston made no reply. But as the cut grew larger, he grew more and more moody, walked more by himself, and grew troubled about the eyes. To hide these signs he drove the men harder and harder.

ONE Saturday morning Gaston came down to the stable where Tom was bringing out his team, and Tom, looking at him by the light of a lantern saw that the troubled look was gone from Gaston's eyes and that he almost smiled.

"Tom Pine," he said with just a touch of the old manner, "I think it is time for you to break loose again."

"Hah?"

"The time has come, Tom Pine, for the thirst to hit you, hard and sudden. You're going to sneak off and quit. You're going to hit town and let 'er roar a little. Is that plain?"

"Plain as a bird's flight to a blind man, Gaston Olaf. What'n'ell you driving at?"

Gaston made sure that they were quite alone.

"I want to see that man, Hale, and you've got to be the go-between. So you quit, and go and stay in town. You tell Hale I want to see him down by the Big Bayou on the La Croix tomorrow night, Sunday, at that bayou he's got marked as a good mill-site on that map of his, you know. Tell him to slip away on the quiet and be there about eight o'clock. Tell him it's just the three of us to know about it."

"All right, Gaston Olaf. Now you go on and tell me what scheme you got."

Gaston shook his head, his jaw set forbiddingly.

"Don't talk like a boy. This is no time for such stuff. Do what you're told and don't talk about it. I want to see Hale at Big Bayou tomorrow night at eight. And don't act like a kid when you get to town, and get drunk and blab all you know."

Tom Pine looked wonderingly after Gaston as the latter strode away toward where the men were beginning work.

"That's a —— of a way to treat a pardner," mused the little man, "but I know you, Gaston Olaf, I know you like a book, and I suspect you've figgered out a big scheme, and I'd be a poor pardner if I didn't obey your orders and quit this beautiful job and go to town and let 'er roar."

Tom did not travel the tote-road when, soon after this, he slipped away unobserved. The craft and guile of the old woodser was Tom's, and he had no notion of risking himself in the vicinity of the old camp building on the creek.

"If I did, that rifle artist might see me, and then I might not be able to let 'er roar according to Gaston Olaf's orders."

So he swung far into the timber away from the creek, circled the big ridge, and made his trail toward Havens Falls run parallel to the tote-road but half a mile to one side. However, half-way to town, his curiosity overcame him. The Big Bayou on the La Croix, where Gaston had appointed his rendezvous with Hale, was constantly in his mind.

What did the bayou have to do with it? Was it possible that a man might get a hint of Gaston's scheme by taking a look at the bayou?

Tom paused, took his bearings and saw that he was about six miles from town, which was just the distance at which the bayou was marked on Hale's map.

"And it ain't more'n three-quarters of a mile over to the La Croix," mused Tom. "I'll step over and take a look."

He found the bayou with little trouble. It was practically a long, narrow lake, lying parallel to the river and separated from it only by a narrow spine of earth perhaps twenty feet high and ten feet wide. The lower end of the bayou was connected with the river by a narrow opening in the bank, through which the river overflowed in high water.. The river along the bayou was narrow and punctuated here and there by jagged black rocks which jutted up above the soft gray ice.

"A hard place to take a drive through," said Tom, studying the scene with knowing eyes, "and that fellow Hale is right about that bayou making a sweet log-pond if they was a mill on it. But what'n'ell has that got to do with getting the start of old Taggart?"

He puzzled his gray head over the problem in vain.

"But Gaston Olaf, he sees," he concluded, as he turned away; and confident of his leader's scheme, though ignorant of what it was, he swung back away from the river and went on his way to town.

He did not seek out Hale immediately upon his arrival in the settlement. He first let 'er roar a little to let people know that he was in town and on a bat. When he had sufficiently advertised this fact he lurched up to Dr. Sanders's office.

"What ho! Drunk again, eh?" greeted the doctor. "Have one with me."

"Look again, Doc," said Tom. "Do I look drunk now?"

Dr. Sanders whistled.

"You certainly looked drunk coming in. Drunk in the legs. Sober in the eye. What's the idea?"

"Where's Hale?"

"Sitting up in his room across the street."

"All right. Have me that drink ready, Doc. I'll be back to get it pretty quick."

He staggered so when he crossed the street that Hulda, meeting him on the stairway, made to bar his way.

"Message from Dr. Sanders to Mr. Hale," said Tom gruffly. "Doctor's business."

"Of, ef et's Dr. Sanders——"

Tom slipped by and found Hale in an armchair, busy with papers and books.

"Thorson says he wants to see you at the big bayou at eight tomorrow night, and tell nobody, and let nobody see you go," he said. "But how'n'ell are you going to make it if your leg's still bunged up?"

"Did Thorson send you in to tell me that?"

"He shore did."

"Then I'll be there," said Hale quietly, and turned to his papers.

CHAPTER XVII

"FOR ROSE HAVENS"

ON SUNDAY evening Gaston lay on a bed of balsam boughs on the spit of land separating the river from the Big Bayou, and with hands folded behind his head stared upward at the troubled April sky. And he smiled. For the sky to his knowing eye had lost the crispness of Winter.

The stars no longer gleamed with the cold glitter of points of brittle ice; in their gleam was a certain tinge of softness, as if the Winter crispness in them had thawed. The clouds that drove northward were not Winter clouds. Snow they contained, perhaps, but to Gaston their textures betrayed the fact that Winter had lost its stern grip on the heavens. The break-up was on its way.

In that northern country Winter reluctantly released its grip only after the calendar counted Spring a month old. But now the signs of the break-up were prominent, and Gaston smiled. For in the waning light of that afternoon he had gone over the Big Bayou and had made sure that his reading of Hale's map was correct, and that the Big Bayou was well fitted to further his scheme.

So now he lay at ease on his balsams waiting for Hale, and smiled at the sky, and thought of Rose.

A buck suddenly jumped from the dark

timber on to the white strip of snow along the river, stood for an instant listening, snorted and like a shadow fled across the ice of the river and disappeared in the darkness beyond.

"Something coming," thought Gaston. "That buck was scared."

Many minutes later he caught the sound of a wary footfall in the woods. The steps came nearer. A dark figure came slowly up the bank. Gaston waited until he saw the short, limping figure outlined against the white snow and called:

"All right, Hale. This way."

He lay stretched at ease in his comfortable position without moving, while Hale fumbled forward in the darkness. By this time he knew Hale well enough to expect that he would keep the appointment, still, at the sight of him limping along in the darkness, obviously out of place and helpless in the woods, Gaston was surprised.

Hale was a town man, and crippled at that, and the woods at night were no place for such, but here he was, coming along quietly, doggedly, as he did most things. Gaston felt one of his old impulses to slap the little man on the back, to cheer him, to call him the game little man that he was. But always with Hale there came thoughts of Rose. So Gaston lay without moving his hands from behind his head and said simply—

"How'd you come out?"

"Rode my little pony up the road, tied him in the brush, and walked over."

"Where's Taggart's Indian?"

"In town."

"Huh! Then I s'pose he trailed you out."

"Hardly. I started in the other direction —down toward La Croix. There is a decent element in La Croix, too. I go down there occasionally. We are trying to organize for the Spring election—to get a decent sheriff if we can. Indian Charley saw me go, but he didn't follow."

"How do you know?"

"I stopped and back-tracked when I was a mile out of town. Then I circled back of the settlement and came up here."

"And I suppose you tied your nag on this side of the road?"

"No. On the other side. And I made tracks in the opposite direction for a short distance."

Gaston smiled.

"Hale, if I'd caught you young I believe I could have made a fair woodsman out of you." Suddenly he dropped his bantering tone. "How much dynamite can you lay your hands on in the next two weeks—before the break-up, say?"

"Dynamite? Oh, I've got a fairly large stock of that on hand, for stump-blasting."

"Do you notice how this narrow ridge we're laying on separates the river from the Big Bayou?"

"I've noticed it often."

"Almost like a dam-wall. Look at it close. If there was a gap blown in the upper end of the ridge there, at the head of the bayou, the river would swing into it considerably, wouldn't it?"

"Yes."

"And if the river channel was blocked right there where those rocks show, with the gap in this bank just above it, the whole current would swing into the bayou strong, wouldn't it?"

"Yes."

"All right. Can you lay hands on enough dynamite to shoot a gap in this bank?"

"How big a gap?"

"Twenty feet wide might do it—thirty would be better. We'll have to get our dynamite down low, level with the river-bed. Put in say a dozen good shots a couple of feet apart. That would topple her over and the water would carry the dirt away."

Hale calculated for a moment.

"Yes, I can get plenty of dynamite for that."

"And a couple of dirt augers to do the boring with, and a couple of axes and peavies?"

"Yes."

"And two good heavy boom-chains, one about a hundred and fifty feet long, the other about seventy-five?"

"I can get all that stuff, Thorson. Now, will you tell me what it's all for?"

Gaston debated awhile.

"For Rose Havens," he said at last.

Hale looked at him, looked away up the river for a space, then put his hand to his wounded leg.

"I understand, Thorson," he said. "I— I guess I'd better be getting back to town. That's all you wanted to see me about, is it?"

Gaston rose.

"That's all. How about it now? I've turned my cards face up. Are you still willing to furnish me the stuff, and keep this all under cover?"

"Certainly." Hale was hobbling away. "When do you want it?"

"If you'll get it together and have it ready for me where I can get it when I want it, that'll be the ticket."

"All right."

Hale was in the timber. Suddenly Gaston's heart smote him.

"Hold on, old boy!" he cried. "Let me give you a hand to your horse."

"No—no, thanks, Thorson," said Hale promptly. "I—I'd rather go it alone if you don't mind."

Nevertheless Gaston followed him through the timber and saw he mounted his pony and was safely on his way to town. Then he turned and struck off by a roundabout way for Taggart's camp.

"Darn him!" he mused as he hurried along. "I never intended to even mention her, but he's so square I had to give him his warning."

CHAPTER XVIII

THE SPRING BREAK-UP

THAT night it grew warmer. When the men tumbled out for work on Monday morning there was a softness in the air which had not been before. The snow was soft underfoot. In the forest tiny traces of moisture began to ooze between the bark and trunks of the trees, while out upon the white expanse of the snow-covered lake there began to appear dark spots of varying size.

Gaston cast eyes on the lake the first thing that morning. At the sight of the dark spots in the snow he ran quickly out for a closer view. When he came back there was a glimmer of the old battle-light in his eyes and his jaw was set with new grimness.

"The Spring-holes are breaking through, Murphy," he said to the camp boss. "You know what that means."

"Sure. Means the break-up's due in a couple weeks or so."

"It means more than that, Murphy. It means that the end of this job is in sight, because the drive starts the minute the ice starts running, and there'll be no logging here after that."

"Sure; that's what I said. Means we'll be out of here in a couple of weeks."

"It means that this bunch of bums will have to jump from this minute on, that's what it means," said Gaston. "It means that they'll have to hustle in a way to make sure that this job will be cut clean before the break-up comes."

Murphy shrugged his shoulders.

"I haven't got any orders like that. I guess the old man wouldn't holler if there should happen to be a few trees left standing when we duck out."

"Maybe not. Maybe Taggart wouldn't kick. But I—" Gaston smiled—"I certainly would kick myself if I didn't get out every pound of work there's in this crew before we quit. Understand, Murphy? I'm here to get every possible saw-log out of this crew of Taggart's. I'm out to set a record. This is going to be a job that will be camp-talk for years to come."

"You must want awful bad to get solid with the old man."

"You bet!" laughed Gaston. "I want to, long as I live."

He walked among the men that morning and told them frankly that he demanded a record.

"You've only got a couple weeks left to go, but for that time you've got to go like thunder. Make up your mind to that. There's no way of soldiering out of it; you know me. So grab hold and go after that record."

Tom Pine would have been puzzled still more had he been able to see Gaston's conduct for the next two weeks. He now seemed to have but one aim in life—for Taggart's crew to log the last of Rose Havens's white pines before the ice went out. If the work lagged for want of a strong back, a quick pair of hands, or a skilfully wielded ax, he leaped into the breach himself.

"He's crazy," growled Murphy, making his report to Taggart. "Why, when a team gets stuck skidding he grabs hold of the chain and pulls with 'em."

Taggart, who never permitted himself to be seen at the camp, nodded appreciatively at such reports.

"Exactly. That's the kind of men who have steam in them, Murphy, men with no dread of the rope spoiling their sleep. Well, well. When I get a proper hold over Thorson I've no doubt he will be the most valuable fool I have on my pay-roll."

And Gaston Olaf continued to drive and heave and work like one possessed. Had

Taggart been there to see with his deep-set little eyes he might have read in the young man's dynamic demand for results something more than a mere desire to make good on his first job. But Taggart did not see.

Taggart was very careful not to permit the possibility of being seen at or near the camp. Taggart was very careful to let it be known that he had never been at the camp, did not even know for sure where it was; that he trusted entirely to his cruisers and working bosses at this camp. So he did not see; he had his knowledge of Gaston's tactics entirely through the eyes of Murphy; and Murphy saw Gaston only as a man who was making strenuous efforts to "get solid with the old man."

ONE gray, muggy afternoon when snow, ice, trees—the whole world— seemed to be steaming, Gaston walked down the lake to where the river ran out and saw running down the middle of the stream a wide ribbon of black water. In the lake, above the head of the stream, likewise, was an opening of clear water.

At intervals a rotting piece of gray ice cracked loose, slid into the water, and was whisked down-stream. It had grown warmer through the night, and the break-up was threatening.

Gaston looked back at the narrow strip of trees comprising the remainder of Rose Havens's white pines. There remained probably a two days' cut of the timber. Gaston was anxious to remain at the camp until the last tree was down, but as he looked up at the gray, dripping sky he saw that this might not be.

There was a probability of rain in the clouds above, a warm, thawing Spring rain. If it came the ice would go out in a rush, the lake would rise, and the first free logs of the cut would start down the river. As Gaston had several highly important matters to accomplish before such an eventuality, he merely looked around to make sure that he was unobserved and departed from that camp suddenly and for good.

Four hours later Dr. Sanders's dog, Samson, hearing a light tapping on the rear window of the doctor's private sanctum, emitted the ominous growl with which he presaged the coming of his full-throated bark. Dr. Sanders came in to investigate. At first he started at what he saw through the window. A few seconds later he locked the door to the front office, opened the window and assisted Gaston to crawl into the room.

"What ho!" The doctor, being an experienced man, had closed the window and pulled down the curtain before uttering a word of greeting. "H'm, h'm. I say, 'Big Fellow,' you do pick original ways in which to hit town. First on Red Shirt's neck, next with Hale and his bum leg, and now through my back window. I—I'm getting keener for you every time I see you, Thorson. You're original. Have some of the few drops of hooch Tom Pine and I have saved for you."

"Tom's in town, then?"

"Yep. In town and in sorrow. He says that town is no place for him, and if it wasn't for your orders he'd be out in the bush, which is the only fit place for a man to live, according to him."

"Can you get Tom here, Doc, and Hale, without letting any one else know I'm in town?"

The doctor looked Gaston over with half-closed eyes.

"Something in the wind, Thorson?"

"Something in the wind."

"Going to tell me what it is?"

"Going to tell nobody what it is."

"Quite so."

The doctor nodded. He saw that it was a different Gaston, cold, grim, cautious, dogged, who was before him, and he went forth without another word.

Gaston spoke without greetings when Tom Pine and Hale came into the room:

"No need for you to hear any of this, Doc, nor you, Tom; the fewer, the safer. That's right; you two keep watch outside. Well, Hale, have you got that outfit together?"

"Yes."

"Where is it?"

"In the cellar of my store."

"And a couple Winchesters with about two hundred cartridges and grub for a week?"

"I've got them in stock."

"All right. Can you haul it all out there —you know where—tonight?"

"Yes."

"Will you do it?"

"Yes."

Gaston sat silent a moment.

"Hale, are you doing this with a free heart—without anything against me?"

"I think so, Thorson; yes. I am human. I have feelings. But I can truthfully say that I do this without any malice—that I even do it eagerly."

"I don't just see how you can do it, Hale."

Hale looked away.

"I'm Miss Havens's agent—and I can't save her logs for her," he said. "I believe you can. I am glad if you can do it. I am glad to do anything I can to help it along."

Gaston felt very uncomfortable. He rubbed his chin, looked sidewise at Hale, looked at the floor. Suddenly he sat up straight, listening. On the tin roof of the doctor's little building came a soft, rhythmic drumming, pleasant to listen to, suggestive of Spring, of soft, steaming earth, of green things growing.

"Rain," said Gaston quietly.

He rose, relieved. No time for finer feelings now; no time for anything but action.

"She's coming," he said. "The logs will be on running water within twenty-four hours. Hale, we've got to get that stuff out of town and up there as soon as we can without being seen."

Hale nodded. "That can be done right away. Nobody's likely to be out in this rain."

"Then let it be right away. Tom Pine will help you load. I'll meet you fellows on the road some place."

He waited until Hale and Tom had gone, then slid past the curious doctor into the black, wet night. Beside the doctor's building he paused an instant and held his hands out in the rain. He smiled grimly as he felt that the drops were warm.

It was a true Spring rain, starting in with a quiet, steady patter that presaged a heavy rainfall before morning. The ground, now bare and brown in spots, had begun to steam warmly. There was no mistake about it, fortune favored him so far. The break-up was coming suddenly this Spring, and this served his purpose admirably.

Gaston did not start at once up the river. Through the mist and rain the lights from the houses shone hazily, yet one of these lights attracted and held his attention. It shone from the house in the big yard behind the post-office and Gaston stood and stared at it as if fascinated.

"Yes," he mused after awhile, "that's from the dining-room, all right."

He had neglected to button his mackinaw, and the rain was finding its way down his neck, but he failed to notice it. Presently he began stalking slowly toward the hazy light, the softened ground and snow squirting beneath his rubbers.

He took a roundabout way, climbed over the fence and cautiously moved toward the window whence the light shone. The light drew him as a magnet. He stood to one side of the window and peered in.

Rose and her mother were at the table. Gaston looked long and prayerfully. Then he swung away from the light toward the darkness, the wet, the hardships of the woods; and he carried with him a dream which at times intoxicated him with hope, and which again he put from him as something for which he was completely unfitted.

CHAPTER XIX

THE TRAP

WHEN he struck the river road he heard the plump of hoofs and the rumble of wheels ahead of him. Presently he made out Hale's voice, steadying the horses in low tones. Then the deep tones of Tom Pine, who was riding with Hale.

Gaston made no move to overtake the wagon. He was in no mood to ride beside Hale. For Hale persisted in appearing and reappearing in the dream which Gaston was dreaming. Hale would have fitted in the picture which Gaston had seen through the window; but, try as he would, Gaston could not quite see himself as a part of it.

"Hale, there, he's one solid, dependable citizen," he soliloquized as he trudged along. "He's the kind who's got a right to things like that. I'm about as dependable as a single wolf on the travel. And a wolf certainly has no right to things like that."

He plumped ahead, rolling the matter over and over in his mind.

"Oh, well, I suppose a man can change, can't he?" he argued with himself. "Of course, the way I am now I wouldn't have any business thinking of her. But if I can change——"

The dream was on again. He marched forward, lost in his thoughts, until he heard Hale pull up at their rendezvous.

"All right, Hale," he said, coming up to the wagon. "We'll unload right here. Then you get back to town as quick as you can. No use your running chances of being seen out here tonight."

The wagon was swiftly unloaded. Hale turned the team back toward the settlement.

"Anything more, Thorson?" he asked.

"No, thanks."

"All right. Good luck, then. Giddap."

"Hold on." Gaston sprang forward. "Hale, I want to shake hands with you—if you'll do it."

"Why, sure."

Their hands met in the darkness. Gaston searched for an expression of his feelings as the team pulled away.

"By the great stump, Hale!" he called, "I believe you're as good a man as myself."

"And now," said Tom Pine, as Gaston turned back to him, "I suppose you got time to tell me something about what you been doing these last days or so?"

"Later," replied Gaston briskly. "There'll be plenty of time to tell all about that later on. In the meantime we got a little hard bone-labor ahead of us. Packing this load of truck comes first of all. Come on; grab a shoulder-load and follow me. Leave that dynamite box till daylight. We won't run any risks of dropping it in the dark."

Through the darkness and rain Gaston led the way straight to the Big Bayou. At the first coming of daylight they made their last trip, to bring the box containing the all-important dynamite, and to erase as much as possible all traces of their trail. The rain had ceased now, the ice was out, and the river was racing bank-full.

Gaston looked out over the brown, ice-specked flood, with practised eye.

"They'll have the head of her down here tomorrow morning this time," he said.

"Who will?" demanded Tom Pine. "Gaston Olaf, you open your sluices and run me a little information or I'm going to get real sour on you. What are we here for? What are we going to do here? And what's all this scheming about?"

Gaston told him in perhaps a score of plain, simple words. Tom Pine's eyes widened, his mouth opened. He sat down slowly, gasping as if the breath had been knocked out of him.

"Hell's fire and six bits!" he exploded at last.

That was his single and sole expression concerning Gaston's revelations. The piratical boldness of the scheme revealed deprived him of the power of further comment. At times he looked at Gaston with awe, at times a grin wrinkled his face. And when Gaston threw off his mackinaw, Tom Pine promptly did the same, eagerly following his young leader to the tremendous task before them.

FIRST, with the aid of a rude log raft, they stretched the long boom-chain straight across the rock-filled rapids at a point slightly below the head of Big Bayou. So far as log-running was concerned the river thereby was shut off. The chains would act as a net, catching and holding the first logs of the drive among the rocks. The current would do the rest.

Given five minutes' stoppage there in the rocky channel, and a drive would be jammed as certainly as the logs came down. With this accomplished, and with the stream at flood-tide, water and logs would seek for the line of least resistance for a possible way around the obstruction.

Gaston Olaf and Tom Pine went directly from their toil in the icy, rushing water of the rapids, to provide another way for logs and current after the rapids should become jammed. In the narrow point of land separating the head of Big Bayou and the river they delved and mined for the better part of half a day.

"It all depends on this shot," said Gaston, as he tamped stick after stick of dynamite into the holes they had dug below water level. "If we can shoot a channel into the bayou, we've got a chance to win."

"It will do it," said Tom. "It's frozen sand. The charge we're putting in will shoot a twenty-five-foot channel as sure as that's dynamite."

When the last charge was in place they covered the holes to muffle the sound, lighted the fuses and ran for a cover. There was a space of waiting; then, down in the ground, a sudden rumbling, like deep thunder. The mined ground heaved and shook, rose in the air, and spattered the landscape for hundreds of yards around.

Gaston and Tom ran forward. Then

they solemnly shook hands. A channel twenty-five or thirty feet in width had been blown out and the La Croix River was pouring a good portion of its flood into the placid waters of Big Bayou.

"She's as good as set," jubilated Tom Pine. "Yes sir, Gaston Olaf, our trap's as good as set."

"When we get our boom across the lower end of the bayou she is," replied Gaston.

Across the lower end of the half-mile-long bayou they stretched the short boom-chain, thereby making of the bayou practically a mill-pond within which every log of a small drive—a drive similar to Taggart's—might ride in perfect security. This task was completed after the coming of darkness, and when the last spike was driven Tom Pine threw himself on the wet ground and slept like the dead.

Gaston did not sleep. He went up the river until, at the confluence of the La Croix and its west branch he met the head of the drive, slowly moving from the small stream out into the grasp of the larger river's current. It was still dark when he returned to Big Bayou, but he made no attempt at resting. He sat with folded arms, staring grimly up the river, waiting for the daylight of the day that would mark the beginning of war to the death between Devil Dave Taggart and himself.

As the first traces of dawn disturbed the darkness in the east, he built a fire and cooked breakfast. Then he awoke Tom Pine and they ate in silence. It was daylight when the meal was completed. As one they looked toward the river. Far up above the rapids they could see a few black specks bobbing on the rushing water, the first stray logs announcing the coming of the drive. Gaston rose, picked up one of the rifles, loaded it and filled his pockets with cartridges.

"You're not to do any shooting except to save your life," he said. "You just keep the new channel open. That's your job."

"Sure," said Tom Pine. "But—hello! Hear that."

From far up the river a shout came echoing faintly through the morning stillness.

"There she is," said Gaston. "I'll catch 'em at the point above. So long."

"So long," said Tom Pine, and looked on wistfully as Gaston jacked a cartridge into the barrel and stalked up-stream to meet the drive.

CHAPTER XX

HOW TAGGART LOST THE DRIVE

HALF a mile above the new channel which had been blown into Big Bayou, the river narrowed, running swift and deep between high banks. At one point in the narrows a cliff-like rock jutted out over the water, commanding the river above for a mile, or to the nearest curve.

Gaston made his way to behind this rock and lay down. The rock hid him like a natural breastwork. As yet there was nothing in the river above him save a few scattered stray logs. Gaston lay still and watched.

The first rays of the rising sun struck the rock. The gray of dawn lifted from the river, the rosy sunshine gleamed upon the rushing waters, and around the curve above, running free and strong, came the compact head of the drive from the lake.

Gaston Olaf carefully wiped the sights of his rifle, thrust it forward to a rest on the rock, with the muzzle pointing up-stream, and waited. The drive came on steadily, a solid brown carpet of logs, half a mile long and as wide as the river, borne on the crest of the flood that had washed it out of the lake, down the west branch and into the swollen La Croix.

Here and there men bobbed up and down on its heaving surface. On its head rode two men, resting on their pike-poles, and on each bank more men walked along, ready to leap in and work if the logs threatened to jam. There was no need for their services. The drive was riding steadily on high water, with no obstacle in sight to hinder its slow, steady progress.

At four hundred yards Gaston recognized the first man on the drive as the camp boss, Murphy. At three hundred yards he saw that the other drivers were all strangers to him. Taggart, to hide his tracks more thoroughly, had brought in a strange crew of river men to take the logs down the river.

Gaston cocked his rifle and waited. When the head of the drive was two hundred yards away, he began firing slowly, methodically, accurately, sending his bullets so close to the feet of the men that one after another they leaped in fright.

Five shots Gaston fired in as many seconds, and the five men in advance stood aghast at the sudden reports and the sinister *whew* of lead uncomfortably near. Ere they had located the shooter, the five shots were repeated. Chips, water and mud flew in the air so close to them that some actually were spattered. The first volley had stricken them helpless with surprise; the second brought them back to their senses and told them what to do.

They were river-men, they were paid to take chances with logs and water, not with bullets, and as one man they dropped peavies and cant-hooks and ran for cover. Murphy, to his credit, stopped on the bank and peered toward the rock, striving to locate the shooter. A final shot dropped at his heels and he followed the others into the timber.

Gaston quickly reloaded his rifle. The head of the drive was coming on, steadily, safely, nearing the trap he had set for it.

"That's just the first tuning up," he mused. "The real dance will begin a little later."

He was right. River-men are not the kind to submit quietly to gun-fire without seeking to return the compliment, and in the batteau following the drive were a couple of rifles. Presently, from five or six hundred yards up the river came the crack of a shot and a bullet dropped in the water fifty feet away.

"Pretty bad," mused Gaston. "They'll have to do better than that."

A second shot sounded and a bullet struck, splatt! against a near-by tree.

"A little better," thought Gaston, and crouched closer on the stone.

Half a dozen shots more were fired, none of them coming close enough to warrant a return. It was not a part of Gaston's program to hurt anybody, and he merely lay low, satisfied with the fact that the drive each minute was nearing the bayou.

The head of the drive now was in the narrows beneath him, and the swift water had caught the logs and was whisking them on to where Tom Pine was waiting. So long as that went on undisturbed the men above were welcome to waste as many cartridges as they pleased.

It did not last long. The firing stopped abruptly and Murphy appeared, peering around the trunk of a tree on the bank, and waving a bandanna handkerchief as a flag of truce.

"Hold up there! What are you trying to do?" he demanded.

Gaston debated not for a moment his course of action. He drove a bullet through the tree a yard above Murphy's head and chuckled at the fashion in which the foreman got out of sight.

There was a lull. Several minutes went by, and with each minute the drive drew nearer to the Big Bayou. Suddenly the shooting resumed from up the river, two rifles throwing lead at the rock as rapidly as the levers could work. At the same time, far back at the middle of the drive, two men ran out bearing a steel cable, followed by a man bearing a sledge.

"Good idea. Trying to cable half of her up," mused Gaston.

He treated the riflemen to two shots apiece, and, raising his sights, shot carefully near the cable-men. At the third shot the men dropped the cable and ran for cover.

Gaston smiled grimly. The entire drive now was within sweep of his rifle, and his shooting by this time had warned the men against exposing themselves in any effort to halt the logs.

"They've got to put me out of business to win," he muttered, as he watched the logs rushing past. "And if they don't do it in another hour they'll lose."

The firing from up-stream was resumed immediately after the cable-men had been driven to cover. The bullets whined overhead, struck dully against the rock, or chipped slivers from the logs below. The shooting was very bad. Evidently the shooters were thinking more of their own security than of their marksmanship. When it showed signs of improving, Gaston methodically pumped shots in the direction of the rifles. The rest of the time he lay tightly behind the rock, content so long as each minute carried thousands of feet of Rose Havens' pines down toward the Big Bayou.

Half of the drive had passed him when a sudden rattle of shots sounded down the river.

"They've gone around me," muttered Gaston. "They've sneaked through the timber—and Tom Pine is sending them on their way. It's time I got back to Tom."

Sending two final shots up the river, he crawled backward from the rock, keeping his retreat hidden until he was in the timber. Then he ran, as he never ran before, for the head of Big Bayou.

He was just in time. The trap had worked, but it had worked too well. The drive had jammed on the chain-boom in the rapids, and the jam had spread until the channel into the bayou threatened to become choked as well.

"Whitewater men to the front!" bellowed Tom Pine from behind the shelter of a tree, whence he was conducting a long-range drill with a hidden adversary in the timber. "She's beginning to jam, but that fellow out in the bush there'll shoot the eyebrows off you if you try to break her."

Gaston threw down his rifle and grasped a peavey.

"Don't try it, Gaston Olaf!" cried Tom. "Let's go hunt that fellow out first."

"No time." Gaston was running toward the logs. "She'll break through the boom unless she's started into the bayou in a hurry."

A bullet greeted him as he leaped out on the jam. He did not even turn his head. Over the heaving, rising carpet of logs in the new channel he ran, his eyes bent upon but one thing, to find the key-log and wrench it free before the jam should become too solid to move.

The logs tossed and tumbled crazily in the rush of high water in the bayou. Now Gaston stood securely on a log butt, now the butt up-ended and he was in the water.

The rifleman in the woods grew very busy as he saw Gaston's purpose. *Whack, whee!* The bullets thudded against the logs and cut the air around him. He found the key-log, an old dead-head with one butt jammed into the bottom, the other jutting up like a rock, spearing the drive and causing the jam to form about it.

Whack, whee!

In spite of Tom Pine's furious fire the man in the woods was dropping his bullets closer and closer to the frenzied giant toiling among the boiling logs.

Ping!

A pitch-knot, bullet-loosened, flipped up and cut a crease in Gaston's cheek, and blood and perspiration streamed together. He did not trouble to wipe it away, nor did he utter any exclamation. All his strength and breath were in demand as, like one of his Norse ancestors gone berserk, he tossed log after log to one side as he dug for the key-log.

Plump!

Water splashed in his eyes, blinding him for an instant. The gunman had the range now, but he was a little off on his line. *Whack!*

A bullet thudded into the key-log the instant it was bare. Gaston drove the spike of his peavey into the log and heaved. The log merely turned over, held securely by the mud of the bottom.

Gaston looked up. Above his head the logs were rising in tangled tiers. In a few minutes more the jam in the channel would be solid, and the logs in the river, deprived of the line of least resistance, undoubtedly would break through the boom and go on down-stream.

The logs in the channel hung on the key-log as on a hair-trigger. The second that log was released those tangled tiers would spew themselves into the bayou explosively, riding down everything in their way.

Gaston threw away his peavey. A bullet splashed the water at his feet. Carelessly he kissed his hand to the hidden rifle-man, to the logs hanging over his head, to Tom Pine, to the bright, sunny world which he with his young, full life joyed in so tremendously.

He dove into the muddy water where the butt of the key-log was lodged. Down under the water his back went under the log, and with all his strength he heaved upward. Tom Pine saw his face for one clear instant as it came above water, the muddy butt of the key-log clasped in his arms. The rest was a mighty roar as of an explosion, a fury of tumbling, shooting logs, of whipped-up water, of the thunder and indescribable force of a jam suddenly released in a pressure of high, swift water.

Tom Pine dropped his rifle and ran down the bank of the bayou, keeping pace with the first rushing logs.

"'Tain't human," he groaned, "'tain't human for any one to do it and live, but I never see him killed yet."

His quick old eyes found the key-log, and he groaned. No sign of Gaston on it. Then suddenly Tom Pine shouted from the bottom of a heart filled with gladness. On the butt of the log as it went down the bayou he discerned a huge brown hand maintaining a precarious but firm grasp.

Immediately a second hand appeared. Tom Pine sat down, weak with joy as Gaston drew his head above water and gasped for air.

"Is she running in?" were Gaston's first words.

"As fast as water will carry logs," cried Tom. "Gaston—Gaston Olaf, you had me awful blue there for a minute. I didn't think you'd make her—I didn't, for a fact."

So did Tom Pine attest that the feat had been superhuman.

Gaston drew himself up on the log and sat straddle of the butt while he filled his lungs with the precious air. He looked back toward the channel. The logs were moving into the bayou in a steady stream, the rushing water from the river thrusting them in as in a mill-race. Gaston grinned as he pulled himself to his feet and came across the heaving logs to where Tom sat.

"Good enough so far," said he. "Now get the guns and we'll go hunt that fellow who pestered us from the woods."

CHAPTER XXI

"YOU CAN'T LIVE HERE AFTER THIS"

THE firing from the woods had stopped. Gaston and Tom swiftly covered the ground in the direction whence the shots had come, without drawing any fire or discovering any trace of their assailant.

"That's funny," said Gaston. "Back to the river, Tom; they may be blocking the drive."

They hurried back, but there was no one in sight about the river.

"Lay low, Gaston Olaf," warned Tom; "they're prob'ly holding back for a sure crack at us."

For a while they lay behind cover, waiting and watching for the men of the drive to reveal themselves. Five, ten, fifteen minutes went by, and not a man was seen nor a shot fired.

The logs were beginning to jam again in the entrance to the bayou and Gaston once more laid down rifle for peavey and sprang out in their midst.

"If they're still laying for us, we'll soon find out," he said as he set to work.

He cleared the tangle, set the logs to running freely again and came back to shore without drawing a single shot. Tom Pine was scratching his head in puzzled fashion.

"I can't figger it, Gaston Olaf, I can't for a fact," he muttered. "Taggart ain't the kind of timber boss to send down a drive of fine stuff like this without having anyhow a few of the real old, pure-quill river-dogs in the crew, and river-men ain't going to let nobody take a drive away from them without a fight.

"The way they started in swapping lead for lead with you, proves there was some of the old style in this crew. Then this fellow, who was put off here in the woods, he had the right idea. He knew what he was doing when he tried to keep you from breaking that little jam. Why do they give it up sudden now? There ain't over half of their logs in the bayou yet. Why do they quit like this? River-men don't usually drop a fight till the last dog's hung."

"I don't know. I suspect Taggart's hand in it, because the men wouldn't stop fighting unless they'd got orders. We won't bother our heads about that, though. Those logs out there belong to Miss Havens. We're here to see that they get safe and snug into Big Bayou, where they'll be out of Taggart's hands till the news is broken that he's a thief and caught in the act."

It was noon now, and while Tom prepared a meal Gaston kept the logs flowing steadily. After the meal Tom took his turn with the peavey while, rifle in hand, Gaston went up the river to the tail of the drive. He came back grinning.

"Not a man in sight, Tom," he called. "They've even pulled the batteau back up-stream. Taggart has been notified and has called them off, or I'm badly mistaken. The old hound will be up to something pretty soon. Probably send a gang of shooters up here to run us off. Well, we'll sit tight and give 'em back as good as they send."

But no gang of shooters came. For the rest of the day the logs came floating into Big Bayou without let or hindrance, and Gaston and Tom worked them down without the slightest molestation. Evening came, and the bayou was covered with a solid carpet of logs.

As the last straggling sticks of the drive swung through the new channel, Gaston exploded a charge of dynamite in the middle of the jam which had caught on the boom across the river. The blast blew jam and boom to pieces, and the La Croix ceased to pour its waters into the bayou and went rushing bank-high down its old channel. The waters of the bayou promptly sank to their normal placid level, and two million feet of Rose Havens' white pine rode on its bosom as snug and steady as if in the mill-pond awaiting a buyer.

When the last log was in the bayou, when the water was normal, when the boom at the bayou's mouth had been tested, when all was secure, Tom Pine threw his cap on the ground, leaped three feet in the air and whooped.

"We did it! By the great pike pole, we did it! We've snatched a man's sized drive smack out of old Dave Taggart's hands, and the old devil will be laughed out of the woods for the trick we've put on him. Whoop! Let 'er roar, Gaston Olaf, let 'er roar!"

But Gaston Olaf refused to let 'em roar at all. He shook his head, grimly viewing the work of his head, heart and hands, and knowing that it was not done.

"That would be right about any other man in the woods," he admitted. "For any other timber thief to have a drive stolen away from him like this would settle him. The boys would laugh at him till he'd have to pack up his traps and travel. But old Taggart isn't any common man. He's got his hand laid so heavy on this country that they won't even dare laugh at him about this. And we haven't put the trick on him yet, Tom. We'd better save our crow for a while; old Dave'll try to make us eat it before we're through here."

Tom Pine shook his head, disappointed.

"Gaston Olaf, I can't figger you lately. You're changing, somehow. By the great pike-pole! A month ago you'd 'a' been singing over a job like this. Now to hear you talk you'd lost confidence, or something. What's happened to you, boy? Getting old?"

Gaston busied himself preparing supper without offering a reply. Tom Pine watched him closely and sadly.

"I know what's the matter with you," he said at last. "You're Norwegian now and you're thinking of settling down."

"Perhaps I am. What of it?"

"What of it? Why, just this: you ain't made for it, that's all. You're made for the trail, and if you settled down and lived in a house, some day your feet'd get to working and you'd kick open the door and just natur'lly travel."

"You may be right, Tom," muttered Gaston half aloud. "If you are, then it wouldn't be square for me to try to settle

down. Well, drop that. You roll in and get your sleep right after supper. I'll stand watch for the first half of the night. We can't let 'em catch us napping."

THE night passed without incident. Morning came, a bright, lazy Spring morning, and still no sign from Taggart. Tom and Gaston breakfasted, made a circle in the woods on each side of the river and returned without finding trace of a single man.

The forenoon passed and still no one disturbed them. It was well past the middle of the afternoon and Tom was whittling shavings against the time for cooking supper, when a stick was cracked sharply in the woods toward the road. The two watchers methodically picked up their rifles and methodically threw themselves behind cover. More sticks cracked in the woods. Some one was coming boldly toward the bayou, by the noise two or more people, and they were walking without any attempt to hide their coming.

"They've got their nerve, thinking to walk up on us that way," muttered Tom, and as he spoke Rose Havens, Hale, and Taggart, walking together, stepped from the shadows of the timber into the bright sunlight and stood looking down at the log-covered bayou.

Gaston laid down his rifle and stood up.

"Hello, folks!" he called, stepping toward them. Hello, Taggart. There you are— the two million feet of Miss Havens' timber that you were stealing. And here I am— I'm the man responsible for their being here."

From his position on a rise in the bank Taggart looked down at Gaston with an expression of great sadness.

"Thorson," he said, slowly shaking his head, "did you know all the time that we were cutting logs on Miss Havens' timberland?"

Gaston gasped. If ever there was a picture of elderly uprightness, of honesty saddened by a suspicionable error, it was frock-coated, bearded David Taggart, as he stood there in the sunlight with the dark woods at his back.

On one side stood Hale, a little puzzled perhaps, but apparently satisfied; on the other side was Rose, and her face was almost jubilant. Gaston looked from one to the other, and before his amazement would permit him to speak, Taggart continued:

"If you did—as your actions lead me to suppose—didn't you realize what a terrible injustice you were doing me, your employer, by not informing me of the fact?"

Almost ministerial was Taggart as he uttered these words. Unquestionably he had convinced Rose and Hale that his sorrow was genuine; unquestionably he was near to convincing Gaston. But the young giant looked up at the clean sky, at the solemn trees, at the clean water, and his woods instinct whispered to him to be on guard, that something was wrong. Nevertheless he said:

"Taggart, do you mean to say you didn't know that timber was Miss Havens'?"

Solemnly, mournfully Taggart shook his head.

"Thorson, when I first laid eyes on you," he said quietly, "I analyzed you like this: an excellent young man of great possibilities, but too prone to jump at conclusions, too much predisposed to violence." He smiled a little, sadly, pityingly. "I am afraid we must laugh a little at you, Thorson. You have performed a valiant deed—a notable deed—but a rather ridiculous one, considering that it was absolutely unnecessary." He seemed to struggle to control his smile. "As you know, Thorson, I had nothing to do with your camp—never visited it."

Gaston's teeth bit back an exclamation as he thought of Taggart's secret morning visit to Murphy.

"I pay my cruisers good money to locate my camps. The man who located this one is no longer in my employe. He was discharged this morning when, after the report that you had stopped this drive, I investigated and found to my sorrow that we had been cutting Miss Havens' timber. I am not so young as I was. Time was, when I would have fought for these logs until the last court in the land had judged against me. But I'm getting old. I'm not as ambitious as I was. Consequently Miss Havens and Mr. Hale and myself are up here to agree on a fair price for me to pay for the logs I have unwittingly thought were mine."

Gaston smiled back at him now.

"That's all I was after, old timer," he said lightly. "If Miss Havens gets paid, that's all I did this for."

"And I thank you for it, Mr. Thorson," said Rose. "It seems you're forever putting me under obligations which I see no way of repaying. But I would rather have lost every penny of it all if that poor man dies."

Gaston looked at her in amazement, and saw that she was struggling between gratitude and horror.

"What poor man?" he asked after a while.

"Murphy," said Taggart with a click of his jaws. "Oh, yes; you can't do things like this without paying for them, Thorson. Poor Murphy; I'm afraid he is done for. Shot through the hips, when he thought he was well out of range, too. We've hurried him down to La Croix, but there's hardly any hope. A bad, bad business. And so absolutely unnecessary, too."

Once more Gaston's woods-sense whispered to him to be on guard, that something was wrong, but for the life of him he could not sense where the wrong might be.

"If I've hurt a man as bad as that, I suppose the sheriff will be up from La Croix to get me. I'll go down to the settlement to save him coming up here."

"We'll see you through, Thorson," shot out Hale. "It's too bad, but we'll be with you."

"Every cent I've got to defend you if necessary," said Rose. "But I'm so, so sorry it had to happen."

Old Taggart scratched his chin.

"Thorson, I've been thinking that over on the way out here. You quit me cold; you suspected me; you took my drive away from my men, but just the same I'm your debtor for having called this deplorable error of my cruiser to my attention. You did it criminally, but let that go. Through you I find it out in time to rectify it before my name is smirched by suspicion. For that I'll give you a little advice—clear out! Quit the La Croix country. Start upstream, right now, and keep going till you've put this country behind you forever. I'll see that you get away, and I'll fix it with Murphy. Take this as the solemn truth from me. It's your only chance, for you can't live here after this."

Gaston threw back his head and laughed the old wolf full in the face.

"'Can't'! That's a strong word, Taggart. Now you take this from me: neither you nor any other man can tell me where I can or can not live."

8

Taggart's eyes narrowed. His jaws snapped. His head shot forward.

"That settles you, Thorson," he growled. "You're done for. You had your chance, now you haven't got any." He turned abruptly to Hale and Rose. "Now, let us get to business, please, and agree on the price."

Gaston turned abruptly away, swinging into the timber at a pace that made Tom Pine dog-trot to keep up. Something was wrong; something sinister was beneath the surface of all this. He sensed it clearly, but the thing was too deeply hidden for him to see. Taggart was lying. He had been to the camp; he knew where it was. Yet he was preparing to pay for the logs, apparently in good faith. Where was the hitch?

The report about Murphy also puzzled him. He and Tom had scoured the woods up the river and had found nothing to indicate that any one had been hurt. They had heard no cry. If Murphy had been hurt, his companions naturally would have swarmed to avenge him rather than tamely drop the fight. On the other hand, where there was so much shooting there was always the possibility of a stray bullet doing sore damage.

"But a man shot through the hips would bleed," he said suddenly aloud. "And there wasn't a drop of blood where the crew had been tracking around."

"I smelled skunk, too," said Tom Pine. "She's a queer one, but somehow I can't locate the animal. For one thing it looks to me like Taggart was running a bluff to scare you out of the country."

"That's the straight look of it, all right," agreed Gaston, "but Taggart's tracks run too crooked to make such a simple trail. He wants to send me out of the country, that's sure; but there's something behind all that. We'll go down and see Doc Sanders and find out how much Murphy was hurt. Then we'll wait for that sheriff, and keep our eyes peeled for signs."

CHAPTER XXII

TWENTY-FIVE THOUSAND—CASH

"HELLO, pirates!"

Dr. Sanders, hearkening to a light knock on his back window opened the door and let Gaston and Tom slip into his private sanctum. It was well after dark. The pair had taken a roundabout way through the woods, avoiding the road, and had entered the settlement without being observed.

Dr. Sanders slammed the door shut behind them, pulled down the curtain, leaped in the air, and, beating time with both arms, gave three cheers, in a whisper.

"You did it, boys! You've done a doughty deed. All my life I've been hoping somebody would do something like it. Didn't seem fair that all the doughty deeds should have been done before I was born. Now I die happy. Captain Kidd has been outdid, almost before my eyes. Stealing a log-drive, lock, stock, and barrel, from Devil Dave Taggart! Boys, you were born after your time. You darned old pirates and buccaneers, have a drink."

"How badly was Murphy shot up?" asked Gaston, when the ebullient doctor had subsided.

Dr. Sanders raised his eyebrows.

"Let's have that again, please. Somebody shot up?"

"Murphy," said Gaston. "I understand he's plugged through the hips and not much hope for him? I suppose they brought him to you first?"

The doctor shook his head.

"This is the first I've heard of that. Nobody has been shot up in this neck of the woods since Hale got it in the leg, that I know of. Whence this news, Thorson?"

Gaston repeated what Taggart had said concerning Murphy. As he talked, Dr. Sanders's shrewd eyes narrowed to a wink and he rolled his tongue in one side of his mouth.

"I don't say that I see an Ethiopian in the wood-pile," said he, when Gaston had done, "but I do insist I catch a whiff of something dark complècted. Why, if the aforesaid Murphy was sorely wounded, as alleged, was he not taken here for first treatment, at least? Men shot through the hips are poor risks to be toting around the country unnecessarily. To get to La Croix the alleged wounded gentleman must have been taken through this settlement right under my nose. Without boasting professionally, I may say that my reputation for treating gunshot wounds and so forth is not of the poorest, thanks to the activities of Taggart's henchmen. Boys, if there isn't something rotten about that I'll—I'll call my bull-dog 'Maude' for the rest of his life."

"Has the drive-crew come into town?"

"Every mother's son of 'em. Came in yesterday afternoon. Been trying to take the town apart ever since."

"Was Murphy among them? Did you know him?"

The doctor thought for a moment.

"I know him when I see him. Come to think of it, I haven't seen him with the gang."

"Do you know if any team has gone to La Croix? They'd have to take him down with a team if he was that badly hurt."

The doctor shook his head.

"I had a call down the river this morning. Polack settler's wife. Confinement case. The road is pure, undisturbed mud; there hasn't a rig gone down for forty-eight hours."

"Then it's pretty safe to say that Taggart lied about that. He's got something up his sleeve. Well, we'll wait and see what it is. Now, how about the rest of it? Do you know if he's settled up?"

The doctor nodded.

"He has. In me you behold one of the witnesses to the transaction, which has just been completed. Taggart paid Miss Havens twenty-five thousand dollars for her logs, just as they lay in the water—twenty-five thousand dollars!"

Gaston gave a long sigh of relief.

"Good enough. Then the girl's got her money. That's a fair price, considering that Taggart's men did the cutting. Twenty-five thousand——"

"Cash," said the doctor.

"What?"

"Cash-money. Paid in hand, hundred-dollar bills."

Gaston sat looking at the doctor in stupid silence. Somewhere in the back of his head he felt the same throb which up at the bayou had told him there was something wrong about the tale of Murphy's wounding. Twenty-five thousand dollars—cash! The words carried with them the sense of something sinister, but what?

"Twenty-five thousand dollars—cash," he repeated blankly. "Was it good money?"

"I looked at it. So did Postmaster Perkins, and Hale, and three others who weren't Taggart's friends. Fact is he insisted on calling in folks who are Rose Havens's friends to witness the deal. It looked good to us."

Gaston walked the floor in keen discomfort.

"That's an awful lot of money to be kept in a town like this with that gang all drunk." Suddenly he shot out, "What did she do with it?"

"Oh, that's all right. It's safe enough. She put it in Hale's safe; he's express agent, too, you know. Oh, yes, the money's safe and sound enough. No trouble about that. And, say, Thorson."

"Well."

"Somebody was asking if you'd been seen around town."

"Well, I hadn't been."

"So I told her."

"And I haven't been now."

"Eh?"

"You haven't seen me. I'm not in town. I haven't been here. Understand?"

"As much as a pig does of flute-playing. What's the idea now?"

"Just that—I'm not in town. Neither is Tom Pine. Haven't been seen."

The doctor stroked his beard.

"But, Thorson, I was going to add that somebody explicitly ordered me to ask you to call in case I did see you. How about that?"

Gaston was tempted. The desire to see Rose, to hear her speak, was strong upon him. But he put the thoughts of her from him sternly.

"The play still goes as I first made it," he said. "You haven't seen Tom or me at all. Now let us out your back way after making sure that nobody's looking. I've got to think, and this room suffocates me."

He led the way from the doctor's, away from the lights of the settlement, up to the spot on the hill from which he and Tom had slid so opportunely on their first arrival in Havens Falls. The slope was bare now, and half-way up Gaston found a convenient windfall, and seated himself with Tom at his side. Down below them the lights shone from the houses of the settlement. The light from the Havens's window was almost beneath them; but Gaston looked beyond it, down to where the red lights twinkled and the drive-crew roared in the river front.

In the upper part of town—the town proper, where the permanent, respectable citizens of Havens Falls had their stores and homes—it was quiet and dark. Though the dark Spring evening was warm enough to justify open-flung windows and doors after the cooped-up Winter, the houses and stores there were well closed.

In the houses curtains were being drawn. The stores were locked up and darkened. There was no activity. Folk were staying close to their firesides in that part of town; and one had only to look and listen to the noise in the lower end, where the red lights winked, to learn the reason why.

As Dr. Sanders had said, the gang down there was bent upon taking the town apart. When a gang of woodsmen thus descends upon a settlement, quiet, respectable citizens lock up their places of business and remain behind locked doors, that peace and order, and their own heads, may be the better conserved.

While Havens Falls was a small, new settlement, its river front was startlingly adequate and complete. Young, brown-skinned lumber-jacks, ramping with health and craving excitement after months of monotony in camp, came down the river to Taggart's office and drew their checks. Often that check represented six months' toiling, toying with danger, even death; not infrequently a red-cheeked, lusty girl waited somewhere for the young woodsman who was to marry her on his Winter's stake. But one drink wouldn't hurt a man, reasoned young Jack, as he stood outside Taggart's office and looked over the river front, which was so situated that he could not escape seeing it after he had drawn his check. No, one drink with the boys wouldn't hurt. Of course he had promised the girl that there wouldn't be any more of that sort of thing now; but a man must be a pretty poor stick if one drink would hurt him, and besides, he had to say good-by to the boys.

So he would have one drink in the first place on the front. And there the boys were cashing their checks and buying drinks, and young Jack had to be a man and hold his own. Good-by check! Good-by thoughts of a red-cheeked girl that held a man straight!

A week later, perhaps, some bartender, growing tired of seeing Jack hanging around, now that his money was gone, threw him out in the street. And Jack, now bleary-eyed white and yellow, shaky and unshaven, drew his hand across his eyes as a man awakening from a bad dream to a worse reality, begged one drink to steady him, and —went back in the woods.

Yet it was brave and gay while it lasted, especially on a warm, still evening when a drive was down, and a score or more broad-shouldered, blue-shirted river-men took possession of the river-front. In most towns the townspeople laid low till the spasm was over, and the river-men went on their way. In Havens Falls, however, the worst men of the gang were permanent to the settlement, and, as a consequence, what happened in other river towns once a year, there was a permanent, impossible condition.

"They're doing her proud," ventured Tom Pine, as he and Gaston harkened to the turmoil from the saloons. "Yes siree, they certainly are letting her roar for fair."

Gaston nodded grimly. A few short weeks ago he knew quite well that he would have been the leader of the celebration below. Now he saw the thing in a new light.

He measured with his eyes the distance from the red light to the light from Rose Havens's window, and he found it perilously short. He pictured the house as he had sat at table with Rose and her mother, and an exclamation of anger escaped him. That was a home. That was the kind of thing that counted, the right kind of thing, for which men, who were men, worked and saved, and even died to maintain.

His dream came back to him, the dream of such a home, such a woman for his own. And again he tried to put the dream away. What had he—the careless, reckless woods-vagabond—to do with such things?

CHAPTER XXIII

THE MONEY SAVED

"HELLO!" Tom Pine sat up as the shouts from below came nearer. "I believe they're coming up to this end of town."

It was true. The gang, apparently tiring of the saloons for a spell, had wandered into the decent part of town singing, shouting, laughing and cursing. At their coming more curtains were drawn down; lights went out and the houses became dark and still.

"That'll put the scared townfolk under the beds all right."

Gaston made no reply. He was thinking over the words he had heard Taggart speak to Murphy on that secret morning visit to the camp: "A man can't blow a safe and kill a marshal without paying for it, Murphy. That was clumsy—that killing—for an expert safe-blower, Murphy," and suddenly the trail began to grow clear, ridiculously clear. Murphy, safe-blower; $25,-000 in Hale's safe.

The gang below swarmed about Olson's hotel. Mrs. Olson promptly locked her doors and pulled down the curtains. The gang grew in numbers. They surrounded the hotel. On the surface it was all good-natured, rough woodsmen's play, but to Gaston there was something too systematic in the way the men flocked about the hotel.

"Hale lives there," said he suddenly.

"Sure," agreed Tom. "What of it?"

"And he's probably in there now."

"That's a cinch. He'd be crazy to be out tonight."

"That gang will keep him in there."

"Sure. He isn't a fool; he won't show himself."

"So long, Tom," said Gaston, rising noiselessly.

"Hah?"

"So long. I've got something to attend to. You stay here. I know you've got a right to be in anything I'm in, but this is something where one man is as good as two."

He disappeared down-hill in the darkness before Tom could have followed, had he been so inclined, which he was not. He knew Gaston too well to fail to recognize a command.

Gaston went swiftly and unobserved to where Tom and he had cached their rifles on coming into town. He would have much preferred to have a shotgun for night work, but a rifle would have to do.

The darkness of the night favored his plans; it permitted him to hide himself close to the window in the rear of Hale's store, so close that when Black Murphy came and broke in, which he did at a moment when the gang about the hotel and in the street set up such a concerted whooping that no one in town could hear the tinkling of broken glass, Gaston recognized the man on the instant. He laughed silently. He had guessed right. Taggart had lied about Murphy's being wounded to establish an alibi for what was about to happen.

Gaston half rose from his hiding-place under the impulse to capture Murphy and clear himself of the alleged shooting. He caught himself as a better idea unfolded itself. Murphy was small game, very small game. Gaston sat back and waited.

Out in the street the noise became a tornado. A score of men had joined hands and were dancing in a circle, singing at the top of their deep bull voices. It was a regular woodsmen's celebration, but it was a trifle too consistent, the din was a little too incessant, too well sustained. It served its purpose, however, for it was only by listening intently that Gaston, close though he was to the window, caught the sound of a muffled explosion within Hale's store.

After that he had not long to wait. Murphy came out of the window, a small sack under his arm, looked out toward the noisy street to see if he was observed, and came straight toward where Gaston lay hidden.

Gaston held his breath. Was his fine plan going awry? If Murphy came stumbling on to him a sudden blow would lay him out, and restore the contents of the sack to its owner; but that was but a part of Gaston's scheme. He sat as immovable as the stump behind which he was hiding, as Murphy came swiftly on. Then he breathed again. Murphy had passed on the other side of the stump, and was swinging down toward the river.

Gaston, blessing the blackness of the night, rose and followed. He was glowing. This was living! Driving Taggart's men to cut Rose's pines, and then snatching the drive out of Taggart's hands had been good. But this was the real thing: on a dark trail, and no knowing what lay at the end, except that it was sure to be strife and excitement! Gaston felt like singing.

He blessed, likewise, the stars that had kept Murphy from becoming a true woodsman. Murphy was wearing leather shoes. Gaston, in his soft rubber-bottomed "high-tops" could keep within hearing of Murphy's footsteps without revealing the fact that he was following. He dared not keep close enough to have his quarry in sight; he trailed by the sound of Murphy's steps, and he followed as noiselessly as any bobcat of the swamps.

MURPHY made a wide detour, striking for the river at a point a half-mile below the settlement. Near the river his way led to a copse of tag alders, so tightly grown together that, save for a trail which had been cut through, the thicket was impassible.

At the edge of the tangle Murphy hesitated, fumbled a moment on the trail, then stood before an opening which showed where the tiny path ran through the alders. Twenty feet behind him Gaston crouched low and waited.

Murphy began to whistle softly. From somewhere in the thicket came a single low note in reply. Murphy crashed boldly ahead, striking into the path with no effort at concealment, while Gaston, cocking his rifle in the crash of Murphy's first footfall, followed swiftly.

The path ended suddenly in an open space on the bank of the river. Gaston, crawling on hands and knees, was only ten feet behind Murphy as the latter stepped out in the clearing.

Gaston lay tight in the path at the edge of the brush. It was lighter there by the river. He saw that Murphy, with the sack still under his arm, was standing on the brink of the river, where a canoe and paddle lay ready for use. He saw Murphy look around, heard him whistle again.

Then something cried out within Gaston to be on guard. He dropped flat on his face. A revolver spat a streak of flame where his head had been an instant before. He felt a burning sting through his left shoulder, fired at the flash, heard some one grunt, then he was recklessly up and in the open, throwing himself on Murphy as the latter, alarmed, leaped for the canoe.

Murphy was getting away with the money! That was the idea that drove Gaston so carelessly from cover. He grasped the sack with one hand, striking at Murphy with the rifle, as a second shot flashed from the brush.

The world reeled and leaped drunkenly, and split in a hellish splash of flame and blood. He was down on the ground; Murphy was in the canoe, racing madly down the river. But Gaston thrilled and exulted in the mad tumult of the moment as he realized that the lump he was lying on was Murphy's sack.

Rolling over on his back he pumped shot after shot into the brush as rapidly as he could work the lever. Not shot or cry came back. The bullets ripped harmlessly through the tag alders.

"That —— Indian!" thought Gaston "No white man could have seen enough to hit me. White man, and I'd have got him."

He heaved himself up, with his eyes running full of blood, and fired wildly down the river after Murphy. The bullet struck a tree on the other side, and he realized that he was shooting across a curve, and that Murphy had disappeared around the bend.

It had all happened within a few seconds, and now there was the sudden quiet that is the aftermath of an explosion. The river brawled steadily as it swept around the curve; save for that the night was quiet, empty.

Gaston's hand went to his forehead, then to the smear that was running down from his left armpit.

"He got me, the dirty Pigeon-Toe," he muttered. "Got me twice, and good—but I got the money."

He staggered a little as he rose, for the blood from both wounds was running strong and free. The sensible thing to do, he knew, was to bandage the wounds at once to stop the bleeding. But there was the chance that the Indian would come back with help; even the men in town might hear the shooting and come down.

Gaston went into the river. The water was mouth high on him, but with rifle and sack held above his head he waded upstream to open timber, then scrambled out and made his way back to town. The gang was back among the red lights now. Olson's hotel was deserted. Gaston staggered to the door and kicked it open.

"Hale!" he gasped, to the startled Hulda. "Take me to him."

He staggered into the room where Hale was sitting and dropped the sack on the floor before him."

"Money—Rose's," he muttered. "Safe blown—Murphy did it. I saw him. Took it away from him. He's down river—canoe. Ugh!"

The windows of the room shook as he swayed like a sawed pine and went down, the two hundred and twenty pounds of him, with a thump on the floor.

CHAPTER XXIV

A FRESH START

GASTON heard some one speaking when he returned to consciousness. He recognized Dr. Sanders's voice.

"In danger? Seriously wounded? My dear young lady, men builded and grown on the plan of our friend, Thorson, require much more than he got tonight before their earthly existence is even threatened. He's a little weak at present, and he'll have a sore shoulder for a few days, and his open, boyish forehead will always be marred by a scar, but outside of that he's perfectly ready to resume his exciting career. Hello, Thorson—have a nice snooze?"

"Money—money all right?" Gaston muttered sleepily, without opening his eyes, the one thought in his mind.

"Yes, yes!"

He looked up sharply at the new voice. The doctor was slipping out of the door and Rose was standing by his side.

"Why—why did you do it?" she asked tremulously.

Gaston closed his eyes. The vision was too disturbing for a man who had had his skull raked by a bullet.

"Risk your life so recklessly for my money?"

There was so much alarm, so much sternness, and withal so much implied reproof in her tone that Gaston opened his eyes and grinned boyishly.

"Ain't mad are you?"

She had to laugh with him, though tears and reproving words were not far away.

"How can you joke about it?" she protested. "You might have been killed."

"Might," he agreed. "It was a gamble; that's why it was fun to do it."

"Oh! Please don't make so light of it. It horrifies me. Do you think I would have had you do it—risk your life—if I had known? Not if everything we had was lost. Don't think I'm ungrateful; I can't imagine how I can repay you——"

"Hold on there." Gaston half rose in the bed. "You don't think I did it expecting any pay?"

"No. But I don't see why you should do such things for me—almost a stranger to you. Why, you——"

"I did it. Somebody had to do it; it was something that had to be done. I happened to do it. Let it go at that. Now, there's the way you can pay me—if you insist on paying me: just let it go at that. It's done; it's past. Say no more about it."

"But how can I——"

"I mean that," he said doggedly. "I don't like to hear anything about it. I don't want to be rude, but say, Miss Havens, will you do me a favor?"

"You know I will."

"Well, will you forget everything that has happened up to now. Let it slide. And

—can we begin fresh, from now on, to—to get to know each other?"

He was sitting up, leaning toward her eagerly, the impetuous, winning power of youth in his blue eyes and boyish smile; and as she looked at him she trembled a little, with a feeling that when he looked at her like that, in spite of his bandages, she would want to do whatever he wished her to do.

"Begin all over, fresh; you know what I mean, Miss Havens? Will you?"

"Yes," she whispered.

For a moment it was still in the room. Gaston was fumbling for words to utter what was in his mind. Rose nervously turned to go.

"Mother is waiting. I think I—will bid you good night."

"I want you to get to know me differently—and forget the wild, tough kid that I've been," said Gaston, as the words came suddenly.

She smiled gladly. She was very young.

"I shall be glad to—very glad—good night."

"Good night."

Gaston lay back with a serious, questioning look on his face.

"I wonder," he mused, "I wonder if I've got the right?"

When Dr. Sanders entered the room, soon after Rose had left, he found his patient sitting up on the edge of the bed, staring out of the window into the black night.

"Back to the hay, boy," commanded the doctor. "You're a bear and a bull for strength, all right, but that hole through the shoulder's from a .44, and there's torn tissue there that needs perfect quiet or there'll be more bleeding. You only lost about a gallon of blood as it was. Lie down, I say. I'm in no mood to trifle with. Hulda's made me go on the wagon. ——! Did you ever notice what influence women have over men in the Spring? So, there you are. Huh! Pulse way up again. You've got to keep quiet I tell you."

"What did Hale do with the money this time, Doc?"

"Hale is at this moment speeding behind his drivers, well on his way to La Croix. Tom Pine, armed to the teeth, sits in the seat beside him. The bag, containing Rose Havens's twenty-five thousand, and incidentally some of Hale's money, is safe between them. And Hale is driving so hard that there'll be no chance anybody over-taking him before he has that money safe in the bank at La Croix. He decided to take no more chances keeping that much money in this tough town."

"Good. Now, if he could only nail Murphy——"

"Not much chance. I've been hearing some talk about Murphy. He'll never go to La Croix. He's wanted down there. He'll probably leave the river and strike into the woods."

"That's so." Gaston scowled. "Then Taggart's still safe. Well, we made him pay for the logs, anyhow."

"Yep. And I suspect he'll be making somebody else pay for making him pay."

"Oh, sure." Gaston laughed cheerfully. "He'll be on the war-path for my scalp from now on. He told me my only chance was to get out of the country."

"And you decided?"

"Oh, I'm beginning to like this place. It's nice country around here, and the people are friendly. Yes, if there was anything wanting to make me like it it was to have old Taggart or any one else tell me I couldn't stay."

The doctor stroked his beard dubiously.

"Devil Dave won't balk at murder, you know."

"That's understood."

"And he can command any one of a dozen bad men who'd pick you off as quick as they would a deer."

"Sure."

"Taggart'll go war-mad now. He'll make this place harder and rougher than it's been."

"Now, there," said Gaston smiling, "there you say something important, Doc! Can he keep that up? Can he keep on running this country the way he has? Taggart and his gang are hard and tough. They've been too tough for you fellows so far. If they make the town any rougher it'll be too rough for decent people to live in. 'Twouldn't be right to go away and leave a fine piece of country like this in the hands of folks like Taggart and his tribe. Might as well have let the Indians have it. It's too good for that; it's too good for anybody but decent white folks, who want to settle down and— make homes.

"And I've been thinking that it's time I got me a home some place, though I don't know if I can stick in one spot. But I want

to try. And I like this place; it's the first place I ever camped in that I felt like stay-ing with, and I've got a hunch I'm going to stay.

"Of course I wouldn't care to stay if old Taggart continued to run things so the de-cent people would have to leave. But Tag-gart's been driving here, smooth and cocky, for about long enough, it seems to me. He's been sitting back in the wannigan like a king, while his hired men ran his drive over this place, knocking heads under water if they got in the way, and never hitting sand-bars or white-water. About long enough. It's time this fine piece of country was set-tling up, and decent people getting the use of it. It's time for a jam.

"Yes, sir, Doc, I've got a feeling that there's going to be a hard, tight jam about here, with maybe a few fellows getting hurt before she's broken, and when she breaks out, old man Taggart and his outfit, or our-selves, will be sluiced down-stream and out of this country for good."

Dr. Sanders knit his brows.

"H'm, h'm. I see what you mean. H'm, h'm. But you see, Thorson, you'll be the victim Taggart will be laying to put away first of all. You've dared him, and you've beaten him. He won't waste any time getting you—Taggart and his gang. H'm, h'm. You'll have to do some skilful side-stepping to keep yourself—h'm, h'm—above the young green grass."

"You can't side-step when you're fighting a gang, Doc. They'll be on all sides of you."

"H'm, h'm. That's what I say. It'll be hard——"

"So there'd be no use trying to buck Taggart by side-stepping."

"No?"

"No. His gang's too big. But, Doc, did you ever stop to think that there wouldn't be any gang without Taggart?"

"Eh?"

"Taggart's the whole thing. The gang wouldn't be his slaves and so ready to do his dirty work if they weren't sneaks and bums. He picks them that way. He holds some-thing over all of them. They're nothing without him; they'd be afraid to try to rough-house a Sunday-school without Tag-gart to send 'em on."

"Yes, Taggart's the driving power, of course. Well——"

"Well, when the jam comes, which will be pretty soon, I've got to take a running-jump at them before they get the jump on me."

"How?"

"Get Taggart," murmured Gaston, settling down to sleep. "He's the key-log. Get him, and we'll have the jam broken, and everything here all our own way."

But it was not of Taggart, nor of ways and means to combat him, that he dreamed that night; it was a girl who smiled, and a home. He did not sleep well. He could not quite see himself in the dream.

CHAPTER XXV

GASTON'S DREAM

HALE and Tom Pine came back from La Croix at noon next day, horses and buggy covered with mud to testify to the speed of their drive through the night.

"I wouldn't have gone with him without waiting to see you come to," explained Tom, "but Doc swore you was still as good as new, and I figgered what you was after was to see that girl's stake cached safe and sound. We figgered we might catch up with that Murphy fellow and have a few words with him for blowing holes in you, but we found where he'd left his canoe in a bend about three miles below. Left it where the river curves into plain sight of the road. He was scairt, all right. We couldn't stop to trail him, with all that money in the buggy. What I don't see is how you got the coin after he'd shot you, 'less you got him, too?"

"Murphy didn't shoot me," explained Gaston. "It was that Indian of Taggart's. I could tell by the way he grunted when I winged him. Yes, I touched him up a little, shooting wild in the brush. Murphy let go of the dough in a hurry and jumped for his canoe."

Tom Pine growled reprovingly.

"You ought to be kicked, Gaston Olaf; yes, siree, you ought to be kicked. Why'n Sam Hill did you try for to do it alone? If you'd took me along you'd have gobbled Murphy while I was gobbling the Indian."

"I wasn't after Murphy or the Indian. I was after old Taggart himself. That's why I ought to be kicked; I should have known better than suppose that the old man would be careless enough to come after the coin himself."

Tom's eyes and mouth opened full width.

"D'you mean to say, Gaston Olaf—d'you mean to say old Taggart had a finger in that safe-blowing?"

"Sure. He was the whole thing. He made Murphy do the job. I had a hunch that something was wrong up there at the bayou when Taggart was so free and easy about paying for the logs. When we came to town last night and Doc Sanders hadn't heard anything about Murphy being hurt, I began to know Taggart was cooking up some medicine. I remembered that Murphy was a safe-blower, and when Doc told about the money being put in Hale's safe I was on a warm trail.

"I went down to watch Hale's store alone because I thought Murphy would come and blow the safe and take the stake to the old man. I wanted to nail old Taggart with the stuff on him. You can buy a new pair of shoes and kick me any time you want to, Tom. A kid might have known it wasn't the old man's style to deal first-hand with one of his crooks."

Tom Pine sat silent for a long time.

"That was good trailing, Gaston Olaf."

"But my game got away."

"Yep." Tom was silent a moment. "Yep, he got away. And he's a hard one, with long, sharp claws. What you going to do now, Gaston Olaf?"

"Sit around for a few days until my shoulder heals up. Doctor's orders."

"Yep. I mean, after that?"

Gaston looked out of the opened window. A breeze from the south was blowing, and the air was soft, piny, redolent with the scent of an awakening Northern Spring.

Outside, the miracle of the last few days was developing. A landscape, which a week before had been a picture of snow, ice and Winter, now proclaimed that the growing season had begun. From where they sat they could see the mighty river racing down from the north, bank-full, swinging around the bend on which the town was located, with low-murmured warning of the immense power of its brown waters.

Far away the pines showed blue in the hazy air. Along the river the buds on the willows and alders had begun to swell; the tamaracks in the swamp, a week before brown and dry, were tinted a faint gold; a robin was chirping cheerfully near by, and in a clearing a settler with a pick was assuring himself that the frost had gone out of the ground.

"Tom, it looks pretty good, doesn't it?"

Tom nodded.

"She does, Gaston Olaf, she does for a fact."

There was another space of silence.

"I suppose you're hankering to be traveling, Tom?"

"You ain't heard me say anything lately, have you?"

"But you are?"

Tom Pine looked wistfully off to where the blue pines marked the horizon.

"I tell you how it is, Gaston Olaf: you and me, we're partners, and where you stick I stick. I ain't blind, boy; I can see what's happening. You're going to settle down. All right. I settle down too. If you can do it, I can. We'll see. You can't make a canary bird or a barnyard fowl out of an eagle. That's against nature. But—we'll see. What I mean is, what you going to do about old Taggart? He'll be cooking bad medicine for us, Gaston Olaf. Have you got a scheme to handle the old devil?"

Gaston shook his head. His thoughts had been busy with other schemes, other hopes. How could a man be expected to scheme for battle when he had just begun to dream of a gentler, a sweeter form of life than he had ever imagined? Yet the scheming was necessary. The battle must be fought and won before the dream might be realized. Very well. He would put the dreaming aside for the time being. He was a little too much inclined to dream anyway. The road before him was hard and stern. It would not be enough that he might win over Taggart. He must make something of himself, have something of his own before he would have a right. . . .

"No, I haven't, Tom. We've got to handle him before he handles us, though. I've got a few days here in this room, and I can't think much in here—too much like being in jail. You just lay low for a day or two, Tom. Then we'll go out in the timber some place and cook up a scheme."

"That's good talk," agreed Tom. "A man can't see clear when he's got a roof between him and the sky. Well, I promised Hale I'd rub some liniment on his mare's knees. We hit a windfall in the dark last night."

"What's Hale doing now?"

"Oh, he piked straight up to the girl's to put the receipt for the money safe in her hands."

When Tom had gone, Gaston leaned far out of his window. From there he could see the Havens's front yard, and Rose and Hale were walking toward the gate. At the gate Rose stopped, shading her eyes with her hand. Hale paused, and for a while they stood talking, while a pang shot through Gaston's heart.

Hale fitted into the picture. The steadiness, the stanchness, the quiet determination of the man were obvious in his bearing, in the serious poise of his head as he listened to Rose's words. And her confidence and trust in him were bespoken in the way in which she looked at him when she spoke.

Gaston drew back from the window, as if discovering himself in a shameful action.

"Hale's all right; he's got a right," he mused. "But if I can make good I'll have a right too, and then——"

The chain of his thoughts shifted abruptly. He sat in a heavy mood.

"I guess—I guess she'd be happy enough with Hale, all right. Well, I won't make her unhappy, no matter what happens to me."

Rose came with her mother to call on him that afternoon, and Gaston, while deprecating cheerfully Mrs. Havens's motherly solicitude over his hurts, watched closely to catch on Rose's face the look of confidence she had bestowed upon Hale. It was not there. But something else was there, something that compensated Gaston for the absence of the other.

Her eyes lighted up at the sight of him as they failed to do at the sight of Hale. When she looked at him there was a look on her face which others never saw. The look thrilled him and made him eager to be out and doing.

That evening when he looked out of his window and saw her raking the leaves from around the lilac bushes in her yard, he threw the doctor's injunctions to the wind. There was a small shed directly under his window, and from the shed it was an easy drop to the ground. So silently and swiftly did he move that he was vaulting over the fence, coming to her side, before she looked up and saw him.

"MR. THORSON!" she gasped. Then, remonstratingly: "But Dr. Sanders insisted that you be quiet for at least two days more. This is wrong of you, it is reckless. You shouldn't. Why——"

She stopped in confusion, leaning upon the rake in her agitation.

"Just for a minute," he said. "I couldn't stand it any longer in that room. I felt I was in prison."

He looked at her and her eyes went to the ground.

"It's Spring," he laughed. "It's hard to stay indoors in Spring."

She raised her eyes now, looking at him seriously.

"I wonder if you ever are serious in what you say?"

"Serious? You bet." He was serious now. "Why?"

"When people speak seriously they mean what they say."

"Yes. Well?"

"You said you wanted to begin all over, and forget the 'wild, tough kid' that you've been."

"And I do."

"Do you think there is a fair chance to forget when you do wild, reckless things like this?" She slowly resumed her raking. "You—you alarm me when you do things like this. You know that Dr. Sanders wouldn't have ordered you to be quiet unless it was necessary. He knows. You can't go contrary to reason any more than other people without paying for it."

For an instant the old reckless spirit flared within him. It was on the tip of his tongue to speak out boastingly that there was where she was wrong; that because of the way he was made he could do things contrary to reason, things other people might not do, and not pay for them in the least; that he had been doing such things ever since he was grown, and that he had never paid, not once.

But he checked himself. He knew now, on second thought, that he was paying now, that he had paid every time he had dreamed of her and had been unable to fit himself into the picture, and that if he was to have a right to make the dream come true he must regulate his life so that he would be as other people, people who lived in towns, sanely, ordinarily. For a flash the sense of confinement of the room he had just quitted passed over him; but she was before him, leaning on the rake-handle now, her eyes upturned to him, and for the moment he felt that he could do anything—yes, even live in a house, tractable and contented, all his life— for the sake of the look which she gave to him and him alone.

"You're right," he said contritely. "But you'll be patient with me, won't you? You know I've got a lot to learn."

"Of course I will."

Her eyes rose to his and quickly fell again. She began to rake slowly.

"I want to make good," he said huskily. "Will you be patient with me while I'm trying?"

She nodded, slowly raking the leaves over and over again.

"I believe you can do almost anything if you really want to," she said without looking up. "But please do stop and think when you feel moved to do reckless things."

"I will. I've got nothing to do but sit and think, up in that room."

And far into that night he sat in his room and thought. At last he seemed to see his path of life clear before him. No more reckless roaming—steady work, and a home.

He blew out the lamp. Before getting into bed he stole a peep out at the star-filled sky. He could hear the river murmuring at the bend, strong, untamed, restless, happy. He leaned on the casing, studying the sky. By the stars and by the "look" of the woods he knew it to be shortly after midnight. The murmuring of the river grew more distinct. He could picture the brown water as it swung around the bend. A fine river. He had never traveled it. A man might drop a canoe in below the settlement and it would carry him. . . .

Gaston tore himself away from the window sharply. He laughed at the vagrant straying of his thoughts.

"No more of that, old boy. You're settling down and making a little home. That other's all right for a kid; but work, doing something, a home, that's the thing for a man—for you."

And for the time being he honestly believed that it was so.

CHAPTER XXVI

THE FIRST MARSHAL OF HAVENS FALLS

THE second morning following Dr. Sanders had pronounced Gaston free to resume strenuous activities. Soon after Hale came into the room as Gaston was preparing to quit it.

"A man came up from La Croix last night who'd like to meet you."

"Meet me?" said Gaston. "Who can he be?"

"Jim Lonergan."

Gaston Olaf sat up excitedly.

"What! Old 'Iron Trail' Lonergan!"

He had often heard of that grim, persistent railroad builder, who was thrusting his steel rails into that part of the North wherever he discovered a locality that promised farms, settlements and filled freight-cars. It was said that Lonergan looked at scenery and saw tons of freight per annum. His reputation was one of squareness and success.

"What in the world does he want to meet me for?"

"He'll tell you himself."

Hale stepped out and returned with a stocky, square block of a man, white-haired, round-faced, brick-brown from sun and wind, genial and patient. In the first glimpse Gaston saw a resemblance to Hale —Hale as he might be when he was twenty years older. Following came Dr. Sanders, Perkins, the postmaster, and two other of the decent settlers.

Lonergan looked Gaston over leisurely, nodded, and held out his hand.

"They grow 'em big and wide where you come from, I see," he said. "Now, Hale's been telling me a few things about you, and I'm pretty much inclined to take his word. The question to be answered before we go any farther is: Do you figure on staying put in this country?"

"That's my idea," replied Gaston. "Old Dave Taggart says I can't, but I differ with him there."

"Exactly." Lonergan rubbed his hands together. "Thorson, we need you for marshal of the town of Havens Falls."

Gaston slowly rose to his feet. He was at first moved to break forth into scornful laughter. But Hale and Lonergan were watching him seriously, anxiously. Lonergan went on, swiftly and earnestly:

"We need you, Thorson. You've shown that you're the man we've been praying for. You drop down here like a godsend. You know what a hell-hole this settlement is. You know what a town it ought to be, what the country around ought to be for settlers. We can't open it up the way things are. They've got to be changed. We've been waiting for the right man to come along to help us change them, and now he's come. You say you intend settling down here.

Good. Then you owe the settlement a citizen's duty. That duty is to be its first marshal. What do you say?"

"One question," said Gaston suspiciously. "Are you fixing up to make me your gun-expert to shoot off old Taggart legally?"

Lonergan and Hale and the others smiled.

"It'll hardly be necessary to do any shooting—if you're our marshal. Taggart is powerful and dangerous because he has a gang at his beck and call. His gang is dangerous because they know they're safe from the law. Give us a marshal to tame them, and the backbone of the Taggart power is broken. Now, if you'll pardon me for saying it, Thorson, I've got it figured that you intended to make it a private, personal, old-fashioned affair between yourself and Taggart?"

"Of course. He's threatened to run me out of the country. It's got to be."

"And you'd probably win. We'll admit that you would. And law and order would be just as far away. It would only be another shooting scrape. But—if the marshal of Havens Falls broke up Taggart's gang, the law would be established as something men would respect, the way for the railroad would be cleared, and civilization would begin to have its inning. Have I made our meaning clear?"

Gaston nodded.

"But what's the use of talking?" he said, turning to Hale. "As I understand it, Taggart's got his own sheriff of the county, and his grip on the courts is too strong for you fellows to break."

"It was until the other day," said Hale.

"How come?"

"It was until the other morning when you took a drive smack away from Taggart's gang."

Lonergan broke into a quiet laugh.

"Big medicine, Thorson, skookum medicine!" he chuckled. "I've been prowling around this bush longer than you've lived, but that's the best I ever heard. As Hale says, Taggart's grip was too strong to be broken up to then. He was the big chief that nothing could touch. But since then—well, I've spread the news to the far corners of the county, and if there's a white man who isn't laughing every time he hears Taggart's name mentioned, there's something wrong with that man sure. No, sir; Dave Taggart isn't the big chief he was. You did more than save those logs for poor old Havens's girl, Thorson, when you did that trick; you got a peavey into the old man, and if we heave on it hard enough we ought to pry him loose. Come with us, boy. We need you; the town needs you. Well, give us your answer."

"I'll go you," said Gaston. "It's a job that's got to be done."

"Good! You're appointed; that's agreed. We'll have the papers hurried up from La Croix in a day or two."

Lonergan remained while the others departed.

"Can you lay your hands on a few hundred dollars, Thorson?" he asked when they were alone.

Gaston told of the timber claims he and Tom Pine had proved up.

"Sell 'em. Turn 'em into cash. Then buy this forty just back of town. It belongs to me; I'll sell it for whatever you get for your timber."

"That stump land! Why should I buy that?"

"Because that's where the line of the Havens Falls main line is going to run. Five, ten years from now you can name your own price for town lots. That's going to be your pay for making this place fit for white folks to live in—if you do. A few men who're in on the ground floor are going to get decently rich out of this town site, Thorson," he concluded as he arose. "There's no reason why you shouldn't make yourself the big buck of 'em all."

Gaston, left alone, rubbed his eyes. He went to the window and looked out, and all he saw was Rose Havens's garden. It certainly looked as if his dream might come true. Here was Opportunity. Havens Falls would become a town. He would become one of the big, solid citizens of the town. Then he would have the right——

"Hi! Gaston Olaf, dast I come in?"

Tom Pine's gruff voice brought Gaston out of his reverie. The old man came in with the narrowed eyes and soft step that told he was keenly on the alert. He looked Gaston over from top to toe.

"Huh!" he snorted. "What you been doing to yourself? You look as solemn and self-satisfied as if you'd got religion."

"I've got a job," said Gaston.

"A job? You bet you have. You've got a job on your hands that it's time you were waking up to."

"I'm the new marshal of Havens Falls."

Tom Pine cackled.

"I jest heard about that. But that ain't the job I'm talking about. While you been talking with the high mucky-mucks I've been doing a little trailing. The war's started, boy. The sheriff's just got into town. He's come to arrest you for shooting one Murphy. Yes, they're keeping the bluff up, and he's getting a small army together down at McCarthy's to come and take you."

Gaston frowned thoughtfully.

"So the old man's started the ball rolling so soon, has he? I thought he'd wait till I was on my pins. Pretty fair scheme. If that sheriff ever got me in his charge I'd never bother Taggart any more."

"You ain't in no fit shape for a battle, Gaston Olaf."

"No, and the time isn't ripe for a battle." His mind was made up. "We're going to sneak. We're going to run away. Go get our rifles, Tom Pine. I'll meet you on the other side of the ridge."

Tom Pine's look betrayed his surprise.

"By the great pike-pole! Gaston Olaf, you're almost getting sense."

WHILE Tom was securing the rifles, Gaston dropped out of the window, slipped unobserved into the timber, and rounded the big ridge back of town. There in a tiny cedar swamp he was soon joined by Tom, who, noting the perfect cover, nodded his approval.

"We can jest lay up here safe as a bear in his den, me going back for chuck after dark, and nobody ever looking for us so close to town."

"Yes, we can, and then we can do something else, too. Did you happen to hear anything about Taggart?"

"Oh, he wasn't in town, of course. I heard that much."

"Of course he wasn't. He wouldn't be anywhere's around while his hired men are putting me out of business. Come on."

"Hah? You ain't going to hit the trail, Gaston?"

"I guess yes. I've got a hunch I know where Taggart is. He's alone in the woods while his gang is in town tending to me. Do you think I'm going to miss such a chance? Come on."

Avoiding the river, the road, trails, clearings, they swung by a roundabout way through the woods toward the camp where they had worked for Taggart. They forded the west branch above the watch-house, then instead of following the stream Gaston led the way straight into the woods.

It was in the middle of the afternoon when at last they lay flat-bellied under the brush of a hillside and peered down at the little, hidden clearing with Taggart's strange cottage in the center. They had found Taggart's trail, and knew he was before them.

For a long time they lay there in silence, making no sound or movement that might betray their presence to some sharp-eyed watcher down below. So far as they could see, the clearing was deserted; the doors and windows of the house were open, and occasionally a sound came floating up, too faint to be distinguished.

"I guess he ain't there," whispered Tom Pine finally. "And if he was, Gaston Olaf, what's your scheme for handling him? You say you're all for law and order now, and no shooting goes. What then?"

"I'm the marshal of Havens Falls," replied Gaston. "My job is to break up the gang that's making the town a hell-hole. If the gang suddenly wakes up and finds that it hasn't got any Taggart to nerve it up, the job of busting it will be about cut in half."

"So we——"

"We kidnap Taggart and keep him in a nice dry place till the gang's been kicked to pieces and sent floating down-stream."

"All right," Tom Pine nodded quietly. "I ain't surprised at anything you do any more. First we steal a drive, now it's old Devil Dave himself. All right, Gaston Olaf, let's go down and get him."

"We'll wait until dark. We're on his trail out now, so if he leaves he's got to come this way. No hurry."

TO BE CONCLUDED

THE DEVIL'S DUE
by Redfield Ingalls.

MY FRIEND, "Brick" Stoddard, of the United States Marine Corps, told me this of late, as we sat over sundry successive glasses in a plaisance at Coney, scorning the while the efforts of a misguided photo-play director to depict adventure as she is.

Brick had been sent North on sick leave, to recuperate from an island fever, and was doing so after a fashion of his own. Brick, by the way, can talk good American when he wants to, but to do so he considers "putting on dog."

Did the papers print much about what the m'rines done down in Haiti? Made quite a fuss, eh? Well, they ought to. Did they say anything about Jeff Cole gettin' wounded? I bet you don't remember; and I bet more that they didn't.

In the first place, it was strictly unofficial and against orders; and more'n that, Jeff would of about murdered anybody that blabbed. I got my blasted fever at the same time, but the rest of the bunch—O'Toole and Ole and the doc—was luckier.

And it was all account of a fool mulatto native and her kid. I don't blame Jeff for bein' sore on 'em.

Well, the *Washington* was at Cape Hatien when Admiral Bill got orders to be at it to Port au Prince, 'count of their havin' murdered a couple of presidents or something, and kicked holes in the French legation. So we made a flyin' jump and pulled up at the Port late one blazin' hot afternoon near the end of July. Port au Prince was mighty pretty to look at as we came up, with the high green and blue mountains behind, and the city lyin' at their feet like a handful of broken school-chalk dropped on a lawn.

But when we got closer in the boats and got a whiff off shore—holy snakes! Did ye ever take a walk through the Bowery on a hot N'York day? No, that ain't it. Mix that with a real, old-fashioned country slaughter-house in August, and you'll get a sort of idea of what we had to stand all the time we was there.

Well, we put ashore in a hurry, 'cause they was raisin' Cain in town, screamin' and shootin' and yellin' and rushin' around like a mixture of the parrot-house at the Zoo with this here Coney crowd—and then some.

A mob of the natives in white pants and nothin' much else comes rushin' down to the rotten jetty as our boats pull in, howlin' and yellin' and wavin' long, wicked bamboo clubs bound with iron. It looks kind of promisin' at first; but when us m'rines and blue-jackets jumped ashore they sort of lost interest, and tried to pretend that they'd just come down to give us the glad hand.

We hadn't hardly formed up, hustlin' the crowds back, when along comes a native, black as your boot, ridin' on a donkey. He was in the regular white pants, and barefooted same as the rest, but he had on an oh-be-joyful red coat all covered with medals and gold braid, and a plumed hat. He hops off the donkey and marches up to the lieutenant bowin' and scrapin' and spillin' a line of French that beat anything I ever heard.

Jeff Cole was alongside of me, chewin' as usual, and it knocked him all of a heap. Jeff's from Virginia, he is, though he's got the nose and jaw of a Yankee; and he don't hold with color. He didn't say nothin' then, but he near swallowed his gum.

The lieutenant listens a minute—tries his Serene Highness in plain United States, and then beckons to me.

"Stoddard," he says, "you speak French, don't you?"

"Yes, sir," says I, salutin' and steppin' up. Me? Sure I do; leastways, Canuck French. I was raised in Vermont, and I didn't forget none of it workin' in the Maine lumber camps.

So I starts to translate. Medals explains in a lofty and supercillabus manner that he's General Guillaume de something-or-other, and likewise and incidental the examinin' medical officer of Port au Prince; and while he's overwhelmed with honor and adulation 'count of this friendly visit of soldiers of the so-great sister nation of the U. S. A., he positively can't think of lettin' us land before he has made a strict examination of every mother's son.

There's been reports of bubonic plague—"*maladie bubonique*" he called it—in some of the other islands, and the great Republic of Haiti is all fussed up about it, and he personally has had several suspected cases disposed of summary. Furthermore it would be an international calamity for the said U. S. of A. to bring a so-frightful disease into the so beautiful and tranquil country. Therefore, deeply as he regrets it, he must positively——

The lieutenant has been kind of dazed so far, but now he comes to.

"Tell him to can the chatter and beat it!" he raps out. "Fall in, Stoddard. Comp'ny, for'ard!" And we shoos the whole rabble back into town in spite of their yells and wavin' sticks.

I'm only tellin' you this to show you the kind of thing we was up against. There was most as many generals as there was soldiers; they was polite as ——, and talked French more or less like Parisians; they shook hands right or left, indifferent every time they met, but some of the things we seen and the smells—waugh!

 WELL, we starts in disarmin' every soldier and civilian we caught. You couldn't tell 'em apart mostly. The town got kind of quiet after awhile, and we left a bunch of the boys at the French legation to keep order, and finally bivouacked in a market in the north of the place. We cleaned it up all we could, and used about a barrel of disinfectants, but it didn't help much.

After a while we got settled for the night, with a lot of little fires goin'—the smoke kept the mosquitoes and bugs away some—and went to jawin' and foolin' around to rest up before goin' to sleep.

It was still early in the evenin', and hot—sufferin' cats! Mike O'Toole, the devil, had managed to ease in a couple bottles of rum, and that helped a heap.

We was squattin' and lyin' around one of the little fires when the thing I started to tell you about began—me and Jeff and O'Toole and Ole Swanson.

Jeff was masticatin' a hunk of navy twist and runnin' on in his slow voice without enough r's, about the "—— nigrows, suh, that talk French like a sho'nough white man." Lord, how that did get Jeff's goat! O'Toole was hummin' a "come all ye," lyin' flat on his back with a bottle beside him, and Ole Swanson with his placid, round face and fair hair and mustache was stirrin' raw sugar into his rum to make it taste like *arrak punsch*.

As for me, I was puttin' a real edge on my sword-bayonet with a whetstone, which isn't in the regulations, and might of got me into trouble, but is considerable useful in a close scrap. I hate a dull knife, and that's a fact.

Well, we was sittin' there peaceful, when all of a sudden one of the sentries gives a challenge. Then comes a voice that I'd know in a million.

"All right, old man," it says with a kind of a laugh in it. "Surgeon George King, U. S. N., and mighty glad to see you!"

I jumps up and beats it over, and sure enough it was him, big as life, and smilin' like he'd just heard of a new kind of religion. . . . Huh? Mean to say I never told you about Doc King of the old *Albuquerque*, him who was life and soul of our amateur theatricals—the guy that's wrote books on antypology, or whatever you call it? All but got boloed in the Philippines one time tryin' to find out what kind of a god the Moros worship, and then near killed himself curin' a Gugu brat of diphtheria? Sure I did!

Well, it was Doc King, all right, with his hair standin' on end where he'd took his hat off; hawk nose, gray eyes and all. The moon had come up around half-past eight and was pretty high now, showin' him clear as day.

"Why, if it isn't Brick Stoddard!" he sings out, squeezin' my hand till the bones cracked. "Right in the thick of it as usual, eh, Brick?"

Many's the time I've altered a guy's mug for callin' me that—I ain't to blame for my hair. But Lord, you'd take anything from the doc. And his hair's near the color of mine at that!

Well, he comes into the market-place and shakes hands with the lieutenant, and tells him that he's on furlough, and has been in Port au Prince for the last three-four days. Seems he's visitin' Haiti 'count of some girl or other; and I was considerable surprised, for the doc never had much use for women, and especially the kind you'd find in a hole like Haiti. Flora he said her name was; Flora N. somebody-or-other.

Huh? *Fauna?* Say, how t'ell did you know her name? Oh. Well,. I never did think he was like that.

Doc King goes on to tell the lieutenant about the doings in town previous to our coming, which they'd been a considerable sight livelier than we'd suspected—but I guess you read all about that in the papers.

The two of them sit down by the lieut's shelter-tent near our fire and continue their palaver; and O'Toole curses 'em good for it under his breath, seein' that he had to hide the booze, and we go on talkin'.

I never saw a night like that before. That moon was a wonder—it made the sky look right blue, and you couldn't hardly see the stars at all. There wasn't a breath of air stirrin', which maybe was as well for the disinfectants smelled clean at all events.

I said the doc was the start of it; and he was, in a way, for we wouldn't of gone if it hadn't been for him. The real beginnin' came a little later.

We was sittin' there talkin' low, with the natives all over town screamin' and yellin' and singin' at the tops of their lungs, and laughin' and carryin' on like they hadn't a care in the world—a regular "I Should Peeve" club—and us, in spite of the noise and smells and heat, gettin' sleepier and sleepier, when all of a sudden the sentry hollers—

"Who goes there?"

A woman answers him shrill and excited, and the lieutenant looks up from his talk with Doc King and goes over to see what the matter is. The dame keeps on jabbering, and pretty soon the lieutenant yells for me.

I beats it there, and it's a kind of a good-lookin' mulatto, little more than a girl, with the regular cotton dress on that all the native women wear, and her head done up in a white hank'chief. She's standin' near the edge of the market-place, wringin' her hands and gabbling Creole French like a type-writer goin', and her face in the moonlight is all streaked with tears.

The sentry, one of the bluejackets, has gone back on his beat again, and the lieutenant is lookin' worried.

"Ask her what she wants, Stoddard," he snaps.

I does, and she gives a sort of gasp and comes at me with her hands clasped, gabblin' so fast I can't make head or tail of it.

"*Pas si vite*," I tells her sharp-like. "*Qu'est qu'il y a?*"

She pulls it again, and this time I make out, "*Mo' pauv' bébé emporté.*" And then she alludes to a "*loup.*"

"It's something about a wolf carrying off her baby, sir," says I.

"Huh?" says the lieutenant surprised. "Well, bring her over to my tent," and he turns back.

He's a kindly sort of guy about children, havin' some of his own.

The dame follows me like a shot, though she's tremblin' all over. When we come up the lieutenant says:

"Here's something ought to interest you, doctor. Tell him what she says, Stoddard," and I does, the dame standin' there shakin' in her shoes. She was well-shaped, pretty near white, and mighty graceful; but her voice—Lord, it was like an election horn, same as the rest of them native women!

"What's that?" says the doc. "Why, it's impossible!"

Then he gives the mulatto a look, jumps up, pats her on the shoulder, and makes her sit down on a packin' case. The lieutenant gives me a nod, and I try again to find out what's eatin' her.

Well, Ingalls, it was about the hardest job I ever tackled. First place she was spielin' the brand of French a kid would talk; next it was a heap different from Canuck French; and finally she used words now and then that ain't in any human language. However, by makin' her say it over and over I finally got the main part of it, and near jumps out of my skin.

It wasn't a "*loup*" she was talkin' about; so help my Bob, it was a "*loup-garou!*" It made the cold chills chase up and down my back in spite of the awful heat, for I hadn't heard of one of them things since old Père Vaudoin used to tell us ghost-stories when I

9

was a kid in Vermont. And to think of hearin' of them away down there!

"What's the matter, Stoddard?" says the lieutenant. "What's she been telling you?"

"I can't make it all out, sir," I says, wiping my forehead; "but accordin' to her, her baby's been carried off by a kind of a wolf——"

"But I tell you it's impossible!" exclaims the doc. "There aren't any wolves in Haiti."

"Beg pardon, sir," says I, "but it ain't exactly a wolf; it's a sort of spook she's been talkin' about that's part man and part wolf."

"A werewolf?" The doctor actually jumps, thinkin' about his antypology, most like—anthropology? Thanks.

"She's crazy," says the lieutenant disgusted.

Doc King looks at her sharp where she sits shiverin' and sobbin' on the packin'-case, and shakes his head.

"No," he says, "she's sane enough—and in serious trouble, or I never saw a grievin' mother before. What else did she say, Brick?"

"Well," says I, "maybe I didn't get it straight, but she says her baby died three days ago, and the wolf-thing has only just got it tonight. But what I can't make out is that she thinks it ain't dead at all, sir. And she keeps talkin' about a 'goat without horns,' callin' the kid that."

"Of course a kid has no horns," says the lieutenant grinnin'. "Is a kid a baby in French, too?"

"No, sir," I says.

"What's the French for it?" asks the doc, watchin' the mulatto under his hand.

"*Chèvre sans cornes,*" says I; and with that the girl shudders all over, and moans pitiful.

"You see?" says the doc, noddin' at her. "It means something pretty serious to her, anyhow. What else did she say, Brick?"

"All the rest I could make out was that she wants us white soldiers to please for God's sake go and get her baby for her," I says; and crazy as the dame's story was, I couldn't help but feel sorry for her.

Well, the lieutenant couldn't act on any such wild yarn as that, of course, and was for sendin' her away. The doc insists that her trouble is real enough, but can't make a stab at what it is.

"Why doesn't she go after it herself?

Or her folks?" he says. "Ask her, Brick."

I did, and made out that her husband was scared stiff—"So is she," the doc mutters—and had tried to keep her from comin' to us. I asks some more, but only got the same thing over and over—"*Loup-garou emporté mo' bébé pou' chèv sans cornes*," over and over, in a kind of wail that 'ud wring your heart.

"A werewolf carried off her baby for a hornless goat," repeats the doctor disgusted. "Well, it gets mine." He runs his fingers through his hair. "Ask her where the thing came from."

I did.

"*Papaloi*," she says, lookin' at me surprised and as much as to say, "of course, you mut!"

"*Papaloi envoyé*," she adds with a new fit of the shivers.

"Where in thunder's Papaloi?" says the lieutenant.

"Beggin' your pardon, sir," I says, "a Papaloi sent it."

"Then what's a Papaloi?" says the doc.

"Search me," I says. "It ain't French."

"This won't get us anywhere," says the lieutenant, moppin' his face with his hank'-chief. "Marines are handed some funny jobs all right, but they aren't supposed to chase spooks that I ever heard of. Stoddard, chase out and collar the first intelligent-looking native you find, and see if he can explain."

I does, and brings a general. They're near as thick in Haiti as the flies. He was scared at first; but when I explains he chirks up and is honored 'most to death to translate for the so-brave brother-citizens of a sister republic. He gabbles to the girl for a minute, she answerin' back in a tired kind of way, like she was tellin' him something she knew he knew all about already; and then——

Did you ever see a nigger turn pale? They don't of course; the nearest they come to it is a sort of slate-blue.

Well, so help my Bob, that guy actchully went *gray!* Then he fetches a gulp; says she's crazy, and anyhow he can't understand her, and he's got a mighty pressin' engagement, and if we don't mind excusin' him—and he scuttles away like we all had the plague.

"Huh!" says the lieutenant, lookin' after him. "I'm beginning to think, doctor, that you're right. Stoddard, see if you can't get her to explain what a Papaloi is."

I tries to pump her on that line, and she shut up like a clam. Just sat starin' at me with her eyes rollin' and her face workin' and wouldn't say a word!

Doc King watches her, rubbin' his hair the wrong way, which is a trick he has. But the lieutenant gets mad.

"We can't do anything for her if she won't tell us what she wants!" he snaps. "Tell her so; and tell her to go chase herself."

I did, and the girl gets up, wringin' her hands and cryin' like her heart would break. She was scared—I could see that—scared like she had a nightmare, yet tryin' to fight back her fear so as to get us to save her kid. It sure was pitiful!

IT WAS then that the drum began. The lieutenant was sittin' on his camp-stool, chewin' the stem of his pipe, and frownin'; the doc was standin' beside him clawin' at his hair; I was standin' at attention beside the little fire, waitin' for the next orders; and the mulatto was fightin' with herself to make up her mind.

O'Toole and Jeff Cole and Ole were lyin' beside another fire a little ways off, jawin' together and watchin' us in the sharp white moonlight, with their service shirts wide open, and the rest of the detachment was scattered thick all over the market-place, sleepin' or talkin', and others doing sentry-go along the edges. All around was the chatterin', screamin', singin' city, with the mountains loomin' black and solemn over it. It's funny how a scene will stick in your head.

Well, while we're watchin' her, and the poor dame, white as paper for all of the tar-brush, there comes clear and distinct over the noises from somewhere up on the mountain-side the beatin' of a drum—first three sharp strokes, then a sort of roll, but quick and excited.

There was something mighty queer about that drum, something I can't altogether explain. Did ye ever hear 'em poundin' at a Hopi snake dance? Or a hula-hula? Or in a Hindu temple? Well, you've heard 'em go at a real good Oriental dance in a burlesque show with the lid off, haven't cha? You know how the dull "tunk-tunk-tunk" goes right through you, and makes the hair sort of crawl at the back of your neck, stirrin' the devil in you, and yet makin' you sort of afraid?

This drum was the same, only a heap sight worse. I'd never forget it, even if I hadn't found out what it meant. It made me shiver all over, and gave me the feelin' that I wanted to get away from there *pronto* —a long way; and at the same time wanted to get closer! Like a bird and a snake, I guess.

I didn't have time to notice all this then, believe me! But I had plenty of chance to think about it after.

It took the others much the same way. The lieutenant starts and cocks his head, listenin'—he can't hear very good on one side since a Gugu fired his gun beside his head. The doc jumps and turns around to see where it come from. O'Toole crosses himself quick and turns his head so the scar on his cheek showed clear in the moonlight. But the queerest thing was that there came a hush over the whole blame town when that drum started, and for a second there wasn't a sound to be heard but its shivery, pantin' throb.

But the mulatto girl—Lord! She gave a kind of choky gasp and listened with her hands clutchin' at her breast. The noise in the town starts up again, louder and wilder than ever, and then she lets a screech out of her that brought half the bivouac up on their feet, and flings herself down at the doctor's feet.

She grabs him by the knees and starts jabberin' frantic. He backs away, all fussed up; and then she catches her breath and says—seems to force it right out of her —"Voodoo!" and he jumps like he'd been shot.

"My God!" he whispers. "Oh, why didn't I think of that before? It's all right, young woman, we'll look after your baby. Hey, Brick, tell her it's all right, will you?"

And he pulls loose from her hands, goes over to the lieutenant and starts to tell him something in a low voice but mighty strenuous.

The girl had dropped flat; but when I tells her what he said she jumps up with a kind of glory in her face and tries to kiss my hand.

I jerks away, of course, and tells her not to be a fool; and meanwhile I saw the lieutenant start.

"Good God, man, you can't be serious!" he gasps. And then he groans and shakes his head. "Can't help it," he says; "can't be done—I haven't the authority." And

then he says something about "hardly four hundred men—jungle—murder, pure and simple!"

Their voices drop again, and I starts to pump the dame again on my own hook; for if the doc had got wise I sure hadn't. She was ready enough to talk now.

She says her name's Melisse Labeau, and three days before a strange woman had stopped at her cabin for a bite to eat. The woman was a "red," she says, pointin' to the bandanna around her head; while she and her man were "whites," again pointin' to the turban, and don't hold with anything more than fruit and white cocks, or a white goat at most.

I'm givin' you this exactly as she told me —far as I could make out, that is. I understood her all right, but I didn't know what she was talkin' about.

I tells her she'll have to come across with every mortal thing she knows, or we won't be able to do nothin' for her. She bobs her head, shiverin', and all the while, remember, that drum was beatin' away like the blood poundin' in your ears when you've got a fever, and once there comes a faint, high scream at which the girl starts and moans.

She goes on in a hurry to say that the "reds" go in for black cocks and goats, and for big affairs the "hornless goat" she'd been talkin' about. It was then I started to get next, and to go sort of cold and sick all over.

Well, she hadn't thought anything of the strange woman stoppin' at the cabin; even when her baby fell sick sudden that afternoon, and died. The woman was gone by that time anyhow. She grieved over the kid, it bein' her first; and they'd held a funeral. And it was only tonight she'd found out what had really happened.

The dame with the red turban was a *"loup-garou,"* and had poisoned the baby for the Papaloi. The poor girl was cryin' again, with a sort of wild rage that made me feel like a—like a lead nickel with a hole in it, yet wantin' powerful bad to kill somebody.

I tells her to buck up and asks what a Papaloi is. She says he's a priest.

And then I tumbles some more.

"Voodoo?" I says, shakin' inside, and she nods once, still and scared.

I wets my lips—my mouth was powerful dry—and asks her how she knows it was the strange woman that done that, and she tells me. Also what'll happen to the kid if we don't save it—ugh!

All of a sudden the sound of that —— drum changes, and there's another scream, faint, of course, but clear. The mulatto jumps like she'd stepped on a hot coal and grabs me by the arm.

"Quick!" she gasps, and points to where the drum was throbbin' up the mountain, which was all silver and black and mysterious in the moonlight. "Quick, quick!" she pants, tryin' to shake me. My arm was sore for an hour after where she'd caught me.

Doc King and the lieutenant come over and the dame steps back with a look in her eyes same as a she-dog's when you've picked up one of her puppies. They was still arguin', and I butts right in and tells them what she'd told me, short and straight.

The lieutenant doesn't say nothing, but shivers and wipes his forehead; but the doc swears magnificent; and it was the first time I'd ever heard him do it, too. Then he looks the lieutenant square in the eye.

"Well?" he says—just that.

The lieutenant braces himself and throws up his head.

"Doctor," he says, white but steady, "I can't do it—I can't risk the lives of my whole command for anybody's baby."

"What does he say?" says the girl, catchin' my arm again.

I tells her, and she fetches a gasp, and spills a line of talk so fast I can't make out a word. I makes her repeat, and finally get the drift.

"She says," I translates, "that half a dozen of the brave whites will be enough. She knows just where the kid is and will show us, and if we hurry we can steal it back without any danger."

"*Oui, oui!*" she cries. "*Vite!*"

The lieutenant thinks a minute, and throws up his chin.

"Very well," he says. "I have children of my own."

The mulatto tumbles to what he means, all right. She gives a wild sob, throws herself down at his feet, and tries to kiss them. The lieutenant gets red.

"Here, none of that!" he says, backin' away. And then: "Boys! Come here a minute!"

Jeff and Ole Swanson and O'Toole, who've been watchin' the doin's pretty close, come up prompt; and so do maybe half a dozen more of the boys—Tompkins and MacVeigh and some bluejackets.

"Now, boys, it's like this," says the lieutenant in a low voice. "This woman claims that her baby has been kidnaped by the voodoo priests, and is going to be sacrificed tonight where you hear that drum beating." And he adds some details.

There's a sort of hissing gasp goes around.

"I can't send you to rescue it," the lieutenant goes on in the same level voice, "and I can't even permit you to go on your own responsibility. But," he says, "if four or five of you want to volunteer to save the baby, I'll overlook it and do what I can to keep you out of trouble. And remember," he says, "if you don't come back I can't send after you—not till I get reënforcements at least. So far as I know, you will be going into grave danger, perhaps to certain death, and quite possibly court-martial in any event.

"Well, boys," he says sort of grim, "what about it?"

Of course you know what happened. After a second every one took two paces forward and halted. The lieutenant is tickled as if he'd just found a five-spot and says something about the spirit of the navy and specially the m'rines.

"I'll go, of course," says Doc King, careless, and makes a crack about his antypology. "Splendid opportunity to witness voodoo rites at first hand," or something like that, and about getting out of the heat and smells of the town; but all the same I knew his real reason was he wanted to save the baby.

I says I'll go 'count of my speakin' French; the bluejackets and MacVeigh and Tompkins tell about how they love a scrap; Jeff claims he's sore on the natives for talkin' French, and wants to get back at 'em; O'Toole says he's had more experience than anybody there—and I guess he'd had at that; and Ole just says placid:

"Ay tank Ay bane like to vent."

The lieutenant settles on me and Jeff and Ole and Mike O'Toole, us not bein' married; warns us again that we're probably walkin' into a trap or something, and that he can only do his best to prevent a court-martial if we do get back, and gives us all a handshake.

We each took a Krag and bayonet, plenty of ammunition and a full canteen—O'Toole filled his with rum on the sly, which we were mighty glad of later. All except the doc, that is, and he borrowed an automatic from the lieutenant.

And then we started. The girl takes the lead, her face wet with tears, and yet kind of shinin' in the moonlight, and she'd warned us to be mighty careful that none of the natives got next.

II

 I'M NOT going to say much about that night hike of ours through the Haitian jungle, though I'm not likely to forget it for a while. We sneaked out of Port au Prince with the mulatto girl leadin', takin' a lane that smelled to heaven, and keepin' to the black shadows that the moon made.

And then, before you could draw breath, the forest shut down on us black as ink, and with hardly any light even where the moon cut through the branches and creepers and things, though it was near the full.

We went single file, the girl in front, and goin' so fast that we had our work cut out to keep up. In a way it was a heap better there than in the town, for at least we was clear of the amazin' smells, with the heavy, half-stranglin' perfumes of flowers instead. It was quiet, too, except for the noises of small beasts and birds.

But the flies and mosquitoes was pretty bad—that's how I come to get my fever, the doc said later—and the heat! Holy *snakes*, how hot it was! Worse'n the hot room of a Turkish bath with all your clothes and a Winter overcoat on, only steamin' to boot.

Once Ole all but got bit by a *fer-de-lance*, which are as bad as cobras. And once O'Toole tripped over a creeper and went down with his arm in a pool of water, and brought it out covered with leeches. It was sure a picnic!

It was darker'n a movin' picture theayter when you just go in, even after we'd got used to what light there was; but the dame seemed to know her way all right. We could tell we were goin' straight because the blasted drum was goin' steady, with never a pause nor let-up, straight in front of us, till I could of yelled with pure nervousness.

After a while, though—we'd gone maybe three miles then—it began to get fainter instead of louder, as it should of; and pretty soon the doc calls a halt and tells me to ask the dame if we ain't goin' the wrong way.

But she goes up in the air straight off, swears it's all right, and tells us for the love of Heaven to hurry.

That drum was the queerest thing I ever ran into—something like a rattlesnake. When he shakes his tail at you the dry rustlin' seems to come from anywhere but the right place.

At last after we'd gone maybe five miles or so the doc gettin' more and more suspicious and wantin' to stop right there, and the dame more excited and tellin' us just above her breath not to make a sound, and the drum so faint we could hardly hear it at all, we hear a loud singin' break out just ahead and catch a glimpse of a fire.

We went on then, scarcely breathin', and walkin' like we was in our bare feet, and had dropped a package of carpet-tacks in the dark. And a moment later we parts the ferns and creepers, and looks, and there was a big buck native playin' the drum with his palms and fingers, loud and plain as day; and a thunderin' big drum it was, too.

I didn't exactly see the drum first off, though. The whole scene kind of hit me in a heap, and I was a minute or two takin' in the details.

It was a clearin' in the jungle on the side of the mountain, maybe an acre in size, only the shape of a domino. We was at one end. At the other end was a prickly sand-box tree which was the only thing growin' in the clearing, the ground bein' beaten down hard and smooth, and near as level as an asphalt pavement.

In front of the tree a big fire was burnin', yet the jungle was so thick we hadn't seen it fifty feet away. Behind the tree and to one side was a long, low wattle hut, tricked out with red flags and things.

Before the fire was a cage of wooden slats, with something in it that kept movin' around restless. I couldn't make out what it was.

Down both sides of the square and back of the fire around the tree and in front of the hut, standin' and squattin' three and four and five deep, was about two hundred natives, men and women, all chantin' a queer, shivery sort of song, that wasn't very loud, but more monotonous than the drum, all faced inwards, and all rockin' back and forth and every which way, shinin' with sweat in the moon and firelight, and all screwed up to a pitch of excitement that you could fair feel. They was bunched thickest up near the fire, with only a few at our end, with their backs to us, of course. So we could see everything that went on, like we had reserved seats.

And in the hollow square that they made —a space just like the one they leave in a *café dansant* for the people to tango in— there was a native woman as black as your hat, dressed in a sort of red kimono and turban, doin' the coochee-coochee, with her eyes wide, and starin' and spots of foam at the corners of her mouth. She was stout and active as a burlesque queen; but Lord, what a wicked face she had!

The guy with the drum was on one side of the fire, and on the other was another woman, squattin' on the ground and holdin' a black chicken tied up with red ribbons.

What with the leapin', flickerin', roarin' fire throwin' its red light over everything, the silver-white moonlight hittin' spots that the fire missed, and the ink-black shadows and natives, not to mention the coochee dance and the drum and the chantin' and swayin', the scene was the unholiest I ever see in my life—hell, plain hell!

 JUST then somebody grabs my arm and I near jumps out of my skin. It was the mulatto. She was clutchin' with the other hand a little ju-ju bag she'd pulled out of her dress, and her eyes were glarin' in a look that meant plain murder, though at the same time her teeth were chatterin' like she had the ague. She points at the dame cavortin' in the middle of the square.

"*Mamaloi!*" she breathes in my ear; and then with a choke: "*Mamaloi loup-garou— emporté mo' bébé!*"

So this was the she-devil that had poisoned her baby and carried it off! I didn't blame her for that look.

I pipes off the rest of the boys. The doctor was watchin' with his eyes shinin', eager as a pointer when you've started a bunch of partridges. He couldn't think of anything but his entomology, and I remembered the time he'd near got croaked in the Philippines.

O'Toole was crossin' himself industrious, his lips movin'; Jeff was chewin' savage and spittin' like a Maxim gun; and as for Ole, he was watchin' it all so calm and mild and interested that I all but bust out laughin'.

I turned to the red and white and black

hell again and asks the mulatto in a whisper where her kid is. She kind of hesitates and swallows and then says it's probably in the hut.

And then I starts in mentionin' under my breath all the cuss words I knew, and inventin' new ones. Of all the crazy fool expeditions that ever happened, this was the foolest. We might of known that the wench hadn't any sort of a plan for gettin' her kid when she dragged us up here, but was just doin' anything with the ghost of a show to save it.

We five Americans had just about as much chance of gettin' into that hut and out again safe with the brat as of strollin' into the mint at Washington and walkin' off with a million in gold. Lord, I was mad!

I edges over to the doc and tells him. He nods without takin' his eyes from the scene.

"That's what I thought," he breathes. "Simply can't be done, Brick. But we won't go yet for a minute; I want to see what's going to happen next. Shades of hiccups, what an opportunity!"

How's that? Well, that's what it sounded like. Hecate? Yeh; I guess that was it.

Well, we saw what would happen all right. The *Mamaloi*, which I found out after meant priestess, waltzes up to the dame with the chicken, grabs it by the neck, does a whirlin' dervish stunt, and— I'll spare you the details. Then she lets out a screech and falls down in a fit, red froth bubbling from her mouth, while the congregation all jump up and have convulsions, singin' to beat the band, some of 'em tearin' their clothes off and dancin' mother-naked around the fire.

They squat down again, and the doc gasps and runs his handk'chief over his face and around his neck. Then a queer little old man comes shufflin' out of the hut, walkin' like Charlie Chaplin.

"P-p-papaloi!" whispers the mulatto girl, her teeth rattlin' in her head.

The gink hobbles over to where the woman is twitchin' among the feathers, and pretty soon he begins to make the round of the congregation with a saucer, dabblin' their foreheads from it. They rock faster and sing louder as he passes, stickin' out their heads kind of eager, yet scared, to be touched, and the drum keeps goin'—I can hear it yet—ugh!

As he came closer, I got a chance to size him up. He was withered and wrinkled as a man of eighty, and the patches of wool on his head and chin were a dirty white; and yet I had a queer feelin' that he was still on the sunny side of half that age. Maybe it was his eyes.

He had on a red breech-clout and nothin' much else, except some strings of dirty brown beads and bunches of ju-ju bags. The natives hardly dared look at him straight, and I don't wonder, with those eyes. But somehow——

"What the deuce is the matter with him?" whispers the doc beside me; "he's been watchin' the Papaloi like a fox."

For a fact there was something wrong. His Nibs is bent forward as he shuffles along; kind of groans once or twice mixed up with what he's mutterin' as he messes in the dish, and feels his stomach tender once or twice.

He passes our end, markin' the natives' foreheads with a red cross from the dish, goes on up the other side and back into the hut again.

With that the natives get up and do another song-and-dance, and Doc King turns to me.

"Ask this woman," he says just loud enough to hear, "how she expects us to rescue her baby. It's time we got down to cases."

I does, but the dame never says nothin', only looks at the doc pleadin' and wrings her hands, her eyes big and black in the moonlight and her face white, and all screwed up like a kid fixin' to cry. Then she stammers something about the "brave whites," and waits tremblin' to see what we'll do.

It was then I began to get a sort of sinkin' feelin' in my stomach, for I realized jus' what kind of a hurrah's-nest we'd walked into. If we tried to get the brat we'd get croaked; and if we didn't, the mulatto'd raise a holler and give the show away, and we'd get croaked anyhow. It was "heads I win, tails you lose" all right, with us for the goats. Honest, the only thing I could think of was to croak her quick and quiet. But, Lord, I couldn't do that, of course!

The doc shrugs his shoulders disgusted, and passes the word to the bunch to come closer.

"Now, boys," he breathes, "you see how the land lies. I have a hunch that if those devils get wise to us we can kiss ourselves good-by." Of course he didn't say it just like that, but that's what he meant.

"This dame's kid is in that shack behind the fire," he goes on. "There's just a chance that we can creep around through the brush and cut a hole into the shack and snake the kid out that way; but if we make a sound, or they see us move—bluey-bluey!" He said that all right; it was one of his pet expressions.

"It's up to us, boys," he says. "Do we——"

He breaks off and turns to look. So do the rest of us. The natives had fetched a howl all together, like a pack of wolves, and slumped down sitting again. The drum hits up a new gait, wilder and wickeder than ever, and out of the hut comes the Mamaloi, draggin' a bleatin' black goat by one horn.

And the goat—so help my Bob—the goat had on a pair of pants and a shirt!

Behind her hobbles the Papaloi, with something in his arms. He shuffles over and lays it on the cage I told you about, and then I got a fair look at it.

So did the mulatto. I claps my hand over her mouth just in time to be too late.

"'S all off, boys!" I grunts, wishin' I had time to choke that fool dame; but believe me, they didn't have to be told.

I yanks out my bayonet and sticks it between my teeth—handiest place there is in a close scrap—and whips forward my Krag, while the others get ready just as quick, each in his favorite way. And then we wait for the mob.

But they didn't come! Yet it was hardly surprisin', seein' the row they was makin' themselves, that they didn't none of 'em hear the woman squawk. I glanced at her and couldn't help but feel sorry. She was leanin' forward, her hands clutchin' at her breast, and a look on her face!

We waits for a minute, to be sure, all tense and ready, and then I guess we all sighed. I know I done it through my teeth. Then I took out the bayonet and tried to get rid of the taste in my mouth. Next time, I says to myself—and it only goes to show what triflin' things a feller'll think about in the worst possible fix—I'll grease that bayonet with butter.

"Boys," says the doc, speakin' hoarse and wettin' his lips, "we simply can't do anything now, I'm afraid, except hang every man-jack of the devils when the time comes. —ugh!"

Something landed on his back like a ton of bricks. Same on mine. Somebody let out an almighty yell, and the mulatto screeches; and then we're fightin', just plain rough-and-tumble.

It was then that the bloody drum stopped for the first time since it had started.

I MANAGED to get my bayonet into action as a set of fingers squashed my windpipe flat, and wriggled loose; and for a minute I thought we might get away, after all. But just then the whole congregation arrives, screamin' and howlin' like crazy wildcats. The doc's automatic cracks a couple of times, and then—*blam!*

The next thing I was quite certain about was that I was lyin' in a place with firelight comin' in at the door, tied up like a hammock ready to be stowed away, at ankles, knees, wrists and arms. My head's achin' fit to bust. Outside there was the devil's own hullabaloo. Gee, those voodooers was mad because their party had been broke up!

I might as well tell you now what I learned later. The bunch that jumped us from behind was the guards—inner and outer, too, I guess, if they had 'em—which were thick all around the clearin'. How we'd got through them in the first place the Lord only knows—and the mulatto. They'd heard her yell when she seen her baby and slipped up on us like shadows. We hadn't a chance.

But I'm gettin' ahead of myself.

Well, I hears a groan next me and lifts my head a little. And there was the whole bunch of us, laid along the wall of the hut in a row, with the doc at the far end. I was the last in the line, except the mulatto girl, and she was sittin' near me on my right, tied to a post. Her head was buried in her arms, and she was sobbin' heart-broken.

It was sure a filthy shack, that one was. As soon as my head felt equal to it I sat up to be out of the dirt, and wriggled back till I could lean against the wall.

Huh? Sure thing! There's a lot of bunk wrote about how helpless a guy is with a couple of turns of rope around him. You got to tie him to something if you want to keep him in one place.

I sized the place up while I was movin'. As much as I could see was decorated with red flags and pictures cut out of newspapers; and on the wall behind me was a big green snake, painted rough and crude, like a kid had done it. At the end near the doc was a dirty red curtain.

"Hey, doc!" I calls when my head got clearer, which it was hummin' like a Chinese temple-gong.

He lifts his head a bit and grins at me kind of one-sided. I could see, because his face was in a patch of the firelight.

"All there, Brick?" he groans. "Lord, this is a sweet mess! Are you hurt bad?"

"Nothin' but a bump on the bean and a sore throat," I says. Gee, my throat was sore when I tried to talk. It ain't no joke to be choked, believe me! "How about you?" I says.

"Had the wind knocked out of me, that's all," he says, and wriggles up against the wall like me.

I fetched a groan, for besides the ropes cuttin' into me, which were bad enough, and not bein' able to move any to speak of, the filthy shack was hotter'n the jungle had been and smelled worse'n Port au Prince.

Pretty soon the other boys was sittin' up, too, more or less dazed, but with hardly a scratch on 'em. It was really surprisin' how little we was damaged, considerin' the scrap we put up; but seemingly they wanted us alive and kickin'.

For the second time since I knew him the doc sets to and does some cussin' that's perfectly amazin'. He blames himself for gettin' us into this pickle and wonders how, in the name of a number of things I never heard of before, he's goin' to get us out again. We all try to cheer him up and tell him to remember we'd volunteered, but that don't help none.

He falls quiet after a bit, and I listen to the noise outside and try to gather from what I can hear and understand what they're figurin' on doin' with us. But it wasn't, so to speak, encouragin'.

All of a sudden the natives stop their noise, and the Papaloi and Mamaloi come in and give us the up-and-down, grinnin' most unpleasant. Then a couple of bucks follows, showin' the whites of their eyes and carryin' all our equipment and belongin's.

They'd frisked us down to our navy twist and cigarette sacks, and even O'Toole's scapulary, which was danglin' from the end of a scabbard like they was afraid to touch it. The bucks carried the things into a room at the end of the shack, which the curtain hung in front of, left them there and beat it.

Then the priest and priestess say something to each other and go behind the curtain, the old guy lookin' sick and draggin' his feet. I saw that plain enough, spite of the fact that the natives had crowded up around the door to watch, and were shuttin' off most of the firelight. So did the doc. He had been starin' at the Papaloi in a queer sort of way ever since he came in. Just as the curtain dropped behind them he gave a funny sort of gasp. But he didn't say nothin'.

The niggers crowded up around the door and all the chinks—there weren't any windows—and watched us quiet like, only shovin' some for a better look, and mutterin' to each other now and then.

My eyes had got a bit used to the darkness by now, and I could make out a couple of goats in one corner that kept stampin' and "baain'," and some chickens somewhere chuckled or squawked. Then a light flares up behind the curtain. It's quiet there, too.

"Well, byes," says O'Toole cheerful, and I saw he had a fresh scratch on his cheek that crossed his scar, "I'm thinkin' there'll be four fewer m'rines in the corps the maarnin'. If anny of yeez get out, ye might write a line to me ould mother in the Bronx, N'York."

"There's a gyurl," says Jeff Cole, who's next to me; and then he breaks off. "No, never mind," he says, and starts cussin' the natives heartfelt.

"How about you, Ole?" says I.

My head was feelin' a lot better already. I hadn't got much of a bump.

"Ay bane got a vife in Minnesota," says Ole slow and solemn, "but Ay skoll write her mineself if ve get out."

I told 'em who to write to for me, and then we was quiet again, except that O'Toole starts whistlin' "The Girl I Left Behind Me" as if he didn't give a whoop.

The doc, though, never said a thing, just sat scowlin' to himself, his lips movin'. I bet if his hands had been loose he'd about pulled the hair out of his head in the way he had when he was thinkin'.

I went to running over the things I'd like to do to that mulatto if she was a man; Jeff pulls his knees up and drops his head on to 'em as if he wanted to go to sleep, and the other boys groan or curse a little.

And then the curtain lifts and in comes the Papaloi, carryin' a flarin' oil-lamp in one claw and in the other something that looks like a big black pocketbook. He's holdin' this like it was alive and he was afraid it would bite him.

He puts it down on the ground careful and sets the light to one side where he can see us plain. The Mamaloi pokes her head through the curtain to watch, and the natives outside stop their shufflin' and mutterin'.

The old voodoo-man tries to straighten up commandin', but quits with a bit of a groan, and the sweat springs out sudden on his forehead. Then he looks us over slow.

He seems kind of uncomfortable when he comes to Doc King; and no wonder, for the doc was starin' at him in the queerest way, his head stuck forward, his mouth a little open and his eyes kind of glarin', breathin' short and quick.

Pappy shuffles from one foot to the other and then he busts into a song-and-dance in a thin kind of voice, tellin' what a great Papaloi he is and what fools we whites are to butt into his affairs. He runs along like this for a while, me translatin' some of it so the doc can get it; and then all of a sudden he asks who the pocketbook belongs to.

"Tell him it's my medicines, Brick," says the doc, hoarse as a crow and kind of white about the gills. If it had of been anybody on earth but Doc King, I'd of said he was scared.

Pappy looks from him to the case and moves further away from it just as I was beginnin' to translate. He starts to say something else, but the doc cuts in.

"Tell him," he says, wettin' his lips and never takin' his eyes off the old scarecrow, "that we're just the advance party of a regiment that's been sent to clean up this place."

I does, and Pappy snaps back before I've hardly begun that the woods are full of guards, and that even if all the soldiers in the United States came, they wouldn't find us when they got here. I didn't like the way he said it, either. It was too darn positive.

I starts to tell the doc what he said, but he cuts me short as if he didn't give a ——.

"Ask him if he's got a pain in his head, as well as in his belly," he says, after swallowin' hard.

Pappy kind of jumps, claps his hands to his waistline and stares at the doc in a sort of funny way, for all the world the way the natives stared at him!

Then he scowls ferocious while I'm askin'

him in French. He doesn't say nothin' for a minute, with us all watchin'; then he wants to know who the doc is.

"Tell him I'm Dr. George King, M. D., D. S., of the United States Navy," says the doc, quick and sharp and excited. "Ask him if he's begun to feel the pain yet under his left arm. Ask him, Brick!"

Pappy claps a hand to his side and scowls worse than ever. *"Ya—pas de mal,"* he says, but the sweat is beginnin' to run down his wicked old face and he doesn't look happy a little bit.

"He says it don't hurt." I was beginnin' to get anxious. "Say, doc, what——?"

"No," groans the doc, and he looks pretty sick himself. "It don't hurt much—now. But wait till it begins to swell. Ask him if he's sure there isn't any pain there, or a swelling. Oh, Lord, boys, what have I got you into?"

The old bird is feelin' himself cautious, and I see him wince. While I'm talkin' French, Jeff Cole lifts his head.

"What do you-all reckon is the matteh with him, docteh?" he asks, his voice sort of uneasy.

But the doc is leanin' forward with his eyes fairly bulgin' out of his head.

"The spot on his chest there—the purple spot!" he yells. *"My God, he's got it!"* and jerks back as though to get as far away as he could. His face was like a dead man's.

"Got what?" we all want to know; and we was scared proper, 'count of him bein' scared. The mulatto girl was starin' at him, and the natives outside was breathin' hard, their eyes gleamin' white at every chink.

 FOR a minute Doc King was quiet, and then he says in a hopeless sort of way:

"Boys, it's all up with us, even if we get loose unless— But I'll tell you. Don't let him know, Brick. Pass it on, O'Toole. It's——"

And he leans sidewise and says something in a whisper, every mortal person watchin' him breathless, like he was—like he was the hero in the third act.

"Houly Mother av God!" yells O'Toole, goin' white as paper. "Ye can't mane it, docthor dear?"

"Look at him," is all the doc says.

We all look, of course, and if ever I see a sick man it's that voodoo priest, and scared, too. I couldn't see the spot on his chest; but of course the doc was closer than me.

O'Toole whispers to Ole and starts to pray, and Ole kind of collapses and then starts up with a scream and tries to break loose, jerkin' around till he falls over on his side.

"What is it? What is it?" cries Jeff, and Ole gasps something and lies still, breathin' hard.

Jeff just sits there, gettin' whiter and whiter. And then all of a sudden he's taken terrible sick to his stomach.

The sinful old idol has stood watchin' us and shiftin' from one foot to the other and feelin' himself tender; and now he busts out in a rage. What's going to be done to us whites, he screams, for bustin' up the sacrifice, is we're goin' to be left in this place which we've defiled, and it's goin' to be set afire and burned to the ground!

I tells the doc as unemotional as I can, for all I'm half crazy, not knowin' yet what the rest know; and Doc King, who's been sittin' with his head bowed, straightens up sudden.

"Is that right? Did he say that?" he asks, lookin' relieved.

"Yo' gwine fo' be bu'n up alife!" yells the Papaloi in English, dancin' up and down and endin' with a groan.

"Thank God!" says the doc, and he means it. "It'll be a heap pleasanter death, eh, boys?"

"It will thot," says O'Toole, and goes on prayin'.

"Ya," says Ole. "Ay tank Ay bane sick already."

Jeff only groans and drops his head back on his knees again. I heard his jaws begin goin' to beat the band, like he'd got ahold of his favorite plug. I didn't say nothin' for I didn't know, though I suspicioned; and if I was right, I sure agreed.

Well, the way we took it knocked his Nibs all of a heap. He swings around with a grunt and shuffles back through the red curtain, the Mamaloi, who hasn't missed none of this, though she'd kept still, givin' him plenty of sea-way.

The two of them aren't hardly out of sight before a commotion starts among the natives around the door. There's a lot of shovin' and pushin' and excited jabberin' in whispers, and then a young buck comes stealin' in, steppin' quick and noiseless, and scared clean through.

He goes over to the doc.

"Me spik Ingliss," he whispers. "How he is seek?" And he jerks his head at the curtain.

"Bend down," mutters the doc.

The Creole does, and the doc whispers something in his ear. The feller jumps like he'd been stabbed, makes two leaps for the door and plunges out with a hair-raisin' squall.

There's a moment of silence outside, then a volley of shrieks and screams, and in ten seconds there ain't a native in sight. I could hear 'em plungin' through the jungle in every direction, their yells cut off short by the trees.

At the first holler the Mamaloi rushes out from behind the curtain, just in time to see the last of their backs. She stands in the doorway for a minute gapin' like she can't believe her eyes; then she runs back again, givin' the doc a wicked look. She jabbers something to Pappy, and he drags himself out to see for himself. He stares out into the empty clearing with the fire burnin' down and the clean white moonlight over everything; then he turns and looks at us in a scared, uncertain way.

He gasps something to the Mammy, but she comes back at him hard and scornful; and they go back behind the curtain, and come out with their arms full of ju-ju charms and truck which they tote outside, bringin' back some fire-wood and stackin' it along the walls.

Seemingly these two are goin' to complete the arrangements, even if the audience has left. But I noticed that the Mammy kept as far away from him as she could. She was sure shook up. But the old sinner—Lord, he was awful! But I'll give him credit for one thing—he sure had grit.

They finish with the fire-wood without sayin' anything. O'Toole has quit prayin' and is whistlin' cheerful "The Wearin' of the Green." The Mammy takes out the goats and some chickens, while the Pappy carries out some more ju-ju truck and all our things—except the doc's medicine-case, which is still lyin' on the floor in front of him. He groans at almost every step, and sure enough there *was* a swellin' in his armpit! I saw it as he passed.

Pappy comes back with Mammy behind him and goes and gets the flarin' lamp. He takes it over by the door. She's standin' in it, watchin' with a nasty little smile.

O'Toole had stopped whistlin', and all the sound there is is Jeff's jaws goin' on whatever he was chewin'. The doc is watchin' like a hawk.

All of a sudden Pappy straightens up from the firewood and comes back—and he hadn't set it alight! The doc draws a little breath, but don't say nothin'.

"W'at you t'ink I got, me, *hein?*" says Pappy, tryin' to make his voice indifferent and not succeedin' very well.

"What's the good of telling you?" says the doc in a tired way. "You'll be dead inside of an hour."

"Me? Dead? Hah!" says Pappy, but his voice has gone up into a squeak and his eyes are rollin' in his head.

He tries to say something else, but it sticks in his throat, and he takes a step forward.

"Keep away from me!" yells the doc, crouchin' back against the wall. "My God, your neck's swelling, too! *Keep away!*"

I could see by her eyes that the Mamaloi understood enough English to follow, and she's mighty upset. Pappy feels of his neck, his hand shakin', and goes back with the lamp. He hesitates again and turns to the doc.

"Yo' got some med'cine?" he asks with a crafty look.

"Yes!" says the doc, short and sharp. "I've got just enough to keep me and my men from catching it. Why, you fool!" he breaks out. "Don't you know yet what you have? It's bubonic plague!"

Well sir, in the next few seconds there's a heap that happens—and an amazin' bunch of noises. All at the same time the Papaloi staggers back with a strangled sort of shriek and crumples up on the ground. The Mamaloi gives a howl of terror and skips outside, though she waits there, shakin' and gray-blue in the face. The mulatto, who has understood, too, squalls out and tries to break loose from her post. Mike and Ole holler with joy at knowin' that the doc has some dope to keep them from catchin' the plague. Jeff groans and spits and goes on chewin'. And I give something between a gasp and a choke at findin' out at last what's the matter with the voodoo-man. Jeff hadn't told me.

Next second Pappy is up and flings himself on his knees in front of the doc.

"Oh, please!" he wails with a rattle in his throat like a dyin' man. "Oh, *please*, yo'

gimme med'cine. I geeve yo' t'ousan' dol-
laire gol'—two t'ousan'—mekky yo' go
back! Oh, *please!*"

"We-ell," says the doc, kind of slow,
"maybe I could cure you if I used it all."

"Hey, doc!" I yells, and I couldn't believe my ears. "What about us?" I says,
and so do the other boys.

Him a United States officer and goin' to
ditch us white men for the sake of money?
And he never paid no attention to us! Jeff
spits again and hisses:

"Don't you-all do it, docteh. I reckon
I'll be loose in a minute."

A kind of funny look comes over Doc
King's face; and then he says to the Voodoo-man real sharp:

"All right. Tell the woman to cut me
loose."

The Papaloi gives a sob and shrieks out
something. The Voodoo-woman hurries in,
quick and nervous, hesitates a bit, and then
at another string of language from Pappy,
who's still on his knees, goes away around
him and slices through the doc's rope with
a knife. Then she beats it out again in a
hurry, and with a mighty wicked look in
her eye.

But I didn't think much about her then,
for I was kind of stunned. The doc, Doc
King, U. S. N., was goin' to do this thing!

"Doc!" I says, just like that, and he sort
of winced but didn't look at me.

He straightens out his arms with a groan,
and for a few minutes is busy rubbin' them
and his legs into some sort of shape. And
meanwhile Jeff Cole has stopped chewin'
long enough to curse him for a coward.

They were bitter, black words that Jeff
used in his slow Southern drawl, and they
must of cut like a whip-lash. But the doc
never says a thing, only his face set like
flint. The other boys didn't say nothin',
either. Too stunned, I guess. Then Jeff
drops his head again and goes on chewin'.

Then the doc gets up pretty shaky and
gets the wallet, nearly fallin' as he stoops
to get it. He opens the case while the old
devil squats in front of him, starin' like a
sick fish, and picks out a little bottle of yellow fluid and holds it up to the light.

"Yes," he says slow, "I guess I can cure
you." And then like a whip crackin': "I
came here to get this woman's baby. Have
your friend bring it in first!"

Jeff starts beside me and swears soft and
amazed. Then all of a sudden he starts

wrigglin' and twistin' and strainin' to beat
the band, but soft-like so nobody noticed
but me.

Pappy looks kind of startled when the
doc pulls that, but after a minute he gives
in and spiels some more lingo at the woman.
I couldn't make nothin' of it, but Mammy
flounces away into the night and fetches
back a colored baby of maybe a year old,
without a stitch on it, and stark and stiff.
At a nod from the doc—and he looks like
he means to get action *pronto*—she drops it
onto the mulatto's lap and beats it out
again.

The girl gives a shriek of joy soon as she
sees the kid, and begins to croon over it—
say, the way she carried on over that poor
little dead kid was fierce! The doc goes
over, walkin' like his legs were made of
wood, and takes a look, and then he gives
a sort of groan.

"Yo' got um *bébé*," says Pappy with a
twisted grin. "Yo' come too late, *hein?*
Bébé dead. Now gimme med'cine."

But the doc is lookin' at the mulatto girl
murmurin' love-talk to her kid, and his
face has a kind of a funny look. The Papaloi loses his grin.

"Gimme med'cine!" he squawks again.

"Brick," says the doc sharp and without
takin' his eyes from the girl, "ask her if it's
really dead."

For a second I was goin' to refuse, I was
that sore at him; but then I got a sort of
hunch that there was more to it than there
seemed. So, even though the question was
plumb foolish—anybody with half an eye
could tell the kid was past all hope—I asks
her. And b'gosh, she comes back like a
shot!

"She says it's only doped," I tells the
doc pretty short. Can you blame me feelin' that way?

The doc turns to Pappy, and now *he's*
smilin' as dangerous as a bob-cat.

"That baby is not dead," he snaps out
like the first lieutenant reviewin' a hangover squad after shore leave. "Bring it
back to life again and we'll see about curing
you. Get busy!"

THE old devil starts to raise a
howl of protest, but it peters out
before the doctor's eyes. Man, they
were downright bad! Pappy gives him a
mighty black look and yells a third time for
the witchess.

But this time, seemingly, the Mamaloi's goin' to have something to say about it. She'd collected the kid, accordin' to the mulatto, so maybe she feels justified. She gabbles something back at Pappy and I gathered that she'd see him in —— first; but he spills a line of chatter in a thin, high shriek that makes her go weak at the knees.

She stammers something, all out of breath and humble, chases off and comes back with a little pot and some ju-ju stuff. She makes some kind of a mess, chantin' to herself and tryin' to stare the mulatto down, and failin', feeds it to the kid, and beats it. But she shot the doc a look as she passed him that made me feel cold all down the spine, and the doc didn't miss it, neither.

"Now gimme med'cine!" gasps Pappy, who's huddled up on his hunkers, huggin' his knees with his skinny arms. "Queek—queek!" he says.

"Wait till I see how your medicine works," says the doc, dry and sharp; and for a long time—well, it might of been only five minutes—you couldn't hear nothin' but the bunch breathin', the raspin' wheeze of Pappy, who looked like death already and sounded like a leaky locomotive, and Jeff's squirmin' and whispered cussin'. He'd fell over on his side by now and was in the shadow beside Ole. I had an idea that the reason Pappy was so quiet was that he was scared stiff for fear the Mamaloi had accidentally-on-purpose put some of the wrong dope in the dose she gave the kid.

Then I see the doc start and hear him take a long breath; and sure enough, there was a tinge of color in the baby's cheeks! In a minute more the poor little brat begins to stir and to cry feeble. And the girl hollers and hugs it and cries.

"Well, I'll be ——!" says the doc softly. "All right, brother physician, here's your medicine."

And he goes over to Pappy with the little bottle of yellow stuff in his fingers, throwin' a look at Mammy as he passes her. She's standin' in the doorway whettin' the knife thoughtful on her palm.

"Mother av God, docthor!" yells O'Toole. "Yeez aren't really goin' to double-cross us, I dunno?"

But the doc is already stoopin' to dump the precious medicine down the dirty old idol's throat. Pappy says something to Mammy and opens his mouth, his eyes gog-

glin'. Mammy sidles further in, casual and not meanin' anything.

And then the mulatto comes to life.

"*Prends garde!*" she screams. "*Elle va tuer!*"

"Look out, doc!" I yells.

He jumps. There's a tinkle on the hard-beaten floor, and he's starin' down at the busted bottle of medicine that meant health for the Papaloi and safety for all of us from the worst disease goin'!

Again there was a heap that happened all in a bunch. Ole gives a groan of horror. O'Toole hollers to some saint or other. I suddenly notice that I'm cussin' at the top of my lungs.

You must remember that our nerves was all shot to pieces by now; we was hysterical as a bunch of schoolgirls. We all had had a sneakin' hope up to the last moment that the doc was goin' to wiggle out of it somehow. But when that medicine began to seep into the floor—good night!

Well, to go on. The —— old witch stared at the wet spot for a second like he couldn't believe his eyes. Then he staggers to his feet with them bulgin' out of his head, claws the air like, gives one awful howl and pitches over backward, twitchin'.

There's another howl, this time from Mammy. She makes a jump for the mulatto, her eyes glarin' and every tooth in her head bared and gleamin'. There's a considerable flurry for a second, and then she turns and charges the doc.

He side-steps, catches her hand with a kind of twist that sent the knife flyin', and the next I know he's tripped her, and she falls down flat on the Papaloi.

But she's up again in a second, shriekin' like a maniac; rushes out through the doorway and off, her yells dyin' away and swallowed up by the jungle.

The doc didn't wait to see what happened to her, though. He snatched up the knife and cut us all loose, includin' the mulatto. And while we're groanin' and rubbin' ourselves—Lord, how my arms and legs did ache as the blood started circulatin' again—he goes over to the Papaloi, who has stopped twitchin' and is lyin' mighty still, and starts examinin' him as unconcerned as if the gink had been shot or something, instead of bein' dead from bubonic.

"Good God, doc, are you crazy?" I yells. "Surely we've got a chance of not catchin' it if we keep away——"

"This kind of bubonic isn't catching," he snaps. "Don't be a fool, Brick." And then to himself: "All the symptoms—and dead as Adam's cat! Well, I'll be——"

His voice shakes. Then he straightens up and gives us all the once-over with a queer, twisted smile.

"Well, boys," he says, "I guess we'd better go back and make a report."

We staggered out into the deserted clearin', half carryin' Jeff. The fire was hardly more than a heap of hot coals now, and the clean white moonlight was over everything. My good gosh, how good it felt and smelled!

We limbered up a bit, found our equipment with nary a thing missin', and all took a swig of O'Toole's rum, which was sure right where it was needed worst. Then we took and chucked all the ju-ju truck into the hut with the dead man, and the doc stirred up the coals with a dry branch and set the shack afire. When it's goin' good I gave him a hand to heave the big drum in through the blazin' door.

Then the doc looks at that cage I told you about. He hesitates a minute or two over it; but finally it followed the drum. It was then I found out what was in it that had been movin' around. The cage was all splattered with blood, and inside was a big green snake.

And after that we beat it.

Say, Ingalls, what's "suggestive the-rep-a-tricks?" Why, the doc said that next day—the same day, rather—in "sick-bay" while he's tellin' the lieutenant all about it.

Huh? No, I didn't come down with my fever till a couple weeks later; I was in the bay to see how Jeff Cole was gettin' on. The doc had fixed him up pretty good after we got out of the hut.

 HERE, this is gettin' all tangled. You see, we got back into Port au Prince about sun-up, ready to drop with tiredness, sore all over, and still a little scared of catchin' the plague in spite of all the doc could do to explain things and smooth us down. When we got there the lieutenant was just goin' to send a squad after us, regardless of what he'd said.

I got a few hours' sleep aboard the *Washington* on special leave and then, as I said, I went into the sick-bay to see Jeff. While I'm sittin' with him in comes Doc King with the lieutenant, evidently just finishin' tellin' him about it. Near as I can remember he put it like this:

"You see," he says, "while a large part of the power of those voodoo priests lies in their use of poisons, a heap sight more is due to the terror in which the ignorant natives hold 'em. Their superstition is so great that if a Papaloi tells them they're going to curl up and die, they simply do—of sheer fright.

"That's why this particular priest's plague wasn't contagerous. It was mostly a figure of his own imagination." Then he sprung the "the-rep-a-tricks" thing.

The lieutenant didn't get it, either.

"Whaddya mean?" he says.

"Why," says the doc, "all he had to start with was a bad case of indigestion. I guess I kicked my oath of hypocrisy full of holes," says the doc. What's that? Hippocrates? Oh. "But," he says, "it was the only thing to do. Being the same kind of native as the rest, I knew he'd fall for the same kind of bunk he handed out.

"Did you ever hear of the condemned prisoner that died of smallpox in a clean cell where he was told another man had died of smallpox? The 'cure by suggestion' works both ways," he says, "and I reversed it and gave that Voodoo-man a dose of his own medicine. But I had to make the boys believe it, too, or they'd have crabbed my acting. See?"

"Well, but—" says the lieut.

"I know what you're going to say," says the doc kind of sad. "If that old bird hadn't tried his monkey-business at the end, I'd have cured him with that vial of castor-oil just as surely as I'd made him sick, much as I'd have hated to do it. As it was—well, there was no other way."

"And the—er—the witch?" says the lieut.

"I dunno about her," says the doc, shakin' his head. "Maybe—and maybe not. Women are funny."

Huh? "Suggestive therapeutics," eh? Oh, I see. Huh? About Jeff?

Mm'yeah, about Jeff. Well, I dunno's it matters if I tell you. I can lick him. Well, you see, Jeff he has mighty powerful jaw-muscles what with him chewin' all the time. He'd took and gnawed through the rope that was around his hands, and had rubbed himself quite back into shape—just in time to mix in when the Mamaloi made her jump for the mulatto's kid.

Jeff seen this and jumped, too, his mouth all blood from the rough rope. He didn't have time to do nothin' but get in the way; but he done that, all right, and took her knife through the shoulder.

You see, Jeff he hates color worse'n pizen.

He didn't give two whoops and a holler whether the brat got killed or not, he told us after. All he wanted to do was to fool the witch.

Yeh. He's licked a couple o' guys for not believin' him, though.

WHEN OSCAR WENT WILD
by W.C. Tuttle.

Author of "Derelicts of the Hills," "Magpie's Nightbear."

REN MERTON and Sig Watson had spent the night in Piperock and of a consequence were in no shape to appreciate the beauties of the dewy morn, as their horses picked their way up the trail to the top of Overwhich ridge.

"Them Piperock fellers play poker like I sing," stated Sig, as they pulled up their mounts for a breathing spell. "They gits their words and music so mixed that nobody knows what they're tryin' to do. They're uh success, though."

Ren removed his sombrero with an exaggerated flourish and, lifting himself in his stirrups, broke forth in a shrill falsetto:

"Nobode-e-e-e knows how dry I am."

"Shut up!"

"Mama mine, he won't let me sing," wailed Ren. "I lost jist as much as he did and m' head aches jist as hard and he won't let m' sing. What do yuh know about that!"

"Jist don't sing, that's all," replied Sig. "You can say all th' funny things yuh wants to to yoreself, but I'm right here to re-mark that singin'—yore kind uh singin'—ain't in de-mand a-tall. *Sabe?*"

"Always misunderstood," mumbled Ren. "Th' human race ain't never understood me. Mother misunderstood me; father follered suit, and now you—Siggie, my old pal —you turns on me."

"Misunderstood!" Sig turned in his saddle and gazed reflectively at his partner. "Ren Merton, if you was ever entered fer th' human race you shore was scratched. Yore nose ain't right—too long. Yuh got uh bad case uh squints in both uh yore eyes, and yore mouth, which was cut too wide in th' first place, ain't shrunk none a-tall. Shoulders? Say, I sometimes wonder how comes it that yore collar don't slip down and trip yuh. Also, yore right foot is where yore left ought to be."

"Pickled prairie-dogs, that's right!" agreed Ren. "I reckon I shore must a been muddled this mawnin' when I puts on m' boots."

"And also yore hair——"

"You stops at hair!" exploded Ren. "Mebby I've got red hair and mebby she runs uh little to th' rusty shade, but I'll be danged if any feller with fat eyebrows, buffalo-horn mustache and bow legs can taunt me with th' fact. Take uh look in th' glass and you'll see that you ain't no one-to-ten shot in this race yoreself, Sig."

Sig grunted and turned back. The horses seemed to start by mutual consent and plodded off down the hogback.

"I've knowed uh lot uh people," remarked Sig, "who thought they had red hair, but——"

He pulled up his horse.

"Wasn't that a voice, Ren?"

"I reckon not—not uh human one anyway. Go on and finish yore remarks about hair."

"I tell yuh I heard somebody yell!" declared Sig. "It was jist over that ridge, and I'm goin' to see who it was."

 HE SPURRED his horse into a gallop and Ren followed at his heels. They crossed the ridge and swung down into an open timbered swale, interspersed with clumps of willows and jack-pines.

There they saw her. She was tied to a tree and seemed to be exerting every muscle to get loose. She was dressed in a faded calico dress and her dark-brown hair tumbled in confusion about her half-bare shoulders.

The sight of her was a shock to the punchers and they threw their broncos back on their haunches at the sight. The girl didn't see them, and after the first gasp of surprise they sat there and stared at her.

Suddenly she shrank back against the tree and screamed—

"That's not Oscar!"

Like a flash of yellow light a scared cougar had bounded out of the willow thicket near her and crouched low.

Ren acted first. While he hadn't the uncanny skill on the draw attributed to the Western gunman, he was deadly when he did "get his ol' smoke-wagon unhitched." The cougar had barely touched his belly to the ground when Ren's .45 started to spout death and destruction.

Two of the heavy slugs tore through its neck, and the cougar tied itself in a snarling, spitting knot and rolled over dead. When the last shot was fired Ren's horse was nearly over the body of the cougar and Ren was shoving fresh shells into the gun.

The girl looked at Ren in a dazed sort of a way for a moment and then in a tired little voice remarked—

"That wasn't Oscar."

"No, ma'am," agreed Ren foolishly. "That shore wasn't Oscar."

"What happened?" asked a deep bass voice, and Ren turned in his saddle; behind him stood a florid-faced person in a green-corduroy suit and panama, and behind him a narrow-shouldered, sharp-faced man in knickerbockers.

"What happened, I asked?" repeated the florid one.

"It wasn't Oscar," stated the girl for the third time.

"Well, what was it, then?" queried the sharp-faced man.

"I kept grinding until this cowboy person butted in and spoiled it."

"Did you quit then?" roared the florid one. "By Jupiter! You lost a fine chance for some real stuff. But what happened to Oscar, and where in the world did this other lion come from?"

"Did it—I say—where did it?"

Another person had joined the crowd. He was hatless and garbed in the costume of the early settler, fringed and beaded buckskin from his toes to his chin, and his face was ashen. He walked up with an uncertain gait and his breathing gave evidence of recent exertion.

"What happened to you, Jack?" asked the florid one.

"Why, I—uh—I——"

"You met it too, did you?" grinned the thin-faced one, and the fringed one gulped an assent.

"I was—er—just coming through that clump of bushes and I met it. You see I—er—thought perhaps that if I ran I could coax it away from the rest of you."

"Haw, haw, haw!" roared Sig. "You shore ought to git uh hero medal. Didn't yuh know that no self-respectin' cougar would chase uh git-up like that?"

Just then two more men came running down the hill and, seeing the crowd, one of them stopped and cupped his hands.

"Mister Norton!" he yelled. "Oscar slipped his collar and got away!"

"Just my luck!" exclaimed Norton, the florid one. "Here I bring this bunch way up here to finish that film, and that blamed cat gets away and spoils it all!"

"Oscar is uh cougar, I takes it," opined

Ren, rolling a cigarette and looking admiringly at the girl. "I reckon somebody might as well let th' lady loose. Cougars bein' thick, I don't think it's safe to tie ladies to trees anyway."

One of the men cut the ropes which bound her, and the thin-faced man recovered his camera from the willow thicket.

"Miss, I reckon you can have that cougar skin if yuh wants it," remarked Sig. "We ain't got no use fer it, and if yuh wants it I'll have Ren skin it fer yuh."

"I am Miss Reynolds," she replied with a smile. "And I'd love to shake hands with both of you. You gentlemen saved my life, and I haven't words to thank you with."

"Don't mention it, Miss Reynolds," replied Sig. "Little thing like that—why——"

"Slack up yore rope!" rasped Ren. "You never saved anything—not even yore salary, and now yuh tells her that it's uh little thing to save her life." He leaned over an' held out his hand. "Miss Reynolds, I'm uh heap glad to meet yuh. My name's Ren Merton, and if there's anything I can do fer yuh—yuh can have that catskin to remember me by."

She gave him a sweet smile.

"I'd love to have it, Mr. Merton. I'll have one of the men skin it, and every time I put my foot on that rug I'll remember you. I've had my life saved many times on the films, but this being the first time in real life, I just don't know what to say."

"I jist hope yuh won't forget it, anyway," laughed Ren.

"Do you think you'll forget it?" she asked.

"Lady," interrupted Sig, "that hombre can forget anything. I'm th' brains of our outfit, and if yuh wants an intelligent favor done, jist ask me. *Sabe?*"

"I don't know whether you gentlemen are in earnest or not. Do you mean everything you say to each other?"

"I do," replied Sig, with a bow, "but Mr. Merton here never meant anything he ever said. He's notorious fer jist talkin'. As I orates before, Miss Reynolds, if there is anything I can do fer yuh, why——"

"I do wish we could get Oscar," she replied reflectively. "There goes poor old Nortie up the hill with a broken heart, and I know that Jack Markham is awfully put out about it too. You see we've simply got to have a cougar or we can't finish the

picture. I wonder if you could catch Oscar? He's as tame as a kitten and has never been wild. The company raised him—got him from a zoo when he was a little yellow kitten. I know that Mr. Norton would be willing to pay you well if you would catch him."

"Miss Reynolds, we ain't mercenary thataway," replied Sig. "I ain't wastin' no love on that Norton person, and I don't rassel no cougar fer his money, but if you really wants that cat, I'm promisin' it to yuh."

"That's awfully kind of you," she cooed. "If you could catch him and bring him back here tomorrow, I could just love you both. Then we could finish that picture. Really, he is as tame as a kitten."

"Consider him caught," boasted Sig. "Me and Ren will bring him to yore house tomorrow mawnin'. Uh course I could git him alone, but bein' as Ren is with me I'll let him help."

"Meanin'," drawled Ren, "that I ropes that cat and ties him up fer shipment, and Sig writes th' address."

Miss Reynolds insisted on shaking hands with both of them again, and her smile left them both unable to roll a cigarette.

"We're living in those cabins up there in the pines," she explained, "and probably will be there for a few days. You can bring him right up there."

"Yes'm," they both replied, and watched her skip up the hill in the wake of the rest of the party.

About half-way to the top she stopped and threw them a kiss, and then danced out of sight in the jack-pines.

 REN rolled a fresh smoke and studied Sig's rapt expression from under his hat brim. Suddenly he broke into song——

"And that's what made th' wildcat wild."

"Meanin' which?" demanded Sig.

"Oscar," chuckled Ren. "Don't yuh see, Sig? Them velvet optics made Oscar——"

"Listen," snapped Sig. "Confine yore humor to somethin' else. I don't sit here inactive and hear yuh slander them eyes none whatever. *Sabe?* I'm backin' th' lady's play—me."

"Me and you both," replied Ren seriously. "But did yuh ever stop to consider that you gits so danged conceited when uh female person speaks to yuh that yuh promises to do anything? Cougars ain't woodchucks nor snowshoe rabbits, and I'm thinkin' aloud that you've gone plumb out of yore class this time."

"We'll git him," snapped Sig. "One of th' fellers told me that th' last they saw of him he was lopin' up th' trail, and that means he's liable to hive up in our cabin. Bein' as he's uh house-bred animule, it stands to reason that he's goin' to hunt human company soon's he gits hungry or gits scared of th' dark. *Sabe?*"

Ren nodded and they turned their horses and rode on up the trail to their cabin about two miles away. They unsaddled their horses at the corral and then laid down on their bunks for a much-needed rest.

It was almost dark when Ren awoke and looked around the cabin. Sig was gone. Ren got up and was lazily pulling on his boots when Sig came in with a hammer in his hand and a smile on his face.

"Th' sleek hare sleeps while th' sly fox schemes," he quoted dramatically. "I reckon I've laid uh trap fer Oscar."

He hung up the hammer and went out again. A few moments later he was back of the cabin fumbling with the one window. "Help me take this thing out, Ren!" he yelled.

Ren removed the nails from the inside and Sig removed the window and threw in the end of his lariat rope.

"What's th' idea?" asked Ren.

Sig grinned and coiled up the rope.

"Cougar trap. I got this rope fixed so's that when th' cougar gits inside of th' shed, all we got to do is to pull on th' rope and th' door shuts. There's uh quarter uh venison in th' shed and I'm bettin' that Oscar falls fer it, Ren. What do yuh think about it?"

"Sig, yore uh wonder! I'm bettin' that you've already deduced how to tie him up after we gits him inside. I shore honors and respects yuh, old timer, and as uh special mark of respect I allows yuh to prepare our evenin' meal. I'm so hungry I could eat Oscar, I reckon."

Three hours later they sat humped up on their bunk and watched the door of the shed, a splotch of black in the half moonlight, and prayed that the cougar would come before they lost too much sleep.

"Don't light that cigarette here," cautioned Ren. "Go back near th' door. If that cat saw th' light he'd never show up."

Sig tiptoed to the front of the cabin and sat down on a box. Ren sat by the window for a few minutes and then joined Sig.

"Give me yore papers and I'll roll one, too. I reckon it's uh little too early fer Oscar to show up yet."

They smoked in silence for a while and then sneaked back to the window. Sig took one long look at the door and then threw himself backward and heaved on the rope. The door shut with a bang and an unearthly yelp split the stillness of the night.

"Got him!" whooped Sig. "I seen his eyes and slammed that old door right in his face! Whoopee!"

"Good work!" exclaimed Ren. "I'll bet Oscar is plumb scared to death right now."

"Not any he ain't. Oscar's uh tame cougar and, while he may display uh little peevishness at first, he'll be plumb satisfied with that hunk uh meat. Let's go out and see what he's doin'."

They walked around the shed but were unable to size up their catch, as the shed had no windows. They could hear a sniffling at the cracks of the door and suddenly a heavy body was flung against it, but the heavy bar on the outside held it fast.

"Want to go inside and look him over?" queried Ren.

"Not in his present state uh mind, I don't. That cat is shore some irritated and when they gits fussed thataway they're plumb informal. How do yuh reckon we're goin' to acquire his carcass fer shipment?"

"Might git some uh that movie outfit to come up and git him," suggested Ren, but Sig promptly vetoed it.

"And have that beautiful lady think that me and you were afraid of her pet, eh?"

"I'd rather be uh live coward than uh dead hero," stated Ren. "There ain't no honor in th' grave fer me. I got an idea though. Mebby she's good and mebby again she ain't."

"Shoot."

"I'll unfasten th' door and let her open jist a little ways. *Sabe?* Th' cat will try to come out and I'll slam th' door shut when he's half-ways out an' all you has to do is to put two ropes on him. You take one and I'll take th' other and Mr. Oscar is plumb helpless."

"Uh ha," agreed Sig. "That's uh *hy-iu* scheme—if you holds him."

"Aw ——, Sig, he's tame! I'll hold him. All you got to do is to slip th' two ropes on him and give me one. *Sabe?*"

SIG went to the corral and brought back two ropes. He held the nooses handy while Ren removed the bar. He opened the door an inch at a time and braced himself for the rush.

"Come on out, Oscar," pleaded Sig. "Be uh nice li'l cat and come on——"

Oscar came, not sneakingly nor slowly but a rasping, spitting, clawing chunk of deviltry, and Ren shut the door just in time. It caught Oscar at the flank and for a few seconds the air was full of cougar cuss words.

Sig advanced cautiously and managed to get one rope over its head and pulled the noose tight. He handed that rope to Ren, who immediately proceeded to forget that he was there to keep the door tight. He grabbed the rope with both hands, braced himself for the rush and unthinkingly stepped away from the door.

There was a heave and a flash and the cougar sailed over Sig's head and out to the end of that rope. Ren was partly braced for the shock but didn't figure on the velocity of the animal, and when the shock came he went straight up in the air and off across the clearing.

Luckily he lit running and hung on to the rope, and he and the cougar went down the hill, over stumps and through the thickets like a spitting, yelling, yellow comet with a human tail.

They had traveled thus for about two hundred yards when the cougar went on one side of a tree and Ren on the other. They almost met on thé big swing. The cat flipped upside down over a log while Ren almost completed the circle, only stopping when he threw his arms around a tree and hung on. He still held the rope and had presence of mind enough left to proceed to tie that cat up good and tight. The cougar had choked itself nearly to death trying to come up under the log and Ren had little trouble in tying its hind legs so it was helpless.

He rolled a smoke and hobbled back to the cabin. He wondered in a detached sort of way what had become of Sig and why he didn't help him hold it, but as he walked around the cabin he heard Sig's voice imploring him to:

"Hurry up, fer Gawd's sake!"

"What's th' matter?" asked Ren.

"Come over here you danged fool!" wailed Sig. "Can't yuh see I can't hold this door much longer!"

"Hold th—what—why, I'll be danged! Where did yuh git it, Sig?"

"Grab hold uh this door! How do I know where I got it? When you and Oscar paraded off down th' hill I sees uh pair uh eyes shinin' in there and I jist slams th' door in time to catch his neck. Gosh, ain't he a sassy-lookin' animule, Ren? Where's Oscar?"

"Hog-tied to uh log," mumbled Ren. "At least I got uh cougar tied to th' log—I didn't ask his name. I wonder how two of 'em got in at oncet, and which is Oscar?"

"This ain't Oscar," stated Sig with conviction. "No house variety of cougar would have uh face and uh disposition like this one, Ren."

"Hang onto th' door, Sig, while I takes uh board off th' wall and attacks him from behind. You jist keep on squeezin' him and I'll tie him up."

Ren got the hammer and removed a board. The cougar objected at the top of its voice, but in a few minutes Ren had it trussed up and tied off to a rafter.

They went into the cabin, boiled a pot of coffee and had a smoke.

"Well, we don't know which is Oscar, but I reckon Miss Reynolds can pick him out," remarked Ren.

"Said she'd love me if I got him," grinned Sid, "and I've got him."

"Yore hearin' is on uh par with yore brains," drawled Ren. "She said 'us,' and what's more, Siggie, you ain't got him—I've got him. *Sabe?* I risked my whole danged life to git her that cougar. You can put yore location notice on that one in th' shed, but not on Oscar. He's mine, located, filed and patented."

"Is that so!" exploded Sig. "I'm here to orate that it was my scheme which caught it! All you did was to hang on to th' rope and, not bein' overly strong nor active, you permits that li'l cat to haul yuh around, regardless. And now yuh opines that yuh owns Oscar. Not any yuh don't!

"I don't care if yuh did tear yore pants," he continued. "If yuh can't take care of yoreself don't blame me. I've shore treated yuh white, Ren Merton, and now yuh turns and bites th' hand which feeds yuh!"

"Bites yore hand!" snorted Ren, shaking his forefinger under Sig's nose. "Listen: any time I starts bitin' you won't confine yore diagnosis to hands, old timer. I orates openly that as soon as daylight comes I'm goin' down and make uh crate and prepare Oscar fer shipment. *Sabe?* I ain't concernin' myself about that cat in th' shed and hereby waives all rights to him, but I duly informs all present company that I'm uh close corporation when it comes to li'l' Oscar. Let's go to bed."

"Not with you!" snarled Sig. "I'll take uh blanket and go out in th' woods or sleep in th' shed with th' cougar. I hereby refuses to share yore bed and I does it without malice in m' heart. You grieves me deeply, Mr. Merton, and I'm sore at heart and meek-feelin'."

"Hop to it!" grunted Ren, as he rolled into the bunk and stretched wearily. "Don't go near Oscar 'cause I reckon he's fond uh meek things."

Sig took a blanket and went out, closing the door softly. As the door closed, Ren slid out of his bunk and peered out of the window. He chuckled as he saw Sig wander off into the trees, and he sat up and rolled a smoke and seemed to ponder deeply. Suddenly he slapped his leg and pinched out the light of his cigarette.

"By golly!" he chuckled, "won't Sig go high, wide and handsome?"

 THE first tinge of morning showed in the east when Ren slipped out of the cabin and approached the shed. Ten minutes later a tawny figure glided out of the open shed and bounded off into the underbrush. Five minutes later an apparition in rags stumbled out of the shed and leaned uncertainly against the wall.

"Mama mine!" it mumbled. "I must be uh sight. Them danged things won't go away when yuh gives 'em uh chance. I shore am scratched some artistic."

He staggered into the cabin and painfully removed his torn clothing. He tore up some of the shirt for bandages, but there was too much space to cover and he was awfully tired. He sat on the bunk as naked as the day he was born and fumbled for a cigarette in the pockets he didn't have on.

"Well, I'll be teetotally —— !" exclaimed Sig's voice from the doorway but Ren never looked up. "Come on and help me,

Sig. I reckon I'm all cut to shoestrings."

"You ain't alone, Ren."

Ren lifted his head and looked at Sig.

"Pickled prairie-dogs!" he groaned. "What happened to you? Did you—huh—turn Oscar loose?"

"After seven years uh hard fightin' and hardships I manages to break his holt," declared Sig dismally. "I'm jist uh walkin' hunk uh Hamburger steak, Ren, and I feels that when I removes my clothes I'll be no more. That cat jist simply prospected every piece uh meat on my frame. In my war-sack under th' bunk there's uh roll uh stickin' plaster. You wrap me up and I'll do th' same fer you, Ren. I've done played my last joke—absolutely. I suppose th' shed is empty?"

"Uh ha," nodded Ren. "I'm apologizin', Sig."

"Aw, Ren, I reckon misery likes company."

"Well," drawled Ren, "she's got it."

Half an hour later, with adhesive plaster covering most of their bodies they laid down on the bunk and rolled more cigarettes.

"I wonder which one was Oscar?" mused Sig aloud, but Ren was deep in thought and made no answer.

Finally Ren drew a deep breath and turned to Sig.

"Them movie people take big chances, don't they? Jist think about uh girl playin' with Oscar. Tame? Say, I shore hope I never meets uh wild cougar, Sig. That animule shore put his trade-mark on me."

Just then there came a clatter of horse's hoofs outside and Sig limped over to the closed door.

"Hello!" yelled a voice, which they both recognized as that of Norton, the movie director.

"Hello, yoreself!" retorted Sig. "We're takin' our mornin' bath and can't come out."

"That's all right," laughed Norton. "I just came up here to deliver a message to you from Miss Reynolds."

"What was it?" asked Sig quickly.

"She said for you boys not to worry about Oscar because he came back right after you left."

"Must be sore about something," reflected Norton as his horse picked it's way down the narrow trail. "Either they are sore or mighty ungentlemanly, because they never even said 'thank you.'"

THE EDUCATION OF BILLY STREAM

A COMPLETE NOVELETTE
by Frederick William Wallace.

Author of "In the Bank Fog," "Winter Fishing," etc.

BILLY STREAM had arrived home in Anchorville after two years at college, and Captain William Stream, senior, fish merchant, vessel owner, and proprietor of the plant which turned out Stream's famous "Morning-Glory Finnan-Haddies and Fillets—the Nation's Breakfast," was reviewing his son's university career in language which caused the young man to squirm.

"Yer ma was foolish to imagine that the likes o' you 'ud ever be anything," raved the old man. "She had an idea that ye'd git yer degree an' be an engineer or somethin', an' what hev ye done for th' last two years? Ye've wasted yer time an' my money boozin' an' card-playin' an' hellin' around town with yer good-for-nawthin' pals. About all ye learnt was to write home for money. Ye got scrappin' with waiters in resturongs an' I had to pay yer fines; ye were tourin' around the country playin' football an' hockey when ye sh'd have bin studyin' yer books, an' now ye've come home with nawthin' but a bad reputation an' dressed up with yer —— fancy clothes like a blasted picter post-card!"

Billy attempted to speak, but his father checked him.

"Gimme none o' yer guff!" he stormed. "I'm talkin' and you'll listen. I've lost fif-teen hundred dollars over your eddication, an' I'll have it out o' yer hide. I was a fool to ha' sent ye to college. I sh'd ha' sent ye to sea. Ye'd ha' learnt more useful knowledge out on th' Banks haulin' trawls.

"I've had enough o' you at college. Ye'll git them fancy duds off an' git down to th' fish-house. Ye'll work there from seven in th' mornin' to six at night at whatever th' foreman likes to put you at, an' you'll git three dollars a week an' your board at home here. Ef ye git sassy an' sojer your work, I'll kick ye out an' ye'll never darken my doors again."

"Won't you give me something better than that, dad?" pleaded Billy. "Put me in the office or let me take the little vessel and pick up the fish down the shore ports——"

"Put ye in the office?" sneered the elder Stream. "A white-collar job a-slingin' ink! That 'ud suit ye nicely, wouldn't it, but it won't suit me. Ye'd soon be struttin' around town as the young boss, and as for lettin' ye have the little vessel—why, I wouldn't let ye take charge of a dory. You'll go to work in the fish-house or git out o' this."

The old man gave his son a contemptuous glance and stamped out of the room.

Young Billy Stream, a husky, broad-shouldered, handsome fellow of twenty-two, sat silent for a while and felt that he deserved all he got. He had become a star football player, a crackerjack cover-point at hockey, but his college accomplishments ended there. In his studies he was a laggard, but in his social life he was a shining light. He could dance—such fantastics as are common to the all-night cabarets of a college city—and he could drink, smoke and play cards.

He was a noted scrapper, not a bully, but a hard-hitting young demon when aroused, and among the college crowd he was known as an "Indian," a reputation which was well enough in college fights and differences with authorities, but detrimental to his prospects with the faculty.

"Well," murmured Billy after a mental retrospect, "there's no use kicking, for 'that's all shoved behind me—long ago an' far away,' as Kipling says. I'll simply have to knuckle down to the old man or get out."

NEXT morning at seven he reported to the foreman at the Stream Fish Company's plant, and the latter gave the young fellow a contemptuous look and set him to work loading fish-gurry into a scow. Billy pitched in, and being a powerful young buck did the work well, but evidently not well enough for Jack Hemsley, the foreman, who nagged at him all the time. Jack had his orders from the elder Stream, and having no use for Billy rather exceeded his orders.

In the afternoon two young ladies came down the wharf to fish. One of the girls was a particular pal of Billy's, and she stopped to talk to him while he shoveled the gurry off the dock to the scow below.

"Daddy mad, Billy?" she said, smiling.

"Some mad, Ethel," he answered, knocking off for the moment to speak with her. "I've got a fine job here now."

"Oh, but you'll do something better than that, I hope. You must buck up——"

The eagle-eyed foreman spied him resting from his task, and strode over, bawling:

"Now, then, git to work, you! What th' —— d'ye think ye are? None o' yer sojerin'!"

Billy turned very red and faced the big foreman with his eyes blazing. Hemsley was a rough fellow and did not choose his language before ladies, but Stream resented the hectoring tone and the words.

"Be careful how you speak, Hemsley. There are ladies present!"

"I don't care a cuss ef thar were fifty ladies present!" roared Hemsley. "Don't you imagine because there is a skirt on the dock that you kin hev a spell-oh to yarn with them. Git on with yer work, you blasted college dandy!"

This was too much for Billy. Forgetting everything, he hove the shovel down and went for the foreman and socked him one on the jaw.

Hemsley cursed and put up his hands. He was a big fellow and as tough as iron, but while he had the strength, yet he lacked science, and a beautiful fight soon brought all the fish-workers from the sheds to form an appreciative audience.

The scrap was hot and heavy while it lasted. Some of Hemsley's sledge-hammer blows got home and Billy lost a tooth and had one of his eyes bunged up. It served to cool him off, however, and he fought more scientifically. Getting a straight right to Hemsley's jaw, he hit in with his left, and while the man was dazed for a second, gave him the right again smash on the nose.

The foreman saw stars and Billy gave him a crack which knocked him down into the gurry-heap. The foreman was tough and jumped to his feet and grabbed Billy around the waist, and both slimy men wrestled and struggled around the slimy dock.

For a moment they clinched in a deadlock, and Stream remembered the wrestling tricks of the college gym. He made a rapid movement and hove his opponent from him into the gurry-heap again. As he went down, Hemsley swung his rubber-booted foot up and caught Billy a staggering smack on the side of the head.

The young man saw red and hurled himself on the prostrate foreman. Grabbing him by the collar of his shirt, he yanked him to the cap-log of the wharf and hove him down into the scow-load of gurry, in the midst of which he landed with a gurgling plunk.

Panting and sweating, he stood up and became aware of the fact that the spectators had vanished. A savage kick from a rubber-booted foot caused him to jump around and look into the angry face of his father. The foot rose again and

Billy grappled with his enraged parent.

"Don't you try that again, dad!" he panted. "I only gave Hemsley what he deserved."

"—— you!" yelled the old man. "Keep your hands off me, you beach-comber. Git away out o' this. Git out now! You're a disgrace to the town! Clear out, or by Godfrey I'll have you thrown out by the men!"

Billy released his hold.

"Father," he pleaded, "listen to me a minute——"

"Not a word!" roared his parent. "Clear out!"

The young fellow saw the look on his father's face, and having a certain amount of pride, did not feel like doing any cringing before the interested eyes peeping out from the windows of the plant. He turned shortly on his heel, picked up his coat from a spile and strode away. As he walked down the wharf he could hear his father talking to the discomfited Hemsley.

"Why didn't ye hit him with a billet o' wood—the infernal young sculpin."

Feeling sick at heart, Billy Stream left the water-front and walked up the fields.

"Give a dog a bad name and hang him," he muttered, and threw himself down on the grass to think.

"I won't go home," decided he after a mental survey of the case. "Dad is mad and he'll nurse his temper for months. He thinks I'm no good—and, by Jove, I don't blame him for thinking so! I haven't been fair to him or mother. It's up to me to retrieve myself."

He lay for a while looking up at the sky and thinking. The thoughts were not pleasant. He realized that for the past two years he had idled and wasted his time without a thought for the future.

Billy wasn't a bad fellow. He was like a young colt—a little wild, but strong and full of life. The college crowd idolized him for his prowess in athletics, and he liked their admiration. It took away his individuality, however, and he became too much of a good fellow.

The little poker parties and shines which he gave in his rooms brought him popularity, but it was only transient and would not help him in his life-work. He was beginning to realize that now. The commendation, "Billy Stream is a good scout!" would not fetch him any money, and here he was,

twenty-two years of age and only worth laborer's hire—twenty cents an hour.

"I've got to buck up," he resolved. "I'll cut out drinking and fooling and get down to solid work. I'm no good for an office, but I might be some good aboard a vessel. Dad won't have me, but maybe Uncle Ben will. I'll go over to Port Anthony and see him. He'll put me up for a few days anyhow."

Rising to his feet, he cleaned some of the signs of conflict from his person and swung out on the road to Port Anthony and Uncle Ben Anthony.

II

"SO WILL kicked you out?" repeated Ben Anthony, with a smile creasing his bronzed visage.

Uncle Ben ran a small fish-plant in the village of Port Anthony, but unlike his brother-in-law, who was energetic and ambitious, Ben was good-humored and easygoing.

William Stream began as a fisherman and built up an immense plant by dint of sheer hard work. The toil of his early days had ingrained itself into his nature, and he was a hard man, though kind enough at heart. Between him and Ben Anthony there was no love lost, as they were rivals in business. Both men packed and smoked fish for market, and when any of the inland dealers came down to Anchorville, William Stream would show them over his fine plant and draw odious comparisons between it and the establishment of Ben Anthony's at Port Anthony.

"Ye've seen our modern sanitary plant," Stream would say; "now ef you want to look over a wrack of a place go to Port Anthony an' see whar' them Excelsior Brand fish are put up. A dirtier, lousier hole ye never saw, sir. It's fair fallin' to pieces an' sh'd be condemned. I wouldn't eat a fish put up by Ben Anthony for fear I'd be poisoned."

As Port Anthony was a little out of the way, the visitors seldom went there, and it was just as well that they did not, or Stream's words would have been confirmed. Dealers, however, are human and understand the libels of rivals, which understanding allowed Ben Anthony to keep a certain amount of trade from the Stream Fish Company—a trade he would not have kept were the dealers to take the trouble to visit Port Anthony.

"So the old man cut up rough an' hoofed ye?" reiterated Ben Anthony again. "An' ye trimmed Jack Hemsley an' hove him inter th' gurry-scow? Ha! ha! I kin imagine it. Ho! ho! Well, well, boy, I'd give ye a place for that alone. Now, what d'ye want to do—go in the office an' keep th' books?"

"No, uncle," replied Billy. "I think I'll go to sea. I have a fancy that I might make good as a fisherman and take a vessel out as skipper after a while. I've been in the dory before I went to college. I put in a whole Summer with Arthur Thomson in the *Leonora* shacking, and I can rig gear, bait up and haul a trawl fairly good."

Uncle Ben laughed.

"Fishin's hard work, boy. Summertime's not bad, but the Winter haddockin' is a tough proposition. However, ef ye'd like to try it, why, go ahead. My vessel, the *Jennie Anthony*, will be in any day now an' ye kin go in her. Make yer home here with me. I'll do anythin' for ye jest to put one over on Will. Tell me about that scrap ye had with Bully Hemsley!"

A week later, William Stream, senior, heard the news that his son had gone to sea in the *Jennie Anthony* as a fisherman, and he laughed grimly:

"Ha! ha! Gone as a fisherman — th' lazy, good-for-nawthin' sculpin. God help th' man as goes dory-mates with him. He'll hev to do his own work an' Will's as well. A college-eddicated fisherman! Huh!"

He felt exceedingly bitter, the more because Ben Anthony had taken his son to his home, and he said to his wife:

"Don't you go a-writin' to that young whelp, May. Let him work out his own traverse with Ben. We'll see what kind o' stuff's in him, though I cal'late he's too much of an Anthony to amount to much."

Noting the dangerous look in his wife's eyes, he added:

"Th' womenfolk o' that family are the best o' the breed."

Mrs. Stream said nothing, but felt all a mother's sympathy for her son, just then beginning his apprenticeship in the toughest and hardest college in the world—that of the deep-sea fishing fleet.

It was a hard school and Billy Stream cursed the endless monotony of it. The life he had lived in a university town with its pleasures, the dances, theaters and social life; the excitement of the football gridiron and the hockey rink; the fraternal bonhomie of a college crowd—it was all gone, and here he was, overhauling endless hooks on apparently endless trawls, baiting the same hooks with herring, pulling a pair of oars in a heavy dory, hauling the gear, pitching out and gutting cod, haddock and hake, and doing the same work all over again from daylight to dark, day after day.

Waking and sleeping, he lived in a world which swung and pitched with the restless heave of the ocean. He herded in an odoriferous forecastle with a crowd of rough-spoken, though kindly, men, and with them, toiled and fought the ceaseless menace of the sea. Though not at all enamored of a fisherman's life, yet he made up his mind to stick to it, and, knowing how his father would be keeping track of his work, he toiled the harder just to spite the "old man."

After his third trip to the Banks, Johnny Wilson, his dory-mate came aboard one night after visiting Anchorville.

"Saw your old man, Billy," he said.

"Did he speak to you?" queried Stream.

"Sure thing. Came up to me an' says, 'You're Will's dory-mate, ain't you?' I says I was, an' he asks me ef I wasn't tired o' havin' a blasted college guy to look after as well as my own work?"

"What did you say?"

"I ups an' tells him that Billy Stream needed no man to look arter him, an' that you was jest as smart a fisherman as any what shipped out o' the bay."

Billy slapped his dory-mate on the back.

"You're a good sort, old man," he murmured feelingly, "and I won't forget it."

HATING the monotonous toil of the dory, Billy read up on navigation and perfected himself in the art of handling a vessel, with the fixed idea of going out as skipper as soon as possible. To that end, he studied the Bank charts, noted the best fishing bottoms, watched the set of the tides on the various grounds and picked up a vast store of knowledge from his shipmates, men who had fished all over the western ocean. The little learning he had assimilated in science during his two years at college, helped him wonderfully— especially in navigation and weather lore.

The *Jennie Anthony* was a poor vessel for

Winter fishing and Ben Anthony usually hauled her up for the Winter months. She was a bad sea-boat and rather cranky, and the skippers who had ventured out in her in Wintertime usually made but one voyage. Fish prices were high during the Fall that Stream fished in her, and Ben Anthony induced her skipper to keep her fishing as long as possible.

This he did until they took a November snifter in the bay and swept the decks clean of dories, cable and gurry-kid. It was Billy's first experience of a breeze and it failed to frighten him, though it scared the skipper and some of the gang.

While the gale was at its height, Stream, oil-skinned and sea-booted, sat astride of the furled-up mainsail and watched the schooner's behavior. The water came aboard very heavily and the vessel lay-to like a log with no lift in her. The skipper watched her apprehensively and spoke to Billy.

"Reg'lar barge, ain't she?" he growled. "Heaves-to like an' old bucket. Look at her diving!"

"I'd like to try her on the other tack," shouted Billy above the roar of wind and sea. "Let me make an experiment, skipper!"

The other laughed.

"Go ahead, son," he said. "Ef you kin make her lie easier, you're a wonder."

Billy got the gang up and, taking the wheel, wore the ship around.

"Now slack off that jumbo an' the fore-sheet!" he cried. "So! That'll do!"

He took the wheel and watched the compass, putting the helm down slowly. Scanning the run of the sea, he kept a careful eye on the motions of the vessel and finally lashed the wheel.

"We'll try her at that, skipper," he said, and went below.

Half an hour later, the watch came below. "She's lyin' nicely sence Billy fixed her. She ain't makin' near as bad weather of it as she did afore an' it's blowin' jest as hard."

Billy, in his bunk, felt a thrill of pleasure at the words. The men would remember the incident, he knew, and it made him feel strangely confident.

"She's a —— barge in a breeze, anyway," growled the skipper, "an' I'm a-goin' to knock off soon's we git in. She's no vessel for Winter fishin' an' never was."

Stream, however, thought otherwise.

The bulk of the business carried on by Ben Anthony was in dried salt fish. He owned the ninety-five-ton Bank schooner *Jennie Anthony* and two shore-fishing motor-boats, each run by two men. The haddock caught by these craft were smoked and packed for market under the Excelsior Brand, and Ben Anthony shipped them up to various jobbers in the inland cities who disposed of them. The other fish—cod, hake, pollock and cusk—were salted and dried and sold to traveling buyers, who exported them to the West Indies and South America.

The Stream Fish Company was a large organization owning three Banking schooners, the *Leonora*, *Eugenora*, and *Astronora*, fine modern semi-knockabout vessels, each carrying ten dories. In addition they owned a pick-up gasoline schooner which plied between the fishing villages on the bay buying fresh fish, and the company also bought the fares of the motor-boat fishermen running out of Anchorville. The fish handled by them was shipped to market fresh and in a cured state; the mainstay of the business being the marketing of the famous "Morning-Glory Brand of Finnan-Haddies and Fillets, Kippered Herring and Bloaters." To market their products, the company had sales agencies throughout the country.

The *bête noire* of the sales agents was the Excelsior Brand. Every time Ben Anthony procured a stock of fresh haddock, he smoked the fish and his jobbers undersold the products of the Stream Fish Company and played havoc with the market. William Stream, senior, tried many times to put his brother-in-law Ben out of business, but could not manage it, and as Ben had no regular and steady trade in his products, Stream considered that he was an interloper and disorganizer.

When the *Jennie Anthony* tied up to her dock in Port Anthony, the skipper resigned and Ben made preparations to haul her up above high water for the Winter months. Billy then broached his ideas to his uncle.

"Look here, Uncle Ben," he said, "if you could keep the *Jennie* fishing all ˌWinter wouldn't it pay you well?"

"Sure it would," replied Ben, "but who'll go a-fishin' in her? She's cranky an' wet an' no skipper'll take her out Winter fishin'."

"You let me have her," said Billy. "I'll take her out."

Ben Anthony looked hard at the young fellow and then he laughed.

"Waal, by heck, you hev a nerve, son! Three months a-fishin' an' ye want to go skipper on that cranky barge in Winter-time. Ha! ha!"

"Uncle Ben," said the other seriously, "I mean what I say. I put in three months aboard of her just to get the hang of things so's I could take charge of a vessel. Did you think I meant to stick at the grubby drag of work in the dory? Not on your life! I've been keeping my eyes open and learning, and I'm confident of my ability to skipper the *Jennie Anthony*. With ordinary luck, I'll catch fish, too."

"Even supposin' ye can sail an' navigate her," demurred his uncle, "that won't alter the fact that she ain't a Winter fishin' vessel. She's too cranky for heavy weather, an' ye'll never git a gang to sail in her."

"That schooner can be made seaworthy, uncle," replied Billy decisively. "I've been watching her. She's badly ballasted, and if you'll agree, I'll draw off her lines and reballast her properly. With a little money spent on her I can fix her up."

The other waved his hand.

"We've tried that," he said. "We've overhauled her ballast lots of times——"

"Yes," interrupted Billy, "you have. That's just the trouble with you fishermen. You get monkeying about with a vessel and, instead of ballasting her the way the designer meant her to be ballasted, you go ahead on your own ideas.

"That's what you did in the *Jennie*. You've got a big pen of sand placed in her fore-hold—a regular dead-weight in the fore-end of her—that takes all the life out of the vessel. No wonder she's cranky. I'll make a safe bet that her pig-iron and stone ballast was dumped in under her floors and leveled off anyhow. I've done a little yacht sailing up West and I know how much ballast affects a vessel's trim and sailing qualities."

At last, with many misgivings, Ben Anthony gave his consent, and for several days Billy spent his time measuring the schooner and drawing off her lines, a piece of work he credited to the little knowledge he picked up during his two years at college. Procuring the plans of a similar vessel—the original designs of the *Jennie* were lost—he

figured out displacements with certain loads, and with his plan of the *Jennie's* lines and a small wooden half-model, he calculated the centers of buoyancy, gravity and lateral resistance.

When the designs were finished to his satisfaction, he got men to work unloading the schooner's ballast, and personally supervised its replacing. Uncle Ben, as an interested looker-on, felt impressed with the careful manner in which his nephew restowed the ballast in a cigar-shaped form along the keelson fore and aft.

"Now, uncle," said Billy when the ballasting was finished, "we'll alter her sail plan a little. She's got too much headsail. We'll cut the jib, jumbo and foresail down a little and get another reef-band in the fore-sail. In lying to, I think it will come in useful. After a little painting and over-hauling of the rigging, she'll be ready for fishing——"

"Ef you kin git a gang to go in her," interrupted the uncle pessimistically.

"Don't worry. I'll get a gang."

III

WHEN the Anchorville trawlers heard that young Billy Stream intended taking the *Jennie Anthony* out Winter haddocking, there was much doubtful comment. The fishermen all liked Billy—especially after he thrashed Jack Hemsley — but to their unsophisticated ideas, Billy was a "wrong 'un" and full of the crazy notions which comes to those who have been up to a college and absorbed some sort of education.

The fishermen knew the breed of old. They had listened many times to be-spectacled ichthyological professors who had lectured them on fish and fishery subjects, but because these gentlemen had never stood in the bow of a dory and hauled a trawl, they were of no account and not convincing. It is thus with fishermen the world over. They resent ideas propounded to them by men who "read them out of a book."

Billy had not visited his home since the row with his father. He had seen his mother and sister once or twice when the latter drove over to Uncle Ben's, but his parent had evinced no desire to see him. The fact of his linking up with Ben Anthony embittered the harsh old man. When the latter heard that his son was going to skipper the *Jennie Anthony* he laughed grimly and issued an edict, orally of course, that any man who shipped on the schooner would never get a "sight" on the Stream Company's vessels again. This was an error of judgment on Captain Stream's part. Fishermen are singularly independent and refuse to be coerced or restrained from following their inclinations.

Billy Stream found it hard work getting men. His old dory-mate, Johnny Wilson, promised to go with him, and he secured Jim Cline, a half-witted fellow, as cook. When Billy approached the Anchorville and Port Anthony trawlers about shipping with him, they laughed and refused to go. At the end of a week Billy was desperate.

There was a big political meeting held in the Anchorville Hall one night at which many fishermen were present. Just as the conclave adjourned, Billy jumped up on the platform and addressed the crowd.

"Boys," he said, "I want a gang for the *Jennie Anthony*. She's been overhauled and reballasted and is now a fit and able vessel for Winter fishing. I'm a green skipper, I know, but I'll learn, and I'm willing to learn. Anybody that will take a chance, let him come down to Johnny Morrison's pool-room tonight and sign up. Thank you, gentlemen!"

"Anybody that goes with that young fool is crazy!" roared a voice which Billy recognized as his father's. "He's no good an' never will be any good. He's double-crossed his father and will double-cross any man that's fool enough to go with him in that crazy tub o' Ben Anthony's. What does that feller know about sailin' a vessel or ketchin' fish? Take my advice an' keep away from him, boys. Ef he don't drown ye, that crazy cook of his'll pizen ye!"

There was a general laugh at Captain Stream's indictment of his son, but Billy jumped on the platform again, flaming.

"Any man that thinks I'll double-cross him, poison him or drown him, I'll knock the stuffing out of him," he bawled defiantly. "I'll fight any man in the crowd and if I lick him he'll ship with me. Come on, now, who'll take me up?"

Some one did take Billy up. It was the two town policemen who at a sign from the mayor grabbed William and ejected him from the hall as a disturber of the peace. Billy went out quietly and strode off to Morrison's pool-room feeling angry with himself for being such a fool.

At the pool-room, Patrick Clancy sought him out. Mr. Clancy was the town's sporting promoter and owned the local skating-rink.

"Looky-here, Billy," he said. "You play hockey, don't ye? Yes? Well, I've a proposition. Anchorville has always bin licked by the Cobtown boys. Now, ef you'll play for us on Saturday and help lick that Cobtown crowd, ye'll have all the boys with ye. Fishermen are good sports and they'll ship with ye, I'm sure, ef ye help win that game."

Stream laughed.

"I haven't had any practise this season; but go ahead, I'll try."

Clancy turned around to the crowd in the pool-room.

"Boys," said he. "Cap'en Billy Stream is a-goin' to play in the big hockey match against the Cobtown fellers at the Anchorville Rink on Christmas Eve. I told him ef we won, that some o' youse fellers would make up his gang. He's playin' on them conditions, an' I hope ye'll be sports enough to help him out. —— me, ef I could only haul a trawl I'd go mesilf. Now, give him a chance."

Billy came in from Port Anthony on the morning of December twenty-fourth. He had his skates and old college hockey gear with him, but somehow or other he did not feel at all enthusiastic about Clancy's proposition. The idea of getting a fishing crew by prowess at hockey was so absurd that he thought little of it. However, when he arrived in town, he found there was more of a furore over the game than he imagined.

The ingenious Clancy had billed the whole county about the event and, being a skilful press-agent, did not fail to advertise the fact that a college-bred fishing-skipper was going to play a star game in order to get a crew. As a result, fishermen from all up and down the coast came into Anchorville to see the game, and at 7 P. M. the rink was crowded.

The Cobtown men came in on a special train, and a husky crowd they were—hard-muscled young fellows who played a rough, slashing game when science failed to give them victory.

"They're a dirty crowd, Stream," said an Anchorville man to Billy as they climbed into their clothes at the rink. "Most of them are mechanics from the Cobtown

Engine Works and they rough it up in the second half. Our fellows are lighter than they are, most of us being bank-clerks and store-keepers, so we'll look to you at cover-point to help us out."

"I'll do my best," answered Stream, "but remember, boys, combination is everything. Don't hog the puck and play lone-hand games. Pass every time you're tackled, and let your forward men keep in a line across the rink ready to take a pass. Remember that—combination's the thing."

The Cobtown men in black-and-yellow jerseys and stockings were already on the ice and shooting the puck around. When the red-and-white arrayed Anchorville boys appeared, a great cheer greeted them.

"Now, then, Billy Stream!" shouted a man. "The *Jennie* gits a gang ef you play the game!"

Billy took up his position as cover-point when the whistle blew and the referee faced the puck off. The ice was hard, and from the outset the game was fast—too fast for Billy, who lacked practise.

With dull skates on the hard ice, Stream made a poor showing during the first half of the game. Several times the Cobtown men got past him and the Anchorville goal was bombarded with shots which only the skilful goal-tender saved. Once, with the puck at his feet, he fell down on the ice, and a smart Cobtown forward got it and shot a clean goal from the wings. The roar of approval from the Cobtown fans made Billy feel badly, and he cursed his dull skates and lack of practise.

"If the ice only softens up a bit," he murmured, "I'll be able to do something."

The first half had a minute to go, with the score 1—0 in favor of the visitors, when Billy got the puck and the Cobtown men had their goal undefended. With an eye to an off-side play, Stream cautiously carried the puck up the rink, dodged a Cobtown forward, passed to center, received the puck again, dodged the Cobtown point, and saw the goal clear.

"Shoot! Shoot!" roared the Anchorville spectators.

He glanced at the direction of the goal, stiffened up on his stick for the drive to goal, and then ignominiously slipped and fell down on the ice amid the angry howls of the home crowd. The half-time bell rang, and Billy went to the dressing-room with shouts of "Take Stream to the morgue —he's a dead one!" ringing in his ears. One thing alone served to alleviate his chagrin— the ice was getting softer.

In the dressing-room, Clancy hunted around for a new pair of skates, but failed to find any.

"Never mind," said Stream. "I'll do better this next half—the ice is getting softer."

"For Heaven's sake, man, wake up!" almost pleaded Clancy. "If we git trimmed I stand to lose a pile of money. I betted on you—you being a college man and a good hockey player."

The second half of a hockey game is usually the fastest and most exciting. The men have gotten into their stride by then and the deciding goals are won or lost. Stream noted with satisfaction that the ice was softer and that his dull skates cut in better. He took his place with an air of grim determination and stood, a strapping, handsome figure of a man, strong and agile.

The puck was faced off and a Cobtown man got it and came down the rink like a streak of lightning. He passed the Anchorville forwards, the rover, and made a stick play in front of Billy.

To the Cobtown man's surprise, Billy got the puck and started up the ice as quick as a cat. He dodged the Cobtown forwards and their cover-point and then passed to center. The center man, relying on Stream no more after spoiling the last shoot for goal, shot himself and missed. Four times Stream got the puck and went up the ice with it and on passing, the shot was spoiled by his own men.

"I'll play my own game after this," muttered Billy, and he did.

At the Anchorville goal, he got the puck and made a splendid single-handed run through all the Cobtown forwards. The cover-point tried to block him but was easily eluded, and Billy shot—a wonderful unerring drive—which sent the rubber into the Cobtown nets, and the cheers which followed showed how his play was appreciated.

The score stood an even one to one with fifteen minutes to play.

With another goal to get in order to beat their opponents, the Cobtown team started roughing the play and body-checked the Anchorville men heavily. The pace was telling on the home team, and Stream noticed that his men were getting fagged and failed to follow up the puck. Andy Kelly, a bank-clerk, playing as rover for Anchorville, was their best man, and Stream skated up to him.

"How're you feeling?" he asked.

"Pretty fit," replied the other.

"Well then, you follow me and stand by for passes. Our team's breaking up."

"Right-oh! I'm with you!"

A heavily built Cobtown player literally bodied his way down the rink with the puck and knocked his opponents off their feet with his strength and weight. Like a wild horse he came speeding down toward Stream, and it looked as if nothing could stop him.

Billy skated for him. The two bodies met with a clink of steel and the clash of hockey sticks. There was a sullen thud as the Cobtown man drove into the sideboards and sprawled headlong, and Billy came racing up the rink with the rubber disk before him. Glancing around, he noticed Kelly pacing him. He dodged numerous black-and-yellow figures, who slashed at the puck and his stick savagely, and made a lightning pass to Kelly on the right wing.

"Shoot! shoot! Kelly!" screamed the crowd.

The Cobtown point tackled him just as he was about to make a drive for the goal and amid the disappointed roars of the Anchorville fans, the point player secured the puck and started to run the rubber down the rink again.

Like a red-and-white streak, Billy went for him; sticks clashed, and before the Cobtown goal-minder knew what happened, the puck came at him like a shot from a gun and clattered into the net. The spectators yelled with delight and Clancy shouted himself hoarse.

"Good boy, Billy! Only ten minutes more an' we've got them trimmed!"

The puck was faced off again, and Stream found himself the objective of all the Cobtown players. He had the rubber again and was running up the rink when the big fellow, whom he sent sprawling previously, deliberately slashed him over the head with his stick.

Stream fell to the ice like a pole-axed ox and lay prone while shrieks of rage went up from the crowd. The referee blew his whistle; the Cobtown player was sent off the ice for the balance of the game, and Billy was carried into the dressing-room bleeding profusely from a nasty cut on the side of the head.

He revived a minute later and in a daze allowed his head to be bandaged. While he was being attended to, Clancy came bustling in.

"We're trimmed! We're trimmed!" he wailed. "Kelly's the only man on the ice that can stand on his feet—the rest's gone to pieces, and Cobtown hev evened up the score—three to three!"

Stream struggled to his feet.

"Let me out!" he growled savagely, and he staggered out of the room and on to the ice in time to check a rush of the Cobtown forwards.

His head swam with the crack he had received; he could see nothing but the Cobtown goal ahead of him and the puck. He had to get the rubber into their goal once more and he summoned all his strength and energy.

"Another goal and I'll trim them and get my gang!" he murmured subconsciously.

Feeling horribly weak, he sped up the rink, bodying his opponents, leaping over swinging sticks, but keeping the little black disk forever before him.

The opposing team sped after him, but he dodged, doubled and outdistanced them all. They slashed at his stick, but the wrists that held it were wrists of steel—the puck seemed to be contained within an impregnable curve of rock-elm and they failed to get it.

It was a spectacular run from one end of the rink to the other—a gantlet in which five men were eluded as a hare might elude a pack of snarling hounds. And at last he found himself before the Cobtown goal with the tender awaiting his shot as watchful as a cat.

"Shoot! Shoot!" shrieked the excited crowd, and summoning all his strength, Billy shot, and collapsed just as the closing bell rang.

He woke up to find himself lying on his back on a bench in the dressing-room. Clancy was bending over him and forcing brandy between his lips.

"God, boy!" he shouted ecstatically. "What a game! We've trimmed them—th' swabs! Four to three an' you're th' lad what done it. That last bit o' play was a blame marvel. Run through th' hull crowd o' them single-handed an' shot—Lord Harry, what a shot! It was like a bullet an' actually bust th' cussed net. If it had hit that goal-tender it 'ud ha' killed him sure."

"Where's that guy that clipped me?" growled Billy ominously.

"Oh, never mind him," said Clancy. "He's gone."

The door burst open and Ben Anthony and a crowd of Anchorville fishermen swarmed in.

"When ye shippin' yer gang, skip?" shouted one of them.

"Sail on th' second or third of January," replied Stream.

"Give me a sight, by Judas! I'll go jest for th' fun o' th' thing!"

Other voices shouted:

"Me too, by Godfrey! Count me in, Billy! I'll go, even ef the ol' *Jennie* rolls over!"

IV

IT WAS a rare bunch of terriers that sailed to the Banks with Billy Stream — a young, harum-scarum gang, imbued with the sporting instinct, afraid of nothing and ready to take a chance on anything. Through the hockey match, the young skipper secured seventeen men, an eight-dory gang and a spare hand, and two days after the New Year holiday, the *Jennie Anthony*, in Winter rig of four lowers, swung out to sea with the Winter haddocking fleet and made her first fishing set on the northeastern edge of Brown's Bank.

Billy soon realized that commanding a fishing-vessel entailed numerous responsibilities and anxieties: The selection of the fishing-ground; the direction and number of tubs of trawl the men had to set from the dories called for an intimate knowledge of the bottom and the run of the tides; the schooner had to be maneuvered by the skipper and the spare hand when the dories were strung out over four miles of sea, and the former must keep an eye on them all, and attend to them should their gear part or they need help in any way.

Sail-handling and the navigation of the vessel was in the skipper's hands entirely. The men merely obeyed orders, and in that it was absolutely necessary that he gain their confidence and give his commands without hesitation. Stream, with but three months' experience in fishing-vessels, felt that he had a lot to learn.

While the fleet were in sight, Billy felt easy. He would watch them and do what they did. Unfortunately for him, the wind came away heavy one night, and when morning dawned, there wasn't a sail in sight.

"Scattered, I guess," said Billy. "Well, we'll take a sound and fish where we are."

During two gray days, they fished and brought aboard a handsome fare with the ground all to themselves. With sixty thousand pounds of haddock and other ground fish below on ice in the holds, Billy was for swinging off for Port Anthony, but he listened to the men who urged him to hang on a day or two longer and make a "high-line" trip of it. The appearance of the sky, the oily run of the sea and the falling barometer caused him some apprehension, but some of the men averred that such signs did not always mean bad weather.

"Ef you're for swingin' her off every time th' glass falls or th' sky looks greasy, ye'll be in and out o' shelter harbors all th' time," they said, and Billy, allowing for their experience in such things, kept the vessel on the grounds.

It ended in his having to pick the dories up in a moderate gale of rain and sleet. He had just time to get them and the fish aboard when a savage squall struck the schooner and hove her down with the four lowers still on her.

"Haul down yer jib!" he roared from the wheel. "Aft here and sheet in yer mains'l! Now, fellers, get ready to tie the mains'l up. Get your crotch tackles hooked in. Ready? Settle away yer halyards! Roll her up! We'll heave-to under fores'l and jumbo till this blows over."

They dressed the fish down while the *Jennie* bucked and jumped a steep breaking sea, and Stream noted with satisfaction that the schooner rode like a duck.

"She's doin' fine, Skip, sence you ballasted her properly," remarked his old dorymate Wilson. "The ol' *Jennie's* a different craft altogether."

It was blowing hard, but the vessel was lying comfortably, and after giving instructions to the two men on watch to put the vessel about on the other tack at the end of their watch, he went below and turned in. He did not sleep, however, but lay awake listening to the conversation of the men hugging the stove in the cabin.

"Skipper sh'd be puttin' it to her," growled one man. "No use lyin' out here with a trip below."

"Yes," remarked another. " 'Tain't blowin' noways hard. She'd drive along under ridin' sail, fores'l an' jumbo." And so it continued, regular fisherman's gabble which no experienced skipper ever listens to. Billy Stream was green, and he astonished the crowd by tumbling out of his bunk and singing out for all hands to set the riding sail and get the vessel under way.

The *Jennie* made heavy weather of it, and the talkers began to regret their outspoken opinions when the watches came around. The wind hauled northwest and freezing cold, while the spray which whirled over the schooner froze on her decks, sails and rigging. During the night it was "ice-mallets and belaying-pin drill," pounding the ice away.

It froze harder during the day, and the ice made so fast that all hands were unable to clear it. The decks were filmed in ice a foot thick and ropes and standing rigging were encased to the thickness of a man's thigh. The deck-houses, dories, windlass and cables were indistinguishable in the shroud of ice which covered them, and Billy ordered life-lines to be rigged fore-and-aft and ashes scattered upon the slippery decks to prevent the men from sliding overboard.

"This is getting tough," muttered the skipper. "If it makes much more, she'll capsize with the weight of it. Um! Let me see! Cobtown Harbor is thirty miles away. It'll take us seven or eight hours— maybe more—to make it. We can't do it if it keeps cold like this."

The men were getting unusually nervous and frightened and were throwing anxious glances in Stream's direction. The vessel was looking like an iceberg, and the tons of frozen water on her superstructure caused her to roll dangerously.

The men came aft.

"We can't clear her, Skip," they said. "What are you goin' to do? We'll sink soon."

"What do you usually do in a case like this?" asked Billy anxiously.

"How in ——— do we know?" growled a man. "We ain't bin out like this afore. You're skipper here an' you ought to know."

"All right," snapped Stream. "Stand by to wear ship! Slack off yer foresheet!

Git that riding sail down and the mains'l hoisted. Put a single reef in it!"

"What are ye goin' to do?"

"Go ahead an' do as I tell you!" he replied grimly. "Pound that sail clear and get it hoisted."

Setting the reefed mainsail was a terrible job. The great piece of canvas was frozen solid on the sixty-foot boom, and the men pounded it clear, tied the wire-like reef-points, and, after knocking the ice off the halyards, hauled the sail up with lurid oaths.

"There, ——— ye," they growled. "Drive the barge for whatever port yer eddicated skipper kin fetch!"

"Now, get busy with those ice-mallets and keep pounding!" bawled Billy, taking no notice of the remarks.

RUNNING before a heavy sea with the reefed mainsail on her caused the ice-laden craft to perform some hair-curling antics, and the men pounding ice glanced apprehensively every now and again at Stream, who had the wheel. It was ticklish work steering the logy schooner, but Stream was equal to it and held her steady.

"Where are we goin', Billy?" asked Wilson. "Ye ain't headin' for an American port on that course."

"No," replied the skipper. "She's heading right for the open sea." ·

"Where in blazes for?"

"The Gulf Stream, Johnny."

"Th' Gulf Stream!" echoed the other in amazement. "What's the idear?"

"Warmer weather, Johnny," replied the skipper. "In a few hours we'll get into it and this ice'll melt."

When the gang heard the news they laughed the idea to scorn.

"Who ever heard of sich a crazy notion?" said a man. "This is some o' his noo-fangled college idears. Here we are runnin' away to blaze-an'-gone offshore. Let's make him fetch her up an' run for Portland or Boston."

They went aft in a body and suggested it.

"That's no use," replied Billy grimly. "This area of low temperature will prevail all down the New England coast as far south as New York. Just as soon as we run west again we'll strike it. We'll keep to the sou'-southeast until the wind shifts from the northerly board———"

"Aw, that be hanged, Skip!" exclaimed a man. "Ye read that in a book. Fetch her up an' head inshore."

"You go ahead and pound ice," retorted Stream. "I'm master of this craft and I know what I'm doing." The men began to murmur among themselves and Billy recognized the fact that he must assert his authority.

"Here, Johnny Wilson," he cried. "Take the wheel and hold her! Now, fellers, get busy with your ice-mallets and no more guff."

A young fisherman stepped forward.

"Say," he growled. "Who d'ye think ye're talkin' to?"

Stream answered him by a well-directed punch on the jaw and the man fell to the deck. Billy stood over him as he rose to his feet.

"Want another crack?" he snapped.

"Naw!"

"Then don't question my doings. Get to work, the gang of you, and clear that ice away. Refuse, and I'll sail in and lick the lot of you!"

It was a bold speech, and Billy knew it. There were men among his gang who could have eaten him if they were so disposed, but the circumstances were too serious then for men to commence brawling. Besides that, Stream's confident manner impressed them and they went back to their work of ice-pounding without any more words.

Toward evening the temperature rose and the ice began to melt. The wind still breezed hard, but the air became perceptibly warmer and no more ice made on the schooner.

"Aft here, boys, and take in your mains'l," shouted Stream. "We'll heave her to here!"

At midnight the red light of a sailing-vessel appeared on their weather quarter and an ice-coated schooner stormed past.

"What vessel's that?" hailed Billy. "*Regina* of Gloucester! Who's that?"

"*Jennie Anthony* of Anchorville!"

"Hard weather," shouted a voice. "Had to run off here to git clear of ice!"

"By Jupiter!" exclaimed one of Stream's gang. "That's Ansel Watson's vessel. He's a high-line Gloucesterman and I cal'late he knows what he's doing when he runs off here. Skip, ol' dog, I'm sorry I doubted yer idear. You knew what was best, arter all."

Stream said nothing, but when morning broke and showed five fishing-schooners around them hove-to on the edge of the Gulf Stream, he felt that the sight was sufficient testimony to his good judgment. When the wind hauled to the west'ard and they made sail again, Stream had graduated as an able man in the opinion of his gang.

For three days they "warmed it to her" as the saying is, and came storming up the bay and into Port Anthony in fine style. Uncle Ben was over the rail ere the schooner was anchored.

"Thought ye were lost in that breeze," he cried. "H'ard nawthin' of ye sence th' fleet came home. Jupiter! I'm glad t' see ye. How much fish have ye got? Eighty thousand! Good work! There's none to be got now. Nary a vessel or boat out for th' last ten days. Th' fleet jest went out yesterday mornin' an' yer ol' man's crazy to git some fresh stock."

"Is he?" said Billy. "Then sell him our trip."

"At the market price?"

"What was it last?"

"Two and a half cents a pound for haddock."

"Ask him five. If he really needs it to fill his orders, he'll have to pay."

"Wait a second and I'll telephone him," said Uncle Ben. In a minute he came back. "He says it's a hold-up, but he'll take it. That'll make a dandy stock for your gang —over eighty dollars apiece for a three weeks' trip. Billy, you're a high-liner, but ye sh'd ha' heard yer old man cuss at the price. Ye've put one over on him this time, an' what'll make him feel worse is the fact that ye've made good as a skipper and fixed the *Jennie Anthony* up as an able vessel again. Now git acrost to Anchorville with yer trip an' make the old man mad."

Feeling good at the price they were getting, the gang hoisted sail again and the *Jennie Anthony* sailed in to the Stream Fish Company's wharf. Captain Billy went up to his father's office to ratify the sale of the fish and found his parent chuckling to himself over the telephone. When Billy entered, Stream, senior, glanced up, shouted "All right, send them up!" to some one on the other end of the line, and turned to his son with a face stern and saturnine in its expression.

"Hullo, Dad!" exclaimed Billy. "I've

just brought the vessel over with the fish. Five cents for the haddock, you told Uncle Ben, eh?"

"Five cents be ——!" snarled the elder Stream. "D'ye think I'm crazy? I wouldn't give more'n a cent and a half for any fish you'd bring in."

"Didn't you tell Uncle Ben over the 'phone that you'd take our trip at five cents?"

"I might have, but I've changed my mind since."

"You're going back on your word, Dad!" said Billy slowly.

"Am I? Waal, I reckon that's my lookout. A pretty fool I'd be to pay five cents for fish that I kin buy for half the price."

"Yes, but you can't get it now."

"Can't I?" snapped the other. "Don't you worry. I've got all I want. My vessels have jest run in to Cobtown harbor with fifty thousand among them, an' I'm having it shipped up by rail now. Ef you want to sell your trip to me, I'll take it at a cent and a half."

"Why, Dad, that's a cent less than the last market price."

"Take it or leave it then. I'm not anxious to buy!"

Billy was boiling with disgust and rage—so much so that he could hardly speak. His father was enjoying his discomfiture.

"Well, by Godfrey!" said Billy at last. "I always thought my father was an honorable man, but I find his word is worth nothing!"

"You infernal young pup!" shouted Captain Stream, rising. "Git out o' here! I wouldn't take yer fish ef it was given to me. You 'n' Ben thought ye c'd put it all over me, didn't ye? Git aboard that hooker o' yours an' away from my dock or I'll cast yer lines adrift!"

The young skipper turned to go. With his hand on the door, he said:

"You've welshed on this, Dad, but mark my words, I'll pay you back some day." And he went out, inwardly raging.

At the dock he communicated the interview to the gang, and amid the jeers of the shore workers, they cursefully hoisted sail and headed the vessel back to Port Anthony again. When Uncle Ben heard the reason of their return, he swore softly.

"He got me that time, but it was a mean game to play on the men. Never mind, Billy. I'll buy the trip at three cents
11

and smoke them. Git yer hatches off."

That night the premises of the Anthony Fish Company burnt down and morning revealed a heap of smoldering ruins.

V

"MY PLACE was set afire!" said Ben Anthony finally. "It never started in the smoke-house, 'cause the wind was west last night and the smoke-house 'ud be to loo'ard. The fire was set in th' wind'ard buildin' which held nawthin' but three hundred quintal o' dried fish, an' nobody's bin in it fur a week. It was set afire, Billy, an' I believe yer old man had a hand in it to put me out o' business!"

"I don't believe that Dad would do that," dissented Billy. "What'll we do with the *Jennie's* trip of fish? We can't handle it now."

"Um! The only thing I can think of is to telephone Will an' ask him to take it off our hands at his own price," said Uncle Ben dismally. "I'll go 'n' do that now."

Ten minutes later he came down to the vessel almost white with passion.

"Told me he wouldn't take it off my hands to make glue with," stormed Anthony. "Said he was glad that a fire had cleaned my old shacks from off Port Anthony beach and he hoped I'd retire on the insurance money and keep out of the fish business."

"That was cruel," remarked Billy. "Did you telephone any one else about the fish?"

"Yes, I got the Cobtown people on the wire. They wouldn't take them. Your father must have fixed them."

Billy looked serious.

"Um!" he exclaimed. "This is war to the knife! Well, I guess we'll show the old man that we're not dead yet, uncle. You get those ruins cleared up and I'll run this fish across to Bayport. When I come back, we'll hold a council of war."

He got some of the men together and hoisted sail on the schooner for the fifty-mile run to Bayport. Two days later, the *Jennie* shot into port again with her fish still aboard.

"Not a buyer over there would look at our fish," said Billy bitterly. "They've all been fixed by the Stream Fish Company. I couldn't give them away. The old man seems determined to put you and me out of business, but we'll best him. I'll get the gang together to split and salt them and then we'll have a talk."

While the men were discharging the schooner's fare and dressing it for salting, Billy outlined a scheme of future operations.

"Uncle Ben, why not go to work and build a modern fish-plant with smoke-houses, packing-rooms and everything just the same as father's place? You had the name of putting up a better finnan-haddie than the Stream Company."

"To be sure I did," interrupted Ben proudly. "Yer dad could never touch me in smokin' fish. I l'arnt th' proper way from an old Scotchman that used to fish for me. My Excelsior Brand will sell quicker than Morning Glory, 'Th' Nation's Breakfast,' as he calls it."

"Then why don't you develop that business?"

"Too much bother. Salt fish is easier. It don't spile and it kin allus find a market."

"Could you sell all the finnan-haddies you could turn out?"

"Easy. I git piles of orders fur them. Come to the office an' I'll show you letters from jobbers."

Billy went up to the combination store and gear shed in which was the tiny cubicle that Uncle Ben dignified by the name of "office." It contained a base-burner stove, an ancient desk and a safe. The whole place was littered with papers filed upon nails driven into the walls and the desk was jammed full of miscellaneous correspondence. Uncle Ben was clearly no business man and his educated nephew's sense of neatness revolted at the disorder.

Ben's great hands groped among the papers on the desk and he selected some letters from large inland wholesalers offering to purchase considerable quantities of his Excelsior Brand.

"I can see by these that we can build up a good business if it is handled properly," said Stream. "Fix your wharves up; build a good fish-house on it and erect a first-class smoke-house with concrete floors and sides. The other buildings should be well built and nicely painted so as to look good to anybody taking the notion to visit the plant. Let's get out nice boxes; pack the fish in parchment paper and place a little booklet in each box giving hints on how to cook finnan-haddie. Build a new office; get a proper bookkeeper and stenographer in it; have filing cabinets to take care of your papers; procure neatly printed letter paper and bill-heads and write your correspondence by typewriter.

"You keep out of the office and look after the smoking and the outside work. Buy a small gasoline schooner and use her for buying fish down the bay ports; have a good outfitting store and keep gasoline and gear. There's lots of fishermen in Port Anthony but there's nothing to keep them here—they all go over to Anchorville and fish out of that place. I'll take a trip up west and see some of the wholesalers and get them to act as our agents. Let us put up finnan-haddies, smoked fillets, kippers and bloaters. Let's cut in to the Stream Fish Company's trade. We can get it, uncle, if we go after it."

Uncle Ben gasped.

"That's all very well, Billy, but to do what you want'll cost more money than I've got. What's all this a-goin' to cost?"

"I can't say," replied the young skipper, "but I'll soon figure it out. I'll turn to and draw out plans for a new plant and make an estimate of the cost. If you can't finance it all, I'll get you to pay my expenses to go west and get some one with money to invest it in our scheme. Come! Let's dope this thing out."

Overcome by the arguments of his enterprising nephew, and with a strong desire to get back at his brother-in-law whom he believed to have had something to do with the destruction of his plant, Ben Anthony entered into the scheme enthusiastically, and after Stream had seen the *Jennie Anthony's* former skipper and induced him to take the vessel out fishing again now that she was seaworthy, the young fellow took train and left for Montreal without breathing a word to any one of his intentions. Ben Anthony intended to do nothing until he heard from his nephew.

Captain William Stream, senior, heard in due course that Ben was doing nothing in the way of rebuilding his burnt-out premises. He also heard that the *Jennie Anthony* was fishing again under her old skipper and running her trips into another port, and that his son had gone west.

"Got tired of it—th' young cub," mused he contentedly. "I cal'late he had enough o' fishin'. I knew he wouldn't stick—it ain't in him. Waal, th' fire's put Ben out o' business. Th' Stream Fish Company'll hev things its own way now. We'll put th' prices up a cent a pound an' hold them. Ef dealers want my fish they kin pay for them. Ben's junk ain't on th' market to cut prices."

The hard old man felt so good over the news that he allowed his daughter to cajole him into buying an automobile.

BUOYED up with optimism and an enthusiastic faith in the future, Billy Stream landed in Montreal and called on several of the large wholesale fish distributors. They all knew the Excelsior Brand and liked them. The finnan-haddies put up by Ben Anthony had a peculiarly piquant and tasty flavor which was absent in the Stream Company's product, and customers preferred them. There was a good market for all they could supply and any one of the firms he visited would take up an agency and push the sale of the goods.

After looking up their various commercial ratings and a few other things, Billy appointed an up-to-date concern as his distributing agent and promised to let them know when he would be ready to start shipping the fish.

"Get to work as soon as possible, Captain Stream," said the wholesaler. "Your namesake's concern has jacked the price up on us and, as they have no opposition to amount to anything, they've got the market."

Getting an agent was an easier matter than getting money, however, and Billy spent an arduous week interviewing capitalists and exhibiting his plans and outlining the possibilities of his proposition. If he were engaged in promoting an oil-well, a silver mine or a real-estate option, he could have got the money, but a fish business— alas! It was too far away and visionary for the men he interviewed to invest in.

Stream haunted offices, raced around hotels to keep appointments, worked all his college chums for letters of introduction to moneyed men, and got thin and pale with his unavailing efforts. It was fruitless. Ten thousand dollars were as hard to get as ten million.

A trip to Toronto on the money-raising errand took nearly all his money, and when he returned to Montreal after an unsuccessful visit, he had to crave the hospitality of an old college chum and sell his watch in order to procure enough money to take him to Boston. He did not feel like wiring his uncle for funds, and once in Boston he felt sure that he would get a lift over to Nova Scotia upon a coaster or a fisherman.

Feeling decidedly blue, he decided to leave Montreal, and with Jack Anstruther, his college friend, he walked down-town to the railroad depot. It was a cold February evening, the streets were slippery and walking was difficult.

At a busy crossing an old gentleman, dressed rather meanly, attempted to cross the street, and slipped and fell in front of an electric-car which was coming down-hill at a fair rate of speed. The motorman attempted to apply his air- and hand-brakes, but the wheels failed to grip on the slippery rails and the heavy vehicle went charging down the slope with unabated speed.

Spectators shouted in horror; a policeman made a rush, but while he hesitated in fright Stream leaped in front of the car, grabbed a bar with his left hand, and, as it drove down on top of the prostrate man, he reached down and grasped the old gentleman by the coat-collar and held him in a grip of iron.

Before the car could be brought to a standstill, both were dragged several yards in front of the car with their legs trailing under it, but, except for the hurts incidental to scraping along an icy street, neither was injured.

Stream swung the old gentleman to his feet.

"—— you, sir!" shrieked the old fellow. "You've choked me. What the devil do you mean?"

Billy gasped in surprise. After saving the man's life, such a greeting was incomprehensible, and he spluttered:

"—— you! What d'ye mean by goin' to sleep on the car-tracks? Tired of life, or what?"

A crowd had gathered and Anstruther elbowed his way to Stream's side.

"You'll have to hurry, Billy," he said. "Your train goes in two minutes. Golly! That was a nervy thing you did! You must be an awful strong man——"

"Tend to that scurvy old gink and see him home," said Stream hurriedly. "I'll have to run for my train. So long, Jack, and many thanks for your kindness in putting me up. I'll write you."

He gave a glance at the old gentleman, who was surrounded by the crowd, and he struggled through the onlookers and commenced to run for the depot. Some one shouted after him, but as he had only a minute to catch the Boston train, he did not stop.

He swung aboard just as the train was going out of the station, and when he took his seat in the smoker, he had time to survey himself.

"My good boots and the bottoms of my pants all ripped to Hades," he growled, "and my coat torn. Saved the old swab's life and he cussed me for choking him. What d'ye know about that?"

He spent the night in the smoker thinking over the future and his prospects. Things were decidedly blue.

Arriving in Boston, he went down and had breakfast in a "quick lunch" on Atlantic Avenue. He did not sit up at the counter, but entered a partitioned-off compartment. While he was eating he could hear the slurring conversation of two drunken men in the next cubicle, but probably would have taken no notice of it had he not heard the name "Anthony" mentioned. Pausing to listen, he heard a familiar voice speaking in the egotistical bragging manner of "boozy" men.

"Yesh, Tom," it was saying. "I got even with him, see? He licked me, an' made a fool o' me afore th' men, an' you know I ain't th' man any one kin lick an' git away with it, see? He hove me down inter a scow-load o' gurry an' made a proper mug o' me, but I got even with him, tho' he don't know it. You know how?"

"Naw! How d'ye git him, Jack?"

"He was runnin' fish to Ben Anthony after his old man kicked him out fer lickin' me. The old man an' him don't pull, ye see? I owe Ben Anthony one fer gittin' me pinched one time an' I owed this college cub one fer lickin' me, so I jest went over to Port Anthony one night in a dory an' hove a handful o' lighted waste inter Ben Anthony's dried-fish house——"

"*Sh!*" cautioned the other man, who was evidently more sober. "Be careful how ye talk. That's a jail job."

"Aw, ——!" growled the other. "Nobody kin hear me. I ain't shoutin'. So, as I was tellin' ye, th' cussed place burnt down. Ben Anthony's bin put out o' business an' that young swab had t' give up th' vessel. He's gone west——"

"Waal," interrupted the other. "What's yer plan? Ol' man Stream fired ye fer drinkin'. How're ye a-goin' to bleed him?"

"Lissen, son. You were in th' fish-shed that time when ol' man Stream was cussin' Ben Anthony. Remember what he said?"

"Only wished his buildin's 'ud burn down an' git him out o' business. That what ye mean?"

"Sure thing! An' thar were lots h'ard him. Now, I'm goin' over to ol' man Stream an' I'm goin' to say that he hired me to burn Ben Anthony's buildin's down. I'll tell him that you' n' others h'ard him say he wished some one 'ud burn 'em for him——"

"*Sh!*" interjected the other man. "You're talkin' too loud! Here, finish yer cawfee an' let's git out an' aboard th' *Jennie May*."

Stream listened almost breathless at the disclosures he had overheard in this chance conversation. He knew the voices—one was Jack Hemsley's, the foreman he had thrashed—and the other was of a man who used to work around his father's place. Both men were rising to their feet. Stream placed his head drunkenly on the table and snored stertoriously. As the two shambled out, he was conscious that Hemsley's companion glanced in at him.

"Who th' —— is that?" growled Hemsley.

"Another souse—dead to th' world. He h'ard nawthin'." And they passed out.

Stream finished his coffee.

"So they're going over on the *Jennie May*. She'll be going to Anchorville with a load o' hard coal, I guess. Stanley Collins is skipper of her, and I guess he'll give me a lift over as well. I must go down and see him. Even though I'm not friendly disposed to my dad, I won't allow those beachcombers to put a game like that over him, and I'll jug Mister Fire-bug Hemsley for burning Uncle Ben's place."

As he strode down to the coal dock, he felt that his excursion had not proved altogether fruitless.

VI

 CAPTAIN COLLINS of the *Jennie May* laughed heartily when Stream explained his wants.

"Lord Harry! My old packet sh'd git inter th' passenger business. You're the third guy that wants a lift to Anchorville.

Waal, I'm glad t' hev ye, Billy. A coaster kin allus do with a few extry hands in Wintertime. Pick yer bunk an' make yerself to home. We'll go out at noon with the ebbtide."

In the forecastle Billy found Hemsley and his companion, a man named Jones. The former jumped to his feet on seeing Stream and ground out an oath.

"Hullo, Hemsley!" exclaimed Billy heartily. "Going across?"

The man growled an affirmative.

"Well, well," said Billy, "we'll make a regular family party. How's everything at Anchorville?"

"Same's usual," grunted Hemsley sullenly.

Stream could see by the man's demeanor that he was still sore over the thrashing he had got, but Billy treated him as if it had never happened.

They hoisted sail and put to sea, and for two days the weather held fine and they romped up the coast. When they made Matinicus Rock, the weather turned colder and a heavy frost-vapor shrouded the sea, settling down so thickly that it was impossible to see the end of the jib-boom from the windlass. Billy had the wheel from midnight to four, and when relieved by Captain Collins he went down into the cabin and turned into the latter's bunk.

For a while he lay dozing and listening to the drone of the mechanical fog-horn which Hemsley was pumping for'ard, and then turning over in the warm blankets, he went into the deep slumber of sailormen. He was awakened an hour later by a terrific crash which hove him out on the cabin floor.

Grabbing his boots, he hauled them on while a medley of shouts sounded from the deck. The cabin was dark, but he could hear Captain Collins shouting:

"For God's sake, stand by us. We're sinking!"

Another voice, Hemsley's, cried:

"Git th' yawl over. She's cut th' bows off us clean to the forehatch!"

Sea-booted feet tramped overhead, and amid the shouting Billy heard Collins bawling:

"Open th' cabin door, Hemsley! Billy Stream's below in my bunk."

Stream leaped for the gangway ladder and clambered up the steps as Hemsley shoved the hatch back.

"That you, Stream?" he hissed.

"Yep! What's——"

Before he could articulate the question something heavy smashed him on the top of the head and he toppled back into the cabin, senseless, just as the schooner settled in the water to her scuppers.

"He ain't below!" bawled Hemsley. "Must sleep like th' Seven Sleepers."

"—— !" ejaculated the coaster's captain. "She's settling. Into the yawl with you. We can't save him now!" And the five members of the coaster's crew tumbled into the boat and shoved off just as the schooner hove her stern up preparatory to going down by the head.

"Lay to your oars, men!" shouted Collins. "I hear that cursed steamer whistlin' down to loo'ard. Git down to him or we'll be swamped. Poor Billy Stream!"

With a heavy sea running, there was no time for regrets, and the crowd in the yawl pulled hurriedly in the direction of the steamer which had run them down. Within ten minutes they sighted her in the mist and rounded up alongside. A Jacob's ladder was thrown down her steep sides and a voice shouted:

"All saved?"

"Naw, blast ye!" shouted Collins. "Thar's one man gone down in her!"

THE rescued crew were landed next morning in Cobtown Harbor and arrived in Anchorville that night. Captain Stream heard the news of his son's death with genuine emotion and cursed himself bitterly for his harshness toward the boy. Ben Anthony evinced more grief than did Billy's parent, and both were present when Collins told his story.

"Billy came to me in Boston to git a passage acrost," he explained. "I took him as well as Hemsley an' Jones an' let two o' my crew go ashore while th' three o' them 'ud help work th' vessel acrost. Billy was below in my bunk when th' steamer struck us for'ard, an' he went down in her. Hemsley opened th' cabin door an' called to him, but he couldn't ha' heard him. We had only time to git inter th' boat afore she settled."

"Did ye see her go under?" inquired Ben.

"She was awash to her rails when we left her. A vessel with a dead-weight cargo o' coal in her an' her bows shore off don't take long to sink. She must ha' gone down like a stone thirty seconds after we shoved off."

Hemsley was also questioned.

"He couldn't ha' bin in th' cabin," he said, "or else he slept mighty sound. I shouted down to him but got no reply. He might ha' bin for'ard when she was struck. Anyways, he's gone, poor chap. A fine feller, your son, Cap'en Stream. Had th' makin's o' a fine man in him."

Ben Anthony returned home and gave up all idea of rebuilding his plant again, now that his nephew was gone. He was a widower with no children and he had come to look upon Billy in the light of a son. His sorrow was real.

Over at Anchorville strange things were happening. Jack Hemsley—formerly dock foreman of the Stream Fish Company, and discharged for drunkenness—was reinstated in his old berth again and was more or less drunk all the time. The man Jones was placed in charge of the shipping-room and he, like his crony, seldom drew a sober breath.

The office-manager fired them both one day, but to his consternation, Captain Stream told him to leave them alone. The manager wondered, but thought the old man's behavior in the matter was due to the fact that both men were shipmates with his son when he was drowned.

Like many uneducated men, Captain Stream had a horror of the law. The ingenious yarn spun by Hemsley made the old man appear in a damaging light, and the blackmailer assured him that any court would find him guilty of incendiarism.

"It's true enough that I fired th' place," said Hemsley, "but you'd be th' one to gain by it. Burnin' down Ben Anthony's place was good business fur your firm. Ye said out loud right afore th' lot of us on th' wharf that ye wished some one 'ud burn down Ben Anthony's shacks."

Captain Stream winced. He had made these rash remarks to many people.

"And even ef ye had me up in court fur settin' fire to th' buildin's I'd swear you ast me to, an' I kin git Jones t' swear as well. You'd be convicted fur incitin' me to do th' job an' ye'd git ten years in th' penitentiary fur it."

So Hemsley had reasoned, and the old man capitulated. This accounted for his queer actions in employing two worthless characters and placing them in responsible positions.

Three weeks after the foundering of the *Jennie May*, a man, dressed in seamen's dungaree clothes, opened the door of the house where Ben Anthony lived, and entered. Anthony was reading a newspaper in the sitting-room; the housekeeper was engaged in the kitchen, and as it was dark, none saw the stranger approach the house.

"Uncle Ben!"

The old man started at the voice and paled under his tan. Turning fearfully around he gazed with evident horror at the sight of his nephew, Billy Stream. Not the Billy Stream he knew, but an ill-dressed grimy individual with Billy's face, voice and figure.

"Sufferin' codfish!" ejaculated Anthony in an awed tone. "What d'ye want, Billy? Ye ain't come to ha'nt me?"

The apparition laughed and strode across to him.

"Don't be scared, uncle. It's me, all right, alive and well, but awfully hungry and awfully dirty!"

Ben slowly grasped the proffered hand, fully expecting it to vanish, but the feel of solid flesh reassured him that it was real, and that Billy, alive and well, stood before him.

"Waal, I be eternally gosh - swizzled!" cried the uncle, recovering from his fright and shaking the hand heartily. "Lord! but ye scar't me! How in th' name o' all that's sacred did you git here? I thought ye was drownded."

"*Sh!*" cautioned Billy. "I very nearly was, Uncle. What happened to me will never happen again in a thousand years."

"Tell me quick!"

"I was lying in the skipper's bunk aft when the steamer cut the bows off the schooner. I got up after I was hove out on the floor and pulled my boots on. Then I made for the ladder just as Hemsley slid back the hatch. 'That you, Stream?' says he, and when I answered him, he gave me a clip on the head with an iron belaying-pin or something and knocked me back into the cabin, dead to the world. I came to myself when the water poured in and I knew the schooner was sinking, so I swam to the companion-hatch and hung there. The whole vessel must have been under water and I just managed to haul myself through, ready to swim for the surface when she came up again and I found myself above water and jammed in the cabin slide."

"How in blazes c'd she come up an' her loaded with coal?"

"I'll tell you. When the steamer hit her she cut the fore-end clean off the vessel as far aft as the fore-hatch. When she settled, her head went down first and the cargo of coal simply ran out of her. As soon as she dumped it, being a wooden vessel and having no ballast, she came up and floated. I hung to her until daylight and was picked up by a big four-master bound for Philadelphia. I left her there and came up to Cobtown as a fireman in a coal tramp. And here I am."

"And, boy, oh, boy, I'm glad to see ye!" cried his uncle heartily. "Ain't you th' divil for gittin' into scrapes an' out o' them again. Now tell me all what's happened sence I saw ye last. Ye didn't manage to gitny' money up west?"

Stream related the details of his trip until the time he went aboard the *Jennie May*. He did not say anything about the conversation he overheard in Boston, reserving that for a later occasion.

"Why didn't ye wire me for money?" inquired his uncle when he finished. "I'd ha' sent ye all ye wanted. Now, what d'ye plan to do?"

"I can't do much," answered Billy. "There's no use in us attempting to put finnan-haddies on the market unless we can keep up a steady supply and we haven't got the money to do that."

"I've got eight thousand dollars."

"Not enough to do business with, uncle. There's buildings to be erected, men to be employed, boxes to buy, and cash must be paid the fishermen for their fish. Eight thousand dollars won't go very far."

"Then what do you plan to do yourself, Billy?"

The young man hesitated.

"Well, I don't know. I guess I'll go to sea, fishing—coasting or deep-water. I'll wait a day or so."

"Son," said Uncle Ben emphatically, "sooner'n see you do that I'll start business again in a small way an' let you run it. That's what I'll do now, so say no more about it."

After supper, which the startled housekeeper served, Anthony spoke:

"You said Hemsley hit you aboard that vessel?"

"Yes. Where is he now?"

"Waal, it's a funny thing about this Hemsley feller. He's a rum-hound and always was, yet your old man has put him back as foreman again—him an' that sweep Jones—an' both o' them are never sober. Th' manager has sacked them several times, but Will allus puts them on to their jobs again."

Billy laughed.

"Uncle, I must tell you something. It'll explain a lot."

He thereupon related the conversation he had overheard in the Boston "quick lunch."

Anthony's face grew black.

"So he's th' hound, is he? I'll jail him for that, by Godfrey!"

"Can you, though?" said Billy thoughtfully. "It might be hard to prove. I have a bone to pick with him, too. He tried to kill me."

"What'll you do?"

"Uncle, I think if you let me give that man the worst hammering he ever had, it would be the best. He'll skip out mighty quick afterward."

"Your old man won't be sorry, but ef ye're goin' to git Hemsley ye'll need to git him quick. Ef he hears you're back, he'll skip out."

"We'll drive into Anchorville tonight. I'll take a lot of pleasure in beating up that scum—more satisfaction than seeing him jailed."

"I'll go with you, son."

VII

CAPTAIN BILLY STREAM made history in Anchorville that night. People talk about it yet and fishermen relate the incident with gusto in the fo'c'sle o' nights when the vessel is making a passage or lying-to on the Banks.

Jack Hemsley and Jones, half-drunk as usual, were down in Morrison's pool-room with a crowd of fishermen and others when the door opened and Billy Stream and his uncle walked in. The crowd remained spellbound with horror at the sight of a supposedly drowned man walking in to the pool-room, and in their fright they remained transfixed and speechless.

Hemsley, his eyes almost starting from his head, hung on to a table to save himself from falling, and Jones, being the weaker-minded of the two, incontinently fainted and rolled under a bench.

For a moment, Stream stood looking

around the room and then he fixed his eyes on the shrinking, apprehensive Hemsley. At the sight of the man, all the ferocious combativeness of his nature rose and he advanced on him like a tiger that has corraled his prey.

"So you thought you had got rid of me, Hemsley?" he rasped. "Answer me, you hound!"

His fist shot out and smashed the fellow full in the face and the blood spurted from his nose.

"Don't hit him in here, Billy," remonstrated Ben Anthony. "Get him into the stable at the back."

Hemsley was standing stupid-like and making no attempt to put up his hands.

"Boys," said Ben, turning to the wondering mob of men, "this feller Hemsley was shipmates with Billy on that schooner. When she was sinking, Hemsley hit my nevvy on th' head with a belayin'-pin an' left him to drown. He didn't drown, an' he's come back to settle up old scores. 'Sides that, he's payin' a bill o' mine, fur Hemsley is th' man what set my place afire, so drag th' hound outside, boys, an' we'll hev fair play!"

It was a terrible fight. In fact, it couldn't be called a fight—it was a frightful beating at the strong hands of a relentless and powerful man. Hemsley was bigger and stronger than Stream, but in his composition he had a yellow streak a yard wide. True, he made a strenuous resistance, but Billy smashed him unmercifully with cold and calculating blows. When at last the man dropped to his knees, whimpering and whining, gasping for breath and with his face a pulp of blood-stained, bruised flesh, Ben Anthony mercifully pulled his nephew away.

"Let him be, Billy. He's had enough— Hullo, Will!"

Old Captain Stream pushed himself to the front.

"What th' devil's this? Who's that? Hemsley? Who's been hittin' him, eh? Who is it?"

Billy turned around to his amazed father.

"Only me, dad! I've been paying off some old scores," he said calmly. "You can go home and rest easy. Neither he nor Jones will trouble you any more!"

And as he spoke, he pulled on his coat and in company with his uncle climbed into their team and drove away.

"Billy," said Ben after a pause. "I think ye sh'd ha' spoken to yer dad a while."

"No! I didn't feel like it. He's treated us rotten and I won't court his favor. Mother and sis are the only ones I'd like to see and I'll probably see them tomorrow. They'll drive over as soon as they hear I'm back. If they don't, I'll telephone them."

After a clean-up, Billy was handed two letters by his uncle.

"I was jest a-goin' to send them back yesterday. They're from Montreal and addressed to you here."

Billy opened the first one leisurely, and as he did so a slip of paper fell out on the floor. He let it lie for a moment while he read the letter and then he gasped:

"Holy jumping, cod-eyed Christopher Columbus!" he ejaculated. "What d'ye know about that!"

"What's the matter?"

"Remember that old guy I told you about that damned me for pulling him from under a street-car in Montreal? Well, this is from him. Listen: 'Mr. William Stream, Port Anthony, N. S. Dear Mr. Stream: Kindly accept the enclosed with my compliments. My life is worth more to my relations than it is to me, but I consider it is worth at least the amount I am enclosing. I consider it sufficient to compensate you for your trouble in rousing me when "I went to sleep on the car-tracks." Will be glad to see you whenever you happen to be in this city, and thanking you for my life, I remain, yours sincerely, Alvin H. Gardiner.'"

"Where's th' check? What's the amount?" cried Uncle Ben.

Billy picked it up and hastily scanned it.

"Holy sailor! Ten thousand dollars!"

Ben jumped up.

"Are ye sure? It might only be one hundred dollars. They's four noughts in that when they put th' cents in. No, by Godfrey, you're right! It reads 'Pay to William Stream or order, the sum of Ten Thousand Dollars.' Waal, ef that ain't luck. Jupiter! I'm glad for you, son!"

The other letter was from Anstruther.

"Dear Billy," it ran. "You will no doubt be surprised to learn that it was old Senator Gardiner you rescued from under the street-car that night you went away. He is a millionaire flour-mill owner but as mean as Hades. He asked for my card after you ran for your train and next day telephoned for me to come down to his office. I went and he asked all kinds of questions about you and the reason for your visit to Montreal. I told him you wanted to raise ten thousand bones to start a codfish-ball factory or something of that nature, but you couldn't get it. I put it up strong to him as I thought he might lend you the money. He wouldn't give it to you, that's a cinch, for they say he couldn't be pried loose from a dollar with a crowbar. He'll want his old six per cent. if he loans it, but maybe that'll help you out. I may add that he gave me a rotten five-cent cigar when I left him. I'm having it put in a glass case to hang in the Frat House. Best wishes. Your pal, Jack Anstruther."

"Jack's wrong, anyway, uncle. The old man's come across handsomely. I never expected anything."

"Now you'd better bank that money, Billy," said his uncle solemnly. "It's a useful wad to have as a sheet anchor to wind'ard sh'd you git jammed on a lee shore. Ye'll be gittin' married some day——"

"You funny old scout!" cried Billy joyfully. "This ten thousand is what we need for the business. Let's get busy now and make our plans. The Port Anthony Fish Company is going to operate again, and like the Phœnix, it will arise anew, greater than ever, from the ashes of the old."

VIII

CAPTAIN WILLIAM STREAM, senior, was holding a board meeting of the Stream Fish Company. The president, general manager and board of directors were present in the person of himself, for he constituted them all, and the only other member of the board present was his office-manager acting as secretary, ex-officio.

"Ben Anthony is playin' the devil with our business!" reported the president in terse but unparliamentary language.

The secretary nodded dismally.

"Our smoked-fish business is fading away. Nobody seems to order the Morning-Glory Brand now since the Excelsior has been put on the market."

"What d'ye know about them?" growled the old man.

"They've got a fine plant with everything up to date and modern," reported the secretary. "Their smoke-houses are built of concrete and they've got all the latest devices for smoking fish. Their fish-sheds and packing-rooms are splendid. They've a good wharf and handle fish quickly. Their gasoline schooner is faster than ours, and they've got all the best fishermen along the shore selling to them. They've secured the best sales agency in central Canada for distributing their goods, and they've got the railroads and express company lined up to give their stuff preferred treatment and quick despatch.

"I hear they've just contracted for thirty carloads of Excelsior Finnan-Haddies to be delivered to a western dealer. They put up a fine fish and in nice style. Ben Anthony always could smoke a haddie better'n any one I knew. He's looking after that end while your son looks after the general management of the plant. We're dropping out of the finnan-haddie business, and we're likely to lose the fillet, kipper and bloater trade as well. They——"

"Heave-to, you raven!" growled Captain Stream. "One 'ud think by th' way you talk that you're sellin' the Anthony Company's fish. We ain't ruined—not by a long way. Our fresh-fish trade is good an' so's our dried-fish business. An' th' vessels are payin' well. Ben's not touchin' th' fresh fish——"

"I'm not so sure of that," interrupted the secretary. "I heard that your son plans on getting an English steam-trawler out."

"What?" shrieked the old man. "A steam-trawler! He can't buy one. He hasn't the money."

"He won't. He'll charter it and buy the fish."

"He mustn't attempt it. He'll have all the fishermen up in arms. 'Sides that, he'll spile our market. These craft'll bring in' fish when we can't, an' ef he gits to supplyin' the inland dealers regularly, they'll cut us out."

"There's only one thing to do."

"What's that?"

"Get one yourself!"

The president shook his head.

"I can't."

"Why?"

" 'Cos when there was talk o' fetchin' one o' them craft out here afore, I fought it an' made a report that they destroyed th' fishin'-grounds. Ef I was to go back on that, th' fishermen 'ud hang me."

The secretary mused for a minute.

"I have an idea," he said at last.

"Spit it out!"

"Amalgamate!"

"With Ben Anthony an' that young cub? Never!"

The other smiled.

"Captain. Ben's your wife's brother and Billy's your son. He's a smart lad and he's made good. His college training did that. It gave him a broader insight into things. It gave him a pull with people. He can talk intelligently. He understands conditions up west. He's scientific in his methods. Look how he fixed up the old *Jennie Anthony!* By shifting her ballast he made a new vessel out of her. He's a smart sailorman and can lick his weight in wildcats. The fishermen all love him. He's a good sport."

The old man grunted.

"You're getting old, captain. You should be knocking off now and taking it easy. Who's to take your place when you go? Nobody but Billy. You might as well be sensible and live happily with your family for the rest of your life. Billy's a good lad. He licked Hemsley and chased him out of the place. Hemsley——"

"Yes, yes," growled Captain Stream. "Never mind about Hemsley." Then almost plaintively he said. "D'ye think Ben an' Billy will come in with me?"

"I think they may, captain," said the secretary thoughtfully. "I'll try them anyway."

"Don't let on that I sent ye, Jim," cautioned the old man. "I won't knuckle under to either Ben or Billy."

"No, no," answered the other. "Leave it to me. I'll fix it."

The old fisherman lit up a cigar.

"Jim," he said. "You fix up this amalgamation an' I'll give ye a small share in th' business, but, mind ye, don't let on to Ben or Billy that I sent ye."

The meeting then adjourned.

THAT evening, the secretary and manager of the Stream Fish Company sat in Ben Anthony's parlor. Ben and Billy were present and all three smoked cigars and laughed.

"So you talked the dad around, Jim?" said Billy. "Ain't he the proud old joker though? He wouldn't give in to me even if he were dying. Well, well, he's my dad, and I don't think ill of him, though he was a trifle severe on both Ben and me for a time. I'm glad you managed to talk him around. We don't want to be in competition if we can get along together, so you tell dad that we're willing to amalgamate."

The meeting was held on the morrow. Captain Stream, senior, was rather frigid at first, but the evident friendliness evinced by Ben and his son soon had him feeling good. The business was rapidly consummated.

Ben Anthony was given full charge of the smoked-fish business and would manufacture in both smoke-houses as demand dictated. Billy was to take over both plants as general manager. Mr. James Dawson, the secretary, was given a share in the business and supervision over the books and accounting with the title of secretary-treasurer. Captain Stream would retain his position as president, but would take no active part in the concern.

When the deal was concluded satisfactorily, Captain Stream puffed hard on his cigar. He cleared his throat.

"Ahem — Ben — Billy—me—er, th' wife proposed ye come an' hev dinner with us tonight. Maybe ye'll come?"

"Sure we will!" cried Ben Anthony and Billy at once.

"Good! Jim! S'pose ye fetch out that bottle o' champagney water what's in th' safe. We'll hev a little touch to th' health o' th' noo Stream-Anthony Fish Company, Limited!"

THE 500ᵗʰ SHOT
by David L. Mackaye.

THERE have been recruits who have gone to the butts and astonished the old boys by making expert riflemen in their first season, having first heard of that delightful weapon of destruction, the high powered rifle, about two months previously. It may be that they inherit the faculty from their ancestors of 1776; at any rate, they have it, and Henry Howard Maple, of the Thirty-Third United States Infantry, was one of them.

On the other hand there are others who acquire the deadly art by plodding and painful thoroughness, of whom one was Oscar Schmidt, the sergeant-major of Maple's battalion. The Thirty-Third tells of these two men with considerable reverence, though not because it was more reverent than other line regiments. Schmidt was an inspiration to it for twenty years and drilled many generations of its recruits. For the three years before Maple enlisted Schmidt was on the non-commissioned staff of the First Battalion, and so they did not come together until their ambitions on the range led them to.

The Thirty-Third did not average high in marksmen. For seventeen years it was a regiment of one-enlistment men, and its veterans had contracted the habit of reenlisting in other regiments.

Schmidt was an exception. His ideas of loyalty were inflexible. The lower grew its tone, the more his dogged affection clung to it. It had been seventeen years, for instance, since the regiment had been represented on the list of distinguished marksmen, and the sergeant-major's passion was to reach that grade so the colonel could stop weeping in secret over that deficiency, at least. They saw eye to eye in these matters. Both scanned all the new material that arrived. Both saw and appreciated Maple about the same time.

The governors of the American Army have the idea that good shooting makes a good soldier, not goose-stepping or fancy maneuvering. Perhaps for this reason they have proclaimed that whosoever shall hit five hundred consecutive bulls'-eyes shall be raised above his fellow men. These few they bind, one with the other, by the grade of distinguished marksman, and have given it moral and financial standing.

Schmidt had been quartermaster-sergeant of B Company for many years. He was that when his daughter, Dolly, was born; and still that five years later when the uncomplaining Mrs. Schmidt passed to that post where matters of precedence are not settled by army regulations. He consistantly refused a step up until the financial embarrassment that went with Dolly's first long dresses compelled him to accept the higher rank. Maple was assigned to B Company and he found old Schmidt to be a tradition there.

About this time Schmidt was again shooting for the distinguished marksman's medal. During seventeen years of regimental sterility he had considered this a military duty but, although he had reached severel hundred consecutive bulls'-eyes occasionally, an unlucky shot always put him again at the starting point.

Maple was in the midst of his first season and had been a surprise from the start. These phenomena occur not infrequently. Many old sergeants can recite tales of recruits whom they coached in trigger-squeeze, elevation and windage, and the advantages of the peep-sight for two apparently sterile months, only to see them go on the range and string up bulls'-eyes on their very first day.

Maple hung an expert rifleman's badge on his diminutive chest after his first season. When individual firing was over he had thirty consecutive bulls'-eyes to his credit, and Schmidt had fifty-five consecutive bulls'-eyes.

Schmidt then took him aside and explained the matter of becoming a distinguished marksman. This was a sacred rite with the sergeant-major, but his sober voice had not always made the impression on previous candidates that it did on this little recruit. Maple decided from the start that he was going to make this grade.

THE regiment then went into its annual field-training. Schmidt plunged into the interminable clerical work of an active battalion. Maple was determined to become a good soldier and did bayonet practise, plowed up the parade with his little stomach on open-order drill, and chased imaginary foes out of the Missouri basin with vim and gusto. The range had to wait until the following year.

In this interim Dolly Schmidt made Maple's acquaintance and came home and told her father about it. Dolly was ordinarily critical over soldiers, but she declaimed about Maple with a suspicious unreserve.

Her father put down his book and regarded her with his slow intentness. He guarded Dolly with a completeness she never suspected, and paid great attention to any portent of an unusual interest in man. So he did now, before he said, in his queer accent:

"Maple is a goot liddle man. He is a goot shot, too."

Dolly pouted. The sergeant-major was again buried in his book and behind his seeming indifference she did not perceive the ponderous exactitude of his conclusion.

A word about Dolly. She was born in the regiment, had grown up in it and was to it, and to the First Battalion in particular, a Delphic oracle.

The sentimental existence of twelve companies of infantry centered around her with a cleanness only understood when it was remembered that the traditions of her baby face and curls still enshrined her. It might be parenthetically inserted here (because it did in the end, affect the careers of the sergeant-major, Dolly and Maple) that of her admirers she had only one open suitor, and he was a worthless, no-account private by the name of Pudgers.

If Maple reciprocated with an unusual interest in Dolly, he worshiped her from afar, for he certainly burned no incense at her altar with the ostentation of gayer spirits like Private Pudgers. When the next individual firing season commenced, therefore, their romance was merely in bud, waiting for the pungent warmth of range and gunpowder to bring it to its humble bloom.

Sergeant-Major Schmidt went back on the range with the lurking pain of anxiety and anticipation in his heart. His fifty-five consecutive hits of the season before still counted for him, but the four months' lapse might have put his marksman's eye out of focus, or unnerved his finger, and the first shot not in the bull's-eye wiped his slate clean again. He hit, however, and this restored his courage.

No man realized how much agony each shot cost him, except possibly his officers, and no one knew how much joy was his each time the white disk on the target told him he had made bull's-eye "five." He was so close to retirement now that an error in windage or elevation meant a wasted lifetime to him.

A few days later Maple appeared on the range with B Company, and signalized the new season with his thirty-first bull's-eye. He and the sergeant-major were the only candidates left for distinguished marksman after the first two weeks of rifle practise, and they continued slowly to add to their chances.

The command did not expect Schmidt to break until he was in his two-hundreds, and only allowed Maple half that number. Yet he passed it.

In addition, with this race on, it soon became apparent to the company, then to the battalion, and eventually to the regiment, that each spitting cartridge Maple drove through the black was being registered on the tenderer target of the heart of Dolly Schmidt. She appeared more and more on the range when it was told about the Post that Maple was down there shooting fives. No man wrapped up in pride of regiment could feel as she did each time Maple timorously called his shot, as he had been taught to do.

"Maple, five!"

Or when the white disk would rest reverently on the bull's-eye in confirmation, and the range officer would announce—

"Five it is, scorer!"

And the scorer would repeat—

"Five for Maple, sir."

No one noticed that the more this occurred, the madder Pudgers got. This lad had few soldierly qualities to appeal to the daughter of a military man like Schmidt, and he certainly couldn't shoot.

No one liked Pudgers, and it would have been a safe wager any time, that if Dolly had been foolish enough to show an interest in him, the company would have ducked him in a horse-trough in the cavalry lines. But Dolly couldn't be fooled on soldiers. Pudgers never amounted to shucks from the start.

It was all the other way with Maple. His lack of inches may have awakened her maternal instincts; she was only an inch shorter than he, herself.

Old Schmidt said nothing. He had the family eye and maybe saw in Maple what Dolly saw. At any rate, he liked him.

One evening after retreat the sergeant-major trudged home from headquarters, and finding himself alone, moved a chair out to the porch and commenced the silent, reflective survey of the Post that became more frequent with him as his retirement drew near. The infantry parade stretched in front with glowing barracks on one side and sedate officers' row on the other. The evening silence was only accentuated by an occasional melody or song. The drawling challenges of the guard or, at long intervals, the sparkling brilliancy of the guard's bugle, blowing calls, clutched his heart as they did so long ago when he first went into the army. A tear of regret for his coming departure from the regiment stole down his cheek.

Two people came down the walk toward the house and he recognized Dolly's footsteps, for one. They halted just below him. He sensed Maple in the other, but neither of the two said anything for a long time. When Maple broke the silence it was abruptly, almost roughly:

"You told Sergeant Rose you never had a wrist watch or anything like that," he said. "If I make distinguished marksman I get a bonus of a hundred dollars and want to buy you one. Can I?"

There was a moment's fateful silence and Maple desperately repeated—

"Can I?"

"Oh, Mr. Maple," murmured Dolly.

She hesitated for a second and suddenly gathered up her skirts and ran by her father into the house.

Maple stood silently for a spell and then walked off with his head hanging. The sergeant-major continued looking out over the cantonment but the tear on his cheek was destroyed by the momentary fever that parched his throat and caused the flagpole on the parade to perform feats of equilibrium.

Some time after this Pudgers approached Schmidt in his office.

"I want to ask you for a little boost, Sergeant," stated Pudgers. "I'm near the end of my enlistment and I got a swell job waiting for me in Leavenworth when I leave the service. I'm strong for Dolly, you know, and all that. I want to marry her, see? You know yourself there ain't nothin' in it for her if she sticks around and marries a soldier. Now I——"

But Schmidt held up his hand.

"It don't do no goot to talk to me. You speak mit Dolly and hear what she says."

"Yes, but Sergeant," urged Pudgers, "you know I ain't got much pull around the Post. They sorter misunderstand me, see? Dolly's all taken up with that little runt, Maple, you know, and I can't get a look-in. If you was to say something, you know, Sergeant——"

"I says nodings. If you wants to marry mit me, you speaks mit me. If you want to marry mit Dolly, you speaks mit Dolly."

Pudgers was a cautious chap. He realized that as long as Maple was shooting fives he stood as much chance of marrying the battalion sergeant-major as his daughter. He just simply sat around on the range wishing bad luck on Maple.

This, however, had no effect on either contestant. The season neared its end and Maple only had fifty shots to make, the sergeant-major a little more. Old Schmidt did not stay on the range much. He came down when the shooting was light and reported to the officer of the range for practise, fired a clip or two, almost too deliberately, and then returned to his office where he suffered the ordeal over again in retrospect, and alone.

Every shot now was an ordeal to him. He was having a hard time holding himself together.

The sergeant-major would vary this routine a bit when Maple was firing, and stand back and watch the boy for a moment, carefully. His thoughts were his own, but on these occasions he would not leave until he had made sure that Maple was self-possessed and shooting well.

 THE day finally came when Maple had ten to go and Schmidt had five. Schmidt did not shoot that day but came down to watch Maple.

The boy slipped a clip into his rifle and with his beautiful and simple precision fired it into the black, leaving five shots to go. Then on the sixth shot, Schmidt saw Maple aim, and then lower his rifle, his face changing a shade paler. The sergeant-major walked over to the officer of the range and saluted.

"Sir," he said, in his precise way, "dot boy will miss his next shot."

"How do you know, Sergeant?"

"I feel dot he will, sir. He has just had doubts on his aim."

"Very well, Sergeant, thank you. Maple, get off the line! You can finish tomorrow."

"Thank you, sir," cried Maple, and wondered how the captain knew.

So it was that the last day of the shoot arrived, with both candidates absolutely even, and with but five shots between them and the coveted grade. Practically the entire regiment was seated on the bank that sloped up from the firing-line. The sergeant-major and Maple were firing at different targets and they had partners, as usual, firing with them, at their own request. The other men, however, were taken off the line.

Dolly was on the bank also, and Pudgers had taken up his position directly back of Maple's mat. The firing was at five hundred yards, prone.

The sergeant-major fired first, and hit, Maple fired and hit, and both reloaded while their partners shot. The second and third shots for Maple also scored.

Schmidt shot bulls'-eyes up to his very last cartridge, but his bolt jammed on this and he left the line, not so much to repair it as to pull himself together again. Even this slight accident was sufficient to unsteady him.

He did not look at Maple again until he was back of the scorer's desk and when he did, he groaned. The boy had simply gone to pieces. His hand was trembling, his teeth were set, and his face was pale. He fired his fourth shot.

A death-like silence settled on the field. With quick sympathy the men above him knew that he had missed; and the telepathic wave carried to the colonel praying in his office half a mile away for a distinguished marksman this day.

And with the instinct of a man who loves a high-powered rifle, Maple knew, also, that he had missed. The sergeant-major could read it on his face, so he turned his head away and busied himself about his rifle, remembering that he, too, had another shot to fire.

The range officer was not sure whether Maple had missed or not, but he would not ruin the boy's nerve for the last shot, at any rate. He called over as nonchalantly as if they had been at practise work with rookies—

"Maple, call your shot!"

And Maple summoned up all the manhood that was in him, steadied his voice and called it—

"Maple a miss."

Already the red flag that denoted a miss was rising and waving over the butts. Then the white disk appeared and flatted itself against the bull's-eye.

Maple stared. For a moment his senses refused to take in its meaning, and then he realized that he had missed, but that his bullet had hit the top of the butts and ricocheted into the bull's-eye, scoring five.

Eleven hundred men on the bank laughed hysterically. The captain called in his even voice, which concealed some doubt as to the regulations on the matter—

"Maple a five."

"Five for Maple, sir," replied the sergeant scoring.

The perfect mechanism of it keyed Maple up. He reached for his last cartridge and laughed for the first time in the shoot.

Then he saw the shell was covered with green mold. He threw it back and called for a new one.

Pudgers walked forward and handed him one. At the same time Schmidt walked past to his own mat to fire his last shot. His mind retained an automatic impression of Pudgers handing Maple a shell but he did not see the rest of it until after he was down. Then he looked back once. He caught a fleeting glimpse of things, with Pudgers in the fore-front, and on Pudger's face was an evil and meaning gloating.

Back of Pudgers was Dolly with her eyes glued to Maple's rifle arm. The three of them loomed up grotesquely in Schmidt's mind's-eye and suddenly, vividly, the old sergeant understood what Pudgers had done, and why.

Every marksman tests his shell before firing to see if the cartridge is loose in its case, when under no circumstances will it shoot straight. Only on such a shot and under such circumstances would a rifleman forget, and Pudger's face said, just as plainly as his tongue could, that such a shell was in Maple's gun that moment. And Maple's next shot was either going in the bull's-eye or Dolly's heart.

Schmidt turned over to Maple. The boy's eyes were set, his arm was steady as a tripod, the rifle leveled dead on the little black dot five hundred yards away—and his finger was squeezing the trigger. In other words, as all good soldiers there present knew, in one second Maple would have fired his five-hundredth consecutive bulls'-eye.

In that second old Schmidt, the stolid, the plodding, the slow, lived over his nineteen years of military life, counted the agony of his last four-hundred-and-ninety-nine shots. Battalion Sergeant-Major Schmidt, a very fine soldier, suddenly reached the plane of an intellectual giant. He could not stop Maple's shot. He threw himself on his stomach, dropped the rifle in his hand, and fired.

Two rifles snapped as one. All eyes left Maple and turned toward the old idol, Schmidt. Good old Schmidt, the strain had been too much for him. He had gone crazy on the last shot.

There she waves—the gory, red flag that ruins Battalion Sergeant-Major Oscar Schmidt! Poor old war-horse, now he *is* gone! Look at him! Isn't he the sport? He's smiling like he made it anyway.

"O, poor daddy!" shrilled a high young voice over the field, and then—

"Ah!"

Standing upright on its over-worn pole was the white, triumphant disc on Maple's target.

"Sir, Private Henry Howard Maple, distinguished marksman—five hundred consecutive bulls'-eyes, and a —— fine soldier!"

Off went the regiment's lid. The colonel half a mile away knew that the Lord had listened to his prayers.

Under cover of it all, Schmidt stole off the field, leading Private Pudgers by the hand. He led him around the cavalry cantonment, and off the reservation to a deserted powder-shed. There he asked Private Pudgers a question and when Sergeant Schmidt looked like that no man denied him the truth.

Pudgers confessed, and Schmidt heard him in silence. Pudgers didn't know and never did, that Schmidt had fired the last shot into Maple's bull's-eye, and not Maple. No one ever knew that except Schmidt.

Then and there, in a primitive sort of a way, Battalion Sergeant-Major Schmidt taught Private Pudgers how to be a soldier, and after Pudgers had gone through his ordeal and slunk out, the old man laid himself down and cried his heart out.

Off on the parade stood the regiment, company front. Facing it stood Private Maple. The regiment was at the "present."

THE LAW IN LITTLE EGYPT

by Hapsburg Liebe.

Author of "The Silent Torreys," "The Patch," etc.

"BILL, you take the old preacher a ham. Tom, you take the old preacher a bushel o' shelled cawn with the nubbins throwed out, and be shore ye give him Methodist measure. George, you take the old preacher a bushel o' 'taters, and you give him Methodist measure, too. I'll find out whuther ye done it or not, and it'll shore go hard wi' ye ef ye don't do it! Now git! Git! Show me yore heels!"

Thus spake the Law in Little Egypt, which is a settlement lying along Caney River, in the Big Bald Mountain country, considerably less than a thousand miles from the Tennessee-North Carolina State line. And having spoken, the Law crept back into the riotously blooming laurels and disappeared without even the sound of a breaking twig; and the three mountaineers it had halted and spoken to continued on their way homeward, and as they went they said nothing to one another.

They knew that it were far better to obey without question. Other men had dared to disobey, and some of them had been horse-whipped; while another of them had returned to the dust whence he came, and still another now lay on the flat of his back with a blue-lipped hole, through which swift lead had passed, in his left lung.

The correct name for the Law in Little Egypt was Sarah Harrison—but please don't draw a conclusion here. It may be that you'll be surprised inside of three minutes.

Sarah Harrison stole through the blooming laurels and to a dim old trail, followed it silently half a mile through the woodland, stopped at the upper edge of a little clearing, and called sharply:

"Jim!"

A tall and lanky figure with a squirrel rifle in its hands came to a doorway of the log cabin below.

"Put down that gun," ordered the Law, "and come up here."

Jim put his rifle down on the door-step, frowned, and went slowly up through the growing corn and to the snake fence. The other addressed him:

"You owe John Simmons a dollar and a half for one o' old Sade the 'coon-dawg's puppies. When're ye a-goin' to pay him?"

"I'm a-goin' to pay him right now," answered Jim.

"All right; go and do it," said the Law, with twinkling eyes; and Jim went toward the cabin of the man who owned old Sade, the 'coon-dog.

Then Sarah Harrison walked another half-mile through the green woodland, stopped at the upper edge of another little clearing, and called sharply:

"Henry!"

In a doorway of a dilapidated log hut below appeared a little, slender man with mouse-colored hair, the face of a weasel, and fishy blue eyes.

"Come here!" ordered Sarah.

Henry came. He was one of those fellows who will corner you on the day that your mortgages are due, and pick sundry hairs off your coat-collar while he tells you his family secrets. Only Henry had no family. He lived a hand-to-mouth life, with only dogs for company; he hunted fur-bearing game in season, and he dug ginseng and fished. Man's only true friend was a dog, he said; so, in order that he might have many friends, he had many dogs. Mongrels, they were, every one of them, but he loved them none the less for that.

"You tried to gi' me away to Shuriff Connard yeste'day," said the Law. "I'll hosswhup ye, ef ye try to deny it. Ef ye wasn't so danged little, I'd hosswhup ye anyhow. Better not talk to Connard any more. Go back to the house!"

Henry went.

Sarah Harrison disappeared in a way that was almost uncanny, went up on the mountainside, sat down on the leaves and waited patiently for night to come.

When it was quite dark, Sarah Harrison stole down into the settlement, stole up to the back door of an old and rambling and honeysuckle-covered log cabin of three rooms, and rapped lightly and peculiarly—three raps and two, three and two. A candle within was suddenly put out, a meal-bag window-curtain was drawn, and the door creaked open on its wooden hinges. The Law entered, the door creaked back shut and a bar was dropped into place, and the candle was lighted again.

"Bub!" softly cried a glad feminine voice, and a pair of fine brown eyes shone with welcome.

SARAH HARRISON was not a woman. Sarah Harrison had been named too soon. His mother had had five boys, and she had wanted a girl; and when she was disappointed, she wouldn't change the name because she feared it would bring bad luck. They had soon nicknamed him "Bub," and Bub was now the biggest and the strongest and the finest-looking young man anywhere in the Big Bald Mountain country.

The cabin he was in was the home of Old Johnny Barlow, a hill preacher who had grown too old to preach. The girl that had admitted him was Old Johnny's daughter, and his sweetheart. Bub Harrison put his big hands under Hattie's chin, lifted her face a little, bent over and kissed her affectionately and reverently on the forehead.

"Set down, Bub," came a feeble old voice from the chimney-corner; and Bub sat down.

"Bub, I been a-thinkin'," went on the feeble old voice, "what on earth are you a-goin' to do? You cain't go on a-dodgin' from tree to tree from the shuriff, like ye've been a-doin'."

Young Harrison's brows drew thoughtfully.

"I don't know what I'm a-goin' to do," he said a little gloomily. "I could leave here, I reckon, and go away off some'eres whar' I hain't knowed, ef it wasn't for a-doin' without my people and you and Hattie."

"Maybe ye'd better," muttered Old Johnny. "Me and Hattie'll miss ye, a course, and yore people'll miss ye; but—well, I don't know, son. I don't know what to tell ye to do, boy. Ef ye could jest find out for sartain who it was 'at killed that thar nose-talkin' Peele Bailey, 'at'd clear ye, Bub. Hi Footner is shot bad, but he hain't a-goin' to make a die of it, and a-bein' cleared o' killin' Peele'd clear ye o' shootin' Hi."

"Yes, but how am I a-goin' to find out for sartain who killed Peele?"

The old mountaineer shook his head.

"I don't know, son. I don't know. I've thought and thought, and I hain't no nigher a s'lution 'an I was at fust. Yore mother was here today. She wants to see ye, Bub."

"It's dangerous for me to go about home," said Bub. "Shuriff Connard is allus a-watchin' thar. Did George Henderson and Tom Little and Bill Adams bring ye anything today?"

"Yes," smilingly. " 'Taters, and cawn, and a ham—they'd laid off to bring 'em for a long time, they said."

Know you that preachers in the hills are supported, not by salaries, but by donations.

"I see," said Harrison, with twinkling eyes.

He began to look longingly toward a cat-hide banjo that hung on a hickory peg in the log wall. It seemed to him an age since he had played a banjo or heard one played, and, like most hillmen, he loved the instrument. Hattie read his thoughts well. She took down the banjo and gave it to him, and then she sat down on the floor at his feet.

"Play and sing, 'Ella Ree,'" she requested.

"Ella Ree," that old, old song—I think that Ella Ree must have been a poorly dressed, beautiful woman, with sweet, sad eyes. We hillfolk and near-hillfolk, we love that old, old song. After we've become rich, some of us, in coal or in iron or in timberlands, we profess, perhaps, a greater liking for "Ah, I Have Sighed to Rest Me," but—we prick up our ears like young mules on circus day when we hear the banjo and "Ella Ree."

"D'ye reckon it wouldn't gi' me away?" asked Bub. "Shuriff Connard he's some-'eres in this section, Hattie, honey."

He barely heard her say:

"I—don't—know."

But she had asked it, and he would take a risk. He tightened the strings, looked toward the barred door and began to sing, his big fingers beating a jangling though not discordant accompaniment:

Pore Ella Ree-e-e-ee
  In the little churchyard lies;
Her grave is bri-i-ight with draps o' dew,
  But bri-i-ighter were her eyes.

Then carry me back to Tennessee,
  Where the——

Bub rose quickly, put the banjo down and blew out the candle. He had heard the creak of a board in the back porch floor. Then he hastened silently into the next room and to an open window.

The person who made the board creak was the sheriff. For weeks he had been trying to get the drop on Bub Harrison, and failed signally. Bub knew every man, woman and child, every tree and every stone and every laurel bush, for miles around, for Bub had been born out there in the wilds; Bub had a gray squirrel beaten a sea mile for cunning, and a gray squirrel, if you please, is twice as cunning as a fox. Connard was alone. He could have had deputies with him; but four or five men, usually, can not do as much as one when the fugitive is a mountaineer who is unwilling to leave his home section; four or five men may be seen where one man may not. Besides, Connard was a young sheriff, and he was anxious to have the so-called outlaw fall into his own hands.

But now Connard was nonplussed. He had found Bub Harrison quite by accident; he had been about to pass the Barlow cabin, when he had heard Bub's voice singing "Ella Ree."

To go for men to surround the Barlow home was out of the question for several reasons. Those mountaineers who were friendly toward Bub could not be driven to assist in Bub's capture, and those mountaineers who were not friendly toward Bub would be afraid—for Bub might escape. And then the cessation of the song showed that Harrison was alarmed, and Connard did not dare to leave the cabin for fear that Harrison would get away.

So Connard tried to surround the cabin himself. He rapped on the back door and called loudly:

"Open in the name of the law!"

Then he ran around the house to nab Bub at the front door.

But Bub didn't try to make his escape by the front door. Bub knew. At the open window, well hidden in the darkness, Bub watched and waited.

His revolver ready in his hand, the officer went around the house, eyes wide open and keenly alert, several times. Then he did all there was left for him to do—he entered by the back door, which had been opened for him. The candle had been lighted.

"Where is Bub?" Connard demanded, his eyes on the black doorway that led to the cabin's middle room. And at that moment Harrison crept out of the window.

The old preacher and his daughter confronted the sheriff.

"I'm shore I couldn't tell ye jest whar he is," said Old Johnny.

"He was here a minute ago," growled Connard. "You're laying yourself liable for harboring a criminal, you know!"

"Bub ain't no criminal!" declared Hattie angrily.

"Maybe not," replied the officer. "All the same, I've got a warrant for his arrest, and I'm going to arrest him."

Hattie elevated her nose.

"You couldn't arrest a pig!"

Connard smiled tolerantly.

"I'll have to search the house, I guess."

"Bub he ain't in this house," said Hattie, "and you ain't a-goin' to s'arch through it and tear everything up!"

The sheriff went toward the door that led to the middle room, and Hattie very promptly barred the way. Connard gently tried to push her aside, when a big, dark form stole up behind him, shot an arm around him and seized his revolver, wresting it from his hand. It was Bub.

"You'll l'arn some day to take a woman's word, Shuriff Connard!" he cried, turning the revolver upon its owner. "Now set down; me and you's a-goin' to have a little talk right here—we're a-goin' to sort o' hold co'te, so to speak—set down, I say! *Set!*"

The officer sat down. He was no coward; it was good sense to sit down. Bub drew up a chair and also sat down, facing the man who had hunted him so hard.

"Now listen to me, Mr. Connard," began the mountaineer. "I know I'm as good a man as you. I think I'm a durned sight better man 'an you. I believe in laws as much as you do, shuriff. But I don't believe in a-lettin' myself be sent to the pen on sarcumstantial evidence, and so I hain't a goin' to be arrested.

"Shuriff, don't forgit nary word I'm a-sayin'. I set myself up as the Law in Little Egypt acause it needed a law. It didn't have none. I reckon it was jest natcheral for you and everybody else to think it was me killed Peele Bailey, and me shot Hi Footner, acause it happened that them two fellers kicked ag'in me as the Law. But shuriff, I never done it. I hope I may die right here whar I'm a-settin' at ef I done it. And, havin' not done it, I shore hain't a-goin' to suffer for it whilst I'm in my right mind.

"It may be, I know, 'at the sarcumstantial evidence wouldn't be strong enough to send me up, but I hain't a-goin' to resk a-standin' a trial. I don't know, and you don't know, what them Baileys and Footners would swear. One more thing, Mr. Connard: ef you give this here old man here any trouble over him a-lettin' me step into his house, I'll settle with ye. Remember that! You'll find yore gun a-stickin' in a crack o' the back fence, shuriff."

He rose, backed out by way of the back door and disappeared in the thick night. The officer found his revolver sticking in a crack of the fence; he took it and went away.

ANY hillman can find a good hiding-place convenient to his friends and relatives. Bub Harrison, when he left Old Johnny's house, went straight to a rotting, mildewed cabin that stood at the head of a hemlock-filled cove a mile from the settlement. It wasn't long until he was sleeping and dreaming, as he so often dreamed, of Hattie Barlow.

Before the middle of the morning following, Hattie stole up to see him, and she took him something good to eat. Bub kissed her on the forehead, and they sat down together on the rotting, mildewed doorstep.

"Shuriff Connard he's stuck up notices all over the settlement, a-sayin' a big money reward would be paid for you, Bub!" Hattie told her sweetheart.

In truth, it was not a big reward that Connard offered. But to this poor hillwoman it seemed a fortune.

"Ain't that the devil!" exclaimed Bub, his mouth full of fried ham.

"It's a heap wuss'n that," said Hattie. She went on: "I found out somethin' yeste'day, which I didn't have time to tell ye last night. That nose-talkin' Peele Bailey, the day afore he was shot, killed one o' Henry Rumley's dawgs. Could that help ye any, Bub?"

Henry Rumley was the little fellow with the fishy blue eyes, the mouse-colored hair, the weasel's face, and the many canine friends.

"Henry Rumley is the one 'at killed Peele!" exclaimed Bub thickly, because of a mouth full of fried ham, potatoes and corn-cake. "Henry Rumley and Peele never liked one another. Peele thrashed Rumley last Winter for a-takin' a 'coon out o' his trap. But a-provin' 'at Henry killed Peele, 'at's the devil of it, Hattie."

"Allus slip up on a man's blind side, pap allus said," smiled Hattie Barlow. "Pap he allus said all men had a blind side, ef ye could jest find it. Now I wonder what is Henry's?"

"Le's see," said Bub, swallowing. "Henry—Henry believes in signs. I never seen sech a feller to believe in signs. I seen him quit a-fishin' acause he'd accident'ly stepped acrost his pole. Bad luck, he said."

After a moment's thought, Bub went to his feet.

"Hattie, little ole honey-darlin', I be durned ef we hain't done got him!"

For an hour they planned, and at the end of that time Hattie kissed her sweetheart and went homeward.

WHEN Henry Rumley, the superstitious, went to his dilapidated hut from his daily ginseng hunt, late that afternoon, he found a great smear of blood across his door. It was the blood of a squirrel, but Henry Rumley didn't know it. All blood is red.

The fishy eyes widened, and the face that reminded one so much of a weasel's went deathly white. He shrank back from the red smear, and his dogs, afraid, cowered and slunk under the floor, leaving him alone; Henry frequently beat his four-footed friends, true as they were to him, much as he loved them. He stood in the guttered path for a moment, swore many times under his breath, then went around to the other door.

A smear of blood was on that door too!

Again Henry swore. Then he mustered his courage, all that he possessed, and entered the hut. It was growing dusky, and he scratched a match and lighted a half-burned tallow dip. In the feeble yellow glare he saw a cross marked on the floor, and upon closer investigation he found that it had been made of blood!

Henry dropped the candle, smothered a shriek and ran out to the weedy yard. The snowy bloom of the laurels above seemed to him like a multitude of ghosts. A man's hell is lighted in his own soul.

Then there came from somewhere up on the mountainside the cry of one who talked through his nose, as Peele Bailey had done:

"Henry!"

The fishy-eyed little man ran back into his hut, barred both doors as well as he could, found the tallow dip and with fingers that shook violently applied a burning match to the wick. Again there came from somewhere up on the mountainside that weird, nasal-toned cry, and this time it seemed nearer:

"Henry!"

Henry Rumley shrank back against one of the log walls. He bent over, lifted out one of the worn floor-boards and called his dogs to him for company. Even the dogs seemed to feel the presence of some ghastly thing.

Once more there came that terrible, nasal-toned cry, and this time Rumley knew it was nearer, for it was so loud that it was like thunder

"Henry!"

"O Lord!" chattered Henry Rumley, and he sank to his knees on the floor among his dogs, friends who could not offer solace now in this his extremity. "O Lord! O Lord!"

For a few minutes there was a deep and utter silence save for the far-away and mournful cry of an owl, and then there came an old and feeble voice from the direction in which the settlement lay,

"What's the matter wi' ye, Henry, my boy?"

The weasel-faced man recognized the voice as that of the old preacher. He welcomed company now, and especially the company of one like Old Johnny who knew how to pray. He rose, hurried across the room and opened the door. Hattie Barlow's father stepped across the worn sill, limped to a home-made chair and sat down.

"How—how did ye know the' was anything the matter with me?" babbled Henry Rumley.

Old Johnny appeared to be much surprised.

"Why," he said, "didn't ye send for me to come to ye, Henry, my boy?"

"No!"

"Well, 'pon my honor!" and the old preacher suddenly stood up. "Now I wonder ef my old mind is up to playin' me tricks! Henry, I'll be dadblasted ef I didn't hear somebody say, at my front door, this here:

" 'Johnny Barlow, Johnny Barlow, Johnny Barlow! Henry Rumley wants ye quick! Henry Rumley needs ye bad, Johnny Barlow!' And so I come as quick as I could."

Henry Rumley shook like a leaf.

"Look at that—on the floor!" he cried, and he pointed toward the two smears of squirrel-blood that made a cross.

"Why, what is it?" said Old Johnny. "I don't see nothin'—nothin' at all. Henry, you hain't been a-drinkin', have ye, my boy?"

"The cross—don't you see it?" almost screamed Rumley.

"Hain't no cross thar, as I can see," declared the aged mountaineer. "Hain't ye a-tryin' to fool me, son?" smilingly.

"No—no! Look!" And he sat down on the floor, with the candle in his hand, and with a trembling finger pointed to the red marks.

"Why, son, the' hain't a thing thar!" exclaimed Old Johnny. "Not a single, soliturry thing thar!"

Then there came again the cry that had stricken terror to the heart of the younger man. It was a very correct imitation of Peele Bailey's voice. Bub Harrison was holding his nose between finger and thumb:

"Henry! Henry Rumley!"

"Listen! Did you hear that?" babbled the dog-lover.

"Son," smilingly, "I didn't hear nothin' at all. And I've got a good hearin'. Why, what's the matter with ye, son?"

Henry dropped the candle and sank to the floor in a heap. Old Barlow took up the candle and stuck it to a low shelf by means of its own wax. Then he bent over and put a hand gently on Rumley's shoulder, and Rumley flinched at the touch.

"It must be a sign," Barlow said, as if sadly, slipping up, as it were, on Rumley's blind side. "My pore boy, I'm afeard yore time has come. I do wisht ye hadn't ha' killed Peele."

"He killed my best dawg!" whined Henry Rumley—and in another minute he had confessed.

Then there entered several stalwart men and the girl Hattie, who had witnessed, through chinks in the log walls, the confession. Soon Bub Harrison joined them, and there was some rejoicing.

The Law in Little Egypt had vindicated itself.

WILD BILL IN DEADWOOD GULCH

AN ARTICLE by Robert V. Carr.

Author of "The Stronger Call," "Triplets Triumphant," etc.

"**W**ILD BILL was as handsome a man as you could see in a week's ride. And there were good-looking men in the Western country in those days. A weakling was a curiosity. But Bill wasn't merely big and strong; he had grace."

Ellis Taylor Peirce, known to his friends as "Doc," and to the Indians as *Ma-to-O-ye*, (Bear-tracks), was in a reminiscent mood. And Doc in a reminiscent mood is what the miners term "rich diggings." When a man has lived sixty-eight years, and watched the rude frontier camps grow into prosperous cities, it may be taken for granted that he has had a few adventures.

In Doc's case, having been a sheriff, the adventures that he has experienced are as thick as wild plums on a tree in a sheltered draw. Of course he was a Union soldier, and was once elected to the South Dakota Legislature. Best of all, he is a humorist.

We were loafing in the mystic vale of Minnekahta, which is in the town of Hot Springs, South Dakota. Doc had just performed in my honor what he termed "killing a Dutchman." It was fair beer, too; and, believe me, the old corn-cobs held a sweeter taste after the performance of that ancient rite.

And then, having secured a position of ease, the old-timer launched into the story of Wild Bill (James B. Hickok), in Deadwood Gulch.

BOY, I don't know but that there is something in presentiment. When Wild Bill and Charley Utter first looked down into Deadwood Gulch, the greatest gun-fighter the West has ever known seemed to realize that he would never leave the Black Hills alive.

Bill was just straightening up from loosening the rough-locks on the wagon. They were on Breakneck Hill.

"And that's Deadwood Gulch," said Bill gloomily. "Boys, I feel that I will never leave that gulch alive. I do not know of a *living* enemy, but something tells me that this is my last stand."

Charley Utter ridiculed Bill's gloomy sentiments, but the big, brown-haired warrior shook his head sorrowfully.

It was Summer—the Summer of 1876—when Wild Bill and his party entered Deadwood Gulch. They had come up from Cheyenne in the gold stampede. Deadwood then was a clutter of cabins and tents. There was no marble Federal Building, no big Court House and no luxurious hotel. Main Street was a narrow opening between two rows of cabins and tents. The street was full of bumps and hollows, and littered with logs and lumber.

There was little or no law, and the camp was full of reckless men and hard-faced women. Every kind of a game was going full blast, and the nights were red and full of action.

Gold-dust was largely the medium of exchange, and anything less than a dollar was looked on as "chicken feed." Men who might be rich in a day had no time for small change.

The air was full of rumors of gold strikes and Indian killings. Those were feverish days, and rotgut whisky was the remedy for all ailments. Of course, now and then, old Doc Colts filled a prescription, but whisky was the sovereign remedy.

At night on Main Street you could see all kinds of border characters. Some wore red shirts, and others affected buckskins and long hair. A majority of the men, and some of the women, including "Calamity Jane," carried guns. In the Deadwood of 1876 all a man had to do was to crook his finger and trouble would come a-running.

And it was into that uproarious camp that Wild Bill came one Summer day when the aspens were green where the mills now stand, and the pines were singing the same songs that they now sing over his grave.

Of course, we of Deadwood Gulch knew of Bill's reputation as a dead shot and peace officer. We knew of his wiping out of the McCandles gang in Kansas — one man against nearly half a score. We knew of his work as Marshal of Abilene, Kansas, where, in an effort to preserve order, he killed a Texan by the name of Phil Coe. We knew of his record as Marshal of Hays, Kansas, where he killed two soldiers who sought to run the town. We knew that he had killed, in self-defense and as a peace officer, in the neighborhood of forty men, not counting Mexicans and Indians. Lastly, we knew that there was many a hard man in Deadwood Gulch who secretly longed to kill Wild Bill.

A celebrated gun-fighter of those days was the same as a prize-fighter of today—always some man who thinks he is just a little bit better. Bill was the champion gun-fighter of his day, and successfully defended his title against all comers who fought fair. Bill always fought fair; he never killed a man except when forced into it. He was not a trouble-hunter; trouble put in its time hunting him.

Although I never became well acquainted with Wild Bill, I studied him closely as he strolled up and down Main Street, or handled the pasteboards in some gambling-joint. He was an inveterate poker-player, but very careful in his choice of seats. He never sat with his back to a door except once—and that was his last game.

No man could see Wild Bill and not admire him. He was over six feet tall and as straight as a Black Hills pine. His body tapered down from the shoulders like a wedge; he walked with a free, swinging, graceful tread.

His face was habitually calm, and he rarely smiled. I never heard him laugh. He never dissipated. Dissipation means loss of nerve-force, and Wild Bill needed all his nerve-force all the time.

There was a cold expression about his eyes, and his strong, straight nose, with its aquiline tip, gave him a fierce, intense look. He was ever watchful. It seemed that he was continually expecting death. His right hand generally rested on his hip, palm outward, and near the butt of the gun he carried loose in his waistband. He was a light sleeper, and would nap like a dog with one eye open.

Bill's nose being hooked at the tip, his nostrils flared like a thoroughbred's. He had a short upper lip, from which the long, silky mustache curved back almost to the lobes of his ears. His chin was not very large, but the jaw under his ear was exceptionally strong and well muscled. A deadly fighter never has an under-shot bulldog jaw. His strength, like the rattlesnake's, shows at the base of the jaw.

There was great breadth between Bill's eyes, and he had a noble forehead. Back from that classic forehead swept a mane of gold-brown hair, fourteen inches long.

Bill's hands were remarkably beautiful. The fingers were long and tapering and very sensitive. He was most fastidious in the care of his hands, as indeed he was about his dress and person.

In the use of a six-shooter he was ambidextrous. In all of his Kansas fights he used round-barreled 44-caliber cap-and-ball Colts. With those marvelous hands he practised what was known as "the pulse shot"—shooting without aim. His guns seemed to be as much a part of him as his index fingers; and you know that when a man points his finger at an object he instinctively gets a line on it.

Bill's six-shooters were triggerless, with the hammers filed smooth. In action he would throw his guns up and forward, thumbs on the hammers. The weight of the weapons would cock them; he had only to drop them forward in line with the target and let the hammers slip under his thumbs. He rarely fired over two shots at a man. In killing Phil Coe, the Texan, he shot the Southerner just below the heart, at the same time exclaiming, "Too low!"

Bill was not a man the average mortal would want for a close friend. There was always a circle of danger around him. With the exception of Charley Utter, and one or two others, he had no close friends in Deadwood.

We noticed that Bill was fond of children, and very polite to women. There were a few families in Deadwood in those days, and Bill often stopped to play with some youngster. He was married at the time he came to Deadwood, but his wife, a former showwoman, remained in Cheyenne. I never heard of Bill having any children, but he certainly had a soft spot in his heart for the kids. I guess he liked the youngsters because he knew he could trust them.

Square and fair, generous with his money, having little to say, never indulging in jokes or horseplay, ever alert and watchful, a strikingly handsome man, he traveled—at least in Deadwood Gulch—largely a lone trail. And he not quite forty years of age—just in his prime. He did not look thirty.

HERE'S A DEAD MAN!

ON THE morning of the second day of August, 1876, I was picking my way down Main Street. I recall that it was a fine, bright Black-Hills morning. There was the smell of new lumber and fresh dirt in the air. The lower part of the street was full of covered wagons.

A number of men were seated on some logs near a pit in the street. There was not much of a crowd on the street, as most of the men were working on the placer bars or gopher-holing in the hills.

I sauntered along down the street until I came to what was then the "city limits." Suddenly I heard some one call from a clump of near-by spruces, "Here's a dead man!" It was a form of the old call, "Man for breakfast!"

I ran over and found deceased to be a printer from Missouri. His name does not matter, as names did not count much in those days. It wasn't what you had been, but what you were doing that counted in 1876.

A crowd soon gathered, and displayed signs of wanting to hang some one. A big miner exhibited a rope that made me nervous.

Presently a man, whose head was in working order, asked the crowd—

"Hadn't we best find out how this man came to his death before proceeding further?"

"Proceeding further," I may say, meant to give some man a chance to jig on air.

The crowd roared an affirmative to the sensible question, and I knelt down to examine the body more closely. I had had considerable experience in dressing wounds during the war, and, because I had patched up a few of the boys in the camp, they insisted on calling me "Doc." I had never been in sight of a medical college, but was always handy in fixing up hurts and wounds.

I could find no signs of violence on the printer's body. While I was examining the corpse, a real doctor, a German by the name of Schultz, came up; and, seeing me at work, took me for a brother medico. He, too, examined the body, but could find no signs of violence.

But the miners were not satisfied. They wanted a more thorough examination.

"Doctor," said Schultz, "I guess we will have to perform an autopsy—the first in Deadwood."

"All right," I agreed, "but where will we get the instruments? I haven't even a jack-knife."

The German grunted and produced a surgeon's knife, and we opened up the printer. We took out the heart, and Schultz examined it, reeled off a lot of Latin words as long as an old maid's dream, and then passed the organ to me.

As I was not used to handling hearts, I dropped it and it rolled down in a dry ravine. When I recovered it, an old red-shirted Montanian called out to his mate—

"How'd you like to have that feller handle your innards that careless?"

Doctor Schultz declared that the printer came to his death through acute alcoholism.

"That will never do," I objected. "The boys would not know what that meant. We will have to call it 'friction.'"

"Friction?"

"Uh - huh. Friction of rotgut whisky against a tender stomach."

The German was a little puzzled, but my verdict stood. And it satisfied the boys.

We then put everything back in the printer, but discovered that we had no needle and thread with which to sew up the incision. I finally borrowed a jack-knife, whittled out some pine skewers and pinned him together.

We had to get along the best way we could in those days. It was no time for fancy trimmings.

We lugged the printer up to where Ingleside now stands, and dug a grave.

Preacher Smith, killed by Indians a little later, happened along and volunteered to do his best to get the printer into Heaven. I guess he had a hard time of it, for he made a lot of noise.

The parson was praying for all he was worth, fairly hitting the high points, when a man came running up a game-trail, yelling at the top of his voice:

"Wild Bill is killed! Jack McCall shot him in the back of the head!"

The parson kept right on. I gave him a poke in the ribs with my shovel-handle.

"Cut it short, parson," I told him.

"There's another one dead, and you want to save a little Gospel for him."

Leaving the printer half planted, I raced down to Main Street and found an excited crowd around Jerry Lewis's saloon, in which the killing had taken place. I tried the door, but found it locked. I then jumped up on a window-sill, and from that point of vantage secured my first glimpse of the body of Wild Bill.

He was lying on his right side; and so sudden had been his death that he had not even straightened out his legs.

His long, light-brown hair spread out on the floor and away from the pool of blood fed from the bullet-hole in his cheek. The right arm was twisted under him, and the left hand rested on the floor, palm open. Cards were scattered about, and the stools upon which the players had been seated were overturned. It was a dismal-looking hole where Wild Bill died.

"Why hasn't he been laid out?" I asked the crowd.

"We can't get any one to touch him," some one replied.

"I'll prepare his body for burial," I volunteered, "if you'll open the door."

The key was finally located, and I entered the little saloon, followed by as many men as could wedge in. I noticed, for the first time, that Bill had sat with his back to a door.

The murderer, McCall, had been in the game with Wild Bill, Captain Massey, and some others. Being partially drunk, he had had a poor run of luck and flung down his cards in disgust and left the saloon by way of the front door. But he was not so drunk as to fail to note that Wild Bill's back was to the rear entrance.

McCall then reentered the saloon through the back door, and sent a .45 slug crashing into the brain of Wild Bill. The bullet entered the back of the head, came out under the right cheek-bone, struck Captain Massey in the wrist, followed the bone up nearly to the elbow, and badly shattered the arm.

The murderer then ran from the saloon, snapping his gun at the bartender as he leaped toward the front door. The gun missed fire. McCall made an attempt to mount a horse tied in front of the saloon, but the bronco reared and pitched so that he gave it up, and ran up Main Street, snapping his gun at every man in sight.

It was a freak of fate that McCall's gun should contain five worthless loads and one good cartridge. He dodged into Shroudy's meat-market like a mad dog and hid behind a quarter of beef. When any one approached the door, McCall would peer out from his hiding-place and snap his worthless gun.

Finally, Ike Brown walked in on the murderer, regardless of snapping gun, collared him and disarmed him, and placed him under a heavy guard.

Now back to Bill. We loaded the body of the gun-fighter into a spring wagon and pulled it by hand up to Bill's camp, which stood where the Northwestern depot now stands.

With the assistance of a young fellow from Denver—an ex-choir-singer—I prepared the body for burial. I patched up the hole in the head and in the cheek. I folded the strong, graceful hands that had sent so many men into the Beyond. I cut off a lock of the gold-brown hair, in case of inquiring relatives.

Charley Utter secured one of Bill's old cap-and-ball six-shooters; and other friends, whose names I can not now recall, secured little mementoes from the scant personal effects of the great fighter.

Even in death Bill was handsome and immaculate. The loss of blood made him look like a marble statue. It seemed to me as I worked over that magnificent body that the grace it had always shown in life still lingered with it, although the intrepid spirit had departed into that country where all the tracks point one way.

We buried Bill on a hill back of Deadwood, and there he still rests in the shadow of the pines. The presentiment, felt as he looked down on Deadwood Gulch from Breakneck Hill, had come true.

McCall was tried by a miners' jury, which returned the simple verdict of "Not guilty."

There were two factions in the camp, the lawless and the people who wanted law and order. The lawless faction had been running things with a high hand, and desired so to continue. They feared that the law-and-order people might elect Wild Bill marshal of Deadwood. In that event the law-less element knew that unless they walked the chalk-line Bill's deadly guns would go to barking. So they prevailed on McCall to kill Wild Bill.

McCall knew that he did not have a ghost of a show in a fair fight with the fastest gun-juggler in the West; and so, half drunk and crazy with a sense of his own importance, Jack McCall assassinated the man who had always treated him with kindness, and had even lent him money.

The influence of the lawless element was too strong for the jury and they turned McCall loose.

I shall never forget McCall's statement at the trial. I was looking right at him when he made it. I could not look him in the eye, for he was cross-eyed, as well as owning a nose whose bridge had been smashed in with a six-shooter. He was an ungainly, repulsive-looking man.

"Gentlemen," said McCall to the jury in the rude court-room, "I killed Wild Bill. He killed two brothers of mine in Hays, Kansas. I have followed him for years. I wish he had nine lives so I could kill him some more."

I thought at the time McCall was lying. He afterward confessed that he deliberately killed Wild Bill for a little money advanced by the lawless element of Deadwood, and the questionable glory of being able to say, "I am the man who killed Wild Bill."

The night before he was killed I saw Wild Bill lend McCall some money.

McCall left the Black Hills in a hurry, for there were men ready to pick him off, but he was arrested by Federal officials in Laramie, Wyoming. The Black Hills was still an Indian reservation and every person in Deadwood Gulch at the time of the killing of Wild Bill was a trespasser on Indian land. The Government claimed jurisdiction in the McCall case, tried him at Yankton, Dakota Territory, and there a Federal judge sentenced him to be hanged.

On March 2, 1877, Jack McCall (Broken-nosed Jack) mounted the scaffold and swung into eternity. His last words were—

"Let there be no mistake."

And, so far as I know, there wasn't.

RUMOR SUBSTANTIATED
by William R Thompson.

SEATED within the screen-covered veranda of the U. S. Consulate were the three friends, cynical Doc Timkins, Lester Kimble, the coffee-planter and retired lawyer, and old man Bates, the U. S. Consul at Prinzapolca, Republic de Nicaragua. And last, but not least, was the traveling-man, lately arrived and on his first trip to the tropics. He had invited himself to dinner, overstayed his leave, outtalked their patience, and so there was silence among them.

Night had closed in and the rising tide was thundering upon the beach close by. The moon scattered its beams down through the clouds, dotting the sea like golden poppies in a clover-field. The cool night air rustled through the foliage, but now and again some sudden current above would burst through the slender, slanting palms and, shaking loose a hollow coconut husk, send it crashing downward.

Huge fireflies thumped against the screen, night birds uttered low cries that were almost words, and at each new, unfamiliar sound the traveling-man would be startled, look suddenly out into the darkness and quickly whisper, "What's that?" then glance around sheepishly.

So at length he seemed to be casting around for an excuse to break the silence, shifting his feet, clearing his throat, and so forth. Presently, smirking like a parson, he turned to Kimble and said:

"Mr. Kimble, while I journeyed here the steamer captain recounted some very in-

teresting anecdotes relating to one Jasper Cornish, who, as he told it, had been for ten years the political ruler of this Republic, but had recently met with reverses and had barely escaped with his life. And also that rumor now contradicts that he escaped, saying that he is dead. Of course you have your opinions regarding this?"

Kimble, after a moment's hesitation, gave a non-committal reply, saying—

"'Most every one has opinions."

The traveling-man felt the rebuff, but like a nervy salesman, unruffled, tried another tack, and turning to "Doc" inquired as to his opinions.

"Cornish is dead," said Doc bluntly and ready for argument.

"Dead?" echoed the traveling-man with growing confidence. "How do you know that? History states that he escaped."

"Sure," returned Doc. "History states most everything but why he has not been seen or heard from."

"It's quite possible that he escaped and is alive," broke in Kimble, coolly, unable to resist discussing the national rumor. "The evidence is favorable. His blood-stained tunic, with the bullet-hole in the left shoulder and other garments were found in a native hut on the outskirts of the city. Also Mendoza's stiletto. So history sums up, saying that Cornish escaped, dressed in the uniform of his victim, Gen. Mendoza, who disappeared on the night of the day Cornish was last seen."

"That's fair enough," replied Doc with growing animosity, "but what became of

Mendoza's body? Surely, Cornish would not tarry long in that locality, he being in the hurry of escapement. And why are there no authentic reports concerning him?"

"That's simple," smoothly asserted the traveling-man, taking sides with Kimble, and warming up as if he were the center of conversation in a smoking-car. "He's just lying low."

"What-da ye mean, lying low?" snapped Doc. "Here you have been in this Republic about ten minutes and now you try and tell me that Cornish would lie low. Huh! I knew him for ten years, why—oh, nonsense!"

The traveling-man quickly realized that he had underestimated Doc, so he began to hedge, like a crawfish backing water, by saying:

"Well, your standpoint is only rumor, and what does that amount to? Rumor is always fickle and often false. You woo it and it's coy, be heedless and it hovers about like a will-o'-the-wisp. Full of glamour it lures, but once strip the husk to its dry, rattling bones, why—huh, old maids' gossip."

"Rubbish!" roared Doc, violently thumping the table with his fist. "History in this case is nothing more than a rumor, not even fifty-fifty."

And Doc, with that, flopped back in his chair, savagely chewing his cigar, and his eyes glaring with animosity.

Taken aback, the traveling-man fell silent before this retort, though his eyes were filled with unvanquished argument.

At length, Kimble, in an even tone, relieved the tension by renewing the subject, saying:

"Doc, it is obvious that rumor has much evidence for argument and I have given it much thought. But I have never reached any conclusion regarding the whereabouts of Mendoza's body, or the non-appearance of Cornish. And I can not understand why he has not communicated with his friend, the consul. Although I often answer the latter by thinking that he may be drifting around with a total loss of memory, for his defeat must have been bitterly disappointing, and his wound may have developed a brain fever, which is not a rare occurrence in this latitude, as you know.

"So, inasmuch as neither history nor rumor can account as to how the evidence came within the hut, history should be

given the benefit of the doubt. And so then, with the favorable assumption regarding memory and the preference of doubt, as evidence, I can not but believe that Cornish is alive. Do you not agree with me, Consul?"

The consul was lounging in his steamer chair, legs outstretched and head reclining, and watching the smoke of his pipe slowly ascending, as was his habit. He seemed to be deliberating that question, for he had been many years in the tropics, where to be discreet, to listen and to be silent are most valuable assets.

"Oh, well," perhaps he thought, "I shall retire soon, so why not speak plainly?"

For, after a moment, he slowly drawled—

"Well, Kimble, I don't think it's wise to place much faith in the uncertain, and I regret to say that I believe Cornish to be dead."

Doc fell to grinning like a Cheshire cat upon hearing this reply. The traveling-man with a jerk sat upright, utterly astonished. And Kimble, lawyerwise, with his brows drawn together, gazed at the consul, for he was puzzled and sought to fathom the consul's face.

"Yes," he continued, "I believe so. And it took me some time, considerable effort and thought to arrive at this conclusion, although it was much against my desire. But, I found evidence which I believe entirely dispels the statement of history."

"You found evidence," blurted the traveling-man, with open-eyed curiosity. "That's remarkable—very, very. Tell me all about it and Cornish."

The consul, realizing that he was bestraddled with a descendant of the mythological "Old Man of the Sea," smiled slightly and began:

 CORNISH arrived here ten years ago, with the victorious revolutionists.

We became friends, but all that I know of him dates from the night he appeared, dressed in greasy overalls, amidst a cargo of munitions of war that a filibustering ship had hurriedly dumped upon the wharf, up Porta Cortez way. For there and that night he joined the revolutionists led by Gen. Tratina.

He was an educated man, that's certain. He had also been trained in the military arts, that's a decided certainty. But what caused him to turn soldier-of-fortune—who knows? He never volunteered any information, and as a past is not required down here, he's a mystery.

But in action he was a cool, calculating, devil incarnate. The native barefoot soldiers fairly worshiped him, for during the last battle, when his captain became rattled, Cornish, with his rifle, clubbed him down, and then with the "rebel yell" led the soldiers in a successful flanking charge and won the decisive victory. And was Cornish punished for this military crime and mutiny? Certainly not, but instead was given the little salary and abundant honor that belongs to the title of colonel.

Well, time went on and after the first enthusiastic spasm of loyalty in his followers had simmered away, General and President Tratina experienced the cares and worries of his office. Dissatisfaction and envy reared its ugly head among his followers, and although he had confiscated all his enemy's properties—for that seems to be the legitimate right of the victorious—and had lavished them right and left, how could he hope to retain their loyalty? He had nothing more to portion out, so he was filled with worry and sometimes fear, for he knew the breed.

So, feeling the necessity of a stronger man to associate with, he, in their growing intimacy, studied Cornish, found him strong, wonderfully efficient, above mercenary temptation, and seemingly contemptuous of the petty political offices. So then he in one day made Cornish his personal adviser and General-in-Chief, hazarding his all on one turn, hoping that Cornish was strong enough to protect him and safeguard his office.

Cornish was, and, not seeking to further any political schemes of his own, he quelled the sudden riot of indignation and threatened revolt. So, in a short time, the President seemed to take hold of the governmental affairs in a vigorous and aggressive manner. Concessions were granted, foreign capital poured in, the ·revenue and smuggling ceased, education was enforced and the army enlistment lengthened from three months to three years.

For at the outset Cornish was far-sighted. He studied the tropics, the feverish and erratic temperament of the populace, their duplicities, their shallow dignities and childish pretentions; so, during the first few years he reorganized the army and trained them against the morrow, trying to instil into the barefoot half-baked *hombres* the spirit to fight against odds and conquer. And to all appearances he did, for they became silent and intelligent, and the officers competent and loyal.

So, in the ensuing ten years, the country changed from a wild, seething hotbed of revolution into a peaceable, well-regulated, flourishing unit of progress.

But this new order was changing; nothing really ever grows old here except the aging ruins of the Spanish dungeons. Still the order was changing with scarcely a ripple to mark the passing. The suppressed, spasmodic fever of revolt was simmering below the surface.

Well, now, things began to happen. Don't think that I exaggerate, but it takes no great amount of preparation to start a revolution here. In a night man will revert to savagery; a riot—then revolution and ruthless destruction flares forth until chaos reigns. So, given a little money, a leader, much *vino*, a few inflammable words, and the combustion starts amid loud cries of "*Viva! Viva!*" until even the loyal citizens turn traitor for the new cause, which may be worse than the old. They know it, but why they rebel they know not.

But Cornish had an efficient secret service. It kept him informed. Conspiracy was breeding, treason and sedition murmured, and one Don Enrico Mendoza was plotting. So he was not surprised when on the early morning of the presidential election day a telegram in code was handed to him, which read about like this:

Nicoya Barracks.
Revolutionists—leader Enrico Mendoza—crossing frontier. Frontier post deserted to him. Have commandeered two trains. Coming rapidly.
AGUILAR, commanding.

Of course you are familiar with the outcome: how he dynamited the railroad bridge, and placed the troops on either side of the track, just within the jungle's edge across the river. Then he so cunningly concealed the rapid-fire guns that they commanded the track.

His plan was to permit the revolutionists to enter this ambush, and then at the sound of the artillery the flankers would close in and all would be over. And you have heard how the trains that seemingly were loaded with men stopped about a mile from the bridge and how Cornish waited for them to approach.

But that was the moment fate threw in the clutch to destiny's wheel. He waited too long. Some treacherous officer had thrown his lot with Mendoza and informed him of the plan of action; the reinforcements failed to arrive promptly; Mendoza made a detour and attacked in the rear; and then the wheel began to spin.

Cornish quickly reversed the artillery and opened fire as he saw the howling mob of soldiers and citizens bursting out of the city streets just behind him. But who could hope to stem that riotous whirlwind of blazing rifles and flashing machetes. For they, knowing that only a few rapid-fire guns opposed them, swarmed on with a sudden newborn courage and overwhelmed Cornish and his artillerymen. They then sprayed with a hail of lead from the captured guns on the loyal soldiers across the river, who, with charging yells, burst out of the jungle to meet face to face upon an empty track.

That was the last seen of Cornish. He was standing stanch, in his white uniform, surrounded by his crack artillerymen, pumping lead from two revolvers as the mob overwhelmed them.

WELL, about a month after the battle his tunic and the other things were found, and soon rumor began to whisper. So I felt doubtful as to his escape, for he had not reappeared nor had he communicated with me, his best friend.

So then one day I went up to the hut to investigate. The hut is north of here, about two miles. However, before I reached it, after struggling along the slimy trail that winds about the stinking swamps and over the stagnant rivers, I came to a deep, silent, suspicious pool with a rotten foot-log spanning it. I gave it a strength test and in doing so I noticed a shred of cloth hanging on a knot, and by the cloth a crusted section of the log had fallen away. It was probably the result of some sudden weight. So, I swung across on a vine.

Soon I came to the clearing containing the hut. It was standing alone near the center. It had a lonesome appearance and was fast falling away. The low, broad eaves were ragged and almost hidden by the tall coarse grass. The wind had flayed the thatched palm roof until the sun and rain could beat down through the openings.

The whole place seemed creepy and haunted.

And standing on the threshold of this dilapidated hut I gazed in at the slovenly interior. Black lizards scurried away in fright; a scorpion crawled painfully through the gloom toward a spot of sunlight. Old rags and long, slate-colored feathers lay about upon the dirt floor. Near the side a bamboo bed lay overturned and a water-jug and stool near by.

I entered slowly, meditating upon the curious mysteries and contradictions of history—history *versus* rumor, so to speak. So, meditating, with my eyes downcast, I saw trampled into the dirt a leaden bullet. Stooping to pick it up, I found also a copper cartridge-shell, and turning to better light I brushed away the dirt and examined them.

The bullet bore marks that told of clinching teeth and was of the same caliber as the shell. The shell had not been exploded, for it was not powder-blackened, although it had the imprint of a center pin neatly punched in the center.

Now history states that Cornish escaped, dressed in the uniform of his victim, General Mendoza, and shows as proof this evidence, a blood-stained tunic and other garments, also the stiletto, which, it consequently claims, vouches for the presence of Mendoza.

But rumor contradicts, basing its denial upon the hypothetical question as to whether Cornish would dispose of the body, and reasons thus: Cornish would not dispose of the body and could not, being so wounded. Therefore, as Mendoza's body had not been found, neither of them had been there. Here rumor stops and starts speculating.

Well, I agree with rumor in that Cornish is dead, and furthermore I can account for the evidence found, and with the new evidence introduced, namely the rotten foot-log with the section displaced and the shred of cloth hanging beside it, the tooth-marked bullet, the unexploded cartridge-shell and the slate-colored feathers. With these I can circumstantially prove that both are dead.

Of course the following is only a deduction from my imagination and may seem to be far-fetched, but those who are familiar with the tropical people, their dispositions and diabolical modes of procedure and the manner in which nature disposes of objectionable objects in her midst, I think will agree with me in my deductions.

So then, bringing up the evidence in sequence, let us suppose that when Cornish was shot he fell heavily and thereby lost consciousness and that the following begins in the late afternoon of the same day in the hut at the clearing.

CORNISH awoke from his stupor, heavy-lidded and dazed. His gaze slowly wandering about took in the unfamiliar surroundings. He was puzzled. Everything was so dirty and squalid.

When his eyes closed, his brain seemed to reel until he became nauseated like a drunken man. And he was thirsty.

Finally his eyes came to rest upon his person, stretched full length upon the bed. And at last he realized that the red that he saw was blood—his blood. He was covered with it. His face seemed stiff; and feeling with slow, clumsy fingers he found the clots dry and hard.

A dull, steady pain quivered along his nerves and the twitching pain guided his hand to his left shoulder, where he found the wet, clustered clots. Ugh! He was a mess. He groaned aloud in anguish and revulsion.

A dozing sentry, nodding in the shade of the broad eaves without, heard and awoke with a start. Rising, still tightly clutching his ever-ready machete, he peered in through the open doorway.

Cornish saw him and with a sharp intake of breath, sat up and questioned huskily—

"Where am I?"

"*Quien sabe, señor.*"

"Well, who are you?" sharply.

"*Quien sabe, señor,*" again replied the sentry, with the ever-evasive tropical answer, "Who knows."

Cornish lay back. Memory returned and he realized that he had been defeated, was captured, wounded and burning with a fever.

The day was closing. The shadows lengthened and the cool, damp air crept out from the jungle and filled them. The darkness gathered swiftly and the clouds slowly formed in preparation for the nightly shower.

Presently a sound of hurrying footsteps sounded from without and Cornish, looking to the doorway, saw a man standing upon the threshold. And he saw that it was Mendoza, the victorious.

Speaking rapidly in a low, earnest voice, full of feeling and solicitude, Mendoza explained in order that Cornish would be protected and safe from the blood-maddened revolutionists, two men as instructed had brought him here. No one knew. Tomorrow after they had quieted, he would be taken secretly to the palace and cared for. He would soon convalesce and all would be well.

They would be friends, such friends, even as brothers, and together they would serve their beloved people and create a new government. Oh, he would be proud to be associated with such a brave and honorable a man as Cornish. Yes, they would be as brothers, and accomplish much together. Tomorrow they would talk over the situation and begin to plan. Tonight Cornish must be kept quiet and not unduly excited. So he had brought medicine and liquid food in preparation.

Then he saw that Cornish had not been attended to, so he turned to the sentry and cursed him—cursed him with all the soft-spoken eloquence of a Spanish grandee, until the sentry shivered in abject servility. And then with biting insolence he ordered him to disrobe Cornish, wash and bind the wound and prepare the food.

Then, after a moment, Mendoza told of his immediately necessary presence at the palace, for he had secretly left. So with many more gesticulations and condoling words of friendship, he left.

At length Cornish felt the fever abating as the quinine and stimulating food began its work. So he drowsed.

The midnight shower began and the rain pattered gently upon the thatched roof. Cornish awoke, for he lay without covering. Listening to the soothing pattering, his thoughts floated peacefully. It sounded so pleasant, so cool and refreshing. He had not yet begun to ponder over Mendoza's words of friendship. He heard the sentry without, breathing deeply, asleep.

But suddenly he gave a nervous start, for from the darkness a voice whispered, saying:

"It is I—a friend. At dawn turn to the right from the doorway. I will await you. Your 'gringo' friends await you on the beach with a power boat."

And so whispering, the stranger thrust a

revolver into his hand. And then all again was silent save for the pattering rain and the sleeping sentry.

For a moment Cornish was stunned. His heart raced violently. Hope ran riot, and then his brain became a seething vortex of plans and rejections. Then his face flushed with uncontrollable rage, for suspicion had entered his thoughts and he began to reason over Mendoza's words.

Did Mendoza think him a fool? Did he discount manhood and experience? It was only a trick. Shot while attempting to escape. Bah! That was an old one. Better stand him with his back to a wall and be done. He knew the law of the victorious— to exterminate the vanquished leaders. Bah! To —— with their Spanish customs and the niceties of their fiendish etiquette! Let them be done.

And his thoughts became bitter, and black depression filled his pounding temples. But at length his rage quieted. He grew calm, and the thought filtered slowly to his reason—

"Why the revolver?"

So in the darkness he awkwardly began to examine the revolver. Blowing his breath down the barrel he found it clear of obstruction. With his thumb he gently worked the hammer to and fro, testing the spring. He felt of the center firing-pin. It was secure, and each chamber contained a cartridge.

Still he was not satisfied. Some vague premonition of danger and disaster kept surging and hammering at his fever-dulled faculties, kept hovering and pounding until through the seething turmoil the thought burst into form. And, with an anxious throaty sound, he extracted a cartridge, clinched his teeth upon the lead and wrenched it free. Then, spilling the powder upon his naked breast, he felt of the tiny dry cubes. Satisfied, he replaced the empty shell, for safety, let the hammer fall gently upon it and rested, the perspiration of excitement and anxiety pouring from him.

So he thought:

"All was perfect. Five perfect cartridges and a fighting chance. If it was a trick, some one simply invited death. His friends had not failed him, and his name would not be written on the already bloody page of history, in company with that of President Tratini. Even if he were taken to the palace, it would only be a 'cat and mouse game.' "

Confidence returned. So he rested calmly and awaited the dawn.

Soon the pattering rain ceased. The sullen clouds broke away and swung off northward. The stars came out and it was lighter. The deep, regular breathing of the sleeping sentry, sheltered under the low, broad eaves, sounded and the first faint flush of the dawn came stealing down over the jungle top.

Cornish, peering out, saw the dawn. Arising, he groped in the darkness for his shoes. Seated on the bed and awkwardly fumbling with his right hand, he attempted to put them on. But a sudden clumsy movement pained his helpless left arm and with a groan he sat erect, glancing toward the doorway in anxiety about the flying time. And there he saw, silhouetted against the lighter background, the black shape of a man, motionless.

Instantly Cornish was on his feet, revolver in hand, forearm upraised, pointing at the unexpected black shape. Then he softly questioned—

"Is it you, friend?"

There was no reply save that of a stealthy step toward him.

Speculating rapidly, in a fraction of a second Cornish thought:

"It is a trick. No, this was the other sentry; just the customary executioner come at the usual time but unaware of his revolver or plan of escape. One shot would finish him—he could fight off the sleeping sentry in the darkness. But be sure."

So he questioned again sharply—

"Is that you—friend?"

At the same time he took one long quick step to the right, for something caused him to suspect. And even as he stepped he heard the short gasp of breath as the shape brushed by, lunging at him.

 QUICK as a cat Cornish half turned and pulled the trigger. Oh, the instinct of that man, for quicker still he sprang back and away, his left arm swinging wildly, for there had been no blinding flash or deafening report from the revolver.

The momentum of the shape carried it lunging onward, crashing into the stool beside the bed; and with a dull thud the water-jug fell. And again in that fraction of a second Cornish pulled the trigger, aiming at the crashing sound. But there was no report.

Now Cornish was crouching with his back toward the doorway, the revolver gripped close to his naked breast, controlling his suddenly awakened muscles, the surety of his aim and shortening the arc of his fire. Intently he listened for a betraying sound, eyes straining for the shape lost in the darkness, and every muscle on the quiver in expected action.

The shape in its mad rush and confusion of overturning the stool had lost the location of Cornish, so it also waited in silence for a noise. The soft, liquid gurgle of the water flowing from the jug filled the space, and it seemed an hour before Cornish heard the sound as of a foot being gently placed in a puddle of water. And then his eyes, ever ready, turned to the sound, body aligned with eyes and finger, pulled the trigger. Then instinctively realizing that his position had been betrayed, he guided his body in a long, stealthy, crouching step, again to the right, for again nothing but a metallic click had sounded.

Hitherto fear had been unfelt and animal instinct alone had acted and guided his rapid movements. But before this almost supernatural predicament, fear began to rise and overwhelm instinct and cautiousness. It gripped the nerve-center of his stomach, sending chilling, vibrating spasms over his body until his very flesh seemed to crawl and his heart pumped with pulsating, body-racking throbs.

Then his brain awoke and began to question. "What was the matter? The cartridges and revolver were perfect. Had he not examined them? But good God! Three had missed fire and only two remained. Were they——?

Then all of his feverish faculties, all the senses of his virile manhood, seethed and surged. All memories of past action and experiences of sudden danger, lying dormant, crowded to his thoughts, tumbling one over the other in their frenzied haste to serve and try to show the solution for this mysterious enigma. But they could point out no solution, and body, long subjected to will, began to revolt. The empty, chilling, paralyzing sensation of fear grew to the wild, panicky feeling of primeval terror at the silent, stalking enemy, the unseen but lurking death.

But then the will—the terrific will-power of the man—asserted itself and controlled the animal-like body, controlled the fear-formed desire of despair to spring and grapple in the darkness with the unseen, to clutch with his hands and use a man's weapon, his certain strength; to grip, to strain, to throttle and kill. But will was still the master and pounded thoughts again and again—

"You are wounded—control! Control!"

Will-power predominated and the hellish fear subsided. He choked down the animal-like whines of desire that rose in his throat. But the blood thudded in his ears, his pulses raced furiously, and his body was so ridged that it twitched violently and the steel-taut muscles were aching and crying with the strain and calling for action. But he realized that he was between the shape and the lighter doorway, though crouching close to the ground, so he dared not move. And so, with all senses acute, he awaited for another betraying sound.

Soon again he heard the faint, splashing footfall. Again he pulled the trigger, twice, thinking to scatter the shots into the darkness. But nothing save the metallic *click*, *click* followed the efforts, and again betrayed his location, for he heard a quick sardonic laugh from the darkness.

Wildly—his heart most stopped with its spasmodical jerkings—Cornish, praying for a miracle, with such frantic rapidity pulled the trigger, aiming into the darkness, that the cylinder spun with almost a simultaneous clicking sound. Then in one movement — he sensed the coming lunge — he sprang upright, grasping the revolver as a bludgeon, with the butt foremost, arm upstretched full length, right foot to the rear and braced, and knees slightly bent.

And so quickly had the series of movements been executed that again instinct timed and guided his arm, swinging downward and forward with terrific force into the darkness to meet the lunging shape. The revolver crashed with a hollow thud; he realized that, even as he felt an agonizing pain in his breast when the lunging impact carried them falling heavily to the ground.

 THE stars faded in the growing daylight. The slow-moving noises within the jungle quieted, and the baboon ceased his hoarse, grunting cough. Under the sheltering leaves the dewy parrots awoke with a screech. The sun mounted by jerks over the tree-tops, the heat of day descended, and the morning vapors wafted in ghastly, shapeless form about the clearing.

The sleeping sentry, machete in hand and all wet from the splattering rain, shivered and awoke. Rising, he began stretching his stiff limbs one by one. Then, yawning and working his sleep-sodden eyelids, he stepped to the doorway and peered in. Slowly his eyes widened in surprise, and his mouth opened, awestruck, for before him, lying in a pool of fresh blood, was Jasper Cornish, naked, face upward, and with a stiletto sunk to the hilt in his breast. And over and across him, face downward, and in a separate pool, lay a body.

Then the sentry, crossing himself reverently, and with a muttered word, slowly entered. And half in fear he turned over the uppermost body and looked into the face of Don Enrico Mendoza, the victorious. He shivered in aversion and his breath grew rapid. He could not understand. He had heard no shots. And picking up the revolver from beside Cornish, he fell to examining it.

He threw open the cylinder and extracted the empty shell. It was not powder-blackened, still the firing-pin had struck it. And the other shells contained their leaden bullets, but they also had been struck by the firing-pin.

In growing fright he began to mutter to himself, "*Madre de Cristo*," over and over. Then in perplexity his gaze returned to the empty shell and he saw that which in his interest and stupefying amazement he had overlooked, some of Mendoza's blood upon his hand.

With a scream of superstitious horror he threw the shell from him and, whirling in growing terror, ran madly, still tightly clutching the revolver.

The other sentry, just awakening under a lean-to of leaves, heard the cry and saw him running madly, saw his head thrown forward and the whites of his eyes showing in his superstitious terror. So, jumping to his feet, his primitive brain assimilating the fear, he followed, gaining upon the terror-dazed leader.

Dashing madly, they disappeared into the jungle, their cries dying away down the trail. Wildly they ran, pushing and crowding, stumbling and ricochetting against the trees lining the narrow trail, their breath coming in short, throaty gasps.

Crowding madly they sprang to the rotting foot-log spanning the silent pool. Close together, tottering and swaying crazily, their bare toes digging into the moldy surface, they reached the middle.

The leader placed his foot a little off center and the outer rotten crust gave way. He felt the slip and sensed the void underfoot. Quickly whirling, arm swinging in an arc, fingers clutching, he gripped his mate's shoulder.

With a savage cry, his mate struck at the hand and his balance shifted. They tottered a moment, striving to regain equilibrium. Then, struggling and cursing together, they slipped, tearing their clothes on the knots, and with shrill cries slid splashing into the pool below.

The swish of a long black alligator-tail cut the water. The noise of powerful, champing jaws drowned the screams, and the waters closed over the bubbles. The ripples died away from the red blotch under the log. Then all was silent, and a shred of cloth hung motionless from a knot on the log.

THE sun rose to its zenith. The heat of day was oppressive. In the glaring sky a dot appeared descending in an ever-decreasing spiral.

Presently the sky was filled with circular moving specks. And one by one the vultures settled to the earth with long, running hops. Then with the flappings of wings the hideous, beady-eyed, slate-colored birds stood around the house, waiting silently.

When the day started to wane, the old leader began to circle the hut, alone. Its beady eyes ever watchful, its long, hooked bill jerking to and fro in time to its repulsive, scaly legs, it warily stopped at the doorway and peered in. Then with a low, croaking cry it entered and the others rushed to follow. And soon the sound of flapping wings, of hoarse, croaking cries and ravenous noises, of tearing and pulling, came from within the hut.

The shadows lengthened. The vultures ascended, and dusk descended and found the blood-stained stiletto lying upon the dirt floor. Then all was silent.

Blackness again surrounded all. Gleaming eyes shone along the jungle's edge. Soft, cautious footfalls broke the silence, hesitated, then came on.

Soon many eyes pierced the darkness and the soft, approaching patter of paws sounded. Then there was a sniffing and low, guttural snarls within the hut. Then the rustle as of bodies half dragging through the tall grass, that passed and died away crashing through the jungle undergrowth.

All again was silent and within the hut the blood-stained garments lay strewn about near the stiletto.

AS THE consul concluded, the men breathed deeply and stirred. Doc, his face clouded with bewilderment, started to speak, but Kimble held up a restraining hand and said— "Well, Consul, I admire your imagination and reasoning, for your story is very plausible, but——"

Here the traveling-man rose to his feet and interrupted Kimble.

"Yes!" he exclaimed pompously. "Your story is very plausible. But you don't mean to tell me that a man, given a perfect revolver and five perfect, center-fire cartridges, would not get any results when he pulled the trigger. Huh?"

The consul looked at him patiently, and then said dryly: "They were rim-fire cartridges.

TO CRACK A SAFE
by Terence and Patrick Casey

Authors of "The Story of William Hyde."

UNDER a crowd of stars in the wide and silent night, the Kid came along the road where the road dipped down into a little valley. He was hungry. That day, for many weary miles, he had walked without a set-down, without a hand-out, without a chow of any kind. His peaked, pale face was turned not to the crowd of stars, but to the ruts in the road.

He wore a coat that was many sizes too large for him. It had been made for a man. About his slight boy's form, that coat hung so loosely that he looked in the shadowy night like a shriveled-up old man.

But the coat did not hang loosely on the left side. On the left side the coat bulged out oddly. It was as if he had shoved a considerable bundle beneath that coat on the left side. And it was a bundle that moved restlessly at times. At these times, about the bundle, the Kid tightened the clasp of one long-sleeved arm. At the last time, he said:

"Don't git res'less, old feller. There's no use yer sniffin' like yer never et fer a week, and whimperin', and wishin' yer had some eats. It's no use, old-timer. You jes' gotta make up yer mind you git no supper tonight—not even a hand-out. Tonight, Gay-cat, you and me eats wind-puddin', and you jes' make up yer mind to that fac' and be satisfied."

There was a little yellow dog beneath

the boy's coat. As the boy spoke, the dog stuck his sharp yellow nose out of the top of the coat. In his throat he whimpered hungrily, piteously.

"Aw, say now, Gay-cat! Be a sport and quit yer grumblin', will yer? I never et, either, did I? And yer don't hear me complainin'. I'm tryin' to be a good hobo, I am, and eat my wind-puddin' when I'se got ter, see? And it'll soon be dawn, bo. You stay in there, Gay-cat, and jes' wait. It'll soon be dawn and we can strike a farmhouse fer some eats."

But the dog only shoved his yellow and wise old head altogether out of the top of the coat. Nervously he cocked his ragged ears. Of a sudden, he squirmed quickly out over the hugging arm and, dropping to the road, stood tense and excited, barking toward the shadowy slope to one side.

"Sh, Gay-cat!"

The dog quieted with a growl. The Kid listened fearfully. He heard a cavernous yawn as if from some one who slept by the road—some one who had been awakened rudely by the dog's barking.

From out of the echoing night, in a man's gruff voice, came a low guarded call:

"Ho, bo! Ho, bo!"

It was the tramp call. It told what the speaker was and asked if the Kid were a brother.

"Hello, bo," the Kid answered, no longer fearful. "What yer got there?"

"Floppin's fur the night," answered the gruff voice.

"Floppin's, huh? Then I guess we'll pound our ear, too, Gay-cat and me." The Kid left the road, the dog tagging wearily at his heels. "I was jes' snoopin' by when my dog smelled yer sleepin' here."

"Yuh got a dorg? I oughta knowed it was him barkin' what woke me up."

"Sure," the Kid answered proudly. "And he's some dog, too. He smelled yer sleepin', old-timer. He can smell a hobo a mile!"

Making blindly across the slope, the Kid stumbled on to the edge of a gully. The gully was deep between two little knolls of the slope and was soft with a thick tangle of dry grass. Below in the hollow he could see the dark, outstretched figure of a big, heavy man.

The man lay, in a position of complete ease, on his broad back, his arms flung up above his head. His face was in shadow.

The dog sniffed at his legs.

"Them's nuthin' to eat, Gay-cat, old hobo," said the Kid. And he tried to chuckle.

"Gay-cat's some hungry, bo," he explained. "We'se both hungry, Gay-cat and me. We ain't et since mornin'. It's been one horstile town after t'other, bo. Them hayseed bulls has been as thick as the fleas on Gay-cat hisself this day. We'se had tough hobo luck, that's what, old-timer. Every Johnny Tinplate has made us beat it out o' them towns without us even moochin' a measly handout. Say, yer don't happen to have a handout on yer, do yer, pal?"

"What d'yuh think I am, kid," growled the man, "a walkin' free-lunch counter? I ain't et myself tonight. I'm only waitin' fur dawn to breeze down into thet town in the walley and show good kale fur a meal—I'm thet empty inside!"

He grunted sourly, and continued:

"Hobo luck, nuthin'! Yuh hoboin' shif'-less, thet's what. What you need, kid, is to have a couple o' dollars in yer jeans. Git some coin, and then when yuh hit a horstile burg yuh can drill right by them hayseed coppers and buy a square, and them coppers can't say a word. Take thet from me, kid, and yuh won't be shooed out o' no towns no more. Git a road stake."

The Kid sat down beside the supine man, the dog in his lap.

"Mebbe yer is right, old-timer; but that don't buy me nuthin' now. I feel all holler inside. But mebbe a smoke 'ud fix me up, though. Yer hasn't the makin's on yer, has yer?"

"Nope. But d'yuh chaw terbacker? A good chaw o' terbacker 'ud be jest the thing to wet up yer mouth, kid."

"Do I chaw terbacker? Aw, say, bo!"

The man did not move from that position on the flat of his back. Only he fumbled in his trouser's pocket and drew out a ragged oblong of chewing tobacco. He held up one end in his hand, while the Kid leaned over and from the other end bit off a mouthful.

While the Kid leaned over, the man said less gruffly—

"Say, yuh haven't met up along the road with a stiff name o' Swaggerin' Bob?"

"Swaggerin' Bob? No, I ain't never met that bo."

"Bo!" the man snorted. "Bob ain't no bo. He's none o' yer bindle stiffs or back-door moochers. He's a sorter strong-arm stiff and horstile to everybody. Him, he'd be crackin' a safe!"

"Gee!" breathed the Kid. "What a proud and reckless feller!"

Savagely the man rolled his head in the grass.

"'Tain't no use talkin'! Yuh ain't seen my friend so I won't cough on him no more. Me, I guess I'll pound my ear."

In a short time, with the easy adaptability of the true blown-in-the-glass stiff, he was snoring in loud sleep.

It was coming on dawn. The crowd of stars was fading from the sky. Over in the east the sky was tinged with the first color of gray chill dawn.

The Kid drew his huge coat close about himself and his hungry snuggling dog and lay back, in the soft nest of grass, looking up at the brightening sky. He chewed. He chewed manfully. But his stomach still gnawed with a cramping pain. He could not sleep.

A particularly loud snore caused the dog to turn, with cocked ragged ears, to watch the sleeping man alongside. The Kid sat up. The dog fell in a little ball upon the dew-wet grass of the hollow. He gave a startled yelp. Then he unwound and stretched his crooked little legs.

But neither that yelp nor the keenness of dawn disturbed the loud sleep of the man. He still lay in that position of blissful unconsciousness, his arms flung up above his head, his face to the pinking sky.

The Kid could see his face. His was not a hobo's face. There was no stubble of a week's growth smutting his face, nor was his face thin and pale in that unhealthy way peculiar to so many hoboes. His was a broad red face. Down that face from the corner of the left eye, across the mouth, to the cleft in the too-strong chin was a great quarter-inch scar. Against the red health of his face, that scar was a streak of hideous white.

"Gee," said the Kid to himself, "that's some scar he got on his face, that stiff. Must 'a' got it in some drunken fight in the jungles. Fer fancy work with his razor, the bloke what done that sure was a blowed-in-the-glass stiff. I never see'd a hobo carved jes' like that. Bet he got his road name from that white scar—some monniker like 'Scar-face' or 'Split-cheek' or 'White-scar!'

"And jes' look how Whitey-scar pounds

his ear, though! Jes' like a baby, easy-like and without worryin' none where he's gonna mooch the next meal. He's a big fat stiff, too, is Whitey-scar. Ought to be up early huntin' fer scoffin's, 'stead of floppin' like he never slept fer a week."

With sudden thought, the Kid looked down more closely at the man.

"I wonder, now," he said, "I wonder is he a blowed-in-the-glass stiff! Ain't he sleepin' like he had money in his jeans hisself and can buy his scoffin's any old time? And didn't he tell me to git a road stake—to work fer some money? I'll bet he's a guy what works but is temp'rary-like out of a job. He's a fake hobo, that's what—jes' a Gay-cat!"

The boy's voice, as he spoke, lowered to a whisper, as if he feared that the sleeping man might hear. He leaned forward, his mouth half open, his breath sounding in little eager gasps. A thought had leaped full-fledged and with brutal startlingness to his brain. That thought was that he should "roll" the sleeping man. He should go through his clothes and rob him!

It is not a brave thing to rob a sleeping man. It is a coward's trick. Also, it is a true hobo's trick. It is a true hobo's trick because all hoboes are criminals and cowards. They are criminals at heart, but without the courage. Only what they surely can get away with, that only will they do.

The Kid was a true hobo. He had an education only in the ways of hoboes. Nearly all that he knew had been taught him by the roads he tramped, the hoboes he met. Hobo ideals were his ideals; and hobo ideals are strange ideals.

The Kid got to his knees beside the sleeping man. He watched the man's closed eyes. He watched the man's closed eyes with an intense fixed stare. The least flutter of an eyelid would spring him to his feet.

He pulled up the long sleeve of his right arm. He felt along the man's belt. The man's money might be in that belt. It was a likely place. But there were no pockets in that belt, no bulges.

The money might be in the man's shirt-front. The Kid knew that some hoboes carried their stakes in the knot of a bandanna around their necks and over their chests. He leaped closer. His eyes were on the man's eyelids. His eyes never left those eyelids. His lowered head was close to the man's red and scarred face. His breath on that face might awaken the man. He held his breath.

Light as a walking fly, the fingers of his right hand moved from the belt to the brown vest over the man's chest. Through that vest his fingers felt a hard bulge. He breathed once. Here was money hidden.

His eyes on the man's eyelids, his breath held, he felt that hard bulge. Then he got to his feet. Slowly and deliberately he got to his feet. He backed away. His face was death-white with an absolute bloodlessness. There was no need to hold his breath. He had no breath.

Beneath the man's vest, his sensitive fingers had felt the shape of a revolver. It was not a large revolver; its barrel had been sawed down. It was in some sort of cloth sling beneath the vest. On either side of the cloth sling, the vest was padded deeply. That was to round off the bulge of the revolver. It was to lessen, if not wholly conceal, the outlines of that revolver.

The Kid backed up the slope of the gully.

"A yegger!" he breathed in a cold whisper of fear. "A strong-armer! Now I know, I don't monkey with Mr. Whitey-scar. Lucky I found out what he was. I don't want to make no road stake by rollin' him. Him! He might 'a' croaked me with that stick-up gun!"

On top of the knoll to one side of the gully, the Kid whistled for the Gay-cat. As quickly and suddenly as a rabbit, the dog bounded up out of the hollow. He looked open-mouthed and eager up at the Kid, then down at the big blissful head of the sleeping man.

"No, Gay-cat," said the Kid, interpreting that look. "We is gonna leave Mr. Whitey-scar. He ain't like us, Gay-cat. He don't have to wake up early and throw his feet fer scoffin's. He ain't no beggar. He can sleep late, he can, and git money fer his chow out of any old safe he meets, with that stick-up gun he has and a little soup!"

The Kid looked back down the hollow. Across the sleeping man's red face, he saw that long ugly white scar. Into his eyes, as he looked, crept a peculiar expression. Hobo ideals were the Kid's ideals. Like all hoboes, he thought real criminals fine men. He stood in awe of criminals. Admiration and awe—that was the expression in his eyes.

"Gee!" he whispered. "A proud and reckless stiff, jes' like his friend, Swaggerin' Bob!"

Then he turned and, the dog running by his side, fled toward the road.

THE KID fled along the road where the road dipped down between hop-fields that were a thousand leafy trellises, curtaining off the peeping sun. In the flat of the valley near the river was the town.

As he approached the town, he saw standing to one side of the road a little one-storied structure with a corrugated-iron roof. So tiny was that structure that it looked like a tool-house. The Kid saw that it was more than a tool-house. In the exact center of its front door was a square aperture barred with vertical black rods of iron.

"The town lock-up!" breathed the Kid. "Come here, Gay-cat!"

His tail snuggling his back in sudden fright, the dog crept to the boy's side. So the two, boy and dog, slunk by that tiny structure. The boy was a hobo, an outcast. He had all a hobo's fear of the lawful instruments, both animate and inanimate, of that society from which, as a hobo, he was cast out.

The town beyond was a town of four buildings. There were a general merchandise store, a nickelodeon, a saloon and, a little apart from these, a yellow-painted shack that looked like a railroad station. All were labeled with the same name, "J. Curtis Haines." But the yellow-painted shack had the glory of the additional words, "Ranch Office."

The yellow-painted shack stood back from the road in a field overgrown with tall grass and rank weeds and thistles. In the clear gravel sweep before its door, five buckboards were drawn up in line. Through the open door, as he passed by, the Kid saw two clerks working behind a counter. In the rear in a swivel-chair before a huge safe was a tall gray-mustached man who was talking vehemently to the five field bosses who had driven up in the buckboards for the morning orders.

But the Kid did not halt here to ask J. Curtis Haines for a job in his hop-fields. Beyond the bridge over the shallow river and up on the side of the valley, he saw a low whitewashed farmhouse. Toward that he made to ask for a hand-out.

The windows of the farmhouse were open. He could see a Chinese smiling philosophically over a broad cook-stove, crowded with tall pots. But there were no sounds of eating from the open windows of the farmhouse or from the hundred brown-canvas tents of the hop-harvesters across the road.

The Kid understood thereat. It was harvest-time; the hops were being hurriedly picked; and the men had eaten before dawn and at dawn had gone down into the fields.

As the Kid debated with himself whether to ask the Chinese for a late breakfast, he saw a man with a pail in his hands come out of the kiln or oast-house a little up the road, a slim, tall, youngish-looking man with a blue army shirt that draggled its ends outside his trousers.

"I'll strike him fer a meal," he decided. "I'd ruther strike him than a Chinaman, 'cause he's a hop-glomer and sorter like a hobo."

He started up the dusty road, the Gay-cat tagging after him. He approached the man with the draggling blue shirt.

The man wore no hat. His face was brown and pleasing; his eyes of a twinkling gray; and his hair black, with those little tight curls that the Greeks so loved to carve on the artistic heads of their statues. He set down the empty pail and, hands on slim hips, looked at the approaching boy and dog.

"A hobo kid!" he ejaculated. "And by the Lord Jimmy, a hobo dog! Say, kid, what manner of name do you call that strange admixture of dog you've got there—The Survival of the Unfittest?"

He looked down at the dog with the trace of a smile. The Gay-cat was sniffing his legs and cocking his round yellow head at the draggling shirt-tails.

But the Kid did not feel so familiar as that dog. He had judged the slim young man, when he had seen him far off, to be a hop-picker and therefore, by reason of his roving life from one harvest to another, more or less of a hobo. Now he felt, of a sudden, that if the man were a hop-picker, he was no ordinary hop-picker. There was something about the man's words, about the manner with which he threw back his curly head, about that odd twinkle in his gray eyes that made the Kid feel suddenly inferior, suddenly shy. Hunger was gnawing at his stomach; it was no time for bashfulness; yet the Kid felt too abashed to make his request for food.

"No," he gulped; "he's the Gay-cat, my dog. That's all. Jes' Gay-cat."

"Just Gay-cat?" There seemed displeasure in the curly-haired fellow's voice, a royal displeasure. "Well, that's sure a queer name for such a remarkable yellow dog. Really, kid, I don't think it very fine of you to give the little pup that name. It's a no-account name. It means he's not a good rodeo, but only a fake hobo. You can't be a real blown-in-the-glass stiff yourself to give your dog such a shiftless sort of name!"

The Kid was surprised and a great deal touched in his pride.

"Me not a blowed-in-the-glass stiff? Aw, bo! Aw, say now, bo!"

The tall slim young fellow smiled down at the Kid's rueful face. He smiled down at the Kid's rueful face until the Kid smiled back wanly. Thus heartened, the Kid said:

"Yer couldn't set us up to some chow, now could yer—jes' the dog and me? Me and Gay-cat, we ain't et in a long time, bo—since yisterday mornin'. I feel all holler inside. And Gay-cat, he's sniffin' and whimperin' awful. Yer couldn't stack us up to some eats, could yer, boss?"

"Can I? Kid, you've come to the right man this time! Even old Curt Haines with all his rocks couldn't do more for you than give you a feed; and he wouldn't do as much, take it from me, until you had worked and earned your chow. But come on, kid. I'll introduce you to Jim, our Chinee cookey."

He paused suddenly in striding away as if he were struck by a new idea.

"But what name will I give as yours to his Yellow Highness of the Pots and Pans?" he asked whimsically. "What's your monniker, son?"

"Kid."

"Only Kid? Huh, that's no name, that's no hobo monniker! Why don't you get a real name like 'Salt Lake Kid,' or 'Orleans Kid,' or 'Chi Kid?' Those would be monnikers, now! But no self-respecting blown-in-the-glass stiff would want to be called just plain Kid. It's no monniker at all. Why don't you take a monniker? Tell me: where did you come from anyway?"

"I used," the boy faltered, "I used to beg fer 'Frisco Red——"

"'Frisco, huh? You come from 'Frisco?"

"No-o, I——"

The Kid hesitated and looked away. There was something in the man's question that brought up a picture before the Kid's eyes. He saw the cottage up in Grass Valley and his pale little, shawled mother sitting by the window near the bush of white marguerites. She was waiting for his return, he knew, as she had waited for three weary years.

He became aware that the blue-shirted young fellow was speaking.

"I haven't forgotten the last time I was on Howard Street, or warming the benches in Portsmouth Square down in Chinatown. That's a good old town, 'Frisco. And there's a name for you, Kid. You take it. You're 'Frisco Kid from now on—get me?"

Grandly as any Edward or George ever bestowed the garter, just that grandly did the blue-shirted one give the Kid that name. And the Kid received that name humbly, thankfully—with that exaltation a broker or brewer must feel when he is given the privilege to call himself "Sir." Proudly he felt himself to be, then and forever, the 'Frisco Kid!

"Come on," said the slim young fellow. "Now for putting your legs under for a square."

With long strides he walked down the dusty road toward the farmhouse, his shirt-tails flapping over his trousers. His black curly head was thrown back and he whistled a few variegated notes. It was *Musetta's* song from "La Bohème."

The Kid as he followed with the dog, listened to those whistled notes, the notes of a tune he never had heard before; and as he listened he became possessed of a great idea. That idea rose in him like a yeast of admiration. It filled him, at last, to overflowing. He could hold it no longer.

"Say, bo," he called. "I betcha I know what your monniker is! I betcha I know who you are!"

Smiling a little at the naive tone of the boy, the man half turned his head.

"Who am I, 'Frisco Kid?"

"Yer—yer Swaggerin' Bob!"

THE man stopped. He stopped suddenly. He whirled around. A tall upstanding figure, he stood cold and still, his arms stiffly at his sides. There was something ominous in that position of his arms. The Kid did not know why that position of his arms was ominous. But he knew that the man's gray eyes were no longer twinkling. They were dark with the shock of a complete surprise and with, perhaps, a certain terror.

The man's arms were stiffly at his sides for a reason. Under the flapping shirt-tails beneath the man's belt there was a revolver. At the least strengthening of his alarm, he would reach for that revolver. But a swinging arm is never ready to reach for a gun. The man's arms were stiffly at his sides. One lift of his rigid right hand, and the revolver in his belt would be lifted. It would be the matter of an eye-wink.

Thus unconsciously prepared, slowly the man asked a question.

"Why do you say that, Kid?"

But at the change in the man the Kid had lost heart in his idea. He said lamely:

"Aw, yer fixed my name over to 'Frisco Kid, so I thought I'd fix yer name over. Swaggerin' Bob, he's a proud and reckless feller—and yer sorter proud and reckless, so I thought yer might be him. And if yer isn't him—if yer isn't him—aw, Swaggerin' Bob's a kinder proud and reckless name what 'ud seem to fit yer, somehow."

The man laughed oddly. He laughed as if a choking gag had been pulled from his mouth. Very plainly, he was relieved. But he was not altogether relieved.

"Who told you of Swaggering Bob?" he persisted.

"Aw, a friend of his."

"A friend of his?"

"Yes; Whitey-scar. A bo what we shared floppin's with last night. A big, fat stiff what carries a stick-up gun, and is horstile to everybody."

"Whitey-scar? Never met that stiff. Nor do I know your friend, Swaggering Bob, 'Frisco Kid. But if he's as proud and reckless as you say, he'd be worth knowing, I think. He's my kind, your stiff Swaggering Bob is. A fellow might find work for a stiff like him, now."

He looked down at the Kid very seriously.

"As for my name, 'Frisco Kid," he said slowly, "my name at present is 'Slim,' 'Atlanta Slim.' Don't you forget that—understand!"

"No, Slim."

But the Kid would rather have called the tall, slim young fellow, "Swaggering Bob." He felt strangely disappointed.

That disappointment gave a certain quirk of seriousness to his thoughts. As

Slim opened the creaking-hinged gate to the farmhouse, the Kid said—

"I knows I ain't proud and reckless like Swaggerin' Bob, Slim; but if yer got work to do—if yer got work to do, Slim, and is needin' help, mebbe yer could give me a job—huh, Slim?"

"A job? And you a true blown-in-the-glass stiff! What does a hobo like you want a job for, 'Frisco Kid?"

The Kid raised his deep-sunk eyes to Slim. In his deep-sunk eyes, as he looked up at Slim, there was a kind of desperation.

"I knows we'se hoboes," he said. "We'se proud as Sam Hill 'cause we'se blowed-in-the-glass stiffs. But sometimes Gay-cat and me, we don't eat. It ain't our fault, Slim; we knows how to panhandle all right; but it's 'cause the whole country is horstile, and we has no money to buy eats. Once, 'way back in York State, a Galway named Father John Bresnahan, he tole us we oughta put by some money fer a rainy day. But Gay-cat and me, we don't think nuthin' o' that till yesterday. Then all day long them hayseed bulls chase us out o' them towns, and us hungry, too. And last night when we flopped, Whitey-scar, he tole us we oughta git a road stake. 'Then,' he says, 'yer can buy yer eats any old time and them constiboools can't say a word.' So I wanta job where I can earn that road stake and——"

Slim put his arms around the boy's frail shoulder. His arm around the boy's frail shoulder, he looked down at the Kid.

"We'll go in and chow first, my 'Frisco Kid," he said gently, "and then we'll talk about earning that road stake. I'm not sure, but perhaps I have got a job for you—a job like you never thought to work at in all your life. And there's a road stake at the end of it, 'Frisco Kid—a road stake that's big and beautiful with gold!"

They entered the kitchen of the farmhouse. Said Slim with a wave of the hand to the old Chinese:

"Jim, I have here a kid who has not eaten, he says, since the revolution in China. Now I want you to throw a dozen flapjacks into that pale, frail body of his. Also, Jim, a few eggs and ham, some mush, and a baker's dozen of those hot biscuits of yours——"

The Chinese interrupted with a string of frightful oaths.

"You get no more b'eakfast out of me!" he exclaimed. "That clock, it at seven. You chowed at five. Now you want chow again. What you t'ink—make fall-guy out of me? You get every blame' down-on-luck guy on roads and shove him in fo' chow off me. I don' stand it no more!"

"You poor slangy Chinaman!" said Slim grandly. "You've been so many years shooting grub into a lot of roughnecks and bindle stiffs, you've lost all your manners and your fine Chinese sense of decency. I ask you for one meal for one starving kid all alone in a world of chill dawns and long brown roads and hungry sunsets. And you tell me that you have given too many meals to his kind. You balk at too much charity.

"Ah, Jim," sadly, "there is not too much charity in this world. There is not enough. If there was, this motherless little kid would not be a wanderer of long hard roads with only a mournful-eared cur dog for a companion. Nor would I be skulking here in the daylight as a hop-picker, when I'm not a hop-picker at all, only a man who——"

"Allight, allight, Slim," broke in the Chinese, smiling broadly as a mule and showing himself by his quick assent to be another slave of the artful Slim. "I set him up fo' you. I don't care. This nine-tenth guy I feed fo' you in t'ree days; but I don't care, Slim—so long you cut out hot-air talk!"

Slim thought that a good joke. He laughed uproariously. And he continued to laugh while the Chinese brought out plates of food for the boy and plates of food for his dog.

After a bit, he stopped laughing. He watched the Kid eat. At last, he seemed to grow weary of watching the Kid clear the plates of flapjacks, and mush, and ham and eggs, and coffee and biscuits. He stood at an uncurtained window, his back to the Kid, and stared moodily into the white morning.

"I'll do it," he muttered with a shake of his curly head. "I'll declare 'Frisco Kid in on the job."

The Kid scraped back his chair. He got up, wiping his mouth on his long sleeve.

Slim turned around. His face was gray, his voice very gentle.

"You had enough, 'Frisco Kid?"

"Sure, Slim; I'm stuffed like a turkey. But yer don't happen to have the makin's on yer, do yer, Slim? A smoke 'ud top off the meal jes' swell-like!"

The tall slim young fellow passed him the papers and tobacco. Gravely and very deftly, the Kid rolled a cigarette. The tall slim young fellow smiled a little as he watched him.

"Now, my 'Frisco Kid," he said quietly, "now we'll see about that road-stake job of yours."

SMOKING the cigarette contentedly, the Kid walked with Slim back to the kiln. On the ground floor of the huge double-towered kiln was a door like a barn door. That Slim shoved aside. They entered a half-dark place.

By the morning sunlight streaming in over his shoulder, the Kid saw that he was in a large earth-floored room. Over against one wall was a pile of cordwood as high as a table. Against the other wall, set in bricks, were two furnaces for drying the hops spread over the grating-floored loft above. A wood-fire crackled in the furnaces, reddening the iron fronts and spitting out live cinders upon the floor through air-vents near the bottoms. The place was hot and stuffy; yet as the Kid entered after Slim, a voice called sharply from within:

"Close thet door! Do youse wanta let in th' cold?"

Hastily the Kid shoved to the large rusty-wheeled door behind him—so hastily that as the Gay-cat squeezed through his tragic curl of tail was almost pinched off.

"Have a swig, Slim?" said the voice. It came from the top of the cordwood pile, where shadows bulked. "I got a pail o' beer here. Got ut down at th' Portugee's when youse went out with t'other pail an' didn't show back. Say, wot happened to youse? An' Slim, who's thet kid youse got there?"

"Just a hobo kid off the road, 'Yorky.' Bummed me for a meal—that's why I forgot all about getting that beer. But where's the beer you spoke of, Yorky?"

"Over here."

The owner of the voice sat up on top of the cordwood and showed his face. The room was shadowy dark save for the red glow cast by the furnace heads and the live coals upon the earth floor; yet even in that red furnace-light, the man's face was white, unhealthily, morbidly white.

The Kid stood near the door, the Gay-cat squatting on his haunches at his feet. Slim left the Kid. He drew close to the pile of cordwood. He looked down at the shadows in the gloom. He looked down narrowly.

Then he turned his back and walked to the opposite side of the room. Suddenly he kicked open one of the furnace doors. The room leaped vividly all at once with bright light.

Slim whirled around. He backed against the wall beside the open furnace door. He crouched against that wall. At his sides his arms were ominously stiff.

"Who the hell's the other guy here?" he cried sharply. "The new gun—what's he doing here? What's he doing so still and quiet? Yorky—why are you so tight-faced? You —— mugged gun, is this a plant to double-cross me!"

There was anger, a hot anger, in Slim's voice. In his gray eyes was more than anger. In his gray eyes was desperation. He waited. Hunched back against the wall, his arms stiffly at his sides, he waited like one trapped, at bay.

The two men on the cordwood pile were silent. It was as if they had been shocked, by his sudden fierce outburst, into that silence. Then the nearest on the cordwood pile laughed nervously. He was Yorky. He said hastily:

"Oh, there's nuthin' fer youse to git so horstile about, Slim. I'm all right. And this other gun is all right. Youse'll be glad ter meet him, Slim. Stand up, blokey, an' let Slim look youse over!"

Very soberly the other man sat up on top of the cordwood pile and, crawling over Yorky, got to his feet on the earth floor. He stepped forward a bit and faced the firelight and Slim for inspection.

He was a big heavy man with a broad red face and a great ugly white scar that ran down one cheek from the corner of the left eye, across the mouth, to the cleft in the uncompromising jaw.

"Whitey-scar!" breathed the Kid.

The man with the ugly scar faced Slim in an attitude of ease and indifference. But it was an attitude that only affected at ease and indifference. His arms were folded across his chest. The Kid knew, as he watched him, that under those folded arms was a sawed-down revolver concealed.

"I'm all right, buddie," said that man to Slim. "I'm a good gun. I'm no fingers or elbow or stool. I'm one o' the good people."

The man spoke English; yet undoubtedly he is not intelligible to you who read. You understand English to be sure, but you understand the English of the upperworld only. He spoke in the bastard English of the underworld.

The underworld has a language of its own. It is a secret language. It is a language designedly invented to keep those not of the underworld from understanding what those of the underworld mean when they speak that secret language.

A "gun" in that secret language means a criminal. "Fingers" are policemen; detectives, "elbows." "Stools" are stoolpigeons who go down into the underworld as men of that underworld and who then report the doings of the underworld to the police. They are spies of the law who, by the upperworld and the underworld, are despised and hated as betrayers of men.

The "good people" are the pick of the pickpockets, of the second-story men, of the safe-crackers. That is their own name for themselves. By "good" is meant that they make crime pay. They are the brainy, clever, daring and dangerous criminals.

The scarred man was one of the good people, self-avowed. He was one of the brainy, clever, daring and dangerous criminals.

Slim looked him over closely.

"Scar-face Mike Hagan!" he exclaimed suddenly. "Why you mugged gun, anybody's blind that wouldn't know you! I'd know your beauty mark a block. But I heard you tried to yegg a peter in Toledo and was nabbed. I heard you were in stir for ten years. And here you are—Scar-face Mike, the best peterman in the Middle West! When did you get out, Mike? I won't ask how!"

"Me?" said the other. "Oh, I got out three months ago. And I'll tell yuh this, Atlanta Slim, as they call yuh 'round here: no screw or warden shook my fin when I made my gitaway from thet stir. They could only hold me on the inside fur six months.

"And I'll tell yuh sumthin' else, Atlanta Slim. I never heard yer monniker afore; I have no quarrel with yer monniker—Atlanta Slim bein' as good as most; but I knows a name what 'ud fit yuh better'n thet. It's the name of a high-class yegg, a peterman so well knowed he don't need no white scar like me so guns will know him. But I won't say yer old monniker, Slim boy, fur there's a man badly wanted by the Burns

men fur a couple o' bank safes drilled, and by the Govamint elbows, too, fur a bunch o' post-offices what found their peters were cigar-boxes when Slim boy put the soup to 'em!"

"You may be right, Scar-face," Slim halfadmitted cautiously. "But what have you been doing since you got out?"

The man's red face went a darker hue with sudden passion. Against that dark hue, the terrible scar was death-white, ghastly.

"I've been down and out—down and out since I made my gitaway from stir! I've bin no better'n a hobo. I've bin on my hunkers, I tell yuh. I've bin wanderin' here and there, on the rods and blinds and in John O'Briens. Yes; and I've had to walk—walk the roads like a dirty bindle stiff!"

He raised his clenched hands in impotent rage.

"Oh, it's bin a hard long three months fur me—a starvin' dirty three months! No money, no drinks, no decent chow. I've bin bummin' my eats—panhandlin' like a bo fur nickels and dimes. I ain't poured one skee into me. Five-cent grease joints fur coffee and—thet's bin my limit. Park benches and city lots and haystacks fur months. Oh, I've bin on my hunkers, down and out, I tell yuh—me, Scar-face Mike Hagan thet slept in the swellest hotels in Philly and York and Chi, and at Augustin' and Del Monte when I pulled down a good clean swag! Black luck——"

"You've lost your nerve, Scar-face." Slim said quietly, as if sounding out the man.

"Me, a yegg with science, lost my nerve? What about St. Joe and Chi, Slim. Yes, and thet little burg out in lower Illinois—Simpson? Three times I tried it and three times sumthin' went wrong. But Simpson—thet was the place. I'd joined out with a feller name o' Blondy, a bo what I had picked up in a box-car goin' West. He said he did peterwork; knew most o' the swell mobs in Louie and York and Chi, too. He said the post-office in thet little one-horse town o' Simpson was good pickin's.

"We broke in one night. The place was full o' post-office elbows. That guy Blondy had coughed on me. He had got me trapped. He was a stool, —— him! But I went through the winder backward, and before I went I got *him!* I broke his head with one swack o' my gun—and he won't ferget me soon!"

As if to include every one present in what he was about to say, he turned to the listening man on the cordwood pile.

"Guns," he said, "ef ever yuh meets a lanky yaller-haired bo named o' Blondy, what says he does peterwork and knows all the good people—croak him! He's a Govamint elbow, workin' as a tramp. I hit him a good one, but I ain't satisfied none. I'm sure horstile, I tell yuh. I'd like to cook—to kill that stool!"

Slim was thoughtful.

"Never met your friend Blondy," he said seriously. "But I do know the road is thick with stools these days. A yegg's got to have nerve with all these spies pretending they're guns and leading on the real yeggs to break in peters, and then nabbing them or giving them away to the fingers. A yegg never knows, nowadays, which one of the guns who cracks a safe with him is going to betray him. Sometimes he is betrayed and is sent up for twenty or thirty years. And sometimes, Mike, he never knows who it was betrayed him!"

Slim fell thoughtfully silent. He turned away from Scar-face and looked through the open furnace door into the crackling flames. Behind him in the gloom Scar-face stood, a heavy and somber look on his face.

"Black luck!" he muttered gruffly. "Black luck I've had ever since I made my gitaway from stir. I've bin on my hunkers with black luck."

Slim whirled on him sharply.

"It's time for your luck to change! Your luck's going to change, Scar-face Mike— 'cause you're going to do a safe-cracking job with the guy called 'Atlanta Slim'!"

Scar-face Mike Hagan drew back. Startled by the suddenness of Slim's action, the suddenness of Slim's words, he drew back as a man instinctively draws back when menaced by a clenched fist. Then the meaning of Slim's words leaped into his brain. His close-set eyes brightened. His scar-cleft mouth opened like the mouth of an eager dog.

"Work to do!" he cried. "Yuh got a safe to crack! And yuh'll let me in on the deal! Slim boy, to hear yuh say thet is better'n a swig of whisky to me—me thet's bin thirstin' fur a safe to crack, like it was a woman!"

Swiftly he stepped forward. He held out his huge hand. Slim shook his hand on the partnership.

A CHANGE swept over the man's broad red face. The eager look dropped from his face like shed skin. His broad red face became engraved, of a sudden, with lines of caution. With furtive eyes, he looked past Slim at Yorky and the Kid.

With the hand that gripped Slim's hand, he made a peculiar signal. It was a signal as peculiar to the underworld as is the language of the underworld. It was a crook's signal with a certain secret meaning.

With his index finger, as his hand gripped Slim's hand, Scar-face Mike Hagan tapped the back of Slim's hand twice. That meant—

"I want to talk with you alone."

Slim's black eyebrows drew together. He was surprised at the request and a little puzzled. He swept the red-lighted shadows of the room with his gray eyes. Suddenly his brow smoothed. He laughed shortly.

"Oh, Yorky's all right, Scar-face. Don't be leary about shooting your mouth off before him. Why Yorky's a peterman as good as the best, though you can see he's still a bit pale from a recent rest-cure at Sing Sing. We're all one mob here, Scar-face."

"But the kid there?" objected Scar-face. He scowled at the little fellow, pressed back in the gloom against the door.

"Yes, him," said Yorky. "Youse is shootin' off yer mouth consid'able afore him, Slim. Me, I don't trust no kids at all. As soon as a bull gives him th' third degree, a kid will toin stool an' peach on us guns an' th' whole works, an' send us up. I'm scared o' kids, Slim. I done time enough in stir an' I knows wot ut's like. I bin in stir too much fer one man."

Slim lifted his hand for silence. He turned around and stepped nearer the Kid. Putting his hand under the Kid's chin, he tilted up the peaked pale face. Thoughtfully he looked into the deep-sunk eyes of the Kid.

"Frisco Kid," he said. "Frisco Kid that I've fed and named and taken for my chum and buddie—you wouldn't give me away to the bulls? And these guns who are my mob, you wouldn't act as stool against either of them—would you, Kid?"

"No, Slim," said the Kid in a desperate whisper.

Slim put his arms around the boy's frail shoulder. His arm around the boy's frail shoulder, he turned and faced the others proudly.

"Behold!" said he with a return of his grand manner. "Behold, you low-browed guns! Let me introduce to you the 'Frisco Kid. A walker of roads and a beggar at back doors and a talker of the hobo tongue, he was, until Slim saw him and thought him cute and pitied him, he looked so homeless and forlorn, the —— little ——"

Slim never finished. A look almost like that of bodily anguish swept his face. His arm tightened about the boy's frail shoulder.

"Guns," he began again, "Guns, I'm not kidding you. I'm telling you something. I'm telling you that this is my last job. After this job, I quit gun work for good. I'll be no thieving hiding-out yegg any longer. In this job, I'll make my stake— that fortune I hoped to earn as a merchant prince when I was a dreaming boy.

"How do I know? I've got a hunch. I've adopted 'Frisco Kid and that measly cur dog he calls the Gay-cat for mascots. With the Kid and his dog for mascots, I can't fail in this last job. One look at him and I knew he brought my luck. One look at him and I said, 'I'll take him with me to Europe on this haul, and show him all the old churches and the pleasant, sweet old lanes and all the pictures in the great picture galleries!' That's my dream, guns!" His face was frank and enthusiastic and boyish. "'Frisco Kid's one of our mob from now on. I've adopted him for my buddie!"

"Slim, d'yuh mean to say yuh declarin' thet kid in on the mob?" asked Scar-face gruffly. "D'yuh mean he's to share on this haul with the best o' us?"

Slim shook his curly head.

"No," he said. "You, Scar-face, and Yorky and I will split the haul even between us. We'll share thirds. But the Kid wants to earn a road stake. Now you guns have nothing to do with that. The Kid's my buddie. I'll give him half of my share. Whether we go to Europe or not afterward, I'll give him half of my share. That will be his road stake."

The two men woke the room with gruff mumbles of dissent. Slim's promise seemed so preposterously prodigal!

Slim regarded them not. He had another one of his ideas. As usual, it controlled him seriously and utterly. He turned once more to the Kid. Once more he put an arm around the Kid's frail shoulder.

"But my Frisco Kid," he said softly, "I haven't taken you into consideration at all. Do you want to be the buddie of a fellow like me? Do you want to stick with me through this job and go with me where I go afterward and share with me my good fortune?—Slim and the Kid, buddies together! Do you, Frisco Kid?"

The boy in the over-large coat looked up into the gray, thoughtful eyes of the man. His own eyes were serious, very serious.

"Sure, I do, Slim," he said, "if Gay-cat is buddies too!" He nodded his head. To himself he added, "Sure, I do, Swaggerin' Bob!"

FROM far off, a rumble of sound shook through the ground and slid through the interstices of the rough-board structure. The men listened. That rumble of sound thrummed heavily in their ears. They listened with pale, strained faces.

"What's thet?" asked Scar-face. "Thet don't sound like no train!"

His only immediate answer was the steady increase of that sound. It was the distance-dulled sound of mules' hoof-beats on the dust-carpeted road, the creaking of heavy wheels on axles, the cracking of long mule-skinners' whips — all the blended noises of an oncoming procession of wagons.

"Thet?" said Yorky of a sudden. "Why thet is only a bunch o' skinners comin' up with hops from Ranch Number Four."

The face of Scar-face broadened with comprehension and a vast relief. Ranch Number Four was just across the river and had no kiln of its own for drying and purifying the hops.

But Slim's eyebrows remained drawn together. It was as if he did not accept Yorky's explanation. He puzzled. He seemed, at last, to come to some conclusion of his own. He smiled. There was in his smile something of superiority and something that was sardonic.

"Listen, guns," he said. "Listen close, especially you, Mike. I'm giving you the plans!"

His back to the still open furnace he faced them in the red glow.

"It's like this: Down in the flat of the valley across the bridge, there is a little yellow shack like a railroad depot. That's the ranch office of old Curt Haines who is the whole gee in these parts. In that ranch office is the safe we're going to crack. Guns, in that safe is $30,000 in gold!"

Outside, the rumble of the teams had grown louder and nearer, as if they were toiling up the road between the farmhouse and the kiln. That rumble now thrummed through the red-lighted room like a formidable blast of wind. Scar-face raised his gruff voice:

"Thirty thousand dollars in gold! Why the harvest ain't hardly started yet! Slim, how comes all thet money round a hop-ranch at the beginnin' o' the season?"

"True words, them!" put in Yorky. "Scar-face is right, Slim, though I hadn't knowed enough ter ast about ut afore!"

Slim smiled in that superior sardonic fashion.

" 'Frisco Kid," he said quietly. "Open that door!"

With implicit obedience to Slim's command and a valiant surge of strength, the Kid shoved open the great rusty-wheeled door at his back. The white fingers of the day came in and poked into the eyes of the men. As if from the mouth of a tunnel, they looked out into the sparkling morning sunlight.

Drawn up before the door of the kiln was a two-horsed farm-wagon and behind that, down the dust-carpeted road, strung farm-wagon after two-horsed farm-wagon. Each wagon was crowded with men. They were brown men. They were brown men, long and starveling of limb, with heads wrapped in red and yellow and white turbans.

Yorky cried out. He cried out in a great voice—

"Th' ragheads!"

"Now do you understand?" said Slim. It's the ragheads, all right—a whole army of Hindoo laborers. Old man Haines has imported them to finish harvesting his crops!"

"But th' whites? Youse mean, Slim, thet Haines is goin' ter toin out all th' whites?"

"Sure, Yorky—turn out all the whites! Whites are not like these niggers. Whites don't do whatever they're told to do and

for whatever money Haines sees fit to give them. Whites quit when they —— please."

Scar-face stepped closer to Slim.

"Thet thirty thousand dollars in gold is fur payin' the whites off—huh, Slim boy?"

"There's a gun with brains!" said Slim admiringly. "That's it, Mike! But that thirty thousand dollars is not only for this ranch—those hop-picking bums get only a buck and a quarter a day, above their chow. This money is also for Ranch Number Four across the river, and for all the Haines ranches that border this river right down the valley—Ranches Three, Two and One.

"At each ranch to-day, while the whites work all unaware in the hop-valleys, there is arriving quietly just such a train of niggers as that outside. Tomorrow morning the field bosses of each ranch will drive over to that yellow shack down in town, receive a pile of twenties and fives, and at noon pay off and discharge all the whites!"

"But them whites will raise ructions, Slim," objected Yorky. "They'll raise ol' Cain if they're put out fer a parcel o' ragheads. I knows I would."

Even as Yorky spoke, Slim's face lighted up. Once again he was possessed by a new and brilliant idea.

"Guns, I've got it!" he fairly shouted. "We won't wait for the whites to learn the truth tomorrow. We'll whisper about the ragheads in their ears today. That'll get them. They're just big kids, roughnecks. They'll want revenge. It'll be just as Yorky says. They won't think of the money due them—what's a measly half-month's pay to a bunch of hop-picking hoboes when they're ousted by these niggers!

"They're roughnecks, I tell you, boys; natural Reds. They'll see red now. It'll be worse than a strike, worse than any lockout. All they'll want is revenge—revenge on Haines, revenge for his selfishness, arrogance and wealth!"

Slim stepped, in his vehemence, closer to Scar-face.

"We'll help them get that revenge! We'll distribute a little of our nitro among them. We'll start the fireworks! We'll start the fireworks so quick the most cool-headed pickers can't turn back. There'll be ructions tonight, Yorky! Under cover of it all, tonight, we'll crack that safe!"

"Tonight?" Scar-face seemed taken

aback. "Slim boy, yuh don't mean to knock off thet peter tonight!"

"Sure, tonight! Tomorrow the men are fired and paid off. Where's the gold in that peter, then? Tonight's the only time!"

"Yes; I guess so," said Scar-face surlily. "But I didn't expect to be rushed so. I was figurin' on a couple o' nights to—well, say, to prepare sorter."

He seemed inwardly perturbed by the fact that the safe was to be broken open in so short a time. Slim regarded him curiously.

"Scar-face Mike Hagan," he said, "do you want to come in on this peter job?"

The man's surly mood sloughed from him. Against the quick reddening of his broad heavy face, his white scar grew whiter and uglier.

"Do I, Slim boy!" he shouted. He leaped forward. He shoved his red face close to Slim's. "Am I bughouse! Thirty thousand dollars in gold, and me with my black luck! Do I? Sure I wanter git in on this job!"

He shoved his huge hand forward. On the compact, there with the white fingers of the day sparkling upon him, he shook Slim's hand.

THAT night a high fog slid over the mountain-tops to the west and sheeted, as with a monstrous gray blanket, the whole valley with its green treasure of hops. The new moon that had elbowed up, round and yellow, among the crowd of stars, was blotted out. The night fell cold and thick and black.

On the edge of the dark tent-colony on the side of valley, two men and a boy and a dog lay on blankets inside of a tepee tent. There was no light in that tent; it was as dark as the tents about and the night above; yet neither men nor boys nor dogs slept. In subdued and guarded voices, the two men were talking together.

"Thet's good work, Slim," one was saying. "But ef they boins th' hops on this side o' th' river, how are we a-goin' ter git down to the shack? Me, I don't trust them hop-pickin' bums."

"Do you think they're crazy? Their tents are up here. Well, do you think they'll burn the hops on this side of the river and take chances of the fire cleaning out their tents? Not them, Yorky! They'll burn the hops on the other side of the river, but on this side they'll only tear down the vines and trample upon the pods. There'll be no flames licking across the road when we go down!"

"But th' town? Youse gave 'em some o' th' soup, Slim. Wot ef they shoots sky-high thet little shack an' thet peter with all th' gold?"

Slim rolled over to face Yorky in the dark.

"I left that all to Scar-face," he said. "Mike was afraid of just what you suggest—that they might fire the office and the safe by mistake. He said he'd stay behind until the soup was planted under every building but that shack. I was against Scar-face staying behind. I don't know whether he'll be back in time. If the mob gets separated like this, we may not be able to pull off the job!"

There was that in Slim's voice which disturbed Yorky.

"Ain't there sumthin' else, Slim?"

Slim sat up restlessly.

"Well, I'll tell you, Yorky—there is! I'm running this mob; not Scar-face. But what I say doesn't go at all with Scar-face. You saw him when I said we'd crack that safe tonight—it was the same about him staying behind in that town! I was opposed to him staying. But he has stayed, hasn't he?"

"Aw, wot's eatin' youse, Slim!"

"Just this: Scar-face Mike Hagan has something up his sleeve. What it is, I don't know. But I tell you, Yorky, I'm afraid of Scar-face!"

"Youse mean, Slim——"

"That Scar-face Mike Hagan is a stool!"

There was a strained and breathless stillness. Then Yorky laughed nervously.

"Aw, youse is too imagin'ry a guy, Slim," he faltered. "Scar-face, he's a gun—a mugged gun, too. Youse is allus imaginin' things, Slim."

Slim drew a deep breath.

"I hope you're right, Yorky!" he exclaimed earnestly. "That's sure a hard name for such a mugged gun as Scar-face. But I'm afraid of him, I tell you. I'm taking no chances. I've fixed his gun!"

"His gun! Why, Slim, I allus thought he packed his gun on him."

"He did, Yorky, till we went down into that town in our shirt-sleeves so we'd look like the hop-glomers. He left his vest behind. That vest was all padded in front, and between the pads was his gun in a cloth sling. I drew out all the shells."

"But wot ef he gives us away afore we cracks thet peter, Slim?"

Slim's voice showed irritation.

"You don't get him at all, Yorky. He's playing a deep game, that Scar-face. And —— it! What stool is going to come out and betray us before we do the job, when by staying under cover, he can crack the peter with us and then escape while we get nabbed? We get nabbed red-handed, and then we never know it was he gave us away to the fingers. We never try to fix him for it."

"Thet may be his game, all right, Slim. But wot ef he's jerry thet we'se wise ter his game—thet we knows he's a stool? Wot ef he don't come back, Slim?"

"Oh, he'll come back, never fear. Why, he's leary that we may back out of this job altogether. That's why he's helping out now with these hop-glomers — firing the town and the crop across the river. He'll come back just to sic us on to that peter. I know his kind. He's after the rewards offered for me, Yorky. He may have followed me clean West!

"I tell you, Yorky, this helping out in the destruction is all a cloak—a mere blind to hide his hand, to give us nerve. He wants us to go on under cover of the destruction; he wants us to crack that safe. When we're right on the job, when he's sure he's got the goods on us, then, Yorky—then he'll nab us!"

There in the blackness a cold damp beaded Yorky's pasty, white face. He wet his lips.

"Slim—" he gulped— "Slim, I'm scared. I'm losin' my noive. I done time enough in stir. I bin in stir too much fer one man. Wot d'ye say, Slim? Can't we—can't we pass up this job?"

Slim laughed shortly.

"Not Slim, Yorky! This is my last job. There's that thirty thousand dollars in gold! There's the pictures in the big picture galleries and the Kid and the dog and I——"

He broke off huskily. With sudden desperation, he bit out:

"I'll tell you what we'll do! We'll watch him. He'll be easy. He's not even heeled. We'll make him pack the soup. We'll make him do the drilling—get the gold for us. We'll watch him. If he tries any funny work, we'll——"

 A SUDDEN blast of sound drowned Slim's threat. It was a tremendous blast of sound as of dynamite shot off under pressure. It rocked through the ground. From wall to wall of the valley, it boomed.

A bright red light flooded the tent. That bright red light showed out the big, heavy form of Scar-face, crawling on hands and knees under the flap at the rear of the tent.

"Down, guns!" He threw himself, panting, on the blankets. "Thet's the nickelodeon—the start o' the fireworks. Git down, will yuh! Yuh can see right through the tent, yuh simps!"

Within the confines of the tent, the men lay flat on the blankets and close together, like little children huddling from some terror.

Scar-face was breathing heavily, quickly. With each of his breaths came a resounding boom from the flat of the valley below. Those booms came continually. The men counted like a death-watch. They counted ten.

Scar-face laughed harshly:

"The drunken fools! They've gone crazy! They're runnin' amuck with them nitro' sticks! The whisky did the work."

"Whisky!" Slim sat up. "Scar-face, you don't mean——"

"Sure I do! The skee got 'em! I knowed it would. As soon as I broke in thet saloon door, yuh oughta see them stiffs make fur them bottles! Thet was my cue. I faded. I ran some up this walley, I tell yuh. But the skee did the work. They're wild as fire!"

Slim shoved an oilcloth-wrapped bundle toward Scar-face.

"Here's the kit. Everything's in it—the bottle of soup, the rods and the electric flash. Grab your coat and vest, Mike. We gotta act. That whisky may prove too strong. If we don't act quickly now, there may be no shack, no golden peter for us to crack. Come on, guns!"

A rolled-up blanket under his arm, Slim crawled silently out under the flap at the rear of the tent. As similarly burdened and as silently, the others followed. The Kid, the dog under his arm, was the last to belly out. He blinked in the red leaping glare that fired earth and sky.

Below in the valley where the huddle of shanties of Haines Depot had stood, were many immense black holes. About those holes was strewn shapeless farflung wreckage in which fires burned fitfully. But that red glare came from farther away. That red glare came from the hop-fields beyond the river. Running along and dancing upon and leaping up from the thousand high wires to which the hops had been strung, were a thousand-thousand flames.

It was as if the whole world were afire. The heat of those flames had dissipated that gray blanket of fog. They had reddened the moon. The very river was a river of blood.

"They've fired the hops!" breathed Slim. "The drunken glomers!"

"But the office is safe and all the gold!" shouted Scar-face. "Yuh can see the yaller paint on its sides. And the winder, guns! The shock o' them blasts has shattered the winder fur us. It'll be a cinch to git into thet office!"

On the outskirts of the flames, men were rushing about and reeling drunkenly. They looked like little black cinders spit from those flames.

"Go on!" cried out Slim, brandishing his clenched hand in the air. "Wreck things and burn things, you drunken overgrown kids!" He swung on the others. "Come on! We're men. We've got work to do!"

AMID all that glare and hullaballoo and havoc, the little yellow shack seemed quietly asleep. The men threw down their blankets in the field of grass and weeds and thistles and clustered together, stooping, furtive shadows.

Scar-face eyed the Kid.

"Come here, Kid," he said suddenly. "You go and hammer on thet door, while us three go through thet winder!"

"No, you don't, Scar-face!" said Slim quietly. "The Kid stays out of the whole thing. He's not to get nabbed if we are. He stays out here and plays the lookout——"

"Lookout? We don't need no lookout!"

The words were significant.

"—— youse, Scar-face!" cried Yorky, "Slim's runnin' this mob! Wot he says goes!"

Scar-face grunted surlily:

"What's the plan, then?"

"This," said Slim. "Scar-face and you, Yorky, go round to that front door. Bang against that door. While the racket is on, I'll go through that window!"

He turned to the Kid.

" 'Frisco Kid, you wait in this field near the road. Lie down in the weeds so you can't be seen—so any shots will go over your head. If any one comes, yell to me!"

The Kid, the dog under his arm, walked back toward the road.

Scar-face and Yorky were upon the front porch of the shack. They hurled their combined weight against the door. The door shook and groaned, but held firmly.

"Clear out of here!" yelled a voice from within the shack. "Clear out or we'll drill you, you drunken bums!"

The two men simulated the drunken hoppickers they were supposed to be. They shouted and cheered and jeered.

"Thet youse, Curt Haines!" Yorky jeered. "Guardin' th' money ter pay us off termorrow—huh?"

From within the shack a shot cracked out. It shattered through an upper panel of the door. That panel was above the men's heads. But they scattered to either side. Yorky ran far back on the gravel sweep.

Slim dashed forward at that shot. He dashed through the field toward the window. The window was four feet above the field. He took that window feet first. Feet first he crashed through sash and fragments of glass.

Yorky, out on the gravel sweep before the shack, saw him disappear. He ran back toward the porch, calling in subdued but excited tones:

"Scar-face! Slim's got in!"

A cry shrilled out from the shack. It was a cry of surprise, a cry of warning. It broke off in a dull sound. A pistol cracked. Then the hand that pumped that pistol seemed to be held in a terrific struggle. Furniture was scraped about, was overthrown, was rended apart with groaning noises.

The men on the porch forgot to assail the door. They listened. They sweated.

Again the pistol cracked. A resounding thump came from one wall of the shack. It was as though some heavy weight had been hurled against that wall. The shack shook to its very mudsills. There came a scream— a man's scream—a scream as of pain unendurable. It was hideous.

"Slim!" yelled Yorky. "They've broke Slim!"

With one savage kick, he splintered the door into halves. He went through, revolver in hand. After him followed Scar-face.

Outside in the weeds, the Kid waited. The dog was under his left arm. His heart pounded against that dog. Then he heard a panting voice, Slim's voice:

"Come—on in. I—fixed—those two guys. Flash the—light."

Behind the shattered window, a single shaft of white light bored through the blackness within the shack. It came from the flash-lamp in the hands of Scar-face. It was turned full upon Slim.

Slim had been through a hideous fight. His blue army shirt had been torn completely off his back. One torn sleeve draggled from his left wrist. From the waist up his body glistened white in that light, save where it was dirtied by powder smoke and streaked with bloody welts and scratches. His head was bleeding. As the Kid glimpsed him, he tore off the sleeve from his wrist. He wrapped the sleeve about his bleeding head.

"Gee!" muttered the Kid to the dog. "What a proud and reckless feller—that Slim!"

Yorky straightened up behind the window.

"Where's ol' Curt Haines? Didn't I hear he allus guarded his coin hisself afore pay-day? Slim, he didn't slip youse?"

"No, Yorky; he wasn't in here at all. There were only the two guards."

"Thet's all right," said Scar-face suddenly. "Now where's the peter?"

Slim took the electric torch from his hand and flashed it toward the rear of the office. There stood the huge safe. Stumbling over the broken furniture and the unconscious forms on the floor, the men followed Slim toward that safe. Slim knelt down and by the single shaft of light examined closely the door of that safe.

"Let's get to work. We can shoot it in no time. Here, Scar-face. You do the drilling."

"Me?" Scar-face was startled.

But he knelt down beside Slim. Followed the sounds of low directions, low orders; then the grind of drill on steel.

The Kid stood up stiffly in the thicket of weeds near the road. Like a little nervous bird, he cocked his head now to the right, now to the left.

The red glare was dying out of the sky. The fire in the hop-fields far away was

14

lessening for lack of fuel. The wreckage of Haines Depot was only scattered and smoking heaps. Overhead where the blanket of fog had been, was now a slowly thickening blanket of smoke. The night was even blacker than before.

From the little yellow shack came a sudden outburst of voices:

"Hurry up, Scar-face! Rush it, man! Don't take all night on a tin can like that!"

"Shet up, will yuh! Yuh git me all rattled. Where's thet rod?"

The Kid could see neither Slim nor Scar-face. The sill of the window obstructed his vision. But he could see the shadowy form of Yorky bent over the kneeling men with tense watchfulness.

Suddenly Yorky straightened up. He said disgustedly:

"Yer too slow, Scar-face! Me, I thought youse was a yegg!"

"I can't work faster, I tell yuh! These drills are sumthin' fierce. Give me anuther iron!"

"That iron is all right, Scar-face!" cried Slim sharply. "——you, you're stalling!"

Yorky broke in nervously:

"Aw, let's hurry, Slim! Slim, youse open ut!"

"Out of my way!" from Slim.

There came the slight scuffling of feet. Then again the chill grind of steel on steel.

The Kid listened excitedly. To the dog under his arm he breathed in excited little gasps:

"Slim's crackin' her now! Scar-face is too slow. It'll be a cinch fer Slim!"

Suddenly Slim said:

"Where's the soup?"

Just then, the dog that had hung drooping and forgotten under the Kid's left arm came to sudden life. He broke out barking. It was startlingly abrupt. The Kid had heard no one approaching. It was so startlingly abrupt that the Kid dropped the dog in his first panic of fear. The dog ran toward the road. He barked loudly. He barked excitedly.

"Gay-cat! Gay-cat!" cried the Kid. He ran through the weeds after the dog. "Yer'll give us away! Yer'll give Slim away!"

From the shack came oaths and the quick scraping of feet. Said Slim sharply:

"Douse the light! That dog heard something. Yorky, you see who's coming!"

The little shack went black. Some one said:

"I'll go, Slim."

Then the big heavy form of Scar-face appeared through the shattered door. He stepped to the edge of the porch. He peered down the road toward the bridge. Then he stepped back to the door, and listened.

"I'll shoot it anyway!" Slim was saying. "It's all ready but for the blankets. It's my last job. I'll shoot it anyway. Flash on the light, Scar-face!"

"Scar-face took th' torch. He went out——"

"Scar-face? Scar-face took the torch?" Slim's voice shook. "Yorky! He took that torch to signal them! My God!"

A chair crashed over. Yorky screamed out. He screamed out horridly:

"I'll cook—I'll kill thet stool!"

Scar-face at the door raised one hand above his head. In that hand the electric flash-lamp flared. It flared once. A single shaft of white light cleft the blackness. In that black night it was a stark signal.

Yorky leaped through the door. Scar-face jumped from the porch. He dashed straight into the field of weeds. A revolver glinted in Yorky's hand. He raised it, pointed it at the fleeing stool.

The night was loud with a fearful sound. That sound was the pounding of many racing feet. It came from the road. It was near.

With a crash, the revolver dropped from Yorky's hand. He stood swaying on bending knees. He tried to cry out, but he could not cry out. Words struggled in his throat. At last, in a terrible whisper:

"We're trapped, Slim! They're comin'. It's a plant. They've got us! And—I couldn't git thet stool! I lost my noive. I couldn't shoot! I bin too much in stir. And now—they've got me agin! They've got me agin!"

The last was a shriek. With that shriek, Yorky plunged from the porch into the field of weeds.

THE Kid reached the road. He was chasing the barking dog. Coming toward him along the road were the black crowded shapes of men. They carried rifles. Their heads were wrapped in turbans. The Kid leaped back into the field. He ran toward the shack.

"Slim!" he shouted. "They's comin'! The ragheads is comin'!"

A tremendous blast of sound answered him from the shack. It was Slim's last job. In face of everything, Slim had cracked the safe!

Slim was at the door. He walked out into the arms of the ragheads. They closed about him like rats about a bit of food.

A big, heavy form bulked up in the weeds before the racing Kid. It was Scar-face Mike Hagan. As the Kid ran by toward Slim, Scar-face reached out and got the Kid by his overlarge coat. He pulled the Kid back and threw him flat in the weeds.

"They's got Slim!" sobbed the Kid. "The ragheads has got Slim. Slim, he's my buddie. Lemme go to Slim!"

Scar-face put a big hand on each of the boy's frail shoulders. By each of the boy's frail shoulders he held the boy down as in a crushing, terrible machine.

"They've got Slim all right," he said. "But yuh can't go to Slim. They'd nab yuh, too. They'd put yuh in a black hole on bread and water. They'd put yuh there fur life! But I held yuh back. I held yuh back 'cause I didn't want yuh nabbed. I saved yuh!"

But there was in the Kid's soul no answering thrill of gratefulness. His frail shoulders ached under Scar-face's hands. He felt only fear of Scar-face.

"Kid," said Scar-face, "now I'll show yuh how to earn some money. I'll show yuh how to earn thet road stake yuh want so bad!"

He shoved his scarred face closer to the Kid.

"Yuh'll come with me. When Slim's trial comes off, yuh'll git on the witness-stand and tell all yuh knows about Slim. I can't come out in the open and tell on Slim myself. And I knows a lot about Slim; I've follered him fur months! Yes, Kid; I've tracked Slim boy right acrost from thet peter job in the First National in Hartford!

"I don't care about Haines. There'll be only a measly hand-out o' a reward fur Slim in this case. I knowed thet. Thet's why I didn't bother none to save Haines' crop er town. He never knowed all what was comin'—Haines. I jest threw a note, tied to a stick o' wood, through thet winder where ol' Haines was settin' there in the dark, a-guardin' his money. Thet was the time Slim boy thought I was breakin' in the saloon. But thet note, it said only thet some one was goin' to crack his safe, and to watch out and nab him when I flashed the light!"

The Kid listened and, as he listened, he forgot the ache in his crushed shoulders. He lay flat in the weeds and saw only that white-scarred face above him. He was shocked by what that white-scarred face now meant to him. At last, he understood who Scar-face was.

Scar-face Mike Hagan was not one of the good people. He was a professional stool-pigeon. He faked that he was a yegg and betrayed men to get the reward on their heads. And he was telling the Kid to be a stool, also—a stool on Slim!

"Yuh tell all yuh knows about Slim, Kid," he was saying, "all what I said up there in the kiln about them bank safes drilled and post-office peters cracked. Them's the rewards we're after, Kid! And it's all straight goods, too. I knows, I tell yuh. I ain't follered Slim fur months, clear acrost the States, fur nuthin'. I knows a heap about Slim boy!

"But I can't come out in the open and tell all what I knows. I wish I could tell on Slim myself! I ain't skeered o' these yeggs; it's not thet, Kid; they'll go up, sure! It's the other yeggs. I got to work under cover o' bein' a yegg, and I got a lot more work to do. I can't git mixed up in this at all. My life ain't worth a beer ef the other yeggs knows I'm a stool!

"They'd never touch you, though. You're a kid—only a kid. Slim wouldn't let 'em touch yuh. And, Kid, there's a heap o' kale offered fur Slim boy! You and I'll divide the money. But yuh won't have to wait fur yer half, Kid. See—here's a hundred dollars!"

He held up a roll of bills before the boy's eyes.

"A hundred dollars!" he repeated hoarsely. "Yer road stake, Kid! Jest promise me yuh'll tell on Slim!"

From the gravel sweep before the shack came gruff commands in a voice that sounded like the voice of Haines. Then came sounds of marching feet, of men passing back along the road. The ragheads were taking Slim right by that tangle of thistles where the Kid lay.

The Kid lifted up his voice. It was his answer to Scar-face. He lifted up his voice so that the man passing on the road might hear.

"Slim! Slim!" he yelled. "Scar-face is the one that done yer! Scar-face! He's the stool!"

Scar-face leaped afoot. He made a sudden vicious movement toward his vest. He tore out his revolver. The Kid tried to squirm away through the weeds. Scar-face held him flat with one foot on his chest. He pressed the trigger. There was a soundless eternity. He pressed that trigger until his finger was white.

With an oath, he threw the harmless revolver away. He removed his foot from the Kid's chest. He kicked the boy. He kicked the boy until the boy could no longer feel those brutal kicks.

Then he spit into his hand. He spit many times into his hand. He rubbed that moistened hand on the cheek where was that scar. He rubbed and rubbed at that scar. When he drew his hand away from that flaming red cheek, there was no longer a hideous white streak of scar. He had rubbed off the paint of that faked-up mark.

He looked down at the bruised, unconscious form of the boy.

"Now try to cough on Scar-face to Slim!" he said. And he turned and strode away through the weeds.

IT was gray empty dawn when the Kid awoke to the world's sorrow. A warm tongue was moist on his cheek. A whimper sounded in his ears, fear-filled and forlorn. It was the Gay-cat. The dog was whimpering miserably at his lack of life. The dog was licking his face frenziedly. He scooped up the dog into his arms.

"We'se lost Slim, Gay-cat," he said sorrowfully. "But that's no fault of your'n, old hobo. Didn't yer hear them ragheads first? Yer smelled them a mile! Yer sure some watchdog, Gay-cat!"

After a time, the Kid got painfully to his feet. Along the road, away from the wrecked town, he walked, limping at every step like a little broken old man.

Ahead near the blackened hop-fields stood the little tool-house of a jail—too tiny and too useless, perhaps, to be burned or dynamited. But in this dawn a certain use had been found for that little tool-house of a jail. On either side of that barred door, two ragheads squatted, their rifles across their knees.

The Kid forgot his painful bruises. His heart leaped with a great gladness. He ran toward the little jail.

"Slim!" he called. "Slim, it's me!"

The two Hindoos watched him wonderingly. He got on tiptoes and looked through the barred opening in the door.

Within, in that dark and foul-smelling hole, there was the sound of a man stirring. Then there was the sound of Slim's glorious voice—

"Is that you, 'Frisco Kid?"

"Sure, it's 'Frisco Kid, Slim. And Slim—Gay-cat's here, too!"

Slim appeared behind the bars. The Kid saw the manacles on his wrists. He went serious. What a fall had come to his proud and reckless Slim! He went terribly serious.

"He wanted me to tell on yer!" he gulped. "He said he'd give me half the reward——"

"Half the reward?"

"Yes, Slim, fer a road stake. All of a hundred dollars!"

"A hundred dollars? A hundred dollars for me, Atlanta Slim! Oh, the dirty, thieving——"

Slim broke off. He said quietly:

"That would be a lot of money to you, 'Frisco Kid. A hundred dollars would be some road stake, now. But you wouldn't—huh, Kid?"

"Aw, Slim! Aw, say now, Slim!"

Slim breathed hard. His voice when he next spoke was labored:

"My little buddie! I was going to take you with me and show you all the beautiful pictures in the great picture-galleries. I can't do that now; but I can do something else. They haven't frisked me yet, Kid. That's how I happen to have that road stake I promised you!"

He fumbled with one manacled hand in his trousers pocket.

"It's not much—only an ace spot. But it's from Slim who loved you and your little yellow dog. I may never see you again; but this may help you over the road that is hard and long and lonely. Take it, my 'Frisco Kid. Good-by!"

Slim reached his hands out from the dark. There was something in one of those manacled hands. It was a dollar bill.

The Kid could not see that bill. His eyes were blinded with tears. He felt that bill in his hand. With his hand, the bill between, he held on to Slim's hand.

"Good-by, Slim! And Gay-cat—he says good-by too, Slim!"

Blind with tears, hugging the dog and that bill convulsively, the Kid turned away and stumbled up the road—the road down which he had come the dawn before.

Slim peered through the grating after him. Softly he said:

"Yorky ran away! Scar-face turned Judas! But he came back to me—the little hobo kid and his little yellow dog!"

Up on the side of the valley the Kid looked back. There was in his deep-sunk and dewy eyes a wonderful light of triumph.

"No, I couldn't tell on Slim," he said. "Not fer no money. Slim, he was good to me!"

The CAMP-FIRE
A MEETING PLACE for READERS, WRITERS & ADVENTURERS.

WHEN he sent us "The Law in Little Egypt," Hapsburg Liebe sent us this:

There are localities in these hills here that remind one of the old bad West, and more than one of them bears the picturesque name of "Hell." In one of these places a certain man set himself up as the Law, and he had to kill some six or eight men, and then get shot in the back himself—and this is where I got my story. Little Egypt is a real place, but it is not a hell. The aversion the hill-folk have for negroes is interesting. A friend of mine, Tom H——, a drummer, was crossing the mountains with a negro driver, when he was accosted by half a dozen hillmen:

"Hi, friend! Whar'd ye git him?"

Tom H—— realized that his driver was in danger. Quickly he replied: "I'm the sheriff of Washington County, boys, and I'm taking him to jail."

"What did he do?" asked the hillmen; and Tom replied: "Oh, he stole a shote."

"He did!" said the hillmen. "Well, we'll jest hang him for ye, sheriff!" And it was only by the timely intervention of an old mountaineer who had a level head that the driver was saved.

HERE'S a man's letter from General Cliff Sands. Many of you remember the expedition which was prevented from sailing. Also a later venture of a different nature, to which he refers below. I wish to say that, while I felt there was no need of my acting as intermediary, and that printing his letter for you of the Camp-Fire would accomplish his purpose, the formal, signed notes accompanied his letter, and were returned by me to him. I think no one can question his good faith, since he's going far out of his way to meet obligations he could easily avoid and which a less square man might not consider obligations at all. The eight men in question can communicate with General Sands direct.

According to my list there are still eight men who have not yet received reimbursement for money invested in the expedition which failed when I was shot at Bluefields, Nicaragua. Although my being wounded caused my defeat, it is my code that a leader who fails should shoulder the loss, and so have paid all I could out of my own pocket.

I have been unable to get in communication with these remaining eight, and so am forwarding you notes to secure them against loss. These notes are made out for the full sum invested, payable in two years at ten per cent. interest. In those two years these men should all be found.

I have been brought to the verge of bankruptcy and am deeply in debt, but Dr. Dent's operations were successful, and he succeeded in saving both my hands and arms. With the help of leather encasings, I am now able to work with both arms.

Although most of my property is going, by my being unable to meet the mortgage, I am hanging on to one small business which will, in two years, easily pay off the remaining debts of the expedition investors.

I am sending you the notes to hold in trust for the men so, should anything happen to me, they will not lose anything invested.

Ask them to send you their names and receipts from the bank (to prove they are the ones who invested), and fill in their names. At the end of two years I will visit you and check over the list and pay off the notes. Some of the boys have refused to allow me to stand the loss, as you know, but, Mr. Hoffman, I care too much for my men to let them lose anything. I felt happy in giving my blood in trying to win success for them, and feel just as happy in working hard to pay off the last one, so please insist for me that they send in their names.

I hope you will be so kind as to act as the middleman and help us get together.—CLIFF SANDS, Sequim, Wash.

A LETTER, dated March 14th, from one of our number "somewhere in France," from whom we have heard before:

Have been on the move during the past month, and am now in what, I think, is the most Godforsaken part of France. It has been continual rain, snow and mud for some weeks, but the last two days there have been sunshine and signs of Spring. You can understand signs of Spring are now more significant than usual.

I expect to be on the move again this week, and am not sorry, as I think I have the worst quarters now I have had since I left the firing-line. If I am in a decent town any time soon, I will try and send you some little souvenir, if it is only a picture postcard or two. I feel quite proud of having been put on the roll of the Red Heads, but, I doubt if I will ever see another campaign, if I see the end of this one, as I was over a year old when the French and

Germans had their last little disagreement, and it does not look to me as if this business would soon be finished. I don't mind your using any part of my letters you find interesting, though I find it difficult to write an interesting letter and still not use anything the censor might object to.

Early yesterday morning one of our gunners made a good shot and the result was that two of the "opposition," who wanted a look at us, got a much closer view than they wanted. Luckily for them, their fall was not too fast for their necks. They got off with a few cuts and bruises, and the loss of liberty, if they had had any. Naturally enough, they looked somewhat worried, as they had probably been told some weird stories about how the British use prisoners.

I don't see much these days, except the planes coming and going, with often little clouds of smoke in their wake, where the shrapnel has burst. That, with the intermittent fire of guns of all sizes, morning, noon and night, day after day, month after month, with an occasional aeroplane bomb dropped once in a while, makes up the most of what I see and hear at two or three miles from the front line. And if I saw or heard anything more interesting I could not write about it, so there you are.—D. HENDRY.

D. L. MacKAYE, following our custom, with his first story in this magazine, tells us about himself and Hawaii. If I may "butt in," I'd like to take off my hat to Mr. MacKaye's philosophy, and to the Hawaiian Citizen Guard.

I have occupied a humble seat at the Camp-Fire, unobserved for some years, and I just hate to get up and show my ignorance. You know there is a whole lot in the way you look at adventure. I see most of the chaps at the Camp-Fire take it for granted that an adventure is something with a hazard of life. I think life itself is something of an adventure if one goes through with it with an observant eye, an open mind, and a bit of reverence. Anyway, I'm that kind of hero. No one ever fired even a cap-pistol at me. I was a newspaper reporter for six years, and executive officer of the territorial anti-tuberculosis campaign for the past two—I still am. Nothing happened to me in either of them, but the boys I met were mostly the Camp-Fire kind. I got my adventures vicariously.

I AM in my second enlistment as a non-commissioned officer in the line of the Hawaiian Guard. You know Honolulu is the largest garrison town in the United States, and my chums are—and have been—regular Army men. Honolulu as a whole, I imagine, knows the Army better than the rest of the country, more's the pity (and I refer to the country, of course). This is my seventh year in Hawaii. I was born across the bridge from you people, in Brooklyn.

I KNOW you'll be interested in the following data. Hawaii has a population of 224,000 (of which 90,000 are ineligible Japanese), and maintains an active and efficient citizen guard of 5,000 fully equipped men in addition to which coast defense troops will be organized about the time this reaches you. The guard is divided about as follows: Infantry, 4 regiments; cavalry, a troop; engineers, a company; machine-gun companies, 2; signal troops, hospital and medical corps with field ambulances. The first brunt of a Pacific war would fall on Hawaii, which will do its share if the pacifists back home can be pickled in time to let the rest of the country help us out. *Adventure* has certainly done its share.

REMEMBER the *mozo* one of our number sent across Mexico to bring back photographic evidence of just what, if anything, the Japs are doing at Turtle Bay?

Here's a letter from the sender, dated March 25, written in Sonora:

I do not think that I will return to Mexico again unless as a soldier. I can't see any sense in my doing so, until all the country is at peace. The situation here is exceedingly bad. All of Mexico is laughing, offering a passive resistance, and aiding Villa. It will take at the very least 200,000 troops to capture him, and at least thirty years before we can even have a semblance of peace here. The Mexican for the most part is willing, but the small part is what causes the trouble. My man returned from the "other side" a few days ago with no camera, no news, but with a tale of robbery. I guess he is like many another person, and was afraid. *Quien sabe?*

FROM a hospital back of the firing-line, from an old friend of the Camp-Fire:

I have had an awful lot of correspondence, some of which I have been able to answer, others, beyond sending a card of acknowledgment, I haven't. You might tell them from me that I thoroughly appreciate their kindness and good wishes, but time, of which John Bull only allows us a limited quantity, does not permit. If they are sports, they will accept the excuse. (A lame one, I know.) . . . Am in here a bit broke up, but feeling O. K. Will soon be in the running again.—HARRY C. WINTERS, No. 2 Casino Hospital, Somewhere in France.

WE HAVE here an honest gentleman, an adventure, a safe treasure, a missing owner, the echo of war, a mystery—enough to make a fiction story improbable. Yet it is not fiction. At least the letter lies before me, and personally I doubt no least word of it. I hope this printed copy of it reaches the man whose money awaits him.

There is a man for whom I've been looking for eighteen years. The worst of it is, I do not clearly know his name. It was a Scotch name, not Mac-Pherson, but something like it. He commanded a rifle regiment, mounted, in Gomez's Army. One morning in January, 1898, I was coming into the camp with my command, when I met him running out with his command, starting on a raid. He stopped and asked me to go to the house where he had slept and get his money-belt and keep it until he came back.

He never came back. The Spanish got a column between him and us, and we thought he was lost, but, after weeks, we found he had ridden down the length of the island and was with Garcia. When the Americans came and captured Santiago he went home to the States. I had his money. Three times when I have been in New York I have advertised in the paper to find him. I invested his money after waiting a while, and it has done well. I hold it in trust for him.

If your "Lost Trails" can find him with this little information, I shall be very glad to turn the money over to him.

I am just now taking the train for Chicago, and a letter to Fort Dearborn Hotel will reach me there at any time during the next month. Later than that you can reach me at the Queen's Hotel in Toronto.

With very great respect, I am,
Very truly yours,
ALBERTO FUENTES Y BETANCOURT,
Queen's Hotel, Toronto, Canada.

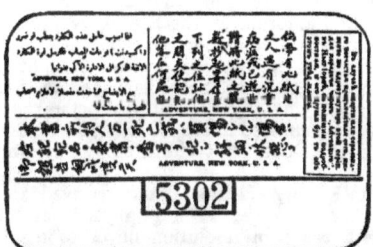

Adventure's Identification Card
(about ¼ actual size)

TO ONE of our number, M. Paul Bean, a merchandise broker, of Providence and Boston, we are all indebted for the fact that our identification cards are now coated with celluloid, and so protected against moisture and rubbing. He carries a card himself, and volunteered to coat the new cards at his plant for less than cost. I'm sure the thanks of all the rest of us go to him for his courtesy and good-fellowship.

Those of you now carrying the old cards are requested *not* to send them in to be exchanged for new ones until the old have worn out or been injured, unless they are starting on some long expedition. We give out these cards gladly, but there is considerable time and labor involved, and we ask you not to add unnecessarily to our work. Each change of card means a general change in our records, for no card number is ever duplicated, and a new card means a new number.

THE celluloid cards will be free like the old ones. No other kind will be issued until further notice. The plan of issuing brass or aluminum cards is temporarily shelved, as such tags are rather expensive even when issued at cost of manufacture and mailing. However, if any of you are sufficiently anxious for them to register in advance as ready to pay twenty to fifty cents for one, send in your name and permanent address on a *post-card, not a letter*. This entails no obligation on your part or on ours. We merely wish a fairly exact knowledge of how many of these metal cards would be wanted. Later we *may* take the matter up. Do *not* send any money now.

And be dead sure you send your notice on a *post-card*. If you notify us in a letter it will be disregarded. This may seem a foolish requirement. It is not. Any other plan would mean so much extra work and confusion in our filing system that we couldn't undertake it. The Camp-Fire, its departments and the various practical services they render, entail more work for us than you have any idea of. We're glad to do it for you, but by glory, you owe it to us in return not to make any extra and unnecessary work for us in doing it for you!

INCIDENTALLY some of you might take the trouble to read carefully the note at the head of each department before you write in and ask us to serve you in that department. Those notes aren't put there for ornament; nor just to give us a chance to talk to ourselves; nor just to fill up space. We could fill the Camp-Fire pages two or three times over each month. Those notes are for the guidance of those who wish to profit by the free service offered. They're meant to be read, and they mean what they say.

YES, sure I'm sore. Wouldn't you be if you were trying to do a favor for a fellow and he thanked you by making you as much trouble as he could, merely through being too lazy or careless to spend two minutes finding out what he was asking of you? Most of you come through all right, and we appreciate it. I'm cussing the minority who don't.

AND if you want to register for a metal card in case they are issued later, put nothing else on that *post-card* except your full name and full permanent address, and "Register me as interested in metal identification cards if issued," or words to that effect. Enclose the post-card, or a card of about the same size and shape, in an envelope, if you prefer.

OUR identification cards remain free to any reader. The two names and addresses and a stamped envelope bring you one.

Each card bears this inscription, each printed in English, French, Spanish, German, Portuguese, Dutch, Italian, Arabic, Chinese, Russian and Japanese:
"In case of death or serious emergency to bearer, address serial number of this card, care of ADVENTURE, New York, U. S. A., stating full particulars, and friends will be notified."
In our office, under each serial number, will be registered the name of bearer, and of one friend, with permanent address of each. No name appears on the card. Letters will be forwarded to friend, unopened by us. The names and addresses will be treated as confidential by us. We assume no other obligations. Cards not for purposes of business identification. Cards furnished free of charge, *provided stamped and addressed envelope accompanies application.* We reserve the right to use our own discretion in all matters pertaining to these cards.
Later we may furnish a metal card or tag for adventurers when actually in the jungle, desert, etc. If interested in metal cards, say so on a *post-card—not* in a letter. No obligation entailed. These post-cards, filed, will guide us as to demand and number needed.
A moment's thought will show the value of this system of card-identification for any one, whether in civilization or out of it. Remember to furnish stamped and addressed envelope and to *give in full the names and addresses of self and friend or friends when applying.*

A LINE from one of us who at the time of writing was in a military hospital in Belfast, Ireland. The handwriting, naturally enough, is too shaky for us to be sure of all the words. The word marked with a star, however, was not omitted because we weren't sure of it.

Just a few lines to *Adventure* for old-times sake, being an old *Adventure* reader, which I still get "when possible." The January number made a hit in the trenches a bit south of Loos and Hallack— "lovely spot."
Am at present lying low, suffering from a severe shock: shell concussion. Was out on a "*Strafing*" expedition (bombing) when, *whiz—bang!* six of us were knocked flat. Unfortunately, two of our crowd got their pass to the Happy Hunting Ground. All in a day's work.
"The ——'s sport" out on that International Sporting Ground, ——?, hike (?), and the everlasting MUD, MUD. Could give you plenty good yarns, but they'd never get by Mr. Censor.
Am at present enjoying life, almost killed with kindness, etc. But I reckon I'll stick it out to the finish. Have met plenty of Yanks out here, and, believe me, some hard nuts. Met a few just over from Old Mexico. Was along with Villa's outfit.
Well, I see you have plenty of talk at Washington yet about Preparedness, etc. Hope they wake up and get some sense. This is not the last war by a ——*-of-sight. I've been looking at Johnny Jap. Britain is playing the game all right. You never see the Japs on the Western front, for reasons known to us all, Anglo-Jap Alliance. Savey.
Well, I'll close now, wishing the best of luck to old *Adventure* and your Red-Headed regiment. (I'm a blond.)—M. LOGIE, 3rd Black Watch.

WILLIAM R. THOMPSON has in this issue the first story he has ever written for a magazine, so when he introduces himself in accordance with Camp-Fire custom what he says will have an extra interest:

Born in Denver, Colorado; 29 years old. Migrated to California at the age of 12 years. Received a partial education at a military academy. At the age of 17 financial reverses brought me to the necessity of labor, but I managed to side-step that by obeying my natural instincts—the wanderlust; so I enlisted in the U. S. N., and spent four years in the Orient, but didn't enjoy any sinecure.

I SERVED my enlistment and received an honorable discharge. Feeling myself ambitious, and with the firm resolution never to reënlist, I started out almost a stranger within my own land, with little money and a half-forgotten partial education, to make good.
I soon found myself employed upon a survey party. My ambition then focused upon a civil-engineering career. I purchased books and studied thousands of questions, accepted the advice of engineers with whom I worked, and jumped from job to job, seeking new experience. At the end of eight years, after traveling and working throughout the Western States and Canada, I found myself an accepted civil engineer and employed in Honduras, C. A., where I heard the story which gave me the idea I revised and embodied in "Rumor Substantiated." It's interesting, so I shall insert it:

ARRIVING in Porto Cortez, I made the acquaintance of the famous soldier of fortune, General Lee Christmas, and heard him relate the following, which I condense:
During a revolution he was wounded and captured by the enemy. While in the hospital, a real friend gave him a loaded revolver, which Christmas did not examine but hurriedly placed beneath the bed-coverings. For several months he convalesced with contentment, for he thought he would have a fifty-fifty chance with any assassin—and assassination is not unusual. Upon his discharge he for the first time examined the revolver, and found that his friend, in his haste, had given him an old rim-fire revolver filled with center-fire cartridges.

AT THE outbreak of the war a comrade and myself proceeded to France aboard one of the supplies ships of the Allies. We then went to London, England. There the English government placed no value upon my military, naval or engineering experience, and so refused my request for official service in their engineering corps. Well, war is one thing, digging trenches another, and taking orders from some 18-year-old son-of-a-duke, who perhaps purchased his rank, quite another, so shook the fog of London from me and returned home.

I have had no remarkable adventures except, perhaps, one. One night while I was a man-o'-war'sman, we (a boat's crew) received orders to arm and array, and reconnoiter on the west coast of Luzon, P. I. As fate would have it, the officer and I proceeded along the beach, while the boat's crew covered our advance. At our approach, bonfires, which had been burning upon the beach, were suddenly put out. I had a revolver and instructions to fire five bullets and then turn the other upon myself, for we were stalking for head-hunters. Nothing happened; they had led a hasty retreat to the tall timbers, thank Heaven. Gee! I was a scared 18-year-old kid!

But, broadly speaking, my life has had some adventure. I have back-packed in B. C., rafted the rivers in the Bitter Roots Mts., waded iguana-infested swamps—but heck, what's the use? That's not adventure nor romance, just plain every-day hard work toward some engineering result. When adventure is mentioned, I can only listen, for, somewhat similar to the cat scratching upon a tin roof, I have been too busy trying to claw my way to the top to have any thrills.

I play chess, admire boxing, am extremely fond of music, and read a great deal. I have two ambitions, one is to become an orange rancher in southern California, and thereby find time to diligently plot to sell to some unsuspecting editor one of my near-poems. And thirdly, achieve the other.

HERE'S another idea for a volunteer regiment. If interested, address Mr. Goff; we'll help if our help's needed. The Red-Heads, Gray-Heads, American Foreign Legion, Highland Brigade, Smoke-Eaters, and the other regiments already suggested are good ideas, and behind them all is the big idea of organizing and naming regiments so that they may profit by the very practical factor of the added esprit de corps that comes of common blood and traditions, physical characteristics, birthplace or home district, training, etc. Legislation on military and defense matters is only in its formative stage, but it's well to lay the groundwork of these special regiments in advance, so that they may be ready to seize their opportunity when it arises. Let me remind you again that from the start it's been those of you who have had actual service on the firing-line who have been first to "see" these regiments, knowing just how important is the practical factor of esprit de corps.

Following Mr. Goff's are other letters, advocating these regiments:

Have been reading about the Red-Headed Regiment. It is a pretty good idea, but I can tell you of another one just as good.

Why not start a regiment composed of men six feet and over? You know how a six-foot man looks in the average regiment. Like a bullfrog in a bunch of tadpoles. They know it, and he knows it, and his chances are that he will stop something hard before long, because he shows up—well, kind of conspicuous. I leave his fighting ability to history.

While we can not boast of any highly-colored polls, still we could give those Red-Heads a run for their money and then some.

I am willing to start it, my qualifications being the following: Six feet six inches in my stockings, which I am afraid will be crowding seven close when I am twenty-two, being eighteen February last; crowding the 240-pound mark close. Those are all for the present. No, there are a few more. Have walked a mile and a quarter in fifteen minutes, can put a rifle bullet where I want it. Know a lot about dynamite.

Seems like there ought to be enough big men to make up a regiment.—HERMAN GOFF, Upper West Main, Amsterdam, N. Y.

Now I would like to say a word about the Red-Heads. Mr. Tom L. Mills, of New Zealand, says their motto should be, "Ginger for Pluck." That, I think, is a good one. And the name of the regiment should be "The Coppernobs." I myself am a red-head, so is the "governor"—in fact, nearly every member of my family is a "fire-top" on the male side, and all soldiers at that. So you can see why I am in favor of them. I am sorry to say that I can't become a member of said regiment. But they (the Reds) are sure some fighters. The best I know of was (or is, which?) "Fighting Mac"— General Sir Hector MacDonald. The man who knocked them down with his bare fists. Lieutenant Gordon McCreagh, East Surrey Regiment (I don't think it is the same one that you know), was a red-head —a man that can give a very good account of himself.—ALBERT H. OFFORD, Santa Monica, California.

OF THE various regiments proposed at our Camp-Fire none is more practical than the Gray-Heads, men over 45, already seasoned in war and still able for garrison, coast-defense and similar duties. Read the following from one of our writers. Major MacFergus's address is in our Information Directory.

The suggestion of Major MacFergus struck me in the right place. A letter from me has been on file in the War Department for two or more years, offering to raise a brigade in California, of men like myself, too old to get into the army, crippled in some way that will interfere with marching but leave them in trim for post duty.

MY IDEA was that such men could hold a line of communication, guard supplies or act as backers for a battery, and they would stay on the job. Good reason, too, if each one had a knee like mine. They couldn't run if they wanted to. But if they were like me they could shoot in a way to make the brigade respected.

The best I have been able to do so far is to get my name down on a list of one thousand men who are pledged to respond to a call of the chief of police when any body of the local Mexican population gets too gay and starts rioting, as they have threatened to do.

WHEN the Spanish War began there were many gray-headed scrappers who ached to take a hand and were bitterly disappointed when they were turned down. This country has a mortgage on my life that it is at liberty to foreclose at any time when it will benefit the land.

Here in Los Angeles there is an organization, just perfected, and now receiving enlistments, that is to have a Summer training camp at Monterey like the one at Plattsburg. Our organization sets the age limit at fifty, but so many old boys have protested bitterly at being shut out by a measly two or four or five years that the limit comes near being the roof now. With only a week of life, the organization now has one hundred and thirty names enrolled.

ONE feature of the local situation that is pleasing is the fact that some of the corporations are offering an extra two weeks of vacation at full pay to their employees. It is expected that over two thousand will join in this locality. Some employers are even paying the expenses of their men while off for training, besides the full pay. Captain J. B. Murphy, U. S. A., has been detailed to handle the camp. He has decreed that the old boys, like myself, are to have instruction in military administration, quartermaster's duty and military law.

In addition there will be lectures on "The Military Policy of the United States," "The Military Problem of the Pacific Coast," "Military Hygiene," and "International Law."

RIFLE and revolver training will be given them if they so elect. The old boys, if enlisted under my plan, could release the same number of hearty young bucks who have good legs and take their duties over effectively. It makes me mad to think that my knee has gone back on me as the result of a little accident. Three years ago I led a bunch of young fellows over thirty-three miles of the Sierra Madre mountain trails, between ten A. M. and eight-thirty P. M., and had the time of my life. Now that gaul-dummed knee says "no," in plain terms, after five miles, just because I mashed the joint some time ago. I can still ride a horse or an auto even if they get fractious, and I prefer the horse. It makes me feel young again to mount some peppery nag that likes to walk on his hind legs or act as if he had a beech-nut under the blanket.— E. E. HARRIMAN, Los Angeles.

TEMPORARY organization of the Red-Headed Regiment in California, Oregon and Washington is in the hands of Les Bentley, San Pedro, Calif. For the general temporary organization, address Fred C. Adams, of Chatham, N. Y., 'as before.

If gifted with red hair, please think over the following non-military suggestion:

IN CONNECTION with the Red-Headed Regiment, I suggested to some of its members the formation of a general order of red-heads, quite apart from the regiment, and having no military purpose, merely a national social order for good-fellowship and mutual benefit. Here is one of the replies that came in. *Adventure* will be glad to help in forming such an organization.

YOUR idea of a Red-Headed order is mighty fine, too, and by all means have it so one may belong to either or both of the organizations. Why not have the Red-Headed order a society of mutual help in all ways, like the Odd-Fellows, Masons, etc., so that any redhead belonging and away from home, would find no trouble in becoming acquainted and obtaining a position, if his standing with the club was good and he was able to furnish proper credentials? There are enough red-heads so they could easily have as strong an organization as any of the secret orders, old or new, and I sincerely hope and believe that, with the Red-Headed Regiment as a beginning, it will be accomplished.

It is, I believe, a thought that has come to every red-head, and why it has lain dormant so long is something I am unable to understand. And then to have it brought at last to the sprouting stage by a non-eligible is the last straw! It sure looks as though we red-heads lack the initiative, inventive genius, or something of that sort. Perhaps all we needed was a "self-starter."

Hoping you will hurry up and get out some membership blanks and let us get in right on this thing, I remain—M. C. BURTON, Ellsworth, Kansas.

REDFIELD INGALLS, with a story in this magazine for the first time, follows Camp-Fire custom and introduces himself:

I was born in Granby, Quebec, the home town of Palmer Cox, creator of Brownies. Since Granby is within sight of the Green Mountains, and since my mother was born in the United States, I'm pretty nearly not a Canadian.

I'VE been a reporter. Also a stenographer. Likewise a machinist, factory-hand, tool-maker, itinerant salesman, free-lance writer, funny-column conductor, spellbinder and magazine editor. I've stood in quicksand fifty feet underground, watching how they sunk a caisson to bed-rock, and been "jingled" for hours afterward by the fourteen or fifteen atmospheres; I've sat on the roof of a ten-story paint warehouse, breathing the fumes of alcohol and turpentine, and watched a two-story hat-factory next door go up in smoke—wondering the while how in thunder I'd get out if we ever caught fire. I've been the thirteenth man on a new auto fire-engine (that had broken down the night before), in making a trial trip at sixty miles an hour through crowded city streets; I've lived through several annual floods, when the St. Lawrence would arise in its Springtime wrath and make wading-boots necessary in order to get breakfast.

But the nearest escape I ever had, happened to a

friend of mine. He was watching some boys on the St. Lawrence play hockey with an impromptu puck one warmish Winter day, when the puck came slithering his way. He put out his foot and stopped it and was about to kick it back when he discovered that it was half a stick of still-frozen dynamite!

LETTER-FRIENDS

Note—This is a service for those of our readers who want some one to write to. For adventurers afield who want a stay-at-home "letter bunkie," and for stay-at-homes, whether ex-adventurers or not, who wish to get into friendly touch with some one who is out "doing things." We publish names and addresses—the rest is up to you, and of course we assume no responsibility of any kind. Women not admitted.

(26) J. B. Vaughan, 169 S. Converse St., Spartanburg, S. C., wishes to hear from people in Africa, Asia, Australia, and especially the South Seas. No soldiers. Will gladly send papers and magazines or perform any reasonable service requested.

(27) Jim Renshaw, Commercial Hotel, Chicago.

(28) R. A. Cooper, Royal Canadian Ordnance Corps, Winnipeg, Manitoba, Can.

(29) S. R. Bevier, carrier 6, P. O., Jackson, Mich. Preferably from those still in the field of adventure.

(30) Hal. Walker, 300 E. 102nd St., New York.

ARRIVALS AND DEPARTURES

Note—The use of this department is free to any of our readers who wishes to announce to his friends and acquaintances his departure with, or return from, an expedition or venture taking him to distant parts for a considerable length of time. Notices from ordinary tourists not admitted. Bear in mind that your notice can not get into the magazine for two months after the magazine receives it. We reserve the right to reject any notice whatsoever and to use our discretion in all matters pertaining to this department. We assume no responsibility of any kind in conducting this department, but shall do our best to make it of value to our readers.

Captain Jack Bonavita is in Los Angeles after his Florida expedition.

Frank A. Hamberry is home at 1323 N. 22nd St., Philadelphia, after eleven months in Africa and Europe, collier and ammunition service, etc.

"The Mysterious Sailor" notifies friends of his departure for Mexico in April, after France, writing from Oklahoma City, March 17th. (Id. card 5435.)

Charles Ashleigh is on a lecture and photographing tour, on foot, over old Santa Fé trail from Kansas City to Los Angeles.

Captain George Ash announces his departure from Key West for U. S. scout duty in Mexico.

BACK ISSUES OF ADVENTURE

May, 1912, to Dec., 1915 (except June, 1915), good condition, 10c each, carriage collect.—D. L. GEESAMAN, Shreve, O.

April, 1913, Aug. to Dec., 1913; 1914 and 1915 complete. $1 a doz., or 10c each, carriage collect.—H. H. NORTHRUP, L. B. 29, North Freedom, Wis.

Complete set from Vol. 1, No. 1, $10, carriage collect.—F. C. McLAIN, 10th and Mechanic Sts., Osage, Iowa.

THE following is a letter written by Patrick Casey, in reply to a reader who asked how much fact there was behind "The Story of William Hyde." The sequel of which Mr. Casey speaks is now in our hands, and will run serially, probably this Fall.

"The story of William Hyde" is almost unalloyed fiction; but no man ever yet wrote without some basis of fact. For instance, I could not write about imaginary inhabitants on the planet Jupiter without giving them some far-fetched characteristics of human beings, because human beings are the only type of living, breathing persons that I know.

Again it is well known how impossible it is to imagine heaven because so few, if any of us, ever have come back to give us some basis of fact.

I mean to say, therefore, that there really is, in Borneo, a field of stones called the Jallan Batoe; but it is our Jallan Batoe in name only. It is not in the crater of an extinct volcano; it is only a disarray of large stones, such as might be found in any country, and not nearly so romantic or so beautiful as that cluster of rocks to be found in our own country, in Colorado—the Garden of the Gods.

The Poonan exist as a primitive race of people, who live in the jungles of Borneo, without roofs over their heads, with only mats for coverings. Their name truly means "Wild Men of the Wilds." But they are not, as we made them, descendants of the Tartars of Genghis Khan.

There really is some basis of fact to the story of the Sending of the Sword, as, according to some authorities, Genghis Khan, or his grandson, Kublai Khan, really did attempt to conquer Borneo.

And William Hyde—I never met him, but many and many a man I have met of his ilk. Once, in working my way down to Honolulu, I chanced upon a fellow-workaway who had not even to his credit so much as a change of socks. But the stories that man could tell! He'd been graduated from a law college in Albany, New York. He'd been in Alaska, rich now, then broke. He said he had a letter from the then new President, Woodrow Wilson, a pal of his! Surely enough, when I met him the day after we landed in the Islands, he was all togged out in new regalia: a straw hat, tan oxfords, silk socks. He was a member of the bar. He introduced me to senators and princes and influential half-breeds of the territory. And it is he, and such happy-go-lucky, take-a-chance, bull artists as he, that have gone to make up the character of William Hyde.

William Hyde is not dead. My brother and I are at work, right now, writing of his further adventures and tragic end in the Jallan Batoe. Also, of the adventures in the Jallan Batoe of Colum Kildare and the remittance man, Fitzhamon, and the Dutch orchid-hunter, Konrade de Jong, and his negro hoss-boy, Harry Christmas. And of Lip-Plak-Tengga, too, and a very beautiful girl called Butterfly of the Dark.

OUR old friend, W. Townend, whose stories we all remember, and who is with the hospital corps of the British army "somewhere in France," sends back this record of his routine life, which is more crowded with adventure than any of his fiction tales. It was written in February. I hope things still go well with him.

Life is somewhat of a whirl these days, and I get little time for letter writing, and none at all for fiction. I am longing to get back to my work, and the war is at present deadly dull—plenty of shelling and not much else. One ought to be thankful for small mercies, and not the least of these mercies is that we are having a wonderful Winter. Already Spring is in the air, and the leaves are showing in the thickets and copses, but we get plenty of rain, of course.

I can't write very much about what we see and do,

but it's a queer, raw side of life: troops and troops and troops; mud, guns, the noise of tramping feet at night; men in muddy garments, goat-skins and steel helmets, shuffling along through the rain from the trenches; little crosses by the roadside, ruined villages, and, of course, always the dead. Have you in New York ever heard of the men who "go over the top"—who know for hours beforehand that those who mount the parapet first are doomed to fall by machine-gun fire, yet who struggle to be first? Some shrink back, others do not. You start off toward the guns that thud away hour after hour. You know that at any moment you may hear shrieking toward you, growing louder and louder, the shell that perhaps will knock you out. Yet you keep on, and try to think of other things: dinner, the day's mail, home, anything. A queer life to be living, isn't it?

We are a Scottish division. We have with us an Irish division, a division from the old regular army, now alas! remade again and again, and a London division, Territorials, and a hard-fighting crowd, too. One can form no real idea of the losses of a modern battle until one has been through it. I have seen a ruined little village, paved with wounded and dead, while later on, in another village, I watched the remnants of a brigade that had made perhaps the most wonderful charge in this war, marching back to refit, and this brigade mustered altogether about as many men as had one of its battalions before they climbed the parapet three days before.

Well, it's late, and I must dry up. Do I bore you with this kind of stuff? I hope not.

As for magazines, if you have any to spare, they would be welcomed out here. If you address any parcel to 15th (Scottish) Division, British Expeditionary Force, care Forwarding Officer, Southampton, England, and put on the cover "For distribution to troops," it will arrive safely. I give you the address of my own division, as we may as well have the benefit of whatever is going. Or you might send the parcel—if not too big—to my own unit: 32nd Sanitary Section, 15th (Scottish) Division, B. E. F.; we will distribute the magazines after having read them ourselves.

I am expecting to get home to London for a few days before very long. It's a weird existence, this. . . .

By Jove! it seems a million years since October, 1914, when we stayed with you at Long Island, doesn't it? I've not written a line since "Tony Mallagh."

Good-by, good luck.—W. TOWNEND.

I'LL call him Bill, because, so far as I know, that is not his name. I've never met him. The tale was sent to me some while ago by another man, whom I do know. I think you'll like it.

Did you hear about that adventure of Bill's at San Ygnacio, Sonora? Bill went down there to confer with the officials of the La Colorada mine about mine-guards against the Yaquis and woke up on the train just before it got to Magdalena, with a beautiful hangover. Noticing a cantina in the brush, he dived out of the car window and made a bee-line for it, and meanwhile the train went on. In the cantina Bill asked for a drink and paid for it. There were about ten or eleven peons in there and one of them asked Bill:

"Are you an American?"

"No, by ——!" said Bill, "I'm a Texan!"

Then the Mexican called Bill a "Texas —— —," and Bill crowned him with a beer-bottle. The others mixed in and for a few minutes Bill had his hands full. He downed several of them and was finally rescued by the *presidente* of the village, who carried him to his house, dressed his wounds and the next day saw him safely to Magdalena.

On his return people were curious about two very beautiful black eyes that distinguished his appearance. I asked him what had happened.

"No, I won't tell you that," he said, "but I'll say this: One gringo can't take Sonora—I've done tried it!"

WAR-CLOUDS are again on our horizon and the storm may have come even before these words reach you. But if not too late, why not make your services quickly available by joining the American Legion? Previous military training is necessary for its Active Service, but men of some eighty-two trades and professions are needed for its Special Service.

INFORMATION DIRECTORY

IMPORTANT: Only items like those below can be printed—standing sources of information. No room on this page to ask or answer specific questions. Recommend no source of information you are not *sure* of. False information may cause serious loss, even loss of life. *Adventure* does its best to make this directory reliable, but assumes no responsibility therefor.

For data on the Amazon country write Algot Lange, care U. S. Consul, Para, Brazil. Replies only if stamped, addressed envelope is enclosed and only at Mr. Lange's discretion, this service being purely voluntary. (Five cent postage in this case.)

For the Banks fisheries, Frederick William Wallace, editor *Canadian Fisherman*, 35 St. Alexander St., Montreal. Same conditions as above.

For the Philippines and Porto Rico, the Bureau of Insular Affairs, War Dep't, Wash., D. C.

For Alaska, the Alaska Bureau, Chamber of Commerce, Central Bldg., Seattle, Wash.

For Hawaii and Alaska, Dep't of the Interior, Wash., D. C.

For Cuba, Bureau of Information, Dep't of Agri., Com. and Labor, Havana, Cuba.

For Central and South America, John Barrett, Dir. Gen., Pan-American Union, Wash., D. C.

For R. N. W. M. P., Comptroller Royal Northwest Mounted Police, Ottawa, Can., or Commissioner, R. N. W. M. P., Regina, Sask. Only unmarried British subjects, age 22 to 30, above 5 ft. 8 in. and under 175 lbs., accepted.

For Canal Zone, the Panama Canal, Wash., D. C.

For U. S., its possessions and most foreign countries, the Dep't of Com., Wash., D. C.

For Adventurers' Club, get data from this magazine.

For The American Legion, The Secretary, The American Legion, 10 Bridge St., New York.

Mail Address and Forwarding—This office, assuming no responsibility, will be glad to act as a forwarding address for its readers or to hold mail till called for, provided necessary postage is supplied.

For cabin-boat and small boat travel on the Mississippi and its tributaries, "The Cabin-Boat Primer," by Raymond S. Spears; A. R. Harding, Publisher, Columbus, O., $1.00.

National School Camp Ass'n; address its Sec'y, care *The Globe*, 75 Dey St., New York.

Red-Headed Regiment, Fred C. Adams, Chatham, N. Y.

Gray-Headed Regiment, address Major Guillermo Mac Fergus, care *Adventure*.

Marine Corps Gazette, 24 E. 23rd St., New York.

ARTHUR SULLIVANT HOFFMAN.

WANTED —MEN

YOUNG man to accompany me on trip through Northwest, Yosemite Valley, Yellowstone Park, and etc., to gather material for short stories and magazine work. American, fair education, must be willing to help finance the trip and share in camp work, as we will "rough it" most of the time. Expect to start about May 1st. An advantageous offer to the right party. Fuller particulars by letter.—Address J. PAIGE, 8 Hall Pl., Albany, N. Y.

YOUNG man wanted as partner traveling the U. S., photographing in a tint and outdoor work. Have good proposition to good man. Write giving age, experience, references, etc.—Address HUBERT McCLURE, Chandler, N. D.

TWO or three men of good habits, to go on a prospecting -trip in Lower California. I have a good placer proposition. Each man to share expenses.—Address WILLIAM C. TURGENS, 114 South Street, San Antonio, Texas.

Inquiries for opportunities instead of men are NOT printed in this department.

YOUNG man about 25, to take trip down Mississippi in canoe. Will spend the Winter hunting and fishing on Gulf. Eventually go to Central America. Must be able to rough it and furnish half the outfit.—M. W., 326, care *Adventure*.

LOST TRAILS

WHITE, HUGH E., was with several others on trip from Atlanta to Key West, in quest of Gypsy kidnapers. I believe I have information as to whereabouts of article we sought, but am unable to finance expedition. The kid was found last Summer.—L. T., 323, care *Adventure*.

SPIEGELHALDER, TYLER (Sergeant William Tell Savage), of Louisville, Kentucky. Honorably discharged from Marine Corps, July 28, 1907, at Marine Barracks, Naval Station, Culebra, Porto Rico. His sister, Myra, and nephew want information.—Address PERCY G. FENNER, Milton, Wis.

KIRBY, BEN (Society Ben), last seen at Canadian Boundary in North Dakota. Supposed to be in Kentucky, and Albert Nelson (Buddy), supposed to be in Wisconsin or Illinois. Their old pal, Blackie, would like to hear from them to make plans for Summer.—Address JERRY WOODS, care WILLIAM COHRING, 294 North Mutter Street, Philadelphia, Pa.

MILLER, WILLIAM ADDISON, last heard of San Francisco, November, 1914. Broke horses in Hawaii Islands for government. He bought and sold horses in West, also worked on ranch at Little Horse Creek, Wyo. 32 years, black hair and eyes, six feet.—Address M. M. HILLS, care *Adventure*.

Inquiries will be printed three times. In the January and July issues all unfound back names will be printed again.

HART, JACK, left Myillenes, Chile, about March, 1911. In Norwegian barque, *Cissi*, for Port Natal. He is known to some as "Silent Jack," from Hutchinson, Kansas. —Address AKSEL ANDERSEN, Correo, Antofagasta, Chile.

PIGGOTT, ARTHUR W., last heard of San Francisco. Ex-Quartermaster clerk in Havana, Corregidor and San Francisco (formerly sergeant in field artillery in Mariannao, Cuba). Good news and proposition.—Address J. L. PEDE, 226 Upper Santa Rosa Avenue, Sausalito, Cal.

BONNER, FRED; send address at once. Know something to your advantage, very important. Do you remember that incident out West near Spokane? Not heard of since 1906.—Address VALENTINE ADAIR, care MR. WILLIAM SIMPSON, 6217 Lancaster Ave., Philadelphia, Pa.

COLLINS, ALFRED (Eleric), son of Daniel H. Collins. Left Philadelphia for mining fields of California 20 years ago, via Florida.—Address LYDIA COLLINS, 5329 Reinhart Street, Philadelphia, Pa.

JOHNSON, ERNEST E., last heard of North Carolina. Plumber, steamfitter and pipe-caulker. Worked Jacksonville, Fla., 1911. Brother wants news of whereabouts.—Address GEORGE JOHNSON, 43 Henry Street, Stamford, Conn.

GRAY, CURTIS C., last seen Denver, September, 1915. Think he has gone to Canada. Write regard to plans for Spring.—Address J. H. STREETER, 408 West 58th Street, New York City.

LORRAINE, FRANK, last heard of U. S. Army. Age 22, height 5 ft., dark blond hair, prominent features, scar about 1½ inches on left forefinger.—Address L. T. 325, care *Adventure*.

Please notify us at once when you have found your man.

SUMMERS, THOMAS M. Parents would like to hear from him.—Address REV. AND MRS. B. F. SUMMERS, Las Vegas, Nevada.

FOSTER, BEN, and E. D. Cook. Have proposition in view for you. Communicate with me.—Address G. F. DIXON, Gen. Del., Cristobal, C. Z.

SWEENY, HENRY A., last heard of in France. Worked in New York as a cook. Perhaps enlisted in English army.—Address W. F. SWEENY, 2029 Routt St., Pueblo, Colo.

COY, ALEXANDER ROBERT, last heard of around Pueblo, Colo., or Miss Mollie Coy, last seen in San Diego, Cal. Information would be gratefully received by their brother.—Address S. T. COY, Wilton, Sac. Co., Cal.

OLD comrades of the 70's that were in the Adobe Wall Pocket Cañon and Yellow House Fight. Am an old buffalo hunter; went by the name of "Moccasin Jim."—Address JAS. W. STELL, Austin Colo.

AVIRETTE, John A., communicate with me for something important in Mexico. Want your present address.—Address WM. BROCKWAY, care MANGANESE MINING Co., 118 Prado Narana, Cuba.

Please notify us at once when you have found your man.

STUMPF, JULIUS, last heard from Tres Hermanos Tampico, Tamp., Mexico, working for Huarteca Petroleum Company.—Address FRED H. GRAMBERGER, Fairburg, Ill.

PRICKETT, STONE J. (Rattlesnake Bill), last heard of in Northern Idaho.—Address E. C. ROSE or ED. E. GARDNER, Metaline, Washington.

EBERT, GERTRUDE VIOLA, last heard of in orphan home at or near Wabash, Indiana.—Address C. O. EBERT, Buchanan, Va.

Please notify us at once when you have found your man.

NAUGLER, OWEN V., last heard from was river driving on the Kennebec, Maine, June, 1914. 25 years, 6 feet.—Address WILLIAM NAUGLER, New Ross, N. S.

MAHONEY, DAN; Noonan, Jack, McDonald. Remember Bachimha.—Address L. T. 324, care *Adventure.*

WOOD, EDWARD, father, last heard of 1888 in Boston, Mass. My two sisters were with him at same time. —Address AL. WOOD, Box 556, Winslow, Arizona.

WIETHALER, FRED, left home in Wisconsin 1906. Information as to whereabouts will be appreciated.— Address CHARLES WIERTHALER, So. Milwaukee, Wis.

CARSON, J. G. (Jack), last heard from Katalla, Alaska, 1906.—Address HARRY R. SHAFER, or MRS. ETHEL GREY, Oroville, Washington.

TOWNE, GEORGE H., born Monmouth, Maine, 1870. Communicate with sister Grace, care *Adventure.*

CRAWFORD, GEO. H., in Searchlight, Nevada, in bum times of 1905-1906. Resident of Jamestown, N. Y.—Address ANDREW J. DAVIS, care *Adventure.*

BERRIDGE, CHARLES ANDREW, last heard of on board *S. S. Lenape*, going to Palm Beach, Florida. Very ill. Can any one give information regarding him.— Address "LYNA," care *Adventure.*

KUNZE, ARTHUR, in Greenwater, Cal., in bum times 1907. Resident Salt Lake City, Utah.—Address ANDREW J. DAVIS, care *Adventure.*

Inquiries will be printed three times. In the January and July issues all unfound back names will be printed again.

THE following have been inquired for in "Lost Trails." They can get name of inquirer from this magazine:

A.—C. ABERNATHY, SUMMER; Adair, Wm. L.; Adams, Eddie, signwriter; Adams, Will Holden, Vicksburg, Miss.; Aldridge, Harry C., Singer Mfg. Co.; Allen, Robert, Hamilton City, Cal.; Allen, Martin Danon; Alston, William E.; Alva, Stockwell, Grand Rapids, Mich.; Ammann, Joseph, Grand Is., Nebr., Feb., 1909; Anderson, Carl O.; Anderson, Joe, Manila, P. I., 1901; Aniba or Kennedy, Alfred; Arhens, Helen Breckenridge; Armbruster, Joseph Anthony; Arrington, Tommy; Asher, Orlie, Detroit, Mich., 1911-1912; Ash, Capt. George, Missoula, Mont.; Ashenfelter, Loyd E.; Avery, J. F., of Ramseur, N. C.; Bagley, Thomas H.; Baker, Edward E.; Baker, Mrs. Maude, left Dallas 1900; Barber, Wallie; Barnes, William Henry; Barrette, Miss Cora Mabel; Basye, Thomas T.; Beaton, A. W., Quincy, Ill.; Beaver, Fred; Bedell, Percy John, Spokane, Wash.; Bee, Taver, Mexico, 1901-1902; Behrend, Otto F.; Belt, Dr. H. P.; Bennett, Ross; Bennett, Richard P., Mt. Clemens, Mich.; Bens, Joseph, "Jupp;" Benson, Harry, Mansfield Center, Conn.; Bergholen, Fred; Best, F. P., Mexico, 1910, Cuba 1912; Black, Beb, alias "Big Ben;" Black, Leslie, Huntly, Mont.; Blackham, N. A.; Blankman, Charles H.; Bleckier, Thomas; Bly, Royal R. (Richard or Dick), Spokane, Wash., 1909; Bolton, Leonard; Bossard, Raymond D.; Boulton, Frederick E.; Bowhan, W. H.; Brackney (wants to establish connections); Bradford, Frank William; Bradley, Alonzo; Brantley, John William; Breed, Riley H., Winnipeg, Manitoba in Fall of 1909; Brice, M. E.; Brink, Clifford; Brooks, Al. H., rancher, Canada; Brown, Arthur, Oklahoma City; Brown, Edward G., "The Dalles Country," Oregon; Brown, James; Brown, Marion M., Portland, Me.; Brown, traveling mate from Portland to Weed in 1912; Brownell, Richard; Brue, Charles (White); Brush, Don; Buckner (Blume); Burke, Edgar, in Hamburg, 1912-13; Burnett, Alice; Burns, William, tailor of Dubuque; Butcher, Bob; Butler, Jack (Ormondi); Challender, Claude; Chamberlain, Carlyle D.; Butterbaugh, Christian; Butts or Olstrom, Godfrey; Byrd, L. B.; Cain, G. W.; Canavan, David; Campbell, Joseph N.; Carr, David H.; Carrico, Ralph; Carroll, Martin; Carl, B. S.; Case, John; Child, George, American Navy, 1876; Christensen, A. G., South America; Clough, Mr. and Mrs. Frank, British Honduras, 1910; Coates, John F.; Cockrill, Arthur R.; Colburn, Johnny; Cole, Clyde W., San Francisco; Cole, Egbert L.; Comfort, James, Lepanto, Ark.; Comstock,

Orns, H.; Conley, Mark Frances; Connelly, Jim; Cooke, Albert; Cook, Elliott, goes under name of George Coburn; Cook, William, Jolo, 1903-04; Cooper, J. Howard; Costelloe, Jack; Cotler, William T., Lake Fisher, 1890; Coughlin, Dr. Jeremiah; Gowen, J. Gordon; Cox, John Arthur; Craft, James M.; Crane, Roland Henry; Cravens, James S., Springfield, Mo.; Cravens, Reecie, B. Prices Branch, Mo.; Crawford, John and Lee; Crockett, Louis Henry; Crompton, James, Leeds, Mass.; Crosby, Si.; Cross, James Kenneth, New York, 1909; Cross, Frederick, Dayton, Ohio; Culp, Simon P.; Culver, Billy, Birmingham, Ala., 1910; Cumery, Bessie; Cunningham, Patrick, Michael and James.

D.—I. DABYMPLE, CHARLES S.; Daley, Walter, Tampico, Mex., 1912; Darst, Red (Memphis Red— Redshear); Davenport, James; Davenport, Phil.; Davenport, William L., Dexter, Texas; Davidman, Max; Davis, James P., Harper, Kan., 1901; Davis, Warren; Davies, Guy; Davis, E. L., formerly of Winnipeg; Dawnie, George M.; De Brenil, Aramand; Deckard, Ed. (Wessel); Dennis, Lee A.; Denson, John, Hozen, Ark.; Deny Brothers; Dewitt, E. L.; Dies, Arthur W.; Digel, Julius C.; Drennan, John Matthew; Dobbert, Ed. (Kid); Dorrity or Dougherty, John; Douglas, Foster W., "Dong"; Downer, Simond (Tom), Lincoln, Nebr., 1909-10; Downer, Vearne; Downing, Flora; Downy, Stephen; Dowst, Arthur A., Sept., 1911, Seattle or Tacoma, Wash.; Driebelles, Jack; DuGuay, William; Duncan, George Riley; Dwight, L. H.; Dyer, Michael; Eckles, Warren; Elliot, Robert (Bob); Ellingsen, Frithjof; Ellis, Harry; Elmsie, Donald E.; Ensign, W. H.; Engesser, Conrad A.; Ethridge, Mrs. Celia; Evans, Frank Ewell, Leighton; Fairbanks, Frank G.; Fairfax, Donald C.; Farnsley, A. A.; Fedoroski, Karol; Fields, Harry R.; Finley, Sam, Tonopah, Nev., 1909; Fisher, Joseph, Great Falls, Mont.; Fitzgerald, Garret; Flewelling, Ernest; Flores, Jose Timoleon; Floyd, Harry; Floyd, Norris; Flynn, James; Foley, Mike L.; Follett, Bob; Foster, John Frank; Foy, George Havelock Willing; Frain, James, St. Louis, 1875; Frain, Roderick; Frank, E. S.; Francis, Henry, Trenton, Samoa; Frager, Clifford, Foraker, Okla.; Franklin, Wm. W., Hamilton, Nev., 1883; Freeman, Al. Chapman, Kans., 1898; Fullmer, Frank F., Moose Jaw, Sask.; Fuller, S. J.; Gallaway, Karl H., St. Louis, Feb., 1913; Galloway, James R.; Gallup, Cordia, known as Leon Burt; Gardner, Frank, Garnache, William J., Puerto, Mexico, 1913; Gattey, Capt., G. G., 1901-04; Gaylord, C. W.; Gazzale, Andrew Mellers; Gebbs or Gibbs, Rebel Junta Courier; Gillbertson, Joseph; Gillespie, Boe W.; Gillespie, Gene, "Manhattan"; Gogg, Ikey; Goldstein, S. A.; Goodwin, James Alexander, 36th U. S. V.; Gordan, John; Gottlieb, Edward; Grace, E. Leslie, Durham, Natal, Vinong, S. Africa; Grace, Mike, Rocky Mts., 1900; Graham, Charles A., left Toronto, August, 1913; Graham, Dan., 32 years; Graves, "Jim"; Greenwood, Charles; Growman, Harry; Gulliver, Iquique, '98; Hall, Charles T., Hamilton, Charles; Hamilton, Thomas K., Braintree, Mass.; Hamm, Robert E., Hallettsville, Tex., 1899; Hammerschmidt, Raimund, Dallas, Texas; Hammond, Paul C.; Hampton, Paul; Hammond, Warry; Hanser, Edward; Hardy, John; Harlow, Robert Pinkney; Harper, John; Harris, Joe, Webster, N. D., 1909; Harson, Wm.; Hart, Jack, once of 5th U. S. Cavalry; Haskinson, Gordon; Hayes, "Bob"; Hayman, Charles Fisher; Heckenhauer, Karl H.; Hellman, H. H.; Herbert, Jack; Hess, Erskine (Erk); Heyer, Milton Albert, Fargo, N. D., 1909; Hiatt, Claud; Hill, John Warren; Hiliman, Frank, Winnipeg, Can., 1911; Hinckley, Roy and Harry; Hinds, John Hamilton, Philadelphia; Hines, Ralph or "Shorty Hines"; Hayden, Charles; Hoeker, Louis; Hoffman, Frank L.; Hoffman, S. G.; Hoffman, Clint, stowaway, Closeburn; Holbrook, Dis (civil engineer) Holbrook; Elmer, H., late of Marine Corps; Holden, Willis A.; Holgate, Clem (Sunny); Holland, Frank; Hollis, Bach; Hoover, Ferris E., of Downers Grove, Ill.; Howard, John, scout in Montana during Indian war; Howlett, Lee.; Howlette, H. J.; Hudson, Charley, Monroe, Wash.; Huffman, J. L.; Huggart, George H.; Hughes, Henry; Hull, Harry H.; Hutchinson, George; Ingersoll, Harry G.; Ingram, Robert W.; Irvin, Howard, of Maitai, Ill.; Irving, James D.; Irvin, E. T.

J.—L. JACKSON, CLIFFORD P., Havana, Cuba; Jame, J. R.; Jasper, Key West, Hexdco; Jay, Wilburn, Madero Foreign Legion; Jefferson, Carl; Jenkins, Earl; Jenkins, Thomas Clayton, Aberystwyth, Wales; Jewell, Geo. H.; Jessup, Theodore V.; "Jew Sam" (last name forgotten); Johnson, A. E.; Johnson, Charles H., prospector, carpenter; Johnson, James Belton, St. Louis, Mo., 1868; Jones, Wm. H. (Bill); Juan (message in Spanish), Juno, A. E., El Paso, Texas, 1906; Kanthar, Paul M. T.; Kaplan, Paul, Kemmerer, Wyo., 1914; Kellar, William S., Tampa, Fla.; Kemp, driver in Oakland; Kennedy, George F.; Kennedy, Frank, naval hospital at Los Anamas, Colo., 1913; Kern, Max, Cuba, 1907-08; Kernohan, Frank; Keys, Levy, left Farmers Sta., Highland Co., Ohio, 1859; King, Frank M., Paris, Texas, 1915; Kinzman, Martin;

Kirpatrick, Clyde, M.; Klemann, Robert, Laredo, Texas; Knight, Chas. L., Cuba, 1907-08; Knight, Charles, Spokane, Wash.; Knight, Joe (Cop); Knudsen, Fred, Red Rock, Balmoral; Koynors, C. H. (Spud); Kretz, Willie, Beaumont, Texas, 1910; Lambert, H. L.; Lane, Martin, U. S. A., Klondike; Lantz, Samuel Joseph, Mexico, 1913, Oregon, Jan., 1914; Lassen, Capt. Lorenz; Lavell, Prof. Cecil F.; Lawler, Slim; Law, Gordon; Leach, O. L. (Slim); Lear, John, Everett, Wash.; Lee, John R., Amsterdam, N. Y.; Leight, T. G.; Leslie, Blayney, left Chicago about 1894; Levy, Samuel; LeVonde, William; Lewis, Harrison H. (Jr.); Lighthowler, George W.; Lindsay, Charles; Linn, Robert Hamilton; Litchfield, H.; Lloyd, Edmund, Box, John and George; Lockard, Harry; Logue, Dan., St. Paul, Minn., 1910; Long, Harry; Long, John Wesley, native of Canada; Loomis, Johney; Lounsbury, Herbert Harley; Lovett, Charles, seaman; Lyons, William C.

Please notify us at once when you have found your man.

M—N. McARDLE, JAMES; McAuliffe, George; McArthur, William; McBride, Douglas; McCandles, Alexander; McCarthy, Dan, rigger on Victoria Falls Bridge, Nyanza; McClellan, William; McClintock, Harry K.; McCormack, 1912-13, on construction work in Mexico; McDaniels, Taylor; McElvain, William; McFall, Joseph, formerly of Chicago; McGonigal, Ed., U. S. S. *Lancaster*; McGuire, Thomas James; McIntyre, J. J., of Brandon, Man.; McIntosh, James W.; McKay, Raymond; McKenney, Hugh; McKinley, Harry; McKinzie, J. W., formerly U. S. N.; McLay, Charles; MacDonald, John Ava; MacDonald, R., British Hussars, U. S. Cav.; McLaughlin, Dr. C. H., late of Canton, O.; MacNeill, Jack V. (Robbie); Mackie, Ed.; Macpherson, J. W.; Maddus, John F.; Maffei, Heck (Curley); Maples, Clem M.; Marlook, Dan (Shorty); Margolin, Louis, Kansas City, Mo., 1910; Marine, Colonel Chas. A.; Marsh, Memer (Lee or de Chantles); Marshall, Robert; Martel, Dick, Hemosillo; Mauzey, Jack; Mason, Joseph Ernest; Mason, William J.; Matthews, Will Fred, Helena, Mont.; Maxwell, William; Maynell, Charles, New York, 1893; Mazurette, Alfred F., last heard of Montreal 1892; Meade, Dan; Meek, Harold C., last heard of in Denver, Colo., in 1907; Megie, Benjamin F.; Meisel, John; Meissner, Pete, Grajervo; Mendoza, Richarde; Mentusha, Big; Merle, Eugene; Meyrick, Lieut. Archibald; Miller, Frank; Miller, Henry Chapin; Miller, Jacob; Miller, T. H. Wingfield, Kansas, June, 1906; Miller, R. H., Toro Point, C. Z., 1913; Miller, William, electrician; Milligan, Archie; Moleres, Edward; Monroe, Joe R.; Moore, Frank L., Seattle, Wash.; Moore, J. A. (Jack), Tremedoc, North Wales, Eng.; Moreland, John L., Gila Bend, Ariz., Oct. 1, 1912; Morgan, Earl, Boston, Mass.; Morgan, William Hare, last heard of in Boulder, Wyo.; Moriarty, John F.; Morissey, Warren, last heard of in Northwest; Morine, Col. Charles A.; Morine, Capt. C. D.; Moore, William; Morris, Frank; Morrisey, John, left Ottawa, for States; Morris, Thomas, George Dixon; Morrow, Joseph; Moulder, Joe; Moyer, Ted; Mudd, Clarence; Mullen, H. E. (Mac); Mullen, Thomas; Murray, Michael, late of Tralee, Ireland; Nelson, Fred; Nichols, Samuel R., last seen in Washington, D. C.; Nicholson, Harry A. or Nickerson; Niell, H. (Nielson); Nolan, Jack; Nolan, Michael, born in Kilkenny; Nugent, Richard Thomas; Nylander, C. W.

Please notify us at once when you have found your man.

O—R. O'BRIEN, WM. F., Oakland, Cal.; O'Callaghan, Dennis Charles; O'Flaherty, Joseph H.; O'Neal, Frank; Ogden, known as Tex or Two-Bar Slim; Olsen, Abbey; Orpen, William M.; Ott, Charles; Owen, G. P.; Owen, Robert; Owen, Allan H.; Owen, G. P.; Owens, Clyde; Paige, Frederick; Parker, O. B., formerly of Mexico; Parker, Ross; Parker, Capt. F. T.; Parker, Jess, cowpuncher; Patterson, Robert J., of Cleveland, O.; Pavilla, Jack, of "Jacky Wonders;" Pedder, Richard; Penault, Frank, High River, Alberta; Penney, J. C., left Vallejo, Cal.; Pennock, Dr. Walker; Peralto, Jose L.; Perry, Mark M.; Perry, Thomas Balantyne; Peters, W. Milton, with D. B. W., 1906; Pettinger, Eugene; Pettit, James R.; Phillips, J. R.; Phillpot, Shirley M.; Pickens, Osmer; Pinney, Bertie; Piper, E. E., Hot Spring, Wash., 1912; Pittenger, Fred; Pogoda, Albert; Pohl, Bernard H., San Diego, Cal., Jan., 1912; Polter, Caloin B.; Poole, Charles W.; Pope, Billy, Texas; Portwood, Alf., blacksmith; Prince, Ben., Memphis, Tenn. Pritzart, Albert; Prunty, F. W., well-driller; Raansvaal, Isaac, Co. I. 9th U. S. I.; Rae, Clarence; Raeder, Edward J.; Radcliffe, Col. John; Randall, W. S.; Ray, Carol D.; Raven, Frank A.; Reardon, John Patrick; Redpath, Adam; Reeves, Paul V.; Reilly, John A.; Reitmeie, Charley; Remes, Alexander or "Allie," East Exeter, Me.; Reynolds, William;

Reynolds, William P., stationed at Tucuran, 1902-1904; Rhode, Gust, left Grant Co., Herman, Minn.; Rice, Andrew, 49-'er; Rice, Hark (Serrott); Rice, Charles B.; Richard, Charlie E., last heard from in Cardiff, Wales; Richardson, Frank Eply; Richard, Mrs. Lauretta; Rider, Wm., Corp. G Co., 41st U. S. Vol.; 1900; Rimer, J. D.; Roach, Henry; Roberts, Joe, Chicago, Ill.; Robertson, Charlie; Robertson, Harry G., Customs, Manila; Rogers, George John; Rogers, Henry, Memphis, Tenn., March 11, 1915; Rogers, Peter, of Manchester; Rogerson, William L.; Romandovski, Ella von (Baron Eugene Karl); Rose, Jack, Melbourne, Australia, 1913; Rowe, Glen S.; Rowe, Theodore; Russell, Charles B.; Tyan, Charles, Meacham, Ore.; Tyan, William; Tyan, Billy; Tyerson, Daniel Sherman, Ariz.

Inquiries will be printed three times. In the January and July issues all unfound back names will be printed again.

S—Z. SABIN, CARL AND STEELE; Sarries, James H.; Sawyer, Walter; Scates, James A.; Scheidell, John; Schnell, Fred B.; Schener, Nich; Schwerin, William H.; Scott, F. B.; Scott, Fred; Scott, Johnson W., track foremen, K. C. S. Ry., Noble, Pa.; Scott, Norwood, of Lansdown, Pa.; Scully, John J., bricklayer; Seery (Family name) Sellers, Edwin Henderson; Semple, James E., of Philadelphia; Seigel, "Dutch"; Servin, Martin; Seton, Capt. Robert Arthur, Venezuela, 1899; Shannon, James and Wm.; Sharpe, Melburn (Curly); Shea, Timothy; Shea, W. A.; Sheehan, James, Orenco, Ore., 1911; Sheern, Thomas Eugene, Shakespear, N. M., 1888; Shepherd, Richard L.; Shepard, W. C.; Sherwood, Dote; Sherwood, F. A.; Shinn, J. W., or G. W., Mo., 1869; Shumaker, Robert F.; Smith, R. I.; Snodgrass, R. L.; Sipes, Hubert E.; Smedegard, James; Smith, Francis Basil; Smith, J. J., formerly with R. R. Club at Tucson, Ariz.; Smith, Oscar, Australian; Smith, William McK., Portland, Ore., Dec., '14; Smith, William Chalmers, Mexico; Snider, M. E.; Snowberger, Kirk R.; Snyder, Bill; Synder, William, last heard of in U. S. N.; Sorentzen, Paul *alias* Sam Wilson; Spang, Chester; Spencer, Alma; Spiering, August Frederick Wm.; Starlight, Capt.; Starnes, Edwin G.; Stauey, Frank N., of Half Moon Bay Cal.; Stanbaugh, Lester, Taft, 1913; Stearns, Herman; Stephens, Will, Ottawa, Ont., Can.; Stevens, Claude; Steven, Mrs. J. S.; Stewart, E. B.; Stewart, W. J. (Bill); Stockton, Walter; Stout, E.; Stokes, P. A.; Strong, S. O. "Struthers"; Sullivan, Frank; Summers, Thomas, M.; Sutherland, Charlie; Sutton, Edward Hepper; Swarm, E. A.; Sweidert, "Dutchy"; Sykes, Grover C.; Taylor, H. E.; Taylor, James C.; Theisen, Peter Frank; Thomas, Willis; Los Angeles, 1913-14; Thompson, Frank J.; Thompson, Jim F.; Thomson, Roscoe; Thomson, Corp. John, 2nd Canadian Mounted Rifles, Boer War; Thurber, E.; Ticek, Wm. G.; Timmanus, Frank E.; Tippit, W. A.; Tobisen, Charles J.; Tombs, Albert; Townsend, Harry S.; Treasdale, A.; Trauhauf, Harold A.; Travis, Joe; Treat, Roy M.; Trevor, Roland (Scotty); Troughton, J. J.; Turner, Charles N.; Turnard, Frank Albert; Underwood, L. T.; Van Auker, Caesar; Van Wagoner, "Dutch"; Vanderdasson, Jim; Wagner, Rudolph (Ruddy); Walker, Charles T.; Wallenstein, William J.; Walters, George (Greasy); Walton, Jack; Washburn, Bert; Watson, A. E.; Watson, Louis, Black Mt., N. C.; Weaver, Joseph C.; Weiner, Oscar; Weyman, Jack; Whalley, Thomas; Wheeler, Joseph, Henry, Milwaukee, 1886; Whelan, Frank, Cal., 1913; Wickens, Fred; Wiley, Elsworth; Wiley, Miles G.; Will, John Andrew; Williams, Babe; Williams, C. E.; Williams, Elizabeth Matilda; Williams, Jack, of Tientsin, China; Wilson, Col. Robert B.; Wilson, Charles Livingston; Wilson, Sadie; Willbern, Walter P.; Willis, A. Holden; Wings, Claud C.; Wise, Johnny; Wittenkamp, Ove.; Wixon, Joe B.; Wolf, Don W.; Wooler, Dick; Wright, James William; Yarborough, Lawrence Seven (Honnie); Young, Dale L.; Zeh, William Anton; Zappert, Walter.

Please notify us at once when you have found your man.

MISCELLANEOUS:—Friend, who answered ad, which appeared in *Adventure* during 1913; any boys of the 4th or 36th Co., U. S. C. A. C., 1911 to 1913; any of the boys on the tug *Tatoosh*, 1911, G. A. M.; comrades of Co. D, 17th Infantry, Mindanao, P. I.; comrades serving in Co. I, of the 40th U. S.; first or second mates on the barquentine *Emily Waters*; O'Connor, A. S.; Ross, Bob; Dan Damme, Jimmie; Kufeke, Hans; Griffiths, Jack; Harries, Julian; Gardiner, Jack, once in E and C Troops, B. S. A. P.; comrades A Co., American Insurrectos, 1900-11; comrades of the 17th B. T. A.; James Elias; Kenny, John; Miller, Henry; "Windy" Bache; "Ballyhoola"; "Star Pointer" Brumby, or any of the boys that were in Troop G, 5th Cav., at Aibonita;

any one who served in Troop L, 4th U. S. Cav., in Philippines July, 1899-1901; Greer, James; Bunch, Wm.; Witmer, Ed. A.; Higgins, Chester C., of the same troop; any member of Troop A, 1st U. S. Cav., 1887-1892; comrades of 17th Field Artillery, who served in Philippines; any soldier member of National Military Home, Dayton, Ohio, 1909, 1910, 1911; comrade B Co., 7th Inf., Jan. 15, 1897, to Oct. 27, 1898; comrades who served in the 34th Inf., Co. B, in the Philippines during the year of 1899; boys of Troop 9, 13th Cav., 1908-11; also those in Parhm & Dean Lumber Camp, N. Bronxville, Me., winter of 1913; members of K Co., of the 18th Inf., during 1900 to 1902; men with U. S. forces during the China Relief Expedition of 1900; Hospital Corps, 23rd U. S. Inf., 40th U. S. V.; comrades in Co. E, 20th Inf., Troop E, 7th U. S. Cavalry; comrades on Culzean, 1875-9; boys in army, navy or marine corps in the China Relief Expedition of 1900-1901; any one 4th Texas Vol. Inf. in Spanish War; comrades Co. G, 5th Inf., in Central and Western States; all members of Co. M, 1, 2; comrades Co. G, 41st Inf., and Capt. Graves' Co., 20th Inf.; corporal discharged Sept.2-12, from Troop F, 13th Cav.; comrades L, 1st Reg., Maryland Vol. Inf., during war with Spain; comrades 30th and 4th Inf., from 1867 until 1885; Spade Tail, Joe Bennett, George Ligars, Chicken Gardner, or any of the bunch of 18th U. S. Inf.; Reckless, where are you; J. P. C.; J. L. F.; Brook, Hens of Glen; Bonavita, Capt. Jack; Will, mail at Sydney; Goff, or Geof, last name unknown; Urita, veterinary surgeon; A. J.; Don; Ross, Mrs. Wm.; Nesbitt, Capt. V. C., and other comrades of Marsden, M. M.; old shipmates British bark *Lyderhorn*; Tressider, Percy; "Lintic" O'Shea, "El Rayo" comrades of; Van Leue, comrades of Capt. F. E.; brother last seen in 1909; orphan inquiring as to her identity; brothers, father, sister, Frazier, John, last seen of in the navy; Frazier, Marion, first seen in oil field of California; Carrett, Wm., last heard of in Ventura, Cal.; Frazier, Mr., last heard of in the Borax fields of California as supt. of mines; Nelda, Miss Winnifred, Wilson, Francis and their father of the Mexican Central R. R. Company; Rampby, Will F.; Clare, William; Steurtzel, Count; Leach, Doc; F. Balance or Harry Balance; Fritz K, Babson, Schooner; Birch, M. C., W. Ekin or Pilary, J. M.; Bed, O. K. (alias Canadian Red); Sands, Gen. Cliff, or members of proposed expedition; Col. C. A. Morine, last heard of Tilden, Butte Co., Col.; Hammond, W. E.; Clark, S. M.; Stoddard, R. F.; Courish, Andrew, Dona Ana; N. M. 1898, also Mike Grace, somewhere in Rocky Mts., 1900, and Frank Whelan, California, 1913; any one who worked J. F. Marshall's and John Bruggar's paper-box shops; members of Madero's Foreign Legion during 1911; shipmates on Hamburg-American Line June 2nd to 21st, 1913; members of Stanley-Pryce and Masby outfits in Lower California during 1910-11; DuBois, Percy H.; Plum, R. R.; Enscoe, Joe; Carruthers, Chas.; Selig, Lester; Hogan, Thos. L.; Osbourne, Andy, once in Evening Star; H. G. G.; boatswain's mate Holyoke, Semour Relief Expedition; Boer comrades of Jolen Bussanich, at Ladysmith and along Tugela, also Murry, John; Morroqs, Tom; McTigh, James; Ryan, Jack; Brew, Jimmy; Howard, Jess; Little Mack and Padgett, George, who were in Chihauhua, Mexico, in '07; Studabaker, Davy; "Bonnie" Bowen; Van Ochs and "Venius" Philips; Foster, Jim, Milwaukee, St. Paul; Lafon, Moore, Louisville; Mylett, Manchester, N. H.; McLain, Butte; pay sergeant Benham, John, all of 4 R. P. R's Transvaal; Maquire, Red, and McHenry, San Francisco, Cape Town; Norton, Ed, New Orleans, Cape Town and Durlan; Shea, Will Bill, Texas; O'Brien, Red, Los Angeles; Providence, Daly, Beira, P. E., Africa; Sullivan, Whitey, Boston, Philippines and Orange Free State; Peterson, William (Pete); Watson, Will; Ahl, Bill; English, "Jess"; Vose, Jack; Seay, Clif; Rooney, Bill; Fry, Joe; Baldwin, "Baldy"; Chapman; Kennedy; Molleter; Benner; McKinney; Tyson; Keinricks; Carlysle, Bill; Knode; Appleton; Wilkes; Butler; Davis; Vanlemberg; Jenkins; Rice; Bergin; Sullivan; Weinell; Armstrong; Shay; Shendel, and other knights of the "Big Stick," who worked for the W. E. Company in Bangor, Me., after the fire April 30, 1911. Any one who served in 3rd Special Service Batt., Halifax, N. S., 1899-1900.

Please notify us at once when you have found your man.

LAWRENCE STEWART, S. N. Morgan, Christian A. Damm, Mrs. Maude Thomas, George A. Blanchard, please send us your present addresses. Mail sent to us at addresses given us doesn't reach you.—Address A. S. HOFFMAN, care *Adventure*.

NUMBERS 56, 68, 73, 76, W 93, W 167, W 140, W 150, W 153, W 183, W 184, W 189, W 195, W 203, W 211, W 212, W 215, W 231, W 250, C 189, C 205, L. T. 207, L. T. 284, C 293, W 311. Please send us your present addresses. Letters forwarded to you at addresses given us do not reach you.—Address A. S. HOFFMAN, care *Adventure*.
